THE RED ROOM

TRANSLATION BY ELLIE SCHLEUSSNER

AUGUST STRINDBERG

2016 by McAllister Editions (MCALLISTEREDITIONS@GMAIL.COM). This book is a classic, and a product of its time. It does not reflect the same views on race, gender, sexuality, ethnicity, and interpersonal relations as it would if it was written today.

CONTENTS

THE RED ROOM 1
  AUGUST STRINDBERG AS NOVELIST 1
  INTRODUCTION TO STRINDBERG'S BOOKS 6
  CHAPTER I. A BIRD'S-EYE VIEW OF STOCKHOLM 9
  CHAPTER II. BETWEEN BROTHERS 17
  CHAPTER III. THE ARTISTS' COLONY 23
  CHAPTER IV. MASTER AND DOGS 31
  CHAPTER V. AT THE PUBLISHER'S 44
  CHAPTER VI. THE RED ROOM 51
  CHAPTER VII. THE IMITATION OF CHRIST................... 62
  CHAPTER VIII. POOR MOTHER COUNTRY 66
  CHAPTER IX. BILLS OF EXCHANGE 74
  CHAPTER X. THE NEWSPAPER SYNDICATE "GREY BONNET" 78
  CHAPTER XI. HAPPY PEOPLE 84
  CHAPTER XII. MARINE INSURANCE SOCIETY "TRITON" 91
  CHAPTER XIII. DIVINE ORDINANCE 98
  CHAPTER XIV. ABSINTH... 104
  CHAPTER XV. THE THEATRICAL COMPANY "PHŒNIX" 113
  CHAPTER XVI. IN THE WHITE MOUNTAINS 121
  CHAPTER XVII. NATURA... 131
  CHAPTER XVIII. NIHILISM 133
  CHAPTER XIX. FROM CHURCHYARD TO PUBLIC-HOUSE ... 140
  CHAPTER XX. ON THE ALTAR..................................... 149
  CHAPTER XXI. A SOUL OVERBOARD 153
  CHAPTER XXII. HARD TIMES 157
  CHAPTER XXIII. AUDIENCES 162
  CHAPTER XXIV. ON SWEDEN..................................... 167
  CHAPTER XXV. CHECKMATE 180
  CHAPTER XXVI. CORRESPONDENCE......................... 191
  CHAPTER XXVII. RECOVERY...................................... 197
  CHAPTER XXVIII. FROM BEYOND THE GRAVE 200
  CHAPTER XXIX. REVUE 206

AUGUST STRINDBERG AS NOVELIST
From the Publication of "The Son of a Servant" to "The Inferno" (1886-1896)

A celebrated statesman is said to have described the biography of a cardinal as being like the Judgment Day. In reading August Strindberg's autobiographical writings, as, for example, his *Inferno*, and the book for which this study is a preface, we must remember that he portrays his own Judgment Day. And as his works have come but lately before the great British public, it may be well to consider what attitude should be adopted towards the amazing candour of his self-revelation. In most provinces of life other than the comprehension of our fellows, the art of understanding is making great progress. We comprehend new phenomena without the old strain upon our capacity for readjusting our point of view. But do we equally well understand our fellow-being whose way of life is not ours? We are patient towards new phases of philosophy, new discoveries in science, new sociological facts, observed in other lands; but in considering an abnormal type of man or woman, hasty judgment or a too contracted outlook is still liable to cloud the judgment.

Now, it is obvious that if we would understand any worker who has accomplished what his contemporaries could only attempt to do, we must have a sufficiently wide knowledge of his work. Neither the inconsequent gossip attaching to such a personality, nor the chance perusal of a problem-play, affords an adequate basis for arriving at a true estimate of the man. Few writers demand, to the same degree as August Strindberg, those graces of judgment, patience, and reverence. And for this reason first of all: most of us live sheltered lives. They are few who stand in the heart of the storm made by Europe's progress. Especially is this true in Southern Europe, where tradition holds its secular sway, where such a moulding energy as constitutional practice exerts its influence over social life, where the aims and ends of human attainment are defined and sanctioned by a consciousness developing with the advancement of civilisation. There is often engendered under such conditions a nervous impatience towards those who, judged from behind the sheltered walls of orthodoxy, are more or less exposed to the criticism of their fellows. The fault lies in yielding to this impatience. The proof that August Strindberg was of the few who must stand in the open, and suffer the full force of all the winds that blow, cannot now be attempted. Our sole aim must be to enable the reader of *The Son of a Servant* to take up a sympathetic standpoint. This book forms *part* of the autobiography of a most gifted man, through whose life the fierce winds of Europe's opinions blew into various expression.

The second reason for the exercise of impartiality, is that Strindberg's recent death has led to the circulation through Europe of certain phrases which are liable to displace the balance of judgment in reviewing his life and work. There are passages in his writings, and phases of his autobiography, that raise questions of Abnormal Psychology. Hence pathological terms are used to represent the whole man and his work. Again, from the jargon of a prevalent

Nietzschianism a doctrine at once like and unlike the teaching of that solitary thinker descriptions of the Superman are borrowed, and with these Strindberg is labelled. Or again, certain incidents in his domestic affairs are seized upon to prove him a decadent libertine. The facts of this book, *The Son of a Servant*, are true: Strindberg lived them. His *Inferno*, in like manner, is a transcript of a period of his life. And if these books are read as they should be read, they are neither more nor less than the records of the progress of a most gifted life along the Dolorous Way.

The present volume is the record of the early years of Strindberg's life, and the story is incomparably told. For the sympathetic reader it will represent the history of a temperament to which the world could not come in easy fashion, and for which circumstances had contrived a world where it would encounter at each step tremendous difficulties. We find in Strindberg the consciousness of vast powers thwarted by neglect, by misunderstanding, and by the shackles of an ignominious parentage. He sets out on life as a viking, sailing the trackless seas that beat upon the shores of unknown lands, where he must take the sword to establish his rights of venture, and write fresh pages in some Heimskringla of a later age.

A calm reading of the book may induce us to suggest that this is often the fate of genius. The man of great endowments is made to walk where hardship lies on every side. And though a recognition of the hardness of the way is something, it must be borne in mind that while some are able to pass along it in serenity, others face it in tears, and others again in terrible revolt. Revolt was the only possible attitude for the Son of a Servant.

How true this is may be realised by recalling the fact that towards the end of the same year in which *The Son of a Servant* appeared, viz., 1886, our author published the second part of a series of stories entitled *Marriage*, in which that relationship is subjected to criticism more intense than is to be found in any of the many volumes devoted to this subject in a generation eminently given to this form of criticism. Side by side with this fact should be set the contents of one such story from his pen. Here he has etched, with acid that bites deeper than that of the worker in metal, the story of a woman's pettiness and inhumanity towards the husband who loves her. By his art her weakness is made to dominate every detail of the domestic *ménage*, and what was once a woman now appears to be the spirit of neglect, whose habitation is garnished with dust and dead flowers. Her great weakness calls to the man's pity, and we are told how, into this disorder, he brings the joy of Christmastide, and the whispered words of life, like a wind from some flower-clad hill. The natural conclusion, as regards both his autobiographical works and his volume of stories, is this: that Strindberg finds the Ideal to be a scourge, and not a Pegasus. And this is a distinction that sharply divides man from man, whether endowed for the attainment of saintship, for the apprehension of the vision, or with powers that enable him to wander far over the worlds of thought.

Had Strindberg intended to produce some more finished work to qualify the opinion concerning his pessimism, he could have done no better than write the novel that comes next in the order of his works, *Hemso Folk*, which was given to the world in the year 1887. It is the first of his novels to draw on the natural beauties of the rocky coast and many tiny islands which make up the splendour of the Fjord whose crown is Stockholm, and which, continuing north and south, provide fascinating retreats, still unspoilt and unexplored by the commercial agent. It may be noticed here that this northern Land of Faery has not long since found its way into English literature through a story by Mr. Algernon Blackwood, in his interesting volume, *John Silence*. The adequate description of this region was reserved for August Strindberg, and among his prose writings there are none to compare with those that have been inspired by the islands and coast he delighted in. Among them, *Hemso Folk* ranks first. In this work he shows his mastery, not of self-portraiture, but of the portraiture of other men, and his characters are painted with a mastery of subject and material which in a sister art would cause one to think of Velasquez. Against a background of sea and sky stand the figures of a schoolmaster and a priest—the portraits of both depicted with the highest art,—and throughout the book may be heard the authentic speech of the soul of Strindberg's North. He may truly be claimed to be most Swedish here; but he may also with equal truth be claimed to be most universal, since *Hemso Folk* is true for all time, and in all places.

In the following year (1888) was published another volume of tales by Strindberg, entitled *Life on the Skerries*, and again the sea, and the sun, and the life of men who commune with the great waters are the sources of his virile inspiration. Other novels of a like kind were written later, but at this hour of his life he yielded to the command of the idea—a voice which called him more strongly than did the magnificence of Nature, whose painter he could be when he had respite from the whirlwind.

Tschandala, his next book, was the fruit of a holiday in the country. This novel was written to show a man of uncommon powers of mind in the toils of inferior folk—the proletariat of soul bent on the ruin of the elect in soul. Poverty keeps him in chains. He is forced to deal with neighbours of varying degrees of degradation. A landlady deceives her husband for the sake of a vagrant lover. This person attempts to subordinate the uncommon man; who, however, discovers that he can be dominated through his superstitious fears. He is enticed one night into a field, where the projections from a lantern, imagined as supernatural beings, so play upon his fears that he dies from fright. In this book we evidently have the experimental upsurging of his imagination: supposing himself the victim of a sordid environment, he can see with unveiled eyes what might happen to him. Realistic in his apprehension of outward details, he sees the idea in its vaguest proportions. This creates, this informs his pictures of Nature; this also makes his heaven and hell. Inasmuch as a similar method is used by certain modern novelists, the curious phrase "a novel of ideas" has been coined. As though it were a surprising feature to find an idea expressed in novels! And not rarely such works are said to be lacking in warmth, because they are too full of thought.

After *Tschandala* come two or three novels of distinctly controversial character—books of especial value in essaying an understanding of Strindberg's mind. The pressure of ideas from many quarters of Europe was again upon him, and caused him to undertake long and desperate pilgrimages. *In the Offing* and *To Damascus* are the suggestive titles of these books. Seeing, however, that a detailed sketch of the evolution of Strindberg's opinions is not at this moment practicable, we merely mention these works, and the years 1890 and 1892.

Meanwhile our author has passed through two intervals in his life of a more peaceful character than was usually his lot. The first of these was spent among his favourite scenes in the vicinity of the Gulf of Bothnia, where he lived like a hermit, writing poetry and painting pictures. He might have become a painter of some note, had it not come so natural to him to use the pen. At any rate, during the time that he wielded the brush he put on canvas the scenes which he succeeded in reproducing so marvellously in his written works. The other period of respite was during a visit to Ola Hansson, a Swedish writer of rare distinction, then living near Berlin. The author of *Sensitiva Amorosa* was the antithesis of Strindberg. A consummate artist, with a wife of remarkable intellectual power, the two enfolded him in their peace, and he was able to give full expression to his creative faculty.

Strindberg now enters upon the period which culminates in the writing of *The Inferno*. From the peace of Ola Hansson's home he set out on his wedding tour, and during the early part of it came over to England. In a remarkable communication to a Danish man of letters, Strindberg answers many questions concerning his personal tastes, among them several regarding his English predilections. We may imagine them present to him as he looks upon the sleeping city from London Bridge, in the greyness of a Sunday morning, after a journey from Gravesend. His favourite English writer is Dickens, and of his works the most admired is *Little Dorrit*. A novel written in the period described in *The Son of a Servant*, and which first brought him fame, was inspired by the reading of *David Copperfield*! His favourite painter is Turner. These little sidelights upon the personality of the man are very interesting, throwing into relief as they do the view of him adopted by the writer of the foregoing pages. London, however, he disliked, and a crisis in health compelled him to leave for Paris, from which moment begins his journey through the "Inferno."

A play of Strindberg's has been performed in Paris—the height of his ambition. Once attained, it was no longer to be desired; accordingly, he turned from the theatre to Science. He takes from their hiding-place some chemical apparatus he had purchased long before. Drawing the blinds of his room he bums pure sulphur until he believes that he has discovered in it the presence of carbon. His sentences are written in terse, swift style. A page or two of the book is turned over, and we find his pen obeying the impulse of his penetrating sight.... Separation from his wife; the bells of Christmas; his visit to a hospital, and the people he sees there, begin to occupy him. Gratitude to the nursing sister, and the reaching forward of his mind into the realm of the alchemical significance of his chemical studies, arouse in him a spirit of mystical asceticism. Pages of *The Inferno* might be cited to show their resemblance to documents which have come to us from the Egyptian desert, or from the narrow cell of a recluse. Theirs is the search for a spiritual union: his is the quest of a negation of self, that his science might be without fault. A notion of destiny is grafted upon his mysticism of science. He wants to be led, as did the ascetic, though for him the goal is lore hidden from mortal eyes. He now happens upon confirmation of his scientific curiosity, in the writings of an older chemist. Then he meets with Balzac's novel *Séraphita*, and a new ecstasy is added to his outreaching towards the knowledge he aspires to. Vivid temptations assail him; he materialises as objective personalities the powers that appear to place obstacles in the way of his researches. Again we observe the same phenomena as in the soul of the monk, yet always with this difference: Strindberg is the monk of science. Curious little experiences—that others would brush into that great dust-bin, Chance—are examined with a rare simplicity to see if they may hold significance for the order of his life. These details accumulate as we turn the pages of *The Inferno*, and force one to the conclusion that they are akin to the material which we have only lately begun to study as phenomena peculiar to the psychology of the religious life. Their summary inclusion under the heading of "Abnormal Psychology" will, however, lead to a shallow interpretation of Strindberg. The voluntary isolation of himself from the relations of life and the world plays havoc with his health. Soon he is established under a doctor's care in a little southern Swedish town, with its memories of smugglers and pirates; and he immediately likens the doctor's house to a Buddhist cloister. The combination is typically Strindbergian! He begins to be haunted with the terrible suspicion that he is being plotted against. Nature is exacting heavy dues from his overwrought system. After thirty days' treatment he leaves the establishment with the reflection that whom the Lord loveth he chasteneth.

Dante wrote his Divine Comedy; Strindberg his Mortal Comedy. There are three great stages in each, and the literary vehicle of their perilous journeyings is aptly chosen. Readers of the wonderful Florentine will recall the familiar words:

"Surge ai mortali per diverse foci la lucerna de mondo."

"There riseth up to mortals through diverse trials the light of the world."

And they have found deeper content in Strindberg's self-discoveries. The first part of his *Inferno* tells of his Purgatory; the second part closes with the poignant question, Whither? If, for a moment, we step beyond the period of his life with which this study deals, we shall find him telling of his Paradise in a mystery-play entitled *Advent*, where he, too, had a starry vision of "un simplice lume," a simple flame that ingathers the many and scattered gleams of the universe's revelation. His guide through Hell is Swedenborg. Once more the note is that of the anchorite; for at the outset of his acceptance of Swedenborg's guidance he is tempted to believe that even his guide's spiritual teaching may weaken his belief in a God who chastens. He desires to deny himself the gratification of the sight of his little daughter, because he appears to consider her prattle, that breaks into the web of his contemplation, to be the instrument of a strange power. From step to step he goes until his faith is childlike as a peasant's. How he is hurled again into the depths of his own Hell, the closing pages of his book will tell us. Whatever views the reader may hold, it seems impossible that he should see in this Mortal Comedy the utterances of deranged genius. Rather will his charity of judgment have led him to a better understanding of one who listened to the winds that blow through Europe, and was buffeted by their violence.

We may close this brief study by asking the question: What, then, is Strindberg's legacy for the advancement of Art, as found in this decade of his life? It will surely be seen that Strindberg's realism is of a peculiarly personal kind. Whatever his sympathy with Zola may have been, or Zola's with him, Strindberg has never confounded journalism with Art. He has also recognised in his novels that there is a difference between the function of the camera and the eye of the artist. More than this—and it is important if Strindberg is to be understood—his realism has always been subservient to the idea. And it is this power that has essentially rendered Strindberg's realism peculiarly personal; that is to say, incapable of being copied or forming a school. It can only be used by such as he who, standing in the maelstrom of ideas, is fashioned and attuned by the whirling storms, as they strive for complete expression. Not always, however, is he subservient to their dominion. Sometimes cast down from the high places whence the multitudinous voice can be heard, he may say and do that which raises fierce criticism. A patient study of Strindberg will lay bare such matters; but their discovery must not blind our eyes to the truth that these are moments of insensitiveness towards, or rejection of, the majestic power which is ceaselessly sculpturing our highest Western civilisation.

HENRY VACHER-BURCH.

INTRODUCTION TO STRINDBERG'S BOOKS

An American critic says "Strindberg is the greatest subjectivist of all time." Certainly neither Augustine, Rousseau, nor Tolstoy have laid bare their souls to the finest fibre with more ruthless sincerity than the great Swedish realist. He fulfilled to the letter the saying of Robertson of Brighton, "Woman and God are two rocks on which a man must either anchor or be wrecked." His four autobiographical works, *The Son of a Servant, The Confessions of a Fool, Inferno,* and *Legends*, are four segments of an immense curve tracing his progress from the childish pietism of his early years, through a period of atheism and rebellion, to the sombre faith in a "God that punishes" of the sexagenarian. In his spiritual wanderings he grazed the edge of madness, and madmen often see deeper into things than ordinary folk. At the close of the *Inferno* he thus sums up the lesson of his life's pilgrimage: "Such then is my life: a sign, an example to serve for the improvement of others; a proverb, to show the nothingness of fame and popularity; a proverb, to show young men how they ought *not* to live; a proverb—because I who thought myself a prophet am now revealed as a braggart."

It is strange that though the names of Ibsen and Nietzsche have long been familiar in England, Strindberg, whom Ibsen is reported to have called "One greater than I," as he pointed to his portrait, and with whom Nietzsche corresponded, is only just beginning to attract attention, though for a long time past most of his works have been accessible in German. Even now not much more is known about him than that he was a pessimist, a misogynist, and writer of Zolaesque novels. To quote a Persian proverb, "They see the mountain, but not the mine within it." No man admired a good wife and mother more than he did, but he certainly hated the Corybantic, "emancipated" women of the present time. No man had a keener appreciation of the gentle joys of domesticity, and the intensity of his misogyny was in strict proportion to the keenness of his disappointment. The *Inferno* relates how grateful and even reverential he was to the nurse who tended him in hospital, and to his mother-in-law. He felt profoundly the charm of innocent childhood, and paternal instincts were strong in him. All his life long he had to struggle with four terrible inner foes—doubt, suspicion, fear, sensuality. His doubts destroyed his early faith, his ceaseless suspicions made it impossible for him to be happy in friendship or love, his fear of the "invisible powers," as he calls them, robbed him of all peace of mind, and his sensuality dragged him repeatedly into the mire. A "strange mixture of a man" indeed, whose soul was the scene of an internecine life-long warfare between diametrically-opposed forces! Yet he never ceased to struggle blindly upwards, and Goethe's words were verified in him:

"Wer immer strebend sich bemüht

Den Können wir erlösen." "Who never ceases still to strive, T is him we can deliver."

]

He never relapsed into the stagnant cynicism of the out-worn debauchee, nor did he with Nietzsche try to explain away conscience as an old wife's tale. Conscience persistently tormented him, and finally drove him back to belief in God, not the collective Karma of the Theosophists, which he expressly repudiated, nor to any new god expounded in New Thought magazines, but to the transcendent God who judges and requites, though not at the end of every week. It seems almost as if there were lurking an old Hebrew vein in him, so frequently in his later works does he express himself in the language of psalmists and prophets. "The psalms of David express my feelings best, and Jehovah is my God," he says in the *Inferno*.

At one time he seems to have been nearly entering the Roman Catholic Church, but, even after he had recovered his belief, his inborn independence of spirit would not let him attach himself to any religious body. His fellow-countryman, Swedenborg, seems to have influenced him more deeply than anyone else, and to him he attributes his escape from madness.

His work *Inferno* may certainly serve a useful purpose in calling attention to the fact, that, whatever may be the case hereafter, there are certainly hells on earth, hells into which the persistently selfish inevitably come. Because our fathers dealt with exaggerated emphasis on unextinguishable fires and insatiable worms, in some remote future, some good folk seem to suppose that there is no such thing as retribution, or that we may sow thorns and reap wheat. Strindberg knew better. He had reaped the whirlwind, and we seem to feel it sometimes blowing through his pages.

In the *Blue Books*, or collections of thoughts which he wrote towards the end of his life, the storm has subsided. The sun shines and the sea is calm, though strewn with wreckage. He uses some very strong language towards his former comrades, the free-thinkers, whom he calls "denizens of the dunghill." One bitterness remains. He cannot forgive woman. She has injured him too deeply. All his life long she has been "a cleaving mischief in his way to virtue." He married three times, and each marriage was a failure. His first wife was a baroness separated from her husband, whom he accuses of having repeatedly betrayed him. His second wife was an Austrian. In the *Inferno* he calls her "my beautiful jaileress who kept incessant watch over my secret thoughts." His third was an actress from whom he parted by mutual consent. All his attempts to set up a home had failed, and he found himself finally relegated to solitude. One of his later works bears the title *Lonely*. His solitude was relieved by visits from his children, and he was especially fond of his younger daughter, giving her free use of his library. On May 14, 1912, he died in Stockholm, after a lingering illness, of cancer, an added touch of tragedy being the fact that his first wife died, not far away, shortly before him.

He was an enormous reader, and seems to have possessed a knowledge almost as encyclopædic as Browning's. While assistant librarian in the Royal Library at Stockholm he studied Chinese; he was a skilled chemist and botanist, and wrote treatises on both these sciences. He was a mystic, but had a certain dislike of occultism and theosophy. A German critic, comparing him with Ibsen, says that, whereas Ibsen is a spent force, Strindberg's writings contain germs which are still undeveloped. He is a lurid and menacing planet in the literary sky, and some time must elapse before his true position is fixed. To the present writer his career seems best summed up in the words of Mrs. Browning:

"He testified this solemn truth, by frenzy desolated,

Nor man nor nature satisfies whom only God created";

or in those of Augustine: "Fecisti nos ad Te, Domine, et irrequietum est cor nostrum donec requiescat in Te."

C.F.

"Courbe la tête fier Segambre; adore ce qui tu as brûlé; brûle ce qui tu as adoré!".

CHAPTER I. A BIRD'S-EYE VIEW OF STOCKHOLM

It was an evening in the beginning of May. The little garden on "Moses Height," on the south side of the town had not yet been thrown open to the public, and the flower-beds were still unturned. The snowdrops had worked through the accumulations of last year's dead leaves, and were on the point of closing their short career and making room for the crocuses which had found shelter under a barren pear tree; the elder was waiting for a southerly wind before bursting into bloom, but the tightly closed buds of the limes still offered cover for love-making to the chaffinches, busily employed in building their lichen-covered nests between trunk and branch. No human foot had trod the gravel paths since last winter's snow had melted, and the free and easy life of beasts and flowers was left undisturbed. The sparrows industriously collected all manner of rubbish, and stowed it away under the tiles of the Navigation School. They burdened themselves with scraps of the rocket-cases of last autumn's fireworks, and picked the straw covers off the young trees, transplanted from the nursery in the Deer Park only a year ago— nothing escaped them. They discovered shreds of muslin in the summer arbours; the splintered leg of a seat supplied them with tufts of hair left on the battlefield by dogs which had not been fighting there since Josephine's day. What a life it was!

The sun was standing over the Liljeholm, throwing sheaves of rays towards the east; they pierced the[2] columns of smoke of Bergsund, flashed across the Riddarfjörd, climbed to the cross of the Riddarholms church, flung themselves on to the steep roof of the German church opposite, toyed with the bunting displayed by the boats on the pontoon bridge, sparkled in the windows of the chief custom-house, illuminated the woods of the Liding Island, and died away in a rosy cloud far, far away in the distance where the sea was. And from thence the wind came and travelled back by the same way, over Vaxholm, past the fortress, past the custom-house and along the Sikla Island, forcing its way in behind the Hästarholm, glancing at the summer resorts; then out again and on, on to the hospital Daniken; there it took fright and dashed away in a headlong career along the southern shore, noticed the smell of coal, tar and fish-oil, came dead against the city quay, rushed up to Moses Height, swept into the garden and buffeted against a wall.

The wall was opened by a maid-servant, who, at the very moment, was engaged in peeling off the paper pasted over the chinks of the double windows; a terrible smell of dripping, beer dregs, pine needles, and sawdust poured out and was carried away by the wind, while the maid stood breathing the fresh air through her nostrils. It plucked the cotton-wool, strewn with barberry berries, tinsel and rose leaves, from the space between the windows and danced it along the paths, joined by sparrows and chaffinches who saw here the solution of the greater part of their housing problem.

Meanwhile, the maid continued her work at the double windows; in a few minutes the door leading from the restaurant stood open, and a man, well but plainly dressed, stepped out into the garden. There was nothing striking about his face beyond a slight expression of care and worry which disappeared as soon as he had emerged from the stuffy room and caught sight of the wide horizon. He turned to the side from whence the wind came, opened his overcoat,[3] and repeatedly drew a deep breath which seemed to relieve his heart and lungs. Then he began to stroll up and down the barrier which separated the garden from the cliffs in the direction of the sea.

Far below him lay the noisy, reawakening town; the steam cranes whirred in the harbour, the iron bars rattled in the iron weighing machine, the whistles of the lock-keepers shrilled, the steamers at the pontoon bridge smoked, the omnibuses rumbled over the uneven paving-stones; noise and uproar in the fish market, sails and flags on the water outside; the screams of the sea-gulls, bugle-calls from the dockyard, the turning out of the guard, the clattering of the wooden shoes of the working-men—all this produced an impression of life and bustle, which seemed to rouse the young man's energy; his face assumed an expression of defiance, cheerfulness and resolution, and as he leaned over the barrier and looked at the town below, he seemed to be watching an enemy; his nostrils expanded, his eyes flashed, and he raised his clenched fist as if he were challenging or threatening the poor town.

The bells of St. Catherine's chimed seven; the splenetic treble of St. Mary's seconded; the basses of the great church, and the German church joined in, and soon the air was vibrating with the sound made by the seven bells of the town; then one after the other relapsed into silence, until far away in the distance only the last one of them could be heard singing its peaceful evensong; it had a higher note, a purer tone and a quicker tempo than the others—yes, it had! He listened and wondered whence the sound came, for it seemed to stir up vague memories in him. All of a sudden his face relaxed and his features expressed the misery of a forsaken child. And he was forsaken; his father and mother were lying in the churchyard of St. Clara's, from whence the bell could still be heard; and he was a child; he still believed in everything, truth and fairy tales alike.[4]

The bell of St. Clara's was silent, and the sound of footsteps on the gravel path roused him from his reverie. A short man with side-whiskers came towards him from the verandah; he wore spectacles, apparently more for the sake of protecting his glances than his eyes, and his malicious mouth was generally twisted into a kindly, almost benevolent, expression. He was dressed in a neat overcoat with defective buttons, a somewhat battered hat, and trousers hoisted at half-mast. His walk indicated assurance as well as timidity. His whole appearance was so indefinite that it was impossible to guess at his age or social position. He might just as well have been an artisan as a government official; his age was anything between twenty-nine and forty-five years. He was obviously flattered to find himself in the company of the man whom he had come to meet, for he raised his bulging hat with unusual ceremony and smiled his kindliest smile.

"I hope you haven't been waiting, assessor?"

"Not for a second; it's only just struck seven. Thank you for coming. I must confess that this meeting is of the greatest importance to me; I might almost say it concerns my whole future, Mr. Struve."

"Bless me! Do you mean it?"

Mr. Struve blinked; he had come to drink a glass of toddy and was very little inclined for a serious conversation. He had his reasons for that.

"We shall be more undisturbed if we have our toddy outside, if you don't mind," continued the assessor.

Mr. Struve stroked his right whisker, put his hat carefully on his head and thanked the assessor for his invitation; but he looked uneasy.

"To begin with, I must ask you to drop the 'assessor,'" began the young man. "I've never been more than a regular assistant, and I cease to be even that from to-day; I'm Mr. Falk, nothing else."

"What?"

Mr. Struve looked as if he had lost a distinguished friend, but he kept his temper.[5]

"You're a man with liberal tendencies...."

Mr. Struve tried to explain himself, but Falk continued:

"I asked you to meet me here in your character of contributor to the liberal *Red Cap*."

"Good heavens! I'm such a very unimportant contributor...."

"I've read your thundering articles on the working man's question, and all other questions which nearly concern us. We're in the year three, in Roman figures, for it is now the third year of the new Parliament, and soon our hopes will have become realities. I've read your excellent biographies of our leading politicians in the *Peasant's Friend*, the lives of those men of the people, who have at last been allowed to voice what oppressed them for so long; you're a man of progress and I've a great respect for you."

Struve, whose eyes had grown dull instead of kindling at the fervent words, seized with pleasure the proffered safety-valve.

"I must admit," he said eagerly, "that I'm immensely pleased to find myself appreciated by a young and—I must say it—excellent man like you, assessor; but, on the other hand, why talk of such grave, not to say sad things, when we're sitting here, in the lap of nature, on the first day of spring, while all the buds are bursting and the sun is pouring his warmth on the whole creation! Let's snap our fingers at care and drink our glass in peace. Excuse me—I believe I'm your senior—and—I venture—to propose therefore...."

Falk, who like a flint had gone out in search of steel, realized that he had struck wood. He accepted the proposal without eagerness. And the new brothers sat side by side, and all they had to tell each other was the disappointment expressed in their faces.

"I mentioned a little while ago," Falk resumed, "that I've broken to-day with my past life and[6] thrown up my career as a government employé. I'll only add that I intend taking up literature."

"Literature? Good Heavens! Why? Oh, but that *is* a pity!"

"It isn't; but I want you to tell me how to set about finding work."

"H'm! That's really difficult to say. The profession is crowded with so many people of all sorts. But you mustn't think of it. It really is a pity to spoil your career; the literary profession is a bad one."

Struve looked sorry, but he could not hide a certain satisfaction at having met a friend in misfortune.

"But tell me," he continued, "Why are you throwing up a career which promises a man honours as well as influence?"

"Honours to those who have usurped the power, and influence to the most unscrupulous."

"Stuff! It isn't really as bad as all that?"

"Isn't it? Well, then I must speak more plainly. I'll show you the inner working of one of the six departments for which I had put down. The first five I left at once for the very simple reason that there was no room for me. Whenever I went and asked whether there was anything for me to do, I was told No! And I never saw anybody doing anything. And that was in the busy departments, like the Committee on Brandy Distilleries, the Direct Taxation Office and The Board of Administration of Employés' Pensions. But when I noticed the swarming crowd of officials, the idea struck me that the department which had to pay out all the salaries must surely be very busy indeed. I therefore put my name down for the Board of Payment of Employés' Salaries."

"And did you go there?" asked Struve, beginning to feel interested.

"Yes. I shall never forget the great impression made on me by my visit to this thoroughly well-organized department. I went there at eleven[7] o'clock one morning, because this is supposed to be the time when the offices open. In the waiting-room I found two young messengers sprawling on a table, on their stomachs, reading the *Fatherland*."

"The '*Fatherland*'?"

Struve, who had up to the present been feeding the sparrows with sugar, pricked up his ears.

"Yes. I said 'good morning.' A feeble wriggling of the gentlemen's backs indicated that they accepted my good morning without any decided displeasure; one of them even went to the length of waggling the heel of his right foot, which might have been intended as a substitute for a handshake. I asked whether either of the gentlemen were disengaged and could show me the offices. Both of them declared that they were unable to do so, because their orders were not to leave the waiting-room. I inquired whether there were any other messengers. Yes, there were others. But the chief messenger was away on a holiday; the first messenger was on leave; the second was not on duty; the third had gone to the post; the fourth was ill; the fifth had gone to fetch some drinking water; the sixth was in the yard 'where he remained all day long'; moreover, no official ever arrived before one o'clock. This was a hint to me that my early, inconvenient visit was not good form, and at the same time a reminder that the messengers, also, were government employés.

"But when I stated that I was firmly resolved on seeing the offices, so as to gain an idea of the division of labour in so important and comprehensive a department, the younger of the two consented to come with me. When he opened the door I had a magnificent view of a suite of sixteen rooms of various sizes. There must be work here, I thought, congratulating myself on my happy idea of coming. The crackling of sixteen birchwood fires in sixteen tiled stoves interrupted in the pleasantest manner the solitude of the place."

Struve, who had become more and more interested[8] fumbled for a pencil between the material and lining of his waistcoat, and wrote "16" on his left cuff.

"'This is the adjuncts' room,' explained the messenger.

"'I see! Are there many adjuncts in this department?' I asked.

"'Oh, yes! More than enough!'"

"'What do they do all day long?'"

"'Oh! They write, of course, a little....'"

"He was speaking familiarly, so that I thought it time to interrupt him. After wandering through the copyists', the notaries', the clerk's, the controller's and his secretary's, the reviser's and his secretary's, the public prosecutor's, the registrar of the exchequer's, the master of the rolls' and the librarian's, the treasurer's, the cashier's, the procurator's, the protonotary's, the keeper of the minutes', the actuary's, the keeper of the records', the secretary's, the first clerk's, and the head of the department's rooms, we came to a door which bore in gilt letters the words: 'The President.' I was going to open the door but the messenger stopped me; genuinely uneasy, he seized my arm and whispered: 'Shsh!'—'Is he asleep?' I asked, my thoughts busy with an old rumour. 'For God's sake, be quiet! No one may enter here unless the president rings the bell.' 'Does he often ring?' 'No, I've never heard him ringing in my time, and I've been here twelve months.' He was again inclined to be familiar, so I said no more.

"About noon the adjuncts began to arrive, and to my amazement I found in them nothing but old friends from the Committee on Brandy Distilleries, and the Board of Administration of Employés' Pensions. My amazement grew when the registrar from the Inland Revenue Office strolled into the actuary's room, and made himself as comfortable in his easy-chair as he used to do in the Inland Revenue Office.

"I took one of the young men aside and asked him[9] whether it would not be advisable for me to call on the president. 'Shsh!' was his mysterious reply, while he took me into room No. 8. Again this mysterious shsh!

"The room which we had just entered was quite as dark as the rest of them, but it was much dirtier. The horsehair stuffing was bursting through the leather

13

covering of the furniture; thick dust lay on the writing-table; by the side of an inkstand, in which the ink had dried long ago, lay an unused stick of sealing-wax with the former owner's name marked on it in Anglo-Saxon letters; in addition there was a pair of paper shears whose blades were held together by rust; a date rack which had not been turned since midsummer five years ago; a State directory five years old; a sheet of blotting-paper with Julius Cæsar, Julius Cæsar, Julius Cæsar written all over it, a hundred times at least, alternating with as many Father Noahs.

"'This is the office of the Master of the Rolls; we shall be undisturbed here,' said my friend.

"'Doesn't the Master of the Rolls come here, then?' I asked.

"'He hasn't been here these five years, and now he's ashamed to turn up.'

"'But who does his work?'

"'The librarian.'

"'But what is his work in a department like the Board of Payment of Employés' Salaries?'

"'The messengers sort the receipts, chronologically and alphabetically, and send them to the book-binders; the librarian supervises their being placed on shelves specially adapted for the purpose.'"

The conversation now seemed to amuse Struve; he scribbled a word every now and then on his cuff, and as Falk paused he thought it incumbent on him to ask an important question.

"But how did the Master of the Rolls get his salary?"

"It was sent to his private address. Wasn't that simple enough? However, my young friend advised me to present myself to the actuary and ask him to introduce me to the other employés who were now dropping in to poke the fires in their tiled stoves and enjoy the last glimmer of the glowing wood. My friend told me that the actuary was an influential and good-natured individual, very susceptible to little courtesies.

"I, who had come across him in his character as Registrar of the Exchequer, had formed a different opinion of him, but believing that my friend knew better, I went to see him.

"The redoubtable actuary sat in a capacious easy-chair with his feet on a reindeer skin. He was engaged in seasoning a real meerschaum pipe, sewn up in soft leather. So as not to appear idle, he was glancing at yesterday's *Post*, acquainting himself in this way with the wishes of the Government.

"My entrance seemed to annoy him; he pushed his spectacles on to his bald head; hiding his right eye behind the edge of the newspaper, he shot a conical bullet at me with the left. I proffered my request. He took the mouthpiece of his meerschaum into his right hand and examined it to find out how far he had coloured it. The dreadful silence which followed confirmed my apprehensions. He cleared his throat; there was a loud, hissing noise in the heap of glowing coal. Then he remembered the newspaper and continued his perusal of it. I judged it wise to repeat my request in a different form. He lost his temper. 'What the devil do you want? What are you doing in my room? Can't I have peace in my own quarters? What? Get out, get out, get out! sir, I say! Can't you see that I'm busy. Go to the protonotary if you want anything! Don't come here bothering me!'

"I went to the protonotary.

"The Committee of Supplies was sitting; it had been sitting for three weeks already. The protonotary was in the chair and three clerks were keeping the minutes. The samples sent in by the purveyors lay scattered about on the tables, round which all disengaged clerks, copyists and notaries were assembled. In spite of much diversity of opinion, it had been agreed to order twenty reams of Lessebo paper, and after repeatedly testing their cutting capacity, the purchase of forty-eight pairs of Grantorp scissors, which had been awarded a prize, had been decided on. (The actuary held twenty-five shares in this concern.) The test writing with the steel nibs had taken a whole week, and the minutes concerning it had taken up two reams of paper. It was now the turn of the penknives, and the committee was intent on testing them on the leaves of the black table.

"'I propose ordering Sheffield doubleblades No. 4, without a corkscrew,' said the protonotary, cutting a splinter off the table large enough to light a fire with. 'What does the first notary say?'

"The first notary, who had cut too deeply into the table, had come across a nail and damaged an Eskilstuna No. 2, with three blades, suggested buying the latter.

"After everybody had given his opinion and alleged reasons for holding it, adding practical tests, the chairman suggested buying two gross of Sheffields.

"But the first notary protested, and delivered a long speech, which was taken down on record, copied out twice, registered, sorted (alphabetically and chronologically), bound and placed by the messenger—under the librarian's supervision—on a specially adapted shelf. This protest displayed a warm, patriotic feeling; its principal object was the demonstration of the necessity of encouraging home industries.

"But this being equivalent to a charge brought against the Government—seeing that it was brought against one of its employés—the protonotary felt it his duty to meet it. He started with a historical digression on the origin of the discount on manufactured goods—at the word discount all the adjuncts pricked up their ears—touched on the economic developments of the country during the last twenty years, and went into such minute details that the clock on the Riddarholms church struck two before he had arrived at his subject. At the fatal stroke of the clock the whole assembly rushed from their places as if a fire had broken out. When I asked a colleague what it all meant, the old notary, who had heard my question, replied: 'The primary duty of a Government employé is punctuality, sir!' At two minutes past two not a soul was left in one of the rooms.

"'We shall have a hot day to-morrow,' whispered a colleague, as we went downstairs. 'What in the name of fortune is going to happen?' I asked uneasily. 'Lead pencils,' he replied. There were hot days in store for us. Sealing-wax, envelopes, paper-knives, blotting-paper, string. Still, it might all be allowed to pass, for every one was occupied. But a day came when there was nothing to do. I took my courage in my hands and asked for work. I was given seven reams of paper for making fair copies at home, a feat by which 'I should deserve well of my country.' I did my work in a very short time, but instead of receiving appreciation and encouragement, I was treated with suspicion; industrious people were not in favour. Since then I've had no work.

"I'll spare you the tedious recital of a year's humiliations, the countless taunts, the endless bitterness. Everything which appeared small and ridiculous to me was treated with grave solemnity, and everything which I considered great and praiseworthy was scoffed at. The people were called 'the mob,' and their only use was to be shot at by the army if occasion should arise. The new form of government was openly reviled and the peasants were called traitors.[A]"

[A]Since the great reorganization of the public offices, this description is no longer true to life.

"I had to listen to this sort of thing for seven months; they began to suspect me because I didn't join in their laughter, and challenged me. Next time the 'opposition dogs' were attacked, I exploded and made a speech, the result of which was that they knew where I stood, and that I was henceforth impossible. And now I shall do what so many other shipwrecks have done: I shall throw myself into the arms of literature."

Struve, who seemed dissatisfied with the truncated ending, put the pencil back, sipped his toddy and looked absent-minded. Nevertheless, he thought he ought to say something.

"My dear fellow," he remarked at last, "you haven't yet learned the art of living; you will find out how difficult it is to earn bread and butter, and how it gradually becomes the main interest. One works to eat and eats to be able to work. Believe me, who have wife and child, that I know what I'm talking about. You must cut your coat according to your cloth, you see—according to your cloth. And you've no idea what the position of a writer is. He stands outside society."

"His punishment for aspiring to stand above it. Moreover, I detest society, for it is not founded on a voluntary basis. It's a web of lies—I renounce it with pleasure."

"It's beginning to grow chilly," said Struve.

"Yes; shall we go?"

"Perhaps we'd better."

The flame of conversation had flickered out.

Meanwhile the sun had set; the half moon had risen and hung over the fields to the north of the town. Star after star struggled with the daylight which still lingered in the sky; the gas-lamps were being lighted in the town; the noise and uproar was beginning to die away.

Falk and Struve walked together in the direction of the north, talking of commerce, navigation, the crafts, everything in fact which did not interest them; finally, to each other's relief, they parted.

Falk strolled down River Street towards the dockyard, his brain pregnant with new thoughts. He felt like a bird which had flown against a window-pane and now lay bruised on the ground at the very moment when it had spread its wings to fly towards freedom. He sat down on a seat, listening to the splashing of the waves; a light breeze had sprung up and rustled through the flowering maple trees, and the faint light of the half moon shone on the black water; twenty, thirty boats lay moored on the quay; they tore at their chains for a moment, raised their heads, one after the other, and dived down again, underneath the water; wind and wave seemed to drive them onward; they made little runs towards the bridge like a pack of hounds, but the chain held them in leash and left them kicking and stamping, as if they were eager to break loose.

He remained in his seat till midnight; the wind fell asleep, the waves went to rest, the fettered boats ceased tugging at their chains; the maples stopped rustling, and the dew was beginning to fall.

Then he rose and strolled home, dreaming, to his lonely attic in the north-eastern part of the town.

That is what young Falk did; but old Struve, who on the same day had become a member of the staff of the *Grey Bonnet*, because the *Red Cap* had sacked him, went home and wrote an article for the notorious *People's Flag*, on the Board of Payment of Employés' Salaries, four columns at five crowns a column.

CHAPTER II. BETWEEN BROTHERS

The flax merchant, Charles Nicholas Falk—son of the late flax merchant, one of the fifty elders of the burgesses, captain of the infantry of militia, vestryman and member of the Board of Administration of the Stockholm Fire Insurance, Charles John Falk, and brother of the former assessor and present writer, Arvid Falk—had a business or, as his enemies preferred to call it, a shop in Long Street East, nearly opposite Pig Street, so that the young man who sat behind the counter, surreptitiously reading a novel, could see a piece of a steamer, the paddle-box perhaps, or the jib-boom, and the crown of a tree on Skeppsholm, with a patch of sky above it, whenever he raised his eyes from his book.

The shop assistant, who answered to the not unusual name of Andersson, and he had learnt to answer to it, had just—it was early in the morning—opened the shop, hung up outside the door a flax tress, a fish and an eel basket, a bundle of fishing-rods, and a crawl of unstripped quills; this done, he had swept the shop, strewn the floor with sawdust, and sat down behind the counter. He had converted an empty candle-box into a kind of mouse-trap, which he set with a hooked stick; immediately on the appearance of his principal, or any of the latter's friends, the novel on which Andersson was intent dropped into the box. He did not seem afraid of customers; for one thing it was early in the morning and for another he was not used to very many customers.

The business had been established in the days of the late King Frederick—Charles Nicholas Falk had inherited this statement from his father, to whom it had descended from his grandfather; it had flourished and earned a good deal of money until a few years ago; but the disastrous chamber-system killed trade, ruined all prospects, impeded all enterprise, and threatened all citizens with bankruptcy. So, at least, Falk said; others were inclined to believe that the business was mismanaged; to say nothing of the fact that a dangerous competitor had established himself close to the lock. Falk never talked of the decline of the business if he could help it, and he was shrewd enough carefully to choose occasion and audience whenever he touched upon *that* string. If an old business connexion expressed surprise, in a friendly way, at the reduced trade, he told him that his principal business was a wholesale trade in the provinces, and that he was looking upon the shop merely in the light of a sign-board; nobody doubted this, for he had, behind the shop, a small counting-house where he generally could be found when he was not in town or at the Exchange. But it was quite another tale if any of his acquaintances, such as the notary or the schoolmaster, for instance, expressed the same friendly uneasiness. Then he blamed the bad times, the result of the new chamber-system; this alone was to blame for the stagnation of trade.

Andersson was disturbed in his reading by two or three boys who were standing in the doorway, asking the price of the fishing-rods. Looking out into the street he caught sight of our Mr. Arvid Falk. Falk had lent him the book, so that it could safely be left on the counter; and as his former playfellow entered the shop, he greeted him familiarly, with a knowing look.

"Is he upstairs?" asked Falk, not without a certain uneasiness.

"He's at breakfast," replied Andersson, pointing to the ceiling.

A chair was pushed back on the floor above their heads.

"He's got up from the table now, Mr. Arvid."

Both young men seemed familiar with the noise and its purport. Heavy, creaking footsteps crossed the floor, apparently in all directions, and a subdued murmur penetrated through the ceiling to the listeners below.

"Was he at home last night?" asked Falk.

"No, he was out."

"With friends or acquaintances?"

"Acquaintances."

"Did he come home late?"

"Very late."

"Do you think he'll be coming down soon, Andersson? I don't want to go upstairs on account of my sister-in-law."

"He'll be here directly; I can tell by his footsteps."

A door slammed upstairs; they looked at each other significantly. Arvid made a movement towards the door, but pulled himself together.

A few moments later they heard sounds in the counting-house. A violent cough shook the little room and then came the well-known footsteps, saying: stamp—stamp, stamp—stamp!

Arvid went behind the counter and knocked at the door of the counting-house.

"Come in!"

He stood before his brother, a man of forty who looked his age. He was fifteen years older than Arvid, and for that and other reasons he had accustomed himself to look upon his younger brother as a boy towards whom he acted as a father. He had fair hair, a fair moustache, fair eyebrows, and eye-lashes. He was rather stout, and that was the reason why his boots always creaked; they groaned under the weight of his thick-set figure.

"Oh, it's only you?" he said with good-natured contempt. This attitude of mind was typical of the man; he was never angry with those who for some reason or other could be considered his inferiors; he despised them. But his face expressed disappointment; he had expected a more satisfactory subject for an outburst; his brother was shy and modest, and never offered resistance if he could possibly help it.

"I hope I'm not inconveniencing you, brother Charles?" asked Arvid, standing on the threshold. This humble question disposed the brother to show benevolence. He helped himself to a cigar from his big, embroidered leather cigar-case, offering his brother a smoke from a box which stood near the fire-place; that boxful—visitors' cigars, as he frankly called them, and he was of a candid disposition—had been through a shipwreck, which made them interesting, but did not improve them, and a sale by auction on the strand, which had made them very cheap.

"Well, what is it you want?" asked Charles Nicholas, lighting his cigar, and absent-mindedly putting the match into his pocket—he could only concentrate his thoughts on one spot inside a not very large circumference; his tailor could have expressed the size of it in inches after measuring him round the stomach.

"I want to talk business with you," answered Arvid, fingering his unlighted cigar.

"Sit down!" commanded the brother.

It was customary with him to ask people to sit down whenever he intended to take them to task; he had them under him, then, and it was more easy to crush them—if necessary.

"Business? Are we doing business together?" he began. "I don't know anything about it. Are you doing business? Are you?"

"I only meant to say that I should like to know whether there's anything more coming to me?"

"What, may I ask? Do you mean money?" said Charles Nicholas, jestingly, allowing his brother to enjoy the scent of his good cigar. As the reply, which he did not want, was not forthcoming, he went on:

"Coming to you? Haven't you received everything due to you? Haven't you yourself receipted the account for the Court of Wards? Haven't I kept and clothed you since—to be strictly correct, haven't I made you a loan, according to your own wish, to be paid back when you are able to do so? I've put it all down, in readiness for the day when you will be earning your livelihood, a thing which you've not done yet."

"I'm going to do it now, and that's why I'm here. I wanted to know whether there's still anything owing to me, or whether I am in debt."

The brother cast a penetrating look at his victim, wondering whether he had any mental reservations. His creaking boots began stamping the floor on a diagonal line between spittoon and umbrella-stand; the trinkets on his watch-chain tinkled, a warning to people not to cross his way; the smoke of his cigar rose and lay in long, ominous clouds, portentous of a thunderstorm, between tiled stove and door. He paced up and down the room furiously, his head bowed, his shoulders rounded, as if he were rehearsing a part. When he thought he knew it, he stopped short before his brother, gazed into his eyes with a long, glinting, deceitful look, intended to express both confidence and sorrow, and said, in a voice meant to sound as if it came from the family grave in the churchyard of St. Clara's:

"You're not straight, Arvid; you're not straight."

Who, with the exception of Andersson, who was standing behind the door, listening, would not have been touched by those words, spoken by a brother to a brother, fraught with the deepest brotherly sorrow? Even Arvid, accustomed from his childhood to believe all men perfect and himself alone unworthy, wondered for a moment whether he was straight or not? And as his education, by efficacious means, had provided him with a highly sensitive conscience, he found that he really had not been quite straight, or at least quite frank, when he asked his brother the not-altogether candid question as to whether he wasn't a scoundrel.

"I've come to the conclusion," he said, "that you cheated me out of a part of my inheritance; I've calculated that you charged too much for your inferior board and your cast-off clothes; I know that I didn't spend all my fortune during my terrible college days, and I believe that you owe me a fairly big sum; I want it now, and I request you to hand it over to me."

A smile illuminated the brother's fair face, and with an expression so calm and a gesture so steady, that he might have been rehearsing them for years, so as to be in readiness when his cue was given to him, he put his hand in his trousers pocket, rattled his bunch of keys before taking it out, threw it up and dexterously caught it again, and walked solemnly to his safe. He opened it more quickly than he intended and, perhaps, than the sacredness of the spot justified, took out a paper lying ready to his hand and evidently also waiting for its cue, and handed it to his brother.

"Did you write this? Answer me! Did you write it?"

"Yes!"

Arvid rose and turned towards the door.

"Don't go! Sit down! Sit down!"

If a dog had been present it would have sat down at once.

"What's written here? Read it! 'I, Arvid Falk, acknowledge and testify—that—I—have received from my brother, Charles Nicholas Falk—who was appointed my guardian—my inheritance in full—amounting to—' and so on." He was ashamed to mention the sum.

"You have acknowledged and testified a fact which you did not believe. Is that straight? No, answer my question! Is that straight? No! Therefore you have borne false witness. Ergo—you're a blackguard! Yes, that's what you are! Am I right?"

The part was too excellent and the triumph too great to be enjoyed without an audience. The innocently accused must have witnesses. He opened the door leading into the shop.

"Andersson!" he shouted, "answer this question! Listen to me! If I bear false witness, am I a blackguard or not?"

"Of course, you are a blackguard, sir!" Andersson answered unhesitatingly and with warmth.

"Do you hear? He says I'm a blackguard—if I put my signature to a false receipt. What did I say? You're not straight, Arvid, you are not straight. Good-natured people often are blackguards; you have always been good-natured and yielding, but I've always been aware that in your secret heart you harboured very different thoughts; you're a blackguard! Your father always said so; I say 'said,' for he always said what he thought, and he was a straight man, Arvid, and that—you—are—not! And you may be sure that if he were still alive he would say with grief and pain: 'You're not straight, Arvid, you—are—not—straight!'"

He did a few more diagonal lines and it sounded as if he were applauding the scene with his feet; he rattled his bunch of keys as if he were giving the signal for the curtain to rise. His closing remarks had been so rounded off that the smallest addition would have spoilt the whole. In spite of the heavy charge which he had actually expected for years—for he had always believed his brother to be acting a part—he was very glad that it was over, happily over, well and cleverly over, so that he felt almost gay and even a little grateful. Moreover he had had a splendid chance of venting the wrath which had been kindled upstairs, in his family, on some one; to vent it on Andersson had lost its charm; and he knew better than to vent it on his wife.

Arvid was silent; the education he had received had so intimidated him that he always believed himself to be in the wrong; since his childhood the great words "upright, honest, sincere, true," had daily and hourly been drummed into his ears, so that they stood before him like a judge, continuously saying: "Guilty...." For a moment he thought that he must have been mistaken in his calculations, that his brother must be innocent and he himself a scoundrel; but immediately after he realized that his brother was a cheat, deceiving him by a simple lawyer's trick. He felt prompted to run away, fearful of being drawn into a quarrel, to run away without making his request number two, and confessing that he was on the point of changing his profession.

There was a long pause. Charles Nicholas had plenty of time to recapitulate his triumph in his memory. That little word "blackguard" had done his tongue good. It had been as pleasant as if he had said "Get out!" And the opening of the door, Andersson's reply, and the production of the paper, everything had passed off splendidly; he had not forgotten the bunch of keys on his night-table; he had turned the key in the lock without any difficulty; his proof was binding as a rope, the conclusion he had drawn had been the baited hook by which the fish had been caught.

He had regained his good temper; he had forgiven, nay, he had forgotten, and as he slammed the door of the safe, he shut away the disagreeable story for ever.

But he did not want to part from his brother in this mood; he wanted to talk to him on other subjects; throw a few shovelfuls of gossip on the unpleasant affair, see him under commonplace circumstances, sitting at his table, for instance—and why not eating and drinking? People always looked happy and content when they were eating and drinking; he wanted so see him happy and content. He wanted to see his face calm, listen to his voice speaking without a tremor, and he resolved to ask him to luncheon. But he felt puzzled how to lead up to it, find a suitable bridge across the gulf. He searched his brain, but found nothing. He searched his pockets and found—the match.

"Hang it all, you've never lit your cigar, old boy!" he exclaimed with genuine, not feigned, warmth.

But the old boy had crushed his cigar during the conversation, so that it would not draw.

"Look here! Take another!" and he pulled out his big leather case.

"Here! Take one of these! They are good ones!"

Arvid, who, unfortunately, could not bear to hurt anybody's feelings, accepted it gratefully, like a hand offered in reconciliation.

"Now, old boy," continued Charles Nicholas, talking lightly and pleasantly, an accomplishment at which he was an expert. "Let's go to the nearest restaurant and have lunch. Come along!"

Arvid, unused to friendliness, was so touched by these advances that he hastily pressed his brother's hand and hurried away through the shop without taking any notice of Andersson, and out into the street.

The brother felt embarrassed; he could not understand it. To run away when he had been asked to lunch! To run away when he was not in the least angry with him! To run away! No dog would have run away if a piece of meat had been thrown to him!

"He's a queer chap!" he muttered, stamping the floor. Then he went to his desk, screwed up the seat of his chair as high as it would go and climbed up. From this raised position he was in the habit of contemplating men and circumstances as from a higher point of view, and he found them small; yet not so small that he could not use them for his purposes.

CHAPTER III. THE ARTISTS' COLONY

It was between eight and nine o'clock on the same beautiful May morning. Arvid Falk, after the scene with his brother, was strolling through the streets, dissatisfied with himself, his brother, and the whole world. He would have preferred to see the sky overcast, to be in bad company. He did not believe that he was a blackguard, but he was disappointed with the part he had played; he was accustomed to be severe on himself, and it had always been drummed into him that his brother was a kind of stepfather to whom he owed great respect, not to say reverence. But he was worried and depressed by other thoughts as well. He had neither money nor prospect of work. The last contingency was, perhaps, the worse of the two, for to him, with his exuberant imagination, idleness was a dangerous enemy.

Brooding over these disagreeable facts, he had reached Little Garden Street; he sauntered along, on the left pavement, passed the Dramatic Theatre, and soon reached High Street North. He walked on aimlessly; the pavement became uneven; wooden cottages took the place of the stone houses; badly dressed men and women were throwing suspicious glances at the well-dressed stranger who was visiting their quarter at such an early hour; famished dogs growled threateningly at him. He hastened past groups of gunners, labourers, brewers' men, laundresses, and apprentices, and finally came to Great Hop-Garden Street. He entered the Hop-Garden. The cows belonging to the Inspector-General of Ordnance were grazing in the fields; the old, bare apple trees were making the first efforts to put forth buds; but the lime trees were already in leaf and squirrels were playing up and down the branches. He passed the merry-go-round and came to the avenue leading to the theatre; here he met some truant schoolboys engaged in a game of buttons; a little further a painter's apprentice was lying in the grass on his back staring at the clouds through the dome of foliage; he was whistling carelessly, indifferent to the fact that master and men were waiting for him, while flies and other insects drowned themselves in his paint-pots.

Falk had walked to the top of the hill and had come to the duck-pond; he stood still for a while, studying the metamorphoses of the frogs; watching the leeches; catching a water-spider. Then he began to throw stones. The exercise brought his blood into circulation; he felt rejuvenated, a schoolboy playing truant, free, defiantly free! It was freedom bought by great self-sacrifice. The thought of being able to commune with nature freely and at will, made him glad;

he understood nature better than men who had only ill-treated and slandered him; his unrest disappeared; he rose and continued his way further into the country.

Walking through the Cross, he came into Hop-Garden Street North. Some of the boards were missing in the fence facing him, and there was a very plainly marked footpath on the other side. He crept through the hole, disturbing an old woman who was gathering nettles, crossed the large tobacco field where a colony of villas has now sprung up, and found himself at the gate of "Lill-Jans."

There was no doubt of its being spring in the little settlement, consisting of three cottages snugly nestling among elders and apple trees, and sheltered from the north wind by the pine-wood on the other side of the High Road. The visitor was regaled with a perfect little idyll. A cock, perched on the shafts of a watercart, was basking in the sun and catching flies, the bees hung in a cloud round the bee-hives, the gardener was kneeling by the hot-beds, sorting radishes; the warblers and brand-tails were singing in the gooseberry bushes, while lightly clad children chased the fowls bent on examining the germinative capacity of various newly sown seeds. A brilliant blue sky spanned the scene and the dark forest framed the background.

Two men were sitting close to the hot-beds, in the shelter of the fence. One of them, wearing a tall, black hat and a threadbare, black suit, had a long, narrow, pale face, and looked like a clergyman. With his stout but deformed body, drooping eyelids, and Mongolian moustache, the other one belonged to the type of civilized peasant. He was very badly dressed and might have been many things: a vagabond, an artisan, or an artist; he looked seedy, but seedy in an original way.

The lean man, who obviously felt chilly, although he sat right in the sun, was reading to his friend from a book; the latter looked as though he had tried all the climates of the earth and was able to stand them all equally well.

As Falk entered the garden gate from the high road, he could distinctly hear the reader's words through the fence, and he thought it no breach of confidence to stand still for a while and listen.

The lean man was reading in a dry, monotonous voice, a voice without resonance, and his stout friend every now and then acknowledged his appreciation by a snort which changed occasionally into a grunt and became a splutter whenever the words of wisdom to which he was listening surpassed ordinary human understanding.

"'The highest principles are, as already stated, three; one, absolutely unconditioned, and two, relatively unconditioned ones. *Pro primo*: the absolutely first, purely unconditioned principle, would express the action underlying all consciousness and without which consciousness cannot exist. This principle is the identity A—A. It endures and cannot be disposed of by thought when all empirical definitions of consciousness are prescinded. It is the original fact of consciousness and must therefore, of necessity, be

24

acknowledged. Moreover, it is not conditioned like every other empirical fact, but as consequence and substance of a voluntary act entirely unconditioned.'"

"Do you follow, Olle?" asked the reader, interrupting himself.

"It's amazing! It is not conditioned like every other empirical fact. Oh! What a man! Go on! Go on!"

"'If it is maintained,'" continued the reader, "'that this proposition without any further proof be true....'"

"Oh! I say! What a rascal! without any further proof be true," repeated the grateful listener, bent on dissipating all suspicion that he had not grasped what had been read, "without any *further* reason, how subtle, how subtle of him to say that instead of simply saying 'without any reason.'"

"Am I to continue? Or do you intend to go on interrupting me?" asked the offended reader.

"I won't interrupt again. Go on! Go on!"

"Well, now he draws the conclusion (really excellent): 'If one ascribes to oneself the ability to state a proposition——'"

Olle snorted.

"'One does not propose thereby A (capital A), but merely that A—A, if and in so far as A exists at all. It is not a question of the essence of an assertion but only of its form. The proposition A—A is therefore conditioned (hypothetically) as far as its essence is concerned, and unconditioned only as far as its form goes.'

"Have you noticed the capital A?"

Falk had heard enough; this was the terribly profound philosophy of Upsala, which had strayed to Stockholm to conquer and subdue the coarse instincts of the capital. He looked at the fowls to see whether they had not tumbled off their roosts; at the parsley whether it had not stopped growing while made to listen to the profoundest wisdom ever proclaimed by human voice at Lill-Jans; he was surprised to find that the sky had not fallen after witnessing such a feat of mental strength. At the same time his base human nature clamoured for attention: his throat was parched, and he decided to ask for a glass of water at one of the cottages.

Turning back he strolled towards the hut on the right-hand side of the road, coming from town. The door leading into a large room—once a bakery—from an entrance-hall the size of a travelling trunk, stood open. The room contained a bed-sofa, a broken chair, an easel, and two men. One of them, wearing only a shirt and a pair of trousers kept up by a leather belt, was standing before the easel. He looked like a journeyman, but he was an artist making a sketch for an altar-piece. The other man was a youth with clear-cut features and, considering his environment, well-made clothes. He had taken off his coat, turned back his shirt and was serving as the artist's model. His handsome, noble face showed traces of a night of dissipation, and every now and then he dozed, each time reprimanded by the master who seemed to have taken him under his protection. As Falk was entering the room he heard the burden of one of these reprimands:

"That you should make such a hog of yourself and spend the night drinking with that loafer Sellén, and now be standing here wasting your time instead of being at the Commercial School! The right shoulder a little higher, please; that's better! Is it true that you've spent all the money for your rent and daren't go home? Have you nothing left? Not one farthing?"

"I still have some, but it won't go far." The young man pulled a scrap of paper out of his trousers pocket, and straightening it out, produced two notes for a crown each.

"Give them to me, I'll take care of them for you," exclaimed the master, seizing them with fatherly solicitude.

Falk, who had vainly tried to attract their attention, thought it best to depart as quietly as he had come. Once more passing the manure heap and the two philosophers, he turned to the left. He had not gone far when he caught sight of a young man who had put up his easel at the edge of a little bog planted with alder trees, close to the wood. He had a graceful, slight, almost elegant figure, and a thin, dark face. He seemed to scintillate life as he stood before his easel, working at a fine picture. He had taken off his coat and hat and appeared to be in excellent health and spirits; alternately talking to himself and whistling or humming snatches of song.

When Falk was near enough to have him in profile he turned round.

"Sellén! Good morning, old chap!"

"Falk! Fancy meeting you out here in the wood! What the deuce does it, mean? Oughtn't you to be at your office at this time of day?"

"No! But are you living out here?"

"Yes; I came here on the first of April with some pals. Found life in town too expensive—and, moreover, landlords are so particular."

A sly smile played about one of the corners of his mouth and his brown eyes flashed.

"I see," Falk began again; "then perhaps you know the two individuals who were sitting by the hot-beds just now, reading?"

"The philosophers? Of course, I do! The tall one is an assistant at the Public Sales Office at a salary of eighty crowns per annum, and the short one, Olle Montanus, ought to be at home at his sculpture—but since he and Ygberg have taken up philosophy, he has left off working and is fast going down hill. He has discovered that there is something sensual in art."

"What's he living on?"

"On nothing at all! Occasionally he sits to the practical Lundell and then he gets a piece of black pudding. This lasts him for about a day. In the winter Lundell lets him lie on his floor; 'he helps to warm the room,' he says, and wood is very dear; it was very cold here in April."

"How can he be a model? He looks such a God-help-me sort of chap."

"He poses for one of the thieves in Lundell's "Descent from the Cross," the one whose bones are already broken; the poor devil's suffering from hip disease;

he does splendidly when he leans across the back of a chair; sometimes the artist makes him turn his back to him; then he represents the other thief."

"But why doesn't he work himself? Has he no talent?"

"Olle Montanus, my dear fellow, is a genius, but he won't work. He's a philosopher and would have become a great man if he could have gone to college. It's really extraordinary to listen to him and Ygberg talking philosophy; it's true, Ygberg has read more, but in spite of that Montanus, with his subtle brain, succeeds in cornering him every now and again; then Ygberg goes away and reads some more, but he never lends the book to Montanus."

"I see! And you like Ygberg's philosophy?" asked Falk.

"Oh! It's subtle, wonderfully subtle! You like Fichte, don't you? I say! What a man!"

"Who were the two individuals in the cottage?" asked Falk, who did not like Fichte.

"Oh. You saw them too? One of them was the practical Lundell, a painter of figures, or rather, sacred subjects; the other one was my friend Rehnhjelm."

He pronounced the last few words with the utmost indifference, so as to heighten their effect as much as possible.

"Rehnhjelm?"

"Yes; a very nice fellow."

"He was acting as Lundell's model."

"Was he? That's like Lundell! He knows how to make use of people; he is extraordinarily practical. But come along, let's worry him; it's the only fun I have out here. Then, perhaps, you'll hear Montanus speaking, and that's really worth while."

Less for the sake of hearing Montanus speaking than for the sake of obtaining a glass of water, Falk followed Sellén, helping him to carry easel and paintbox.

The scene in the cottage was slightly changed; the model was now sitting on the broken chair, and Montanus and Ygberg on the bed-sofa. Lundell was standing at his easel, smoking; his seedy friends watched him and his old, snoring cherry-wood pipe; the very presence of a pipe and tobacco raised their spirits.

Falk was introduced and immediately Lundell monopolized him, asking him for his opinion of the picture he was painting. It was a Rubens, at least as far as the subject went, though anything but a Rubens in colour and drawing. Thereupon Lundell dilated on the hard times and difficulties of an artist, severely criticized the Academy, and censured the Government for neglecting native art. He was engaged in sketching an altar-piece, although he was convinced that it would be refused, for nobody could succeed without intrigues and connexions. And he scrutinized Falk's clothes, wondering whether *he* might be a useful connexion.

Falk's appearance had produced a different effect on the two philosophers. They scented a man of letters in him, and hated him because he might rob them of the reputation they enjoyed in the small circle. They exchanged significant glances, immediately understood by Sellén, who found it impossible to resist the temptation of showing off his friends in their glory, and, if possible, bring about an encounter. He soon found an apple of discord, aimed, threw, and hit.

"What do you say to Lundell's picture, Ygberg?"

Ygberg, not expecting to be called upon to speak so soon, had to consider his answer for a few seconds. Then he made his reply, raising his voice, while Olle rubbed his back to make him hold himself straight.

"A work of art may, in my opinion, be divided into two categories: subject and form. With regard to the subject in this work of art there is no denying that it is profound and universally human; the motive, properly speaking, is in itself fertile, and contains all the potentialities of artistic work. With regard to the form which of itself shall *de facto* manifest the idea, that is to say the absolute identity, the being, the ego—I cannot help saying that I find it less adequate."

Lundell was obviously flattered. Olle smiled his sunniest smile as if he were contemplating the heavenly hosts; the model was asleep and Sellén found that Ygberg had scored a complete success. All eyes were turned on Falk who was compelled to take up the gauntlet, for no one doubted that Ygberg's criticism was a challenge.

Falk was both amused and annoyed. He was searching the limbo of memory for philosophical air-guns, when he caught sight of Olle Montanus, whose convulsed face betrayed his desire to speak. Falk loaded his gun at random with Aristotle and fired.

"What do you mean by adequate? I cannot recollect that Aristotle made use of that word in his Metaphysics."

Absolute silence fell on the room; everybody felt that a fight between the artist's colony and the University of Upsala was imminent. The interval was longer than was desirable, for Ygberg was unacquainted with Aristotle and would have died sooner than have admitted it. As he was not quick at repartee, he failed to discover the breach which Falk had left open; but Olle did, caught Aristotle with both hands and flung him back at his opponent.

"Although I'm not a learned man, I venture to question whether you, Mr. Falk, have upset your opponent's argument? In my opinion *adequate* may be used and accepted as a definition in a logical conclusion, in spite of Aristotle not having mentioned the word in his Metaphysics. Am I right, gentlemen? I don't know, I'm not a learned man and Mr. Falk has made a study of these things."

He had spoken with half-closed eyelids; now he closed them entirely and looked impudently shy.

There was a general murmur of "Olle is right."

Falk realized that this was a matter to be handled without mittens, if the honour of Upsala was to be safeguarded; he made a pass with the philosophical pack of cards and threw up an ace.

"Mr. Montanus has denied the antecedent or said simply: *nego majorem!* Very well! I, on my part, declare that he has been guilty of a *posterius prius*; when he found himself on the horns of a dilemma he went astray and made a syllogism after *ferioque* instead of *barbara*. He has forgotten the golden rule: *Cæsare camestres festino baroco secundo*; and therefore his conclusion became weakened. Am I right gentlemen?"

"Quite right, absolutely right," replied everybody, except the two philosophers who had never held a book of logic in their hands.

Ygberg looked as if he had bitten on a nail, and Olle grinned as if a handful of snuff had been thrown into his eyes; but his native shrewdness had discovered the tactical method of his opponent. He resolved not to stick to the point, but to talk of something else. He brought out everything he had learned and everything he had heard, beginning with the Criticism of Fichte's Philosophy to which Falk had been listening a little while ago from behind the fence. The discussion went on until the morning was nearly spent.

In the meantime Lundell went on painting, his foul pipe snoring loudly. The model had fallen asleep on the broken chair, his head sinking deeper and deeper until, about noon, it hung between his knees; a mathematician could have calculated the time when it would reach the centre of the earth.

Sellén was sitting at the open window enjoying himself; but poor Falk, who had been under the impression that this terrible philosophy was a thing of the past, was compelled to continue throwing fistfuls of philosophic snuff into the eyes of his antagonists. The torture would never have come to an end if the model's centre of gravity had not gradually shifted to one of the most delicate parts of the chair; it gave way and the Baron fell on the floor. Lundell seized the opportunity to inveigh against the vice of drunkenness and its miserable consequences for the victim as well as for others; by others he meant, of course, himself.

Falk, anxious to come to the assistance of the embarrassed youth, eagerly asked a question bound to be of general interest.

"Where are the gentlemen going to dine?"

The room grew silent, so silent that the buzzing of the flies was plainly audible; Falk was quite unconscious of the fact that he had stepped on five corns at one and the same moment. It was Lundell who broke the silence. He and Rehnhjelm were going to dine at the "Sauce-Pan," their usual restaurant, for they had credit there; Sellén objected to the place because he did not like the cooking, and had not yet decided on another establishment; he looked at the model with an anxious, inquiring glance. Ygberg and Montanus were too "busy" and "not going to cut up their working-day" by "dressing and going up to town." They were going to get something out here, but they did not say what.

A general dressing began, principally consisting of a wash at the old garden-pump. Sellén, who was a dandy, had hidden a parcel wrapped in a newspaper underneath the bed-sofa, from which he produced collar, cuffs and shirt-front, made of paper. He knelt for a long time before the pump, gazing into the trough, while he put on a brownish-green tie, a present from a lady, and arranged his hair in a particular style.

When he had rubbed his shoes with a bur leaf, brushed his hat with his coat sleeve, put a grape-hyacinth in his buttonhole and seized his cinnamon cane, he was ready to go. To his question whether Rehnhjelm would be ready soon, Lundell replied that he would be hours yet, as he required his assistance in drawing; Lundell always devoted the time from twelve to two to drawing. Rehnhjelm submitted and obeyed, although he found it hard to part with Sellén, of whom he was fond, and stay with Lundell whom he disliked.

"We shall meet to-night at the Red Room," said Sellén, comforting him, and all agreed, even the philosophers and the moral Lundell.

On their way to town Sellén initiated his friend Falk into some of the secrets of the colonists. As for himself, he had broken with the Academy, because his views on art differed from theirs; he knew that he had talent and would eventually be successful, although success might be long in coming. It was, of course, frightfully difficult to make a name without the Royal Medal. There were also natural obstacles in his way. He was a native of the barren coast of Halland and loved grandeur and simplicity; but critics and public demanded detail and trifles; therefore his pictures did not sell; he could have painted what everybody else painted, but he scorned to do so.

Lundell, on the other hand, was a practical man—Sellén always pronounced the word *practical* with a certain contempt—he painted to please the public. He never suffered from indisposition; it was true he had left the Academy, but for secret, practical reasons; moreover, in spite of his assertion, he had not broken with it entirely. He made a good income out of his illustrations for magazines and, although he had little talent, he was bound to make his fortune some day, not only because of the number of his connexions, but also because of his intrigues. It was Montanus who had put him up to those; he was the originator of more than one plan which Lundell had successfully carried out. Montanus was a genius, although he was terribly unpractical.

Rehnhjelm was a native of Norrland. His father had been a wealthy man; he had owned a large estate which was now the property of his former inspector. The old aristocrat was comparatively poor; he hoped that his son would learn a lesson from the past, take an inspector's post and eventually restore the family to its former position by the acquisition of a new estate. Buoyed up with this hope, he had sent him to the Commercial School to study agricultural book-keeping, an accomplishment which the youth detested. He was a good fellow but a little weak, and allowing himself to be influenced by Lundell, who did not scorn to take the fee for his preaching and patronage in natura.

In the meantime Lundell and the Baron had started work; the Baron was drawing, while the master lay on the sofa, supervising the work, in other words, smoking.

"If you'll put your back into your work, you shall come to dinner with me at the 'Brass-Button,'" promised Lundell, feeling rich with the two crowns which he had saved from destruction.

Ygberg and Montanus had sauntered up the wooded eminence, intending to sleep away the dinner hour; Olle beamed after his victories, but Ygberg was depressed; his pupil had surpassed him. Moreover, his feet were cold and he was unusually hungry, for the eager discussion of dinner had awakened in him slumbering feelings successfully suppressed for the last twelve months. They threw themselves under a pine tree; Ygberg hid the precious, carefully wrapped up book, which he always refused to lend to Olle, under his head, and stretched himself full-length on the ground; he looked deadly pale, cold and calm like a corpse which has abandoned all hope of resurrection. He watched some little birds above his head picking at the pine seed and letting the husks fall down on him; he watched a cow, the picture of robust health, grazing among the alders; he saw the smoke rising from the gardener's kitchen chimney.

"Are you hungry, Olle?" he asked in a feeble voice.

"No!" replied Olle, casting covetous looks at the wonderful book.

"Oh! to be a cow!" sighed Ygberg, crossing his hands on his chest and giving himself up to all-merciful sleep.

When his low breathing had become regular, the waking friend gently pulled the book from its hiding-place, without disturbing the sleeper; then he turned over and lying on his stomach he began to devour the precious contents, forgetting all about the "Sauce-Pan" and the "Brass-Button."

CHAPTER IV. MASTER AND DOGS

Two or three days had passed. Mrs. Charles Nicholas Falk, a lady of twenty-two years of age, had just finished her breakfast in bed, the colossal mahogany bed in the large bedroom. It was only ten o'clock. Her husband had been away since seven, taking up flax on the shore. But the young wife had not stayed in bed—a thing she knew to be contrary to the rules of the house—because she counted on his absence. She had only been married for two years, but during that period she had found abundant time to introduce sweeping reforms in the old, conservative, middle-class household, where everything was old, even the servants. He had invested her with the necessary power on the day on which he had confessed his love to her, and she had graciously consented to become his wife, that is to say, permitted him to deliver her from the hated bondage of her parental roof, where she had been compelled to get up every morning at six o'clock and work all day long. She had made good use of the period of her engagement, for it was then that she had collected a number of guarantees, promising her a free and independent life, unmolested by any interference on the part of her husband. Of course these guarantees consisted merely of verbal assurances made by a love-sick man, but she, who had never allowed her emotion to get the better of her, had carefully noted them down on the tablets of her memory. After two years of matrimony, unredeemed by the promise of a child, the husband showed a decided inclination to set aside all these guarantees, and question her right to sleep as long as she liked, for instance, to have breakfast in bed, etcetera, etcetera; he had even been so indelicate as to remind her that he had pulled her out of the mire; had delivered her from a hell, thereby sacrificing himself. The marriage had been a misalliance, her father being one of the crew of the flagship.

As she lay there she was concocting replies to these and similar reproaches; and as her common sense during the long period of their mutual acquaintance had never been clouded by any intoxication of the senses, she had it well in hand and knew how to use it. The sounds of her husband's return filled her with unalloyed pleasure. Presently the dining-room door was slammed; a tremendous bellowing became audible; she pushed her head underneath the bed-clothes to smother her laughter. Heavy footsteps crossed the adjacent room and the angry husband appeared on the threshold, hat on head. His wife, who was turning her back to him, called out in her most dulcet tones:

"Is that you, little lubber? Come in, come in!"

The little lubber—this was a pet name, and husband and wife frequently used others, even more original ones—showed no inclination to accept her invitation, but remained standing in the doorway and shouted:

"Why isn't the table laid for lunch?"

"Ask the girls; it isn't my business to lay the table! But it's customary to take off one's hat on coming into a room, sir!"

"What have you done with my cap?"

"Burnt it! It was so greasy, you ought to have been ashamed to wear it."

"You burnt it? We'll talk about that later on! Why are you lying in bed until all hours of the morning, instead of supervising the girls?"

"Because I like it."

"Do you think I married a wife to have her refusing to look after her house? What?"

"You did! But why do you think I married you? I've told you a thousand times—so that I shouldn't have to work—and you promised me I shouldn't. Didn't you? Can you swear, on your word of honour, that you did *not* promise? That's the kind of man you are! You are just like all the rest!"

"It was long ago!"

"Long ago? When was long ago? Is a promise not binding for all times? Or must it be made in any particular season?"

The husband knew this unanswerable logic only too well, and his wife's good temper had the same effect as her tears—he gave in.

"I'm going to have visitors to-night," he stated.

"Oh, indeed! Gentlemen?"

"Of course! I detest women."

"Well, I suppose you've ordered what you want?"

"No, I want you to do that."

"I? I've no money for entertaining. I shall certainly not spend my housekeeping money on your visitors."

"No, you prefer spending it on dress and other useless things."

"Do you call the things I make for you useless? Is a smoking-cap useless? Are slippers useless? Tell me! Tell me candidly!"

She was an adept in formulating her questions in such a way that the reply was bound to be crushing for the person who had to answer them. She was merely copying her husband's method. If he wanted to avoid being crushed, he was compelled to keep changing the subject of conversation.

"But I really have a very good reason for entertaining a few guests to-night," he said with a show of emotion; "my old friend, Fritz Levin, of the Post Office, has been promoted after nineteen years' service—I read it in the Postal Gazette last night. But as you disapprove, and as I always give way to you, I shall let the matter drop, and shall merely ask Levin and schoolmaster Nyström to a little supper in the counting-house."

"So that loafer Levin has been promoted? I never! Perhaps now he'll pay you back all the money he owes you?"

"I hope so!"

"I can't understand how on earth you can have anything to do with that man! And the schoolmaster! Beggars, both of them, who hardly own the clothes they wear."

"I say, old girl, I never interfere in your affairs; leave my business alone."

"If you have guests downstairs, I don't see why I shouldn't have friends up here!"

"Well, why don't you?"

"All right, little lubber, give me some money then."

The little lubber, in every respect pleased with the turn matters had taken, obeyed with pleasure.

"How much? I've very little cash to-day."

"Oh! Fifty'll do."

"Are you mad?"

"Mad? Give me what I ask for. Why should I starve when you feast?"

Peace was established and the parties separated with mutual satisfaction. There was no need for him to lunch badly at home; he was compelled to go out; no necessity to eat a poor dinner and be made uncomfortable by the presence of ladies; he was embarrassed in the company of women, for he had been a bachelor too long; no reason to be troubled by his conscience, for his wife would not be alone at home; as it happened she wanted to invite her own friends and be rid of him—it was worth fifty crowns.

As soon as her husband had gone, Mrs. Falk rang the bell; she had stayed in bed all the morning to punish the housemaid, for the girl had remarked that in the old days everybody used to be up at seven. She asked for paper and ink and scribbled a note to Mrs. Homan, the controller's wife, who lived in the house opposite.

DEAR EVELYN—the letter ran:

Come in this evening and have a cup of tea with me; we can then discuss the statutes of the "Association for the Rights of Women." Possibly a bazaar or amateur theatricals would help us on. I am longing to set the association going; it is an urgent need, as you so often said; I feel it very deeply when I think about it. Do you think that her Ladyship would honour my house at the same time? Perhaps I ought to call on her first. Come and fetch me at twelve and we'll have a cup of chocolate at a confectioner's. My husband is away.

Yours affectionately,
EUGENIA.

P.S. My husband is away.

When she had despatched the letter, she got up and dressed, so as to be ready at twelve.

It was evening.

The eastern end of Long Street was already plunged in twilight, when the clock of the German church struck seven; only a faint ray of light from Pig Street fell into Falk's flax-shop, as Andersson made ready to close it for the night. The shutters in the counting-house had already been fastened and the gas was lighted. The place had been swept and straightened; two hampers with protruding necks of bottles, sealed red and yellow, some covered with tinfoil and others wrapped in pink tissue paper, were standing close to the door. The centre of the room was taken up by a table covered with a white cloth; on it stood an Indian bowl and a heavy silver candelabrum.

Nicholas Falk paced up and down. He was wearing a black frock-coat, and had a respectable as well as a festive air. He had a right to look forward to a pleasant evening: he had arranged it; he had paid for it; he was in his own house and at his ease, for there were no ladies present, and his invited guests were of a calibre which justified him in expecting from them not only attention and civility, but a little more.

They were only two, but he did not like many people; they were his friends, reliable, devoted as dogs; submissive, agreeable, always flattering and never contradicting him.

Being a man of means, he could have moved in better circles; he might have associated with his father's friends, and he did so, twice a year; but he was of too despotic a nature to get on with them.

It was three minutes past seven and still the guests had not arrived. Falk began to show signs of impatience. When he invited his henchmen, he expected them to be punctual to the minute. The thought of the unusually sumptuous arrangement, however, and the paralysing impression it was bound to make, helped him to control his temper a little longer; at the lapse of a few more moments Fritz Levin, the post-office official put in an appearance.

"Good-evening, brother—oh! I say!" He paused in the action of divesting himself of his overcoat, and feigned surprise at the magnificent preparations; he almost seemed in danger of falling on his back with sheer amazement. "The seven-armed candle-stick, and the tabernacle! Good Lord!" he ejaculated, catching sight of the hampers.

The individual who delivered these well-rehearsed witticisms while taking off his overcoat, was a middle-aged man of the type of the government official of twenty years ago; his whiskers joined his moustache, his hair was parted at the side and arranged in a *coup de vent*. He was extremely pale and as thin as a shroud. In spite of being well dressed, he was shivering with cold and seemed to have secret traffic with poverty.

Falk's manner in welcoming him was both rude and patronizing; it was partly intended to express his scorn of flattery, more particularly from an individual like the newcomer, and partly to intimate that the newcomer enjoyed the privilege of his friendship.

By way of congratulation he began to draw a parallel between Levin's promotion and his own father's receiving a commission in the militia.

"Well, it's a grand thing to have the royal mandate in one's pocket, isn't it? My father, too, received a royal mandate...."

"Pardon me, dear brother, but I've only been appointed."

"Appointed or royal mandate, it comes to the same thing. Don't teach me! My father, too, had a royal mandate...."

"I assure you...."

"Assure me—what d'you mean by that? D'you mean to imply that I'm standing here telling lies? Tell me, do you mean to say that I'm lying?"

"Of course I don't! There's no need to lose your temper like that!"

"Very well! You're admitting that I'm not telling lies, consequently you have a royal mandate. Why do you talk such nonsense? My father...."

The pale man, in whose wake a drove of furies seemed to have entered the counting-house—for he trembled in every limb—now rushed at his patron, firmly resolved to get over with his business before the feast began, so that nothing should afterwards disturb the general enjoyment.

"Help me," he groaned, with the despair of a drowning man, taking a bill out of his pocket.

Falk sat down on the sofa, shouted for Andersson, ordered him to open the bottles and began to mix the bowl.

"Help you? Haven't I helped you before?" he replied. "Haven't you borrowed from me again and again without paying me back? Answer me! What have you got to say?"

"I know, brother, that you have always been kindness itself to me."

"And now you've been promoted, haven't you? Everything was to be all right now; all debts were to be paid and a new life was to begin. I've listened to this kind of talk for eighteen years. What salary do you draw now?"

"Twelve hundred crowns instead of eight hundred as before. But now, think of this: the cost of the mandate was one hundred and twenty-five; the pension fund deducts fifty; that makes one hundred and seventy-five. Where I am to take it from? But the worst of it all is this: my creditors have seized half my salary; consequently I have now only six hundred crowns to live on instead of eight hundred—and I've waited nineteen years for that. Promotion is a splendid thing!"

"Why did you get into debt? One ought never to get into debt. Never—get—into debt."

"With a salary of eight hundred crowns all these years! How was it possible to keep out of it?"

"In that case you had no business to be in the employ of the Government. But this is a matter which doesn't concern me; doesn't—concern—me."

"Won't you sign once more? For the last time?"

"You know my principles; I never sign bills. Please let the matter drop."

Levin, who was evidently used to these refusals, calmed down. At the same moment schoolmaster Nyström entered, and, to the relief of both parties, interrupted the conversation. He was a dried-up individual of mysterious appearance and age. His occupation, too, was mysterious; he was supposed to be a master at a school in one of the southern suburbs—nobody ever asked which school and he did not care to talk about it. His mission, so far as Falk was concerned, was first to be addressed as schoolmaster when there were other people present; secondly, to be polite and submissive; thirdly, to borrow a little every now and then; never exceeding a fiver; it was one of Falk's fundamental needs that people should borrow money from him occasionally, only a little, of course; and, fourthly, to write verses on festive occasions; and the latter was not the least of the component parts of his mission.

Charles Nicholas Falk sat enthroned on his leather sofa, very conscious of the fact that it was *his* leather sofa, surrounded by his staff; or his dogs, as one might have said. Levin found everything splendid; the bowl, the glasses, the ladle, the cigars—the whole box had been taken from the mantelpiece—the matches, the ash-trays, the bottles, the corks, the wire—everything. The schoolmaster looked content; he was not called upon to talk, the other two did that; he was merely required to be present as a witness in case of need.

Falk was the first to raise his glass and drink—nobody knew to whom—but the schoolmaster, believing it to be to the hero of the day, produced his verses and began to read "To Fritz Levin on the Day of his Promotion."

Falk was attacked by a violent cough which disturbed the reading and spoiled the effect of the wittiest points; but Nyström, who was a shrewd man and had foreseen this, had introduced into his poem the finely felt and finely expressed reflection: "What would have become of Fritz Levin if Charles Nicholas hadn't befriended him?" This subtle hint at the numerous loans made by Falk to his friend, soothed the cough; it subsided and ensured a better reception to the last verse which was quite impudently dedicated to Levin, a tactlessness which again threatened to disturb the harmony. Falk emptied his glass as if he were draining a cup filled to the brim with ingratitude.

"You're not up to the mark, Nyström," he said.

"No, he was far wittier on your thirty-eighth birthday," agreed Levin, guessing what Falk was driving at.

Falk's glance penetrated into the most hidden recesses of Levin's soul, trying to discover whether any lie or fraud lay hidden there—and as his eyes were blinded by pride, he saw nothing.

"Quite true," he acquiesced: "I never heard anything more witty in all my life; it was good enough to be printed; you really ought to get your things printed. I say, Nyström, surely you know it by heart, don't you?"

Nyström had a shocking memory, or, to tell the truth, he had not yet had enough wine to commit the suggested outrage against decency and good form; he asked for time. But Falk, irritated by his quiet resistance, had gone too far to turn back, and insisted on his request. He was almost sure that he had a copy of the verses with him; he searched his pocket-book and behold! There they lay. Modesty did not forbid him to read them aloud himself; it would not have been for the first time; but it sounded better for another to read them. The poor dog bit his chain, but it held. He was a sensitive man, this schoolmaster, but he had to be brutal if he did not want to relinquish the precious gift of life, and he had been very brutal. The most private affairs were fully and openly discussed, everything in connexion with the birth of the hero, his reception into the community, his education and up-bringing were made fun of; the verses would have disgusted even Falk himself if they had treated of any other person, but the fact of their celebrating him and his doings made them excellent. When the recitation was over, his health was drunk uproariously, in many glasses, for each member of the little party felt that he was too sober to keep his real feelings under control.

The table was now cleared and an excellent supper consisting of oysters, birds, and other good things, was served. Falk went sniffing from dish to dish, sent one or two of them back, took care that the chill was taken off the stout, and that the wines were the right temperature. Now his dogs were called upon to do their work and offer him a pleasant spectacle. When everybody was ready, he pulled out his gold watch and held it in his hand while he jestingly asked a question which his convives had heard many times—so very many times:

"What is the time by the silver watches of the gentlemen?"

The anticipated reply came as in duty bound, accompanied by gay laughter: the watches were at the watch-maker's. This put Falk into the best of tempers, which found expression in the not at all unexpected joke:

"The animals will be fed at eight."

He sat down, poured out three liqueurs, took one and invited his friends to follow his example.

"I must make a beginning myself, as you both seem to be holding back. Don't let's stand on ceremony! Tuck in boys!"

The feeding began. Charles Nicholas who was not particularly hungry, had plenty of time to enjoy the appetite of his guests, and he continually urged them to eat. An unspeakably benevolent smile radiated from his bright, sunny countenance as he watched their zeal, and it was difficult to say what he enjoyed more, the fact of their having a good meal, or the fact of their being so hungry. He sat there like a coachman on his box, clicking his tongue and cracking his whip at them.

"Eat, Nyström! You don't know when you'll get a meal next. Help yourself, Levin; you look as if you could do with a little flesh on your bones. Are you grinning at the oysters? Aren't they good enough for a fellow like you? What do you say? Take another! Don't be shy! What do you say? You've had enough? Nonsense! Have a drink now! Take some stout, boys! Now a little more salmon! You *shall* take another piece, by the Lord Harry, you shall! Go on eating! Why the devil don't you? It costs you nothing!"

When the birds had been carved, Charles Nicholas poured out the claret with a certain solemnity. The guests paused, anticipating a speech. The host raised his glass, smelt the bouquet of the wine and said with profound gravity:

"Your health, you hogs!"

Nyström responded by raising his glass and drinking; but Levin left his untouched, looking as if he were secretly sharpening a knife.

When supper was over Levin, strengthened by food and drink, his senses befogged by the fumes of the wine, began to nurse a feeling of independence; a strong yearning for freedom stirred in his heart. His voice grew more resonant; he pronounced his words with increasing assurance, and his movements betrayed greater ease.

"Give me a cigar!" he said in a commanding tone; "no, not a weed like these, a good one."

Charles Nicholas, regarding his words as a good joke, obeyed.

"Your brother isn't here to-night," remarked Levin casually. There was something ominous and threatening in his voice; Falk felt it and became uneasy.

"No!" he said shortly, but his voice was unsteady.

Levin waited for a few moments before striking a second blow. One of his most lucrative occupations was his interference in other people's business; he carried gossip from family to family; sowed a grain of discord here and another there, merely to play the grateful part of the mediator afterwards. In this way he had obtained a great deal of influence, was feared by his acquaintances, and managed them as if they were marionettes.

Falk felt this disagreeable influence and attempted to shake it off; but in vain. Levin knew how to whet his curiosity; and by hinting at more than he knew, he succeeded in bluffing people into betraying their secrets.

At the present moment Levin held the whip and he promised himself to make his oppressor feel it. He was still merely playing with it, but Falk was waiting for the blow. He tried to change the subject of conversation. He urged his friends to drink and they drank. Levin grew whiter and colder as his intoxication increased, and went on playing with his victim.

"Your wife has visitors this evening," he suddenly remarked.

"How do you know?" asked Falk, taken aback.

"I know everything," answered Levin, showing his teeth. It was almost true; his widely extending business connexions compelled him to visit as many public places as possible, and there he heard much; not only the things which were spoken of in his society, but also those which were discussed by others.

Falk was beginning to feel afraid without knowing why, and he thought it best to divert the threatening danger. He became civil, humble even, but Levin's boldness still increased. There was no alternative, he must make a speech, remind his companions of the cause of the gathering, acknowledge the hero of the day. There was no other escape. He was a poor speaker, but the thing had to be done. He tapped against the bowl, filled the glasses, and recollecting an old speech, made by his father when Falk became his own master, he rose and began, very slowly:

"Gentlemen! I have been my own master these eight years; I was only thirty years old...."

The change from a sitting position to a standing one caused a rush of blood to his head; he became confused; Levin's mocking glances added to his embarrassment. His confusion grew; the figure thirty seemed something so colossal that it completely disconcerted him.

"Did I say thirty? I didn't—mean it. I was in my father's employ—for many years. It would take too long to recount everything—I suffered during those years; it's the common lot. Perhaps you think me selfish...."

"Hear! hear!" groaned Nyström who was resting his heavy head on the table.

Levin puffed the smoke of his cigar in the direction of the speaker, as if he were spitting in his face.

Falk, really intoxicated now, continued his speech; his eyes seemed to seek a distant goal without being able to find it.

"Everybody is selfish, we all know that. Ye-es! My father, who made a speech when I became my own master, as I was just saying——"

He pulled out his gold watch and took it off the chain. The two listeners opened their eyes wide. Was he going to make a present of it to Levin?

"Handed me on that occasion this gold watch which he, in his turn, had received from his father in the year...."

Again those dreadful figures—he must refer back.

"This gold watch, gentlemen, was presented to me, and I cannot think without emotion of the moment—when I received it. Perhaps you think I'm selfish gentlemen? I'm not. I know it's not good form to speak of oneself, but on such an occasion as this it seems very natural to glance at—the past. I only want to mention one little incident."

He had forgotten Levin and the significance of the day and was under the impression that he was celebrating the close of his bachelor-life. All of a sudden he remembered the scene between himself and his brother, and his triumph. He felt a pressing need to talk of this triumph, but he could not remember the details. He merely remembered having proved that his brother was a blackguard; he had forgotten the chain of evidence with the exception of only two facts: his brother and a blackguard: he tried to link them together, but they always fell apart. His brain worked incessantly and picture followed on picture. He must tell them of a generous action he had done; he recollected that he had given his wife some money in the morning, and had allowed her to sleep as long as she liked and have breakfast in bed; but that wasn't a suitable subject. He was in an unpleasant position, but fear of a silence and the two pairs of sharp eyes which followed his every movement, helped him to pull himself together. He realized that he was still standing, watch in hand. The watch? How had it got into his hand? Why were his friends sitting down, almost blotted out by the smoke, while he was on his legs? Oh! of course! He had been telling them about the watch, and they were waiting for the continuation of the story.

"This watch, gentlemen, is nothing special at all. It's only French gold."

The two whilom owners of silver watches opened their eyes wide. This information was new to them.

"And I believe it has only seven rubies—it's not a good watch at all—on the contrary—I should rather call it a cheap one...."

Some secret cause of which his brain was hardly conscious, made him angry; he must vent his wrath on something; tapping the table with his watch, he shouted:

"It's a damned bad watch, I say! Listen to me when I'm speaking! Don't you believe what I say, Fritz? Answer me! Why do you look so vicious? You don't believe me. I can read it in your eyes. Fritz, you don't believe what I'm saying. Believe me, I know human nature. And I might stand security for you once more! Either you are a liar, or I am! Shall I prove to you that you are a scoundrel? Shall I? Listen, Nyström, if—I—forge a bill—am I a scoundrel?"

"Of course you are a scoundrel, the devil take you!" answered Nyström, without a moment's hesitation.

"Yes—Yes!"

His efforts to remember whether Levin had forged a bill, or was in any way connected with a bill, were in vain. Therefore he was obliged to let the matter drop. Levin was tired; he was also afraid that his victim might lose consciousness, and that he and Nyström would be robbed of the pleasure of enjoying his intended discomfiture. He therefore interrupted Falk with a jest in his host's own style.

"Your health, old rascal!"

And down came the whip. He produced a newspaper.

"Have you seen the *People's Flag*?" he asked Falk in cold murderous accents.

Falk stared at the scandalous paper but said nothing. The inevitable was bound to happen.

"It contains a splendid article on the Board of Payment of Employés' Salaries."

Falk's cheeks grew white.

"Rumour has it that your brother wrote it."

"It's a lie! My brother's no scandal-monger! He isn't! D'you hear?"

"But unfortunately he had to suffer for it. I'm told he's been sacked."

"It's a lie!"

"I'm afraid it's true. Moreover, I saw him dining to-day at the 'Brass-Button' with a rascally looking chap. I'm sorry for the lad."

It was the worst blow that could have befallen Charles Nicholas. He was disgraced. His name, his father's name, was dishonoured; all that the old burgesses had achieved had been in vain. If he had been told that his wife had died, he could have borne up under it; a financial loss, too, might have been repaired. If he had been told that his friend Levin, or Nyström, had been arrested for forgery, he would have disowned them, for he had never shown himself in public in their company. But he could not deny his relationship to his brother. And his brother had disgraced him. There was no getting away from the fact.

Levin had found a certain pleasure in retailing his information. Falk, although he had never given his brother the smallest encouragement, was in the habit of boasting of him and his achievements to his friends. "My brother, the assessor, is a man of brains, and he'll go far, mark my words!" These continual indirect reproaches had long been a source of irritation to Levin, more particularly as Charles Nicholas drew a definite, unsurpassable, although indefinable, line between assessors and secretaries.

Levin, without moving a finger in the matter, had had his revenge at so little cost to himself that he could afford to be generous, and play the part of the comforter.

"There's no reason why you should take it so much to heart. Even a journalist can be a decent specimen of humanity, and you exaggerate the scandal. There can be no scandal where no definite individuals have been attacked. Moreover, the whole thing's very witty, and everybody's reading it."

This last pill of comfort made Falk furious.

"He's robbed me of my good name! My name! How can I show myself tomorrow at the Exchange? What will people say?"

By people he meant his wife. She would enjoy the situation because it would make the misalliance less marked. Henceforth they would be on the same social level. The thought was intolerable. A bitter hatred for all mankind took possession of his soul. If only he had been the bastard's father! Then he could have made use of his parental privilege, washed his hands of him, cursed him, and so have put an end to the matter; but there was no such thing as a brotherly privilege. Was it possible that he himself, was partly to blame for the disgrace? Had he not forced his brother into his profession? Maybe the scene of the morning or his brother's financial difficulties—caused by him—were to blame? No! he had never committed a base action; he was blameless; he was respected and looked up to; he was no scandal-monger; he had never been sacked by anybody. Did he not carry a paper in his pocket-book, testifying that he was the kindest friend with the kindest heart? Had not the schoolmaster read it aloud a little while ago? Yes, certainly—and he sat down to drink, drink immoderately—not to stupefy his conscience, there was no necessity for that, he had done no wrong, but merely to drown his anger. But it was no use; it boiled over—and scalded those who sat nearest to him.

"Drink, you rascals! That brute there's asleep! And you call yourselves friends! Waken him up, Levin!"

"Whom are you shouting at?" asked the offended Levin peevishly.

"At you, of course!"

Two glances were exchanged across the table which promised no good. Falk, whose temper improved directly he saw another man in a rage, poured a ladleful of the contents of the bowl on the schoolmaster's head, so that it trickled down his neck behind his collar.

"Don't dare to do that again!" threatened Levin.

"Who's to prevent me?"

"I! Yes, I! I shan't let you ruin his clothes. It's a beastly shame!"

"His clothes," laughed Falk. "Isn't it my coat? Didn't I give it to him?"

"You're going too far!" said Levin, rising to go.

"So you're going now! You've had enough to eat, you can't drink any more, you don't want me any longer to-night. Didn't you want to borrow a fiver? What?

Am I to be deprived of the honour of lending you some money? Didn't you want me to sign something? Sign, eh?"

At the word sign, Levin pricked up his ears. Supposing he tried to get the better of him in his excited condition? The thought softened him.

"Don't be unjust, brother," he re-commenced. "I'm not ungrateful; I fully appreciate your kindness; but I'm poor, poorer than you've ever been, or ever can be; I've suffered humiliations which you can't even conceive; but I've always looked upon you as a friend. I mean a friend in the highest sense of the word. You've had too much to drink to-night and so you're cross; this makes you unjust, but I assure you, gentlemen, in the whole world there beats no kinder heart than that of Charles Nicholas. And I don't say this for the first time. I thank you for your courtesy to-night, that is to say, if the excellent supper we have eaten, the magnificent wines we have drunk, have been eaten and drunk in my honour. I thank you, brother, and drink your health. Here's to you, brother Charles Nicholas! Thank you, thank you a thousand times! You've not done it in vain! Mark my words!"

Strange to say, these words, spoken in a tremulous voice—tremulous with emotion—produced good results. Falk felt good. Hadn't he again been assured that he had a kind heart? He firmly believed it.

The intoxication had reached the sentimental stage; they moved nearer together; they talked of their good qualities, of the wickedness of the world, the warmth of their feelings, the strength of their good intentions; they grasped each other's hands. Falk spoke of his wife; of his kindness to her; he regretted the lack of spirituality in his calling; he mentioned how painfully aware he was of his want of culture; he said that his life was a failure; and after the consumption of his tenth liqueur, he confided to Levin that it had been his ambition to go into the church, become a missionary, even. They grew more and more spiritual. Levin spoke of his dead mother, her death and funeral, of an unhappy love-affair, and finally of his religious convictions, as a rule jealously guarded as a secret. And soon they were launched on an eager discussion of religion.

It struck one—it struck two—and they were still talking while Nyström slept soundly, his arms on the table, and his head resting on his arms. A dense cloud of tobacco smoke filled the counting-house and robbed the gas flames of their brilliancy. The seven candles of the seven-armed candelabrum had burnt down to the sockets and the table presented a dismal sight. One or two glasses had lost their stems, the stained tablecloth was covered with cigar ash, the floor was strewn with matches. The daylight was breaking through the chinks of the shutters; its shafts pierced the cloud of smoke and drew cabbalistic figures on the tablecloth between the two champions of their faith, busily engaged in re-editing the Augsburg Confession. They were now talking with hissing voices; their brains were numbed; their words sounded dry, the tension was relaxing in spite of their diligent recourse to the bottle. They tried to whip up their souls into an ecstasy, but their efforts grew weaker and weaker; the spirit had died out of their conversation; they only exchanged meaningless words; the stupefied brains which had been whirling round like teetotums, slackened in their speed and finally stopped; one thought alone filled their minds—they must go to bed, if they did not want to loathe the sight of each other; they must be alone.

Nyström was shaken into consciousness; Levin embraced Charles Nicholas and took the opportunity to pocket three of his cigars. The heights which they had scaled were too sublime to allow them to talk of the bill just yet. They parted—the host let his guests out—he was alone! He opened the shutters—daylight poured into the room; he opened the window; the cool sea-breeze swept through the narrow street, one side of which was already illuminated by the rising sun. It struck four, he listened to that wonderful striking only heard by the poor wretch who yearns for the day on a bed of sickness or sorrow. Even Long Street East, that street of vice, of filth and brawls, lay in the early morning sun, still, desolate and pure. Falk felt deeply unhappy. He was disgraced—he was lonely! He closed window and shutters, and as he turned round and beheld the state of the room, he at once began setting it straight. He picked up the cigar ends and threw them into the grate; he cleared the table, swept the room, dusted it and put everything in its place. He washed his face and hands, and brushed his hair; a policeman might have thought him a murderer, intent on effacing all traces of his crime. But all the while he thought, clearly, firmly and logically. When he had straightened the room and himself, he formed a resolution, long brooded over, but now to be carried into effect. He would wipe away the disgrace which had fallen on his family; he would rise in the world and become a well-known and influential man; he would begin a new life; he would keep his reputation unstained and he would make his name respected. He felt that only a great ambition could help him to keep his head erect after the blow he had received to-night. Ambition had been latent in his heart; it had been awakened and henceforth it should rule his life.

Quite sober now, he lighted a cigar, drank a brandy, and went upstairs, quietly, gently, so as not to disturb his sleeping wife.

CHAPTER V. AT THE PUBLISHER'S

Arvid Falk decided to try Smith first, the almighty Smith—a name adopted by the publisher in his youth during a short trip to the great continent, from exaggerated admiration of everything American—the redoubtable Smith with his thousand arms who could *make* a writer in twelve months, however bad the original material. His method was well known, though none but he dared to make use of it, for it required an unparalleled amount of impudence. The writer whom he took up could be sure of making a name; hence Smith was overrun with nameless writers.

The following story is told as an instance of his irresistible power and capacity for starting an author on the road to fame. A young, inexperienced writer submitted his first novel, a bad one, to Smith. For some reason the latter happened to like the first chapter—he never read more—and decided to bless the world with a new author. The book was published bearing on the back of the cover the words: "Blood and Sword. A novel by Gustav Sjöholm. This work of the young and promising author whose highly respected name has for a long time been familiar to the widest circles, etc. etc. It is a book which we can strongly recommend to the novel-reading public." The book was published on April 3. On April 4, a review appeared in the widely read metropolitan paper the *Grey Bonnet*, in which Smith held fifty shares. It concluded by saying: "Gustav Sjöholm's name is already well known; the spreading of his fame does not lie with us; and we recommend this book not only to the novel-reading, but also to the novel-writing public." On April 5 an advertisement appeared in every paper of the capital with the following quotation: "Gustav Sjöholm's name is already well known; the spreading of his fame does not lie with us. (*Grey Bonnet*)." On the same evening a notice appeared in the *Incorruptible*, a paper read by nobody. It represented the book as a model of bad literature, and the reviewer swore that Gustav Sjöblom (reviewer's intentional slip), had no name at all. But as nobody read the *Incorruptible*, the opposition remained unheard. The other papers, unwilling to disagree with the venerable leading *Grey Bonnet*, and afraid of offending Smith, were mild in their criticisms, but no more. They held the view that with hard work Gustav Sjöholm might make a name for himself in the future. A few days of silence followed, but in every paper—in the *Incorruptible* in bold type—appeared the advertisement, shouting: "Gustav Sjöholm's name is already well known." Then a correspondence was started in the *X-köpings Miscellaneous*, reproaching the metropolitan papers with being hard on young authors. "Gustav Sjöholm is simply a genius," affirmed the hot-headed correspondent, "in spite of all that dogmatic blockheads might say to the contrary." On the next day the advertisement again appeared in all the papers, bawling: "Gustav Sjöholm's name is already well known, etc. (*Grey Bonnet*)." "Gustav Sjöholm is a genius, etc. (*X-köpings Miscellaneous*)." The cover of the next number of the magazine *Our Land*, one of Smith's publications, bore the notice: "We are pleased to be in a position to inform our numerous subscribers that the brilliant young author Gustav Sjöholm has promised us an original novel for our next number, etc." And then again the advertisement in the papers. Finally, when at Christmas the almanac *Our People* appeared, the authors mentioned on the title page were: Orvar Odd, Talis Qualis, Gustav Sjöholm, and others. It was a fact. In the eighth month Gustav Sjöholm was made. And the public was powerless. It had to swallow him. It was impossible to go into a bookseller's and look at a book without reading his name; impossible to take up a newspaper without coming across it. In all circumstances and conditions of life that name obtruded itself, printed on a slip of paper; it was put into the housewives' market baskets on Saturdays; the servants carried it home from the tradespeople; the crossing-sweeper swept it off the street, and the man of leisure went about with it in the pockets of his dressing-gown.

Being well aware of Smith's great power, the young man climbed the dark stairs of the publisher's house close to the Great Church, not without misgivings. He had to wait for a long time in an outer office, a prey to the most unpleasant meditations, until suddenly the door was burst open and a young man rushed out of an inner office, despair on his face and a roll of paper under his arm. Shaking in every limb, Falk entered the sanctum, where the despot received his visitors, seated on a low sofa, calm and serene as a god; he kindly nodded his grey head, covered by a blue cap, and went on smoking, peacefully, as if he had never shattered a man's hopes or turned an unhappy wretch from his door.

"Good morning, sir, good morning!"

His divinely flashing eyes glanced at the newcomer's clothes and approved; nevertheless he did not ask him to sit down.

"My name is—Falk."

"Unknown to me! What is your father?"

"My father is dead."

"Is he? Good! What can I do for you, sir?"

Falk produced a manuscript from his breast pocket and handed it to Smith; the latter sat on it without looking at it.

"You want me to publish it? Verse? I might have guessed it! Do you know the cost of printing a single page, sir? No, you don't."

And he playfully poked the ignoramus with the stem of his pipe.

"Have you made a name, sir? No! Have you distinguished yourself in any way? No!"

"The Academy has praised these verses."

"Which Academy? The Academy of Sciences? The one which publishes all that stuff about flints?"

"About flints?"

"Yes, you know the Academy of Sciences! Close to the Museum, near the river. Well, then!"

"Oh, no, Mr. Smith! The Swedish Academy, in the Exchange...."

"I see! The one with the tallow candles! Never mind; no man on earth can tell what purpose it serves! No, my dear sir, the essential thing is to have a name, a name like Tegnér, like Ohrenschlägel, like—Yes! Our country has many great poets, but I can't remember them just at the moment; but a name is necessary. Mr. Falk? H'm! Who knows Mr. Falk? I don't, and I know many great poets. As I recently said to my friend Ibsen: 'Now just you listen to me, Ibsen'—I call him Ibsen, quite plainly—'just you listen to me, write something for my magazine. I'll pay you whatever you ask!' He wrote—I paid—but I got my money back."

The annihilated young man longed to sink through the chinks in the floor when he realized that he was standing before a person who called Ibsen quite plainly "Ibsen." He longed to recover his manuscript, and go his way, as the other young man had done, away, far away, until he came to running water. Smith guessed it.

"Well, I've no doubt you can write Swedish, sir. And you know our literature better than I do. Good! I have an idea. I am told of great, beautiful, spiritual writers who lived in the past, let's say in the reign of Gustav Eriksson and his daughter Christina. Isn't that so?"

"Gustavus Adolfus."

"Gustavus Adolfus, so be it! I remember there was one with a great, a very great name; he wrote a fine work in verse, on God's Creation, I believe! His Christian name was Hokan!"

"You mean Haquin Spegel, Mr. Smith! 'God's Works and Rest.'"

"Ah, yes! Well, I've been thinking of publishing it. Our nation is yearning for religion these days; I've noticed that; and one must give the people something. I have given them a good deal of Hermann Francke and Arndt, but the great Foundation can sell more cheaply than I can, and now I want to bring out something good at a fair price. Will you take the matter in hand?"

"I don't know where I come in, as it is but a question of a reprint," answered Falk, not daring to refuse straight out.

"Dear me, what ignorance! You would do the editing and proof-reading, of course. Are we agreed? You publish it, sir! What? Shall we draw up a little agreement? The work must appear in numbers. What? A little agreement. Just hand me pen and ink. Well?"

Falk obeyed; he was unable to offer resistance. Smith wrote and Falk signed.

"Well, so much for that! Now, there's another thing! Give me that little book on the stand! The third shelf! There! Now look here! A brochure—title: "The Guardian Angel." Look at the vignette! An angel with an anchor and a ship—it's a schooner without any yards, I believe! The splendid influence of marine insurance on social life in general is well known. Everybody has at one time or other sent something more or less valuable across the sea in a ship. What? Well! Everybody doesn't realize this. No! Consequently it is our duty to enlighten those who are ignorant; isn't that so? Well! We know, you and I; therefore it is for us to enlighten those who don't. This book maintains that everybody who sends things across the water should insure them. But this book is badly written. Well! We'll write a better one. What? You'll write me a novel of ten pages for my magazine *Our Land*, and I expect you to have sufficient gumption to introduce the name *Triton*—which is the name of a new limited liability company, founded by my nephew, and we are told to help our neighbours—twice, neither more nor less; but it must be done cleverly and so that it is not at all obvious. Do you follow me?"

Falk found the offer repulsive, although it contained nothing dishonest; however, it gave him a start with the influential man, straight away, without any effort on his part. He thanked Smith and accepted.

"You know the size? Sixteen inches to the page, altogether a hundred and sixty inches of eight lines each. Shall we write a little agreement?"

Smith drew up an agreement and Falk signed.

"Well, now! You know the history of Sweden? Go to the stand again—you will find a cliché there, a wood block. To the right! That's it! Can you tell me who the lady is meant for? She is supposed to be a queen."

Falk, who saw nothing at first but a piece of black wood, finally made out some human features and declared that to the best of his belief it represented Ulrica Eleonora.

"Didn't I say so? Hihihi! The block has been used for Elizabeth, Queen of England, in an American popular edition. I've bought it cheaply, with a lot of others. I'm going to use it for Ulrica Eleonora in my *People's Library*. Our people are splendid; they are so ready to buy my books. Will you write the letterpress?"

Although Falk did not like the order, his super-sensitive conscience could find no wrong in the proposal.

"Well then! We'd better make out a little agreement. Sixteen pages octavo, at three inches, at twenty-four lines each. There!"

Falk, realizing that the audience was over, made a movement to recover his manuscript on which Smith had all along been sitting. But the latter would not give it up; he declared that he would read it, although it might take him some time.

"You're a sensible man, sir, who knows the value of time," he said. "I had a young fellow here just before you came in; he also brought me verses, a great poem, for which I have no use. I made him the same offers I just made to you, sir; do you know what he said? He told me to do something unmentionable. He did, indeed, and rushed out of the office. He'll not live long, that young man! Good day, good day! Don't forget to order a copy of Hoken Spegel! Well, good day, good day."

Smith pointed to the door with the stem of his pipe and Falk left him.

He did not walk away with light footsteps. The wood-block in his pocket was heavy and weighed him down, kept him back. He thought of the pale young man with the roll of manuscript who had dared to say a bold thing to Smith, and pride stirred in his heart. But memories of old paternal warnings and advice whispered the old lie to him that all work was equally honourable, and reproved him for his pride. He laid hold of his common sense and went home to write a hundred and ninety-two inches about Ulrica Eleonora.

As he had risen early he was at his writing-table at nine o'clock. He filled a large pipe, took two sheets of paper, wiped his steel nibs and tried to recall all he knew about Ulrica Eleonora. He looked her up in Ekelund and Fryxell. There was a great deal under the heading Ulrica Eleonora, but very little about her personally. At half-past nine he had exhausted the subject. He had written down her birthplace, and the place where she died, when she came to the throne, when she abdicated, the names of her parents and the name of her husband. It was a commonplace excerpt from a church register—and filled three pages, leaving thirteen to be covered. He smoked two or three pipes and dragged the inkstand with his pen, as if he were fishing for the Midgard serpent, but he brought up nothing. He was bound to say something about her personally, sketch her character; he felt as if he were sitting in judgment on her. Should he praise or revile her? As it was a matter of complete indifference to him, his mind was still not made up when it struck eleven. He reviled her—and came to the end of the fourth page, leaving twelve to be accounted for. He was at his wits' end. He wanted to say something about her rule, but as she had not ruled, there was nothing to be said. He wrote about her Council—one page—leaving eleven; he whitewashed Görtz—another—leaving ten. He had not yet filled half the required space. He hated the woman! More pipes! Fresh steel nibs! He went back to remoter days, passing them in review, and being now in a thoroughly bad temper, he overthrew his old idol, Charles XII, and hurled him in the dust; it was done in a few words, and only added one more page to his pile. There still remained nine. He anticipated events and criticised Frederick I. Half a page! He glanced at the paper with unhappy eyes; he glimpsed half-way house, but could not reach it. He had written seven and a half small pages; Ekelund had only managed one and a half.

He flung the wood-block on the floor, kicked it underneath his writing-table, crawled after it, dusted it and put it in its former place. It was torture! His soul was as dry as the block. He tried to work himself up to views which he did not hold; he tried to awaken some sort of emotion in his heart for the dead queen, but her plain, dull features, cut into the wood, made no more impression on him than he on the block. He realized his incapacity and felt despondent, degraded. And this was the career of his choice, the one he had preferred to all others. With a strong appeal to his reason, he turned to the guardian angel.

The brochure was originally written for a German society, the "Nereus," and the argument was as follows: Mr. and Mrs. Castle had emigrated to America, where they acquired a large estate. To make the story possible, they had sold their land, and, very unpractically, invested the total amount realized in costly furniture and objects of art. As the story required that everything should be completely lost and nothing whatever saved from the shipwreck, they sent off the whole lot in advance by the *Washington*, a first-class steamer, copper bottomed, with watertight bulkheads, and insured with the great German Marine Insurance Company for £60,000. Mr. and Mrs. Castle and the children followed on the *Bolivar*, the finest boat of the White Star Line, insured with the great Marine Insurance Company "Nereus" (Capital $10,000,000), and safely arrived at Liverpool. They left Liverpool and all went well until they came to Skagen Point. During the whole voyage the weather had, of course, been magnificent; the sky was clear and radiant, but at the dangerous Skagen Point a storm overtook them; the steamer was wrecked; the parents, whose lives were insured, were drowned, thereby guaranteeing to the children, who were saved, £1500. The latter, rejoicing at their parents' foresight, arrived at Hamburg in good spirits, eager to take possession of the insurance money and the property which they had inherited from their parents. Imagine their consternation when they were told that the *Washington* had been wrecked a fortnight before their arrival on Dogger Bank; their whole fortune, which had been left uninsured, was lost. All that remained was the life insurance money. They hurried to the Company's agents. A fresh disaster! They were told that their parents had not paid the last premium which—oh, fateful blow!—had been due on the day preceding their death. The distressed children bitterly mourned their parents, who had worked so hard for them. They embraced each other with tears and made a solemn vow that henceforth all their possessions should be insured, and that they would never neglect paying their life insurance premiums.

This story was to be localized, adapted to a Swedish environment and made into a readable novelette; and with this he was to make his début in the literary world. The devil of pride whispered to him not to be a blackguard and to leave the business alone, but this voice was silenced by another, which came from the region of his empty stomach, and was accompanied by a gnawing, stinging sensation. He drank a glass of water and smoked another pipe. But his discomfort increased. His thoughts became more gloomy; he found his room uncomfortable, the morning dull and monotonous; he was tired and despondent; everything seemed repulsive; his ideas were spiritless and revolved round nothing but unpleasant subjects; and still his discomfort grew. He wondered whether he was hungry? It was one o'clock. He never dined before three. He anxiously examined his purse. Threepence halfpenny! For the first time in his life he would have to go without dinner! This was a trouble hitherto unknown to him. But with threepence halfpenny there was no necessity to starve. He could send for bread and beer. No! That would not do; it was *infra dig*. Go to a dairy? No! Borrow? Impossible! He knew nobody who would lend. No sooner had he realized this than hunger began to rage in him like a wild beast let loose, biting him, tearing him and chasing him round the room. He smoked pipe after pipe to stupefy the monster; in vain.

A rolling of drums from the barracks yard told him that the guardsmen were lining up with their copper vessels to receive their dinner; every chimney was smoking; the dinner bell went in the dockyard; a hissing sound came from his neighbour's, the policemen's kitchen; the smell of roast meat penetrated through the chinks of the door; he heard the rattling of knives and plates in the adjacent room, and the children saying grace. The paviours in the street below were taking their after-dinner nap with their heads on their empty food baskets. The whole town was dining; everybody, except he. He raged against God. But all at once a clear thought shot through his brain. He seized Ulrica Eleonora and the guardian angel, wrapped them in paper, wrote Smith's name and address on the parcel, and handed the messenger his threepence halfpenny. And with a sigh of relief he threw himself on his sofa and starved, with a heart bursting with pride.

CHAPTER VI. THE RED ROOM

The same afternoon sun which had witnessed Arvid Falk's defeat in his first battle with hunger shone serenely into the cottage of the artists' colony, where Sellén, in shirt sleeves, was standing before his easel working at his picture which had to be in the Exhibition on the following morning before ten, finished, framed, and varnished. Olle Montanus sat on the bed-sofa reading the wonderful book lent to him by Ygberg for a day in exchange for his muffler; betweenwhiles he cast a look of admiration at Sellén's picture. He had great faith in Sellén's talent. Lundell was calmly working at his "Descent from the Cross"; he had already sent three pictures to the Exhibition and, like many others, he was awaiting their sale with a certain amount of excitement.

"It's fine, Sellén," said Olle, "you paint divinely."

"May I look at your spinach?" asked Lundell, who never admired anything, on principle.

The subject was simple and grand. The picture represented a stretch of drifting sand on the coast of Halland with the sea in the background; it was full of the feeling of autumn; sunbeams were breaking through riven clouds; the foreground was partly drift sand and newly washed-up seaweed, dripping wet and lit by the sun; in the middle distance lay the sea, with huge crested waves—the greater part in deep shadow; but in the background, on the horizon, the sun was shining, opening up a perspective into infinity; the only figures were a flock of birds.

No unperverted mind who had the courage to face the mysterious wealth of solitude, had seen promising harvests choked by the drifting sand, could fail to understand the picture. It was painted with inspiration and talent; the colouring was the result of the prevailing mood, the mood was not engendered by the colouring.

"You *must* have something in the foreground," persisted Lundell. "Take my advice."

"Rubbish!" replied Sellén.

"Do what I tell you, and don't be a fool, otherwise you won't sell. Paint in a figure; a girl by preference; I'll help you if you don't know how to do it. Look here...."

"None of your tricks! What's the good of petticoats in a high wind? You're mad on petticoats!"

"Very well, do as you like," replied Lundell, a little hurt by the reference to one of his weakest points. "But instead of those grey gulls you should have painted storks. Nobody can tell what sort of birds these are. Picture the red storks' legs against the dark cloud! What a contrast!"

"You don't understand!"

Sellén was not clever in stating his motives, but he was sure of his points and his sound instincts led him safely past all errors.

"You won't sell," Lundell began again; his friend's financial position worried him.

"Well, I shall live somehow in spite of it. Have I ever sold anything? Am I the worse for it? Do you think I don't know that I should sell if I painted like everybody else? Do you think I can't paint as badly as everybody else? I just don't want to!"

"But you ought to think of paying your debts! You owe Mr. Lund of the 'Sauce-Pan' several hundred crowns."

"Well, that won't ruin him. Moreover I gave him a picture worth twice that amount."

"You are the most selfish man I ever met! The picture wasn't worth twenty crowns."

"I value it at five hundred, as prices go! But unfortunately inclinations and tastes differ here below. I find your 'Crucifixion' an execrable performance, you find it beautiful. Nobody can blame you for it. Tastes differ!"

"But you spoilt our credit at the 'Sauce-Pan.' Mr. Lund refused to give me credit yesterday, and I don't know how I'm to get a dinner to-day."

"What does it matter? Do without it! I haven't had a dinner these last two years."

"You plundered Mr. Falk the other day, when he fell into your clutches."

"That's true! He's a nice chap; moreover, he has talent. There's much originality in his verses; I have read some of them these last few evenings. But I'm afraid he's not hard enough to get on in this world. He's too sensitive, the rascal!"

"If he sees much of you, he'll get over that. It's outrageous how you spoilt that young Rehnhjelm in so short a time. I hear you are encouraging him to go on the stage."

"Did he tell you that? The little devil! He'll get on if he remains alive; but that's not so simple when one has so little to eat! God's death! I've no more paint! Can you spare any white? Merciful Lord! All the tubes are empty! You must give me some, Lundell!"

"I've no more than I want for myself—and even if I had, I should take jolly good care not to give you any."

"Stop talking nonsense! You know there's no time to lose!"

"Seriously, I haven't got your colours. If you weren't so wasteful your tubes would go further."

"I know that! Give me some money, then!"

"Money, indeed! That's no go!"

"Get up, Olle! You must go and pawn something."

At the word pawn Olle's face brightened; he saw a prospect of food.

Sellén was searching the room.

"What's this? A pair of boots! We'll get twopence halfpenny on them; they'd better be sold."

"They're Rehnhjelm's! You can't take them," objected Lundell, who had meant to put them on in the afternoon when he was going up to town. "Surely you aren't going to take liberties with other people's property!"

"Why not? He'll be getting money for them. What's in this parcel? A velvet waistcoat! A beauty! I shall keep it for myself and then Olle can pawn mine. Collars and cuffs? Oh! paper! A pair of socks! Here, Olle, twopence halfpenny! Wrap them in the waistcoat! You can sell the empty bottles—I think the best thing would be to sell everything."

"Do you mean to say you are going to sell other people's belongings? Have you no sense of right and wrong?" interrupted Lundell again, hoping to gain possession of the parcel which had long tempted him, by means of persuasion.

"He'll get paid for it later on! But it isn't enough yet. We must take the sheets off the bed. Why not? We don't want any sheets! Here, Olle, cram them in!"

Olle very skilfully made a bag of one of the sheets and stuffed everything into it, while Lundell went on eagerly protesting.

When the parcel was made, Olle took it under his arm, buttoned his ragged coat so as to hide the absence of a waistcoat, and set out on his way to the town.

"He looks like a thief," said Sellén, watching him from the window with a sly smile. "I hope the police won't interfere with him! Hurry up, Olle!" he shouted after the retreating figure. "Buy six French rolls and two half-pints of beer if there's anything over after you've bought the paint."

Olle turned round and waved his hat with as much assurance as if he had the feast already safely in his pockets.

Lundell and Sellén were alone. Sellén was admiring his new velvet waistcoat for which Lundell had nursed a secret passion for a long time. He scraped his palette and cast envious glances at the lost glory. But it was something else he was trying to speak of; something else, which was very difficult to mention.

"I wish you'd look at my picture," he said at last. "What do you think of it, seriously?"

"Don't draw and slave at it so much! Paint! Where does the light come from? From the clothes, from the flesh! It's crazy! What do these people breathe? Colour! Turpentine! I see no air!"

"Well," said Lundell, "tastes differ, as you said just now. What do you think of the composition?"

"Too many people!"

"You're awful! I want more, not fewer."

"Let me see! There's one great mistake in it."

Sellén shot a long glance at the picture, a glance peculiar to the inhabitants of sea-coasts and plains.

"Yes, you're right," agreed Lundell. "You can see it then?"

"There are only men in your picture. It's somewhat monotonous."

"That's it! But fancy, that you should see that!"

"You want a woman then?"

Lundell looked at him, wondering whether he was joking, but was unable to settle the point, for Sellén was whistling.

"Yes, I want a female figure," he replied at last.

There was silence, and gradually the silence became uncomfortable: two very old acquaintances in a *tête-à-tête* conversation.

"I wish I knew where to get a model from! I don't want the Academy models, the whole world knows them, and, besides, the subject is a religious one."

"You want something better? I understand! If it were not for the nude, I might perhaps...."

"It isn't for the nude! Are you mad? Among all those men ... besides, it's a religious subject."

"Yes, yes, we know all that. She must be dressed in something Oriental, and bend down as if she were picking up something, show her shoulders, her neck, and the first vertebra, I understand. Religious like the Magdalene! Bird's-eye view!"

"You scoff and jeer at everything!"

"Let's keep to the point! You shall have your model, for it's impossible to paint without one. You, yourself, don't know one. Very well! Your religious principles don't allow you to look for one; therefore Rehnhjelm and I, the two black sheep, will find you one."

"But it must be a respectable girl, don't forget that."

"Of course! We will see what we can do, the day after to-morrow, when we shall be in funds."

And they went on painting, quietly, diligently, until four—until five. Every now and then their anxious glances swept the road. Sellén was the first to break the uneasy silence.

"Olle is a long time! Something must have happened to him," he said.

"Yes, something must be up. But why do you always send the poor devil? Why can't you run your own errands?"

"He's nothing else to do, and he likes going."

"How d'you know? And besides, let me tell you, nobody can say how Olle's going to turn out. He has great schemes, and he may be on his feet any day; then it will be a good thing to have him for a friend."

"You don't say so! What great work is he going to accomplish? I can quite believe that Olle will become a great man, although not a great sculptor. But where the devil is he? Do you think he's spending the money?"

"Possibly, possibly! He's had nothing for a long time and perhaps the temptation was too strong," answered Lundell, tightening his belt by two holes, and wondering what he would do in Olle's place.

54

"Well, he's only human, and charity begins at home," said Sellén, who knew perfectly well what he would have done under the circumstances. "But I can't wait any longer. I must have paint, even if I have to steal it. I'll go and see Falk."

"Are you going to squeeze more out of that poor chap? You robbed him yesterday for your frame. And it wasn't a small sum you borrowed."

"My dear fellow! I am compelled to cast all feelings of shame to the winds; there's no help for it. One has to put up with a good deal. However, Falk is a great-hearted fellow who understands that a man may suddenly find himself in Queer Street. Anyhow, I'm going. If Olle returns in the meantime, tell him he's a blockhead. So long! Come to the Red Room and we'll see whether our master will be graciously pleased to give us something to eat before the sun sets. Lock the door, when you leave, and push the key underneath the mat. By-by!"

He went, and before long he stood before Falk's door in Count Magni Street. He knocked, but received no reply. He opened the door and went in. Falk, who had probably had uneasy dreams, awakened from his sleep, jumped up and stared at Sellén without recognizing him.

"Good evening, old chap," said Sellén.

"Oh! It's you. I must have had a strange dream. Good evening! Sit down and smoke a pipe! Is it evening already?"

Sellén thought he knew the symptoms, but he pretended to notice nothing.

"You didn't go to the 'Brass Button' to-day?" he remarked.

"No," replied Falk, confused; "I wasn't there, I was at Iduna."

He really did not know whether he had dreamt it or whether he had actually been there; but he was glad that he had said it, for he was ashamed of his position.

"Perfectly right, old chap," commented Sellén; "the cooking at the 'Brass Button' is beneath criticism."

"It is, indeed," agreed Falk; "the soup's damned bad."

"And the old head-waiter is always on the spot, counting the rolls and butter, the rascal!"

The words "rolls and butter" awakened Falk to consciousness; he did not feel hungry, only a little shaky and faint. But he did not like the subject of conversation and changed it.

"Well, will your picture be ready for to-morrow?" he asked.

"No, unfortunately, it won't."

"What's the matter now?"

"I can't possibly finish it."

"You can't? Why aren't you at home working?"

"The old, old story, my dear fellow! I have no paint! No paint!"

"But there's a remedy for that! Or haven't you any money?"

"If I had I should be all right."

"And I haven't any either! What's to be done?"

Sellén dropped his eyes until his glance reached the height of Falk's waistcoat pocket, into which a heavy gold chain was creeping; not that Sellén believed it to be gold, good, stamped gold. He could not have understood the recklessness of carrying so much money outside one's waistcoat. But his thoughts were following a definite course, and he continued:

"If at least I had something to pawn! But we carelessly pledged our winter overcoats on the first sunny day in April."

Falk blushed. He had never done such a thing.

"Do you pawn your winter overcoats?" he asked. "Do you get anything on them?"

"One gets something on everything—on everything," said Sellén, laying stress on *everything*; "the only thing needful is to have something."

To Falk the room seemed to be turning round. He had to sit down. Then he pulled out his gold watch.

"How much, do you think, should I get on this watch and chain?"

Sellén seized the future pledges and looked at them with the eye of a connoisseur.

"Is it gold?" he asked faintly.

"It is gold."

"Stamped?"

"Stamped."

"The chain, too?"

"The chain, too."

"A hundred crowns," declared Sellén, shaking his hand so that the gold chain rattled. "But it's a pity! You shouldn't pawn your things for my sake."

"Then for my own," said Falk, anxious to avoid the semblance of an unselfishness which he did not feel. "I want money, too. If you'll turn them into cash, you'll do me a service."

"All right then," said Sellén, resolved not to embarrass his friend by asking indelicate questions. "I'll pawn them! Pull yourself together, old chap! Life is hard at times, I don't deny it; but we go through with it."

He patted Falk's shoulder with a cordiality which did not often pierce the scorn with which he had enveloped himself.

They went out together.

By the time they had concluded the business it was seven o'clock. They bought the paint and repaired to the Red Room.

Berns' "Salon" had just begun to play its civilizing part in the life of Stockholm by putting an end to the unhealthy *café-chantants* life which had flourished—or raged—in the sixties, and from the capital had spread over the whole country. Here, every evening after seven, crowds of young people met who lived in that abnormal transition stage which begins on leaving the parental roof and ends with the foundation of a new home and family; here were numbers of young men who had escaped from the solitude of their room or attic to find light and warmth and a fellow-creature to talk to. The proprietor had made more than one attempt to amuse his patrons by pantomimic, gymnastic, ballet, and other performances; but he had been plainly shown that his guests were not in search of amusement, but in quest of peace; what was wanted was a consulting-room, where one was likely every moment to chance on a friend. The band was tolerated because it did not stop conversation, but rather stimulated it, and gradually it became as much a component of the Stockholm evening diet, as punch and tobacco.

In this way Berns' Salon became the bachelors' club of all Stockholm. Every circle had its special corner; the colonists of Lill-Jans had usurped the inner chess room, usually called the Red Room on account of its red furniture and for the sake of brevity. It was a safe meeting-ground even if during the whole day the members had been scattered like chaff. When times were hard and funds had to be raised at any cost, regular raids were made from this spot round the room. A chain was formed: two members skirmished in the galleries, and two others attacked the room lengthways. One might have said they dredged the room with a ground-net, and they rarely dredged in vain, for there was a constant flow of new arrivals during the evening.

To-night, however, these efforts were not required; Sellén, calmly and proudly, sat down on the red sofa in the background. After having acted a little farce on the subject of what they were going to drink, they came to the conclusion that they must have something to eat first. They were starting the "sexa," and Falk was beginning to feel a return of his strength, when a long shadow fell across their table. Before them stood Ygberg, as pale and emaciated as ever. Sellén, who was in funds to-night, and under those circumstances invariably courteous and kind-hearted, pressed him to have dinner with them, and Falk seconded the invitation. Ygberg hesitated while examining the contents of the dishes and calculating whether his hunger would be satisfied or only half-satisfied.

"You wield a stinging pen, Mr. Falk," he said, in order to deflect the attention from the raids which his fork was making on the tray.

"How? What do you mean?" asked Falk flushing; he did not know that anybody had made the acquaintance of his pen.

"The article has created a sensation."

"What article? I don't understand."

"The correspondence in the *People's Flag* on the Board of Payment of Employés' Salaries."

"I didn't write it."

"But the Board is convinced that you did. I just met a member who's a friend of mine; he mentioned you as the author; I understood that the resentment was fierce."

"Indeed?"

Falk felt that he was half to blame for it; he realized now what the notes were which Struve had been making on that evening on Moses Height. But Struve had merely reported what he, Falk, had said. He was responsible for his statements and must stand by them even at the risk of being considered a scandal-monger. Retreat was impossible; he realized that he must go on.

"Very well," he said, "I am the instigator of the article. But let us talk of something else! What do you think of Ulrica Eleonora? Isn't she an interesting character? Or what is your opinion of the Maritime Insurance Company Triton? Or Haquin Spegel?"

"Ulrica Eleonora is the most interesting character in the whole history of Sweden," answered Ygberg gravely; "I've just had an order to write an essay on her."

"From Smith?" asked Falk.

"Yes; but how do you know?"

"I've returned the block this afternoon."

"It's wrong to refuse work. You'll repent it! Believe me."

A hectic flush crimsoned Falk's cheeks; he spoke feverishly. Sellén sat quietly on the sofa, smoking. He paid more attention to the band than to the conversation, which did not interest him because he did not understand it. From his sofa corner he could see through the two open doors leading to the south gallery, and catch a glimpse of the north gallery. In spite of the dense cloud of smoke which hung above the pit between the two galleries, he could distinguish the faces on the other side. Suddenly his attention was caught by something in the distance. He clutched Falk's arm.

"The sly-boots! Look behind the left curtain!"

"Lundell!"

"Just so! He's looking for a Magdalene! See! He's talking to her now! What a beautiful girl!"

Falk blushed, a fact which did not escape Sellén.

"Does he come here for his models?" he asked surprised.

"Well, where else should he go to? He can't find them in the dark."

A moment afterwards Lundell joined them; Sellén greeted him with a patronizing nod, the significance of which did not seem to be lost on the newcomer. He bowed to Falk with more than his usual politeness, and expressed his astonishment at Ygberg's presence in disparaging words. Ygberg, carefully observing him, seized the opportunity to ask him what he would like to eat. Lundell opened his eyes; he seemed to have fallen among magnates. He felt happy; a gentle, philanthropic mood took possession of him, and after ordering a hot supper, he felt constrained to give expression to his emotion. It was obvious that he wanted to say something to Falk, but it was difficult to find an opening. The band was playing "Hear us, Sweden!" and a moment afterwards "A Stronghold is our God."

Falk called for more drink.

"I wonder whether you admire this fine old hymn as much as I do, Mr. Falk?" began Lundell.

Falk, who was not conscious of admiring any one hymn more than another, asked him to have some punch. Lundell had misgivings; he did not know whether he could venture. He thought he had better have some more supper first; he was not strong enough to drink. He tried to prove it, after his third liqueur, by a short but violent attack of coughing.

"The *Torch of Reconciliation* is a splendid name," he said presently; "it proves at the same time the deep, religious need of atonement, and the light which came into the world when the miracle happened which has always given offence to the proud in spirit."

He swallowed a meat ball while carefully studying the effect of his remark—and felt anything but flattered when he saw three blank faces staring at him, expressing nothing but consternation.

"Spegel is a great name, and his words are not like the words of the Pharisees. We all know that he wrote the magnificent psalm, 'The wailing cries are silent,' a psalm which has never been equalled. Your health, Mr. Falk! I am glad to hear that you are identifying yourself with the work of such a man."

Lundell discovered that his glass was empty.

"I think I must have another half-pint!"

Two thoughts were humming in Falk's brain: "The fellow is drinking neat brandy" and "How did he get to know about Spegel?" A suspicion illuminated his mind like a flash of lightning, but he pretended to know nothing, and merely said: "Your health, Mr. Lundell!"

The unpleasant explanation which seemed bound to follow was avoided by the sudden entrance of Olle. It was Olle, but more rugged than before, dirtier than before and, to judge from his appearance, lamer than before. His hips stood out beneath his coat like bowsprits; a single button kept his coat together close above his first rib. But he was in good spirits and laughed on seeing so much food and drink on the table. To Sellén's horror he began to report on the success of his mission, all the time divesting himself of his acquisitions. He had really been arrested by the police.

"Here are the tickets!"

He handed Sellén two green pawn-tickets across the table, which Sellén instantly converted into a paper pellet.

He had been taken to the police station. He pointed to his coat, the collar of which was missing. There he was asked for his name. His name was, of course, assumed! There existed no such name as Montanus! His native place? Västmanland! Again a false statement! The inspector was a native of that province and knew his countrymen. His age? Twenty-eight years! That was a lie; he must be at least forty. His domicile? Lill-Jans! Another lie; nobody but a gardener lived there. His profession? Artist! That also was a lie: for he looked like a dock labourer.

"Here's your paint, four tubes! Better look at them carefully!"

His parcel had been opened and, in the process, one of the sheets had been torn.

"Therefore I only got one and twopence halfpenny for both. You'll see that I'm right if you'll look at the ticket."

The next question was where he had stolen the things? Olle had replied that he had not stolen them; then the inspector drew his attention to the fact that he had not been asked *whether* he had stolen them, but *where* he had stolen them? Where? where? where?

"Here's your change, twopence halfpenny; I've kept nothing back."

Then the evidence was taken down and the stolen goods—which had been sealed with three seals—were described. In vain had Olle protested, in vain had he appealed to their sense of justice and humanity; the only result of his protestations was a suggestion made by the constable to place on record that the prisoner—he was already regarded in the light of a prisoner—was heavily intoxicated; the suggestion was acted upon, but the word heavily was omitted. After the inspector had repeatedly urged the constable to try and remember whether the prisoner had offered resistance at his arrest, and the constable had declared that he could not take his oath on it—it would have been a very serious matter for the prisoner looked a desperate character—but it had *appeared* to him that he had tried to resist by taking refuge in a doorway the latter statement was placed on record.

Then a report was drawn up, and Olle was ordered to sign it. It ran as follows:

A male individual of sinister and forbidding appearance was found slinking along the row of houses in Northland Street, carrying a suspicious-looking parcel in his hand. On his arrest he was dressed in a green frock-coat—he wore no waistcoat—blue serge trousers, a shirt with the initials P.L. (which clearly proves that either the shirt was stolen or that he had given a wrong name), woollen stockings with grey edges, and a felt hat with a cock's feather. Prisoner gave the assumed name of Olle Montanus, falsely deposed that his people were peasants in Västmanland and that he was an artist, domiciled at Lill-Jans, obviously an invention. On being arrested he tried to offer resistance by taking refuge in a doorway. Then followed a minute description of the contents of the parcel.

As Olle refused to admit the correctness of this report, a telegram was sent to the prison, and a conveyance appeared to fetch Olle, the bundle, and a constable.

As they were turning into Mint Street, Olle caught sight of Per Illson, a member of Parliament and a countryman of his. He called to him, and Per Illson proved that the report was wrong. Olle was released and his bundle was restored to him. And now he had come to join them and——

"Here are your French rolls! There are only five of them, for I've eaten one. And here's the beer!"

He produced five French rolls from his coat pockets, laid them on the table, and placed two bottles of beer, which he pulled out of his trousers pockets, by the side of them, after which his figure resumed its usual disproportions.

"Falk, old chap, you must excuse Olle; he's not used to smart society. Put the French rolls back into your pockets, Olle! What will you be up to next?" said Sellén disapprovingly.

Olle obeyed.

Lundell refused to have the tray taken away, although he had cleared the dishes so thoroughly that it would have been impossible to say what they had contained; every now and then he seized the brandy bottle, absent-mindedly, and poured himself out half a glass. Occasionally he stood up or turned round in his chair to "see what the band was playing." On those occasions Sellén kept a close eye on him.

At last Rehnhjelm arrived. He had obviously been drinking; he sat down silently, his eyes seeking an object on which they could rest while he listened to Lundell's exhortations. Finally his weary eyes fell on Sellén and remained riveted on the velvet waistcoat, which gave him plenty of food for thought for the remainder of the evening. His face brightened momentarily as if he had met an old friend; but the light on it went out as Sellén buttoned up his coat "because there was a draught."

Ygberg took care that Olle had some supper, and never tired of urging him to help himself and to fill his glass.

As the evening advanced music and conversation grew more and more lively.

This state of semi-stupor had a great charm for Falk; it was warm, light, and noisy here; he was in the company of men whose lives he had prolonged for a few more hours and who were therefore gay and lively, as flies revived by the rays of the sun. He felt that he was one of them, for he knew that in their inner consciousness they were unhappy; they were unassuming; they understood him, and they talked like human beings and not like books; even their coarseness was not unattractive; there was so much naturalness in it, so much innocence; even Lundell's hypocrisy did not repulse him; it was so naïve and sat on him so loosely, that it could have been cast off at any moment.

And the evening passed away and the day was over which had pushed Falk irrevocably on to the thorny path of the writer.

CHAPTER VII. THE IMITATION OF CHRIST

On the following morning Falk was awakened by a maid servant who brought him a letter. He opened it and read:

Timothy x. 27, 28, 29. First Corinth. vi. 3, 4, 5.

DEAR BROTHER,

The grace and peace of our Lord J. C., the love of the father and the fellowship of the H. G., etc., Amen.

I read last night in the *Grey Bonnet* that you are going to edit the *Torch of Reconciliation*. Meet me in my office to-morrow morning.

Your saved brother,
NATHANAEL SKORE.

Now he partially understood Lundell's riddle. He did not know Skore, the great champion of the Lord, personally; he knew nothing of the *Torch of Reconciliation*, but he was curious and decided to obey the insolent request.

At nine o'clock he was in Government Street, looking at the imposing four-storied house, the front of which, from cellar to roof, was covered by sign-boards: "Christian Printing office,*Peace*, Ltd., second floor. Editorial office, *The Inheritance of the Children of God*, half-landing floor. Publishing office, *The Last Judgment*, first floor. Publishing office, *The Trump of Peace*, second floor. Editorial office of the children's paper, *Feed My Lambs*, first floor. Offices of the Christian Prayer House Society, Ltd., *The Seat of Mercy*. Loans granted against first securities, third floor. *Come to Jesus*, third floor. Employment found for respectable salesmen who can offer security. Foreign Missions Society, Ltd., *Eagle*, distribution of the profits of the year 1867 in coupons, second floor. Offices of the Christian Mission Steamer *Zululu*, second floor. The steamer will leave, D.V., on the 28th. Goods received against bill of lading and certificate at the shipping offices close to the landing-bridge where the steamer is loading. Needlework society 'Ant Heap' receives gifts, first floor. Clergymen's bands washed and ironed by the porter. Wafers at 1*s*. 6*d*. a pound obtainable from the porter. Black dress-coats for confirmation candidates let out. Unfermented wine (Mat. xix. 32) at 9½*d*. per quart; apply to the porter. (Bring your own jug.)"

On the ground floor, to the left of the archway, was a Christian bookshop. Falk stopped for a few moments and read the titles of the books exhibited in the window. It was the usual thing. Indiscreet questions, impudent charges, offensive familiarities. But his attention was mainly attracted to a number of illustrated magazines with large English woodcuts, displayed in the window in order to attract the passers-by. More especially the children's papers had an interesting table of contents, and the young man in the shop could have told anyone who cared to know that old men and women would pass hours before this window, lost in contemplation of the illustrations, which appeared to move their pious hearts and awaken memories of their vanished—and perhaps wasted—youth.

He climbed the broad staircase between Pompeian frescoes reminiscent of the path which does not lead to salvation, and came to a large room furnished with desks like a bank, but so far unoccupied by cashiers and book-keepers. In the centre of the room stood a writing-table, of the size of an altar, resembling an organ with many stops; there was a complete key-board with buttons and semaphores with trumpet-like speaking-tubes, connected with all parts of the building. A big man in riding-boots was standing at the writing-desk. He wore a cassock fastened with one button at the neck which gave it a military appearance; the coat was surmounted by a white band and the mask of a sea captain, for the real face had long ago been mislaid in one of the desks or boxes. The big man was slapping the tops of his boots with his horsewhip, the handle of which was in the form of a symbolical hoof, and sedulously smoking and chewing a strong regalia, probably to keep his jaws in trim. Falk looked at the big man in astonishment.

This, then, was the last fashion in clergymen, for in men, too, there is a fashion. This was the great promulgator, who had succeeded in making it fashionable to be sinful, to thirst for mercy, to be poor and wretched, in fact, to be a worthless specimen of humanity in every possible way. This was the man who had brought salvation in vogue! He had discovered a gospel for smart society. The divine ordinance of grace had become a sport! There were competitions in viciousness in which the prize was given to the sinner. Paper chases were arranged to catch poor souls for the purpose of saving them; but also, let us confess it, battues for subjects on whom to demonstrate one's conversion in a practical manner, by venting on them the most cruel charity.

"Oh, it's you, Mr. Falk," said the mask. "Welcome, dear friend! Perhaps you would like to see something of my work? Pardon me, I hope you are saved? Yes, this is the office of the printing works. Excuse me a second."

He stepped up to the organ and pulled out several stops. The answer was a long whistle.

"Just have a look round."

He put his mouth to one of the trumpets and shouted: "The seventh trumpet and the eighth woe! Composition Mediæval 8, titles Gothic, names spaced out."

A voice answered through the same trumpet: "No more manuscript." The mask sat down at the organ, and took a pen and a sheet of foolscap. The pen raced over the paper while he talked, cigar in mouth.

"This activity—is so extensive—that it would soon—be beyond my strength—and my health—would be worse—than it is—if I did—not look after it—so well."

He jumped up, pulled out another stop and shouted into another trumpet: "Proofs of 'Have you paid your Debt?'" Then he continued writing and talking.

"You wonder—why—I—wear riding-boots. It's first—because—I take riding exercises—for the sake of—my health...."

A boy appeared with proofs. The mask handed them to Falk. "Please read that," he said, speaking through his nose, because his mouth was busy, while his eyes shouted to the boy: Wait!

"... secondly—(a movement of the ears plainly conveyed to Falk that he had not lost the thread), because—I am of opinion—that a spiritually minded man should not—be conspicuous—by his appearance—for this would be—spiritual pride—and a challenge—to the scoffers."

A book-keeper entered. The mask acknowledged his salutation by a wrinkling of his forehead, the only part of his face which was unoccupied.

For want of something else to do, Falk took the proofs and began to read them. The cigar continued talking:

"Everybody—wears—riding-boots. I won't—be conspicuous—by my—appearance. I wear—riding-boots—because—I'm no humbug."

He handed the manuscript to the boy and shouted—with his lips: "Four sticks—Seventh trumpet for Nyström!"—and then to Falk:

"I shall be disengaged in five minutes. Will you come with me to the warehouse?"

And to the book-keeper:

"Zululu is charging?"

"Brandy," answered the book-keeper in a rusty voice.

"Everything all right?"

"Everything all right."

"In God's name, then! Come along Mr. Falk."

They entered a room the walls of which were lined with shelves, filled with piles of books. The mask touched them with his horsewhip and said proudly:

"I've written those! What do you think of that? Isn't it a lot? You, too, write—a little. If you stick to it, you might write as much."

He bit and tore at his cigar and spat out the tiny flakes which filled the air like flies and settled on the backs of the books. His face wore a look of contempt.

"The *Torch of Reconciliation*! Hm! I think it's a stupid name! Don't you rather agree with me? What made you think of it?"

For the first time Falk had a chance of getting in a word, for like all great men, the mask answered his own questions. His reply was in the negative but he got no further; the mask again usurped the conversation.

"I think it's a very stupid name. And do you really believe that it will draw?"

"I know nothing whatever about the matter; I don't know what you are talking about."

"You don't know?"

He took up a paper and pointed to a paragraph.

Falk, very much taken aback, read the following advertisement:

"Notice to subscribers: The *Torch of Reconciliation*. Magazine for Christian readers, about to appear under the editorship of Arvid Falk whose work has been awarded a prize by the Academy of Sciences. The first number will contain 'God's Creation,' by Hokan Spegel, a poem of an admittedly religious and profoundly Christian spirit."

Falk had forgotten Spegel and his agreement; he stood speechless.

"How large is the edition going to be? What? Two thousand, I suppose. Too small! No good! My *Last Judgment* was ten thousand, and yet I didn't make more than—what shall I say?—fifteen net."

"Fifteen?"

"Thousand, young man!"

The mask seemed to have forgotten his part and reverted to old habits.

"You know," he continued, "that I'm a popular preacher; I may say that without boasting, for all the world knows it. You know, that I'm very popular; I can't help that—it is so! I should be a hypocrite if I pretended not to know what all the world knows! Well, I'll give you a helping hand to begin with. Look at this bag here! If I say that it contains letters from persons—ladies—don't upset yourself, I'm a married man—begging for my portrait, I have not said too much."

As a matter of fact it was nothing but an ordinary bag which he touched with his whip.

"To save them and me a great deal of trouble, and at the same time for the sake of doing a fellow-man a kindness, I have decided to permit you to write my biography; then you can safely issue ten thousand copies of your first number and pocket a clear thousand."

"But, my dear pastor—he had it on the tip of his tongue to say captain—I know nothing at all about this matter."

"Never mind! Never mind! The publisher has himself written to me and asked me for my portrait. And you are to write my biography! To facilitate your work, I asked a friend to write down the principal points. You have only to write an introduction, brief and eloquent—a few sticks at the most. That's all."

So much foresight depressed Falk; he was surprised to find the portrait so unlike the original, and the friend's handwriting so much like that of the mask.

The latter, who had given him portrait and manuscript, now held out his hand expecting to be thanked.

"My regards to—the publisher."

He had so nearly said Smith, that a slight blush appeared between his whiskers.

"But you don't know my views yet," protested Falk.

"Views? Have I asked what your views are? I never ask anybody about his views. God forbid! I? Never!"

Once more he touched the backs of his publications with his whip, opened the door, let the biographer out and returned to his service at the altar.

Falk, as usual, could not think of a suitable answer until it was too late; when he thought of one, he was already in the street. A cellar window which happened to stand wide open (and was not covered with advertisements) received biography and portrait into safe keeping.

Then Falk went to the nearest newspaper office, handed in a protest against the *Torch of Reconciliation*, and resigned himself to starve.

CHAPTER VIII. POOR MOTHER COUNTRY

The clock on the Riddarholms Church struck ten as Falk arrived, a few days later, at the Parliamentary buildings to assist the representative of the Red Cap in reporting the proceedings of the Second Chamber.

He hastened his footsteps, convinced that here, where the pay was good, strict punctuality would be looked upon as a matter of course. He climbed the Committee stairs and was shown to the reporters' gallery on the left. A feeling of awe overcame him as he walked across the few boards, hung up under the roof like a pigeon house, where the men of "free speech listen to the discussion of the country's most sacred interests by the country's most worthy representatives."

It was a new sensation to Falk; but he was far from being impressed as he looked down from his scaffolding into the empty hall which resembled a Lancastrian school. It was five minutes past ten, but with the exception of himself, not a soul was present. All of a sudden the silence was broken by a scraping noise. A rat! he thought, but almost immediately he discovered, on the opposite gallery, across the huge, empty hall, a short, abject figure sharpening a pencil on the rail. He watched the chips fluttering down and settling on the tables below.

His eyes scanned the empty walls without finding a resting-place, until finally they fell on the old clock, dating from the time of Napoleon I, with its imperial newly lit emblems, symbolical of the old story, and its hands, now pointing to ten minutes past ten, symbolical in the spirit of irony—of something else. At the same moment the doors in the background opened and a man entered. He was old; his shoulders stooped under the burden of public offices; his back had shrunk under the weight of communal commissions; the long continuance in damp offices, committee-rooms and safe deposits had warped his neck; there was a suggestion of the pensioner in his calm footsteps, as he walked up the cocoa-nut matting towards the chair. When he had reached the middle of the long passage and had come into line with the imperial clock, he stopped; he seemed accustomed to stopping half-way and looking round and backwards; but now he stopped to compare his watch with the clock; he shook his old, worn out head with a look of discontent: "Fast! Fast!" he murmured. His features expressed a supernatural calm and the assurance that his watch could not be slow. He continued his way with the same deliberate footsteps; he might be walking towards the goal of his life; and it was very much a question whether he had not attained it when he arrived at the venerable chair on the platform.

When he was standing close by it he pulled out his handkerchief and blew his nose; his eyes roamed over the brilliant audience of chairs and tables, announcing an important event: "Gentlemen, I have blown my nose." Then he sat down and sank into a presidential calm which might have been sleep, if it had not been waking; and, alone in the large room, as he imagined, alone with his God, he prepared to summon strength for the business of the day, when a loud scraping on the left, high up, underneath the roof, pierced the stillness; he started and turned his head to kill with a three-quarter look the rat which dared to gnaw in his presence. Falk who had omitted to take into account the resonant capacity of the pigeon house, received the deadly thrust of the murderous glance; but the glance softened as it slid down from the eaves-mouldings, whispering—"Only a reporter; I was afraid it might be a rat." And deep regret stole over the murderer, contrition at the sin committed by his eye; he buried his face in his hands and—wept? Oh, no! he rubbed off the spot which the appearance of a repulsive object had thrown on his retina.

Presently the doors were flung wide open; the delegates were beginning to arrive, while the hands on the clock crept forward—forward. The president rewarded the good with friendly nods and pressures of the hand, and punished the evil-doers by turning away his head; he was bound to be just as the Most High.

The reporter of the Red Cap arrived, an unprepossessing individual, not quite sober and only half awake. In spite of this he seemed to find pleasure in answering truthfully the questions put by the newcomer.

Once more the doors were flung open and in stalked a man with as much self-assurance as if he were in his own home: he was the treasurer of the Inland Revenue Office and actuary of the Board of Payment of Employés' Salaries; he approached the chair, greeted the president like an old acquaintance and began to rummage in the papers as if they were his own.

"Who's this?" asked Falk.

"The chief clerk," answered his friend from the Red Cap.

"What? Do they write here, too, then?"

"Too? You'll soon see! They keep a story full of clerks; the attics are full of clerks and they'll soon have clerks in the cellars."

The room below was now presenting the aspect of an ant-heap. A rap of the hammer and there was silence. The head clerk read the minutes of the last meeting, and they were signed without comment. Then the same man read a petition for a fortnight's leave, sent in by Jon Jonson from Lerbak. It was granted.

"Do they have holidays here?" asked the novice, surprised.

"Certainly, Jon Jonson wants to go home and plant his potatoes."

The platform down below was now beginning to fill with young men armed with pen and paper. All of them were old acquaintances from the time when

Falk was a Government official. They took their seats at little tables as if they were going to play "Preference."

"Those are the clerks," explained the Red Cap; "they appear to recognize you."

And they really did; they put on their eye-glasses and stared at the pigeon house with the condescension vouchsafed in a theatre by the occupants of the stalls to the occupants of the galleries. They whispered among themselves, evidently discussing an absent acquaintance who, from unmistakable evidence, must have been sitting on the chair occupied by Falk. The latter was so deeply touched by the general interest that he looked with anything but a friendly eye on Struve, who was entering the pigeon house, reserved, unembarrassed, dirty and a conservative.

The chief clerk read a petition, or a resolution, to grant the necessary money for the provision of new door mats and new brass numbers on the lockers destined for the reception of overshoes.

Granted!

"Where is the opposition?" asked the tyro.

"The devil knows!"

"But they say Yes to everything!"

"Wait a little and you'll see!"

"Haven't they come yet?"

"Here every one comes and goes as he pleases."

"But this is the Government Offices all over again!"

The conservative Struve, who had heard the frivolous words, thought it incumbent on him to take up the cudgels for the Government.

"What is this, little Falk is saying?" he asked. "He mustn't growl here."

It took Falk so long to find a suitable reply that the discussions down below had started in the meantime.

"Don't mind him," said the Red Cap, soothingly; "he's invariably a conservative when he has the price of a dinner in his pocket, and he's just borrowed a fiver from me."

The chief clerk was reading: 54. Report of the Committee on Ola Hipsson's motion to remove the fences.

Timber merchant Larsson from Norrland demanded acceptance as it stood. "What is to become of our forests?" he burst out. "I ask you, what *is* to become of our forests?" And he threw himself on his bench, puffing.

This racy eloquence had gone out of fashion during the last few years, and the words were received with hisses, after which the puffing on the Norrland bench ceased.

The representative for Oeland suggested sandstone walls; Scania's delegate preferred box; Norbotten's opined that fences were unnecessary where there were no fields, and a member on the Stockholm bench proposed that the matter should be referred to a Committee of experts: he laid stress on "experts." A violent scene followed. Death rather than a committee! The question was put to the vote. The motion was rejected; the fences would remain standing until they decayed.

The chief clerk was reading: 66. Report of the Committee on Carl Jönsson's proposition to intercept the moneys for the Bible Commission. At the sound of the venerable name of an institution a hundred years old, even the smiles died away and a respectful silence ensued. Who would dare to attack religion in its very foundation, who would dare to face universal contempt? The Bishop of Ystad asked permission to speak.

"Shall I write?" asked Falk.

"No, what he says doesn't concern us."

But the conservative Struve took down the following notes: Sacred. Int. Mother country. United names religion humanity 829, 1632. Unbelief. Mania for innovations. God's word. Man's word. Centen. Ansgar. Zeal. Honesty. Fairplay. Capac. Doctrine. Exist. Swed. Chch. Immemorial Swed. Honour. Gustavus I. Gustavus Adolphus. Hill Lûtzen. Eyes Europe. Verdict posterity. Mourning. Shame. Green fields. Wash my hands. They would not hear.

Carl Jönsson held the floor.

"Now it's our turn!" said the Red Cap.

And they wrote while Struve embroidered the Bishop's velvet.

Twaddle. Big words. Commission sat for a hundred years. Costs 100.000 Crowns. 9 archbishops. 30 Prof. Upsala. Together 500 years. Dietaries. Secretaries. Amanuenses. Done nothing. Proof sheet. Bad work. Money money money. Everything by its right name. Humbug. Official sucking-system.

No one else spoke but when the question was put to the vote, the motion was accepted.

While the Red Cap with practised hand smoothed Jönsson's stumbling speech, and provided it with a strong title, Falk took a rest. Accidentally scanning the strangers' gallery, his gaze fell on a well-known head, resting on the rail and belonging to Olle Montanus. At the moment he had the appearance of a dog, carefully watching a bone; and he was not there without a very definite reason, but Falk was in the dark. Olle was very secretive.

From the end of the bench, just below the right gallery, on the very spot where the abject individual's pencil chips had fluttered down, a man now arose. He wore a blue uniform, had a three-cornered hat tucked under his arm and held a roll of paper in his hand.

The hammer fell and an ironical, malicious silence followed.

"Write," said the Red Cap; "take down the figures, I'll do the rest."

"Who is it?"

"These are Royal propositions."

The man in blue was reading from the paper roll: "H.M. most gracious proposition; to increase the funds of the department assisting young men of birth in the study of foreign languages, under the heading of stationery and sundry expenses, from 50.000 crowns to 56.000 crowns 37 öre."

"What are sundry expenses?" asked Falk.

"Water bottles, umbrella stands, spittoons, Venetian blinds, dinners, tips and so on. Be quiet, there's more to come!"

The paper roll went on: "H.M. most gracious proposition to create sixty new commissions in the West-Gotic cavalry."

"Did he say sixty?" asked Falk, who was unfamiliar with public affairs.

"Sixty, yes; write it down."

The paper roll opened out and grew bigger and bigger. "H.M. most gracious proposition to create five new regular clerkships in the Board of Payment of Employés' Salaries."

Great excitement at the Preference tables; great excitement on Falk's chair.

Now the paper roll rolled itself up; the chairman rose and thanked the reader with a bow which plainly said: "Is there nothing else we can do?" The owner of the paper roll sat down on the bench and blew away the chips the man above him had allowed to fall down. His stiff, embroidered collar prevented him from committing the same offence which the president had perpetrated earlier in the morning.

The proceedings continued. The peasant Sven Svensson asked for permission to say a few words on the Poor Law. With one accord all the reporters arose, yawned and stretched themselves.

"We'll go to lunch now," explained the Red Cap. "We have an hour and ten minutes."

But Sven Svensson was speaking.

The delegates began to get up from their places; two or three of them went out. The president spoke to some of the good members and by doing so expressed in the name of the Government his disapproval of all Sven Svensson might be going to say. Two older members pointed him out to a newcomer as if he were a strange beast; they watched him for a few moments, found him ridiculous and turned their backs on him.

The Red Cap was under the impression that politeness required him to explain that the speaker was the "scourge" of the Chamber. He was neither hot nor cold, could be used by no party, be won for no interests, but he spoke—spoke. What he spoke about no one could tell, for no paper reported him, and nobody took the trouble to look up the records; but the clerks at the tables had sworn that if they ever came into power, they would amend the laws for his sake.

Falk, however, who had a certain weakness for all those who were overlooked remained behind and heard what he had not heard for many a day: a man of honour, who lived an irreproachable life, espousing the cause of the oppressed and the down-trodden while nobody listened to him.

70

Struve, at the sight of the peasant, had taken his own departure, and had gone to a restaurant; he was quickly followed by all the reporters and half the deputies.

After luncheon they returned and sat down on the narrow stairs; for a little longer they heard Sven Svensson speaking, or rather, saw him speaking, for now the conversation had become so lively that not a single word of the speech could be understood.

But the speaker was bound to come to an end; nobody had any objections to make; his speech had no result whatever; it was exactly as if it had never been made.

The chief clerk, who during this interval had had time to go to his offices, look at the official papers, and poke his fires, was again in his place, reading: "72. Memorial of the Royal Commission on Per Ilsson's motion to grant ten thousand crowns for the restoration of the old sculptures in the church of Träskola."

The dog's head on the rail of the strangers' gallery assumed a threatening aspect; he looked as if he were going to fight for his bone.

"Do you know the freak up there in the gallery?" asked the Red Cap.

"Olle Montanus, yes, I know him."

"Do you know that he and the church of Träskola are countrymen? He's a shrewd fellow! Look at the expression on his face now that Träskola's turn has come."

Per Ilsson was speaking.

Struve contemptuously turned his back on the speaker and cut himself a piece of tobacco. But Falk and the Red Cap trimmed their pencils for action.

"You take the flourishes, I'll take the facts," said the Red Cap.

After the lapse of a quarter of an hour Falk's paper was covered with the following notes.

Native Culture. Social Interests. Charge of materialism. Accord. Fichte material, Native Culture not mater. Ergo charge rejected. Venerable temple. In the radiance morning sun pointing heavenwards. From heath. times Philos. never dreamt. Sacred rights. Nation. Sacred Int. Native Cult. Literature. Academy. History. Antiquity.

The speech which had repeatedly called forth universal amusement especially at the exhumation of the deceased Fichte, provoked replies from the Metropolitan Bench and the bench of Upsala.

The delegate on the Metropolitan bench said that although he knew neither the church of Träskola nor Fichte and doubted whether the old plaster-boys were worth ten thousand crowns, yet he thought himself justified in urging the Chamber to encourage this beautiful undertaking as it was the first time the majority had asked for money for a purpose other than the building of bridges, fences, national schools, etc.

The delegate on the bench of Upsala held—according to Struve's notes—that the mover of the proposition was *à priori* right; that his premise, that native culture should be encouraged, was correct; that the conclusion that ten thousand crowns should be voted was binding; that the purpose, the aim, the tendency, was beautiful, praiseworthy, patriotic; but an error had certainly been committed. By whom? By the Mother country? The State? The church? No! By the proponent? The proponent was right according to common sense, and therefore the speaker—he begged the Chamber to pardon the repetition—could only praise the purpose, the aim, the tendency. The proposition had its warmest sympathies; he was calling on the Chamber in the name of the Mother country, in the name of art and civilization, to vote for it. But he himself felt bound to vote against it, because he was of the opinion that, conformable to the idea, it was erroneous, motiveless and figurative, as it subsumed the conception of the place under that of the State.

The head in the strangers' gallery rolled its eyes and moved its lips convulsively while the motion was put to the vote; but when the proceeding was over and the proposition had been accepted, the head disappeared in the discontented and jostling audience.

Falk did not fail to understand the connexion between Per Ilsson's proposition and Olle's presence and disappearance. Struve, who had become even more loud and conservative after lunch, talked unreservedly of many things. The Red Cap was calm and indifferent; he had ceased to be astonished at anything.

From the dark cloud of humanity which had been rent by Olle's exit, suddenly broke a face, clear, bright and radiant as the sun, and Arvid Falk, whose glances had strayed to the gallery, felt compelled to cast down his eyes and turn away his head—he had recognized his brother, the head of the family, the pride of the name, which he intended to make great and honourable. Behind Nicholas Falk's shoulder half of a black face could be seen, gentle and deceitful, which seemed to whisper secrets into the ear of the fair man. Falk had only time to be surprised at his brother's presence—he knew his resentment at the new form of administration—for the president had given Anders Andersson permission to state a proposition. Andersson availed himself of the permission with the greatest calm. "In view of certain events," he read, "move that a Bill should be passed making his Majesty jointly and severally liable for all joint-stock companies whose statutes he has sanctioned."

The sun on the strangers' gallery lost its brilliancy and a storm burst out in the Chamber.

Like a flash Count Splint was on his legs:

"*Quosque tandem, Catilina!* It has come to that! Members are forgetting themselves so far as to dare to criticize Government! Yes, gentlemen, criticize Government, or, what is even worse, make a joke of it; for this motion cannot be anything but a vulgar joke. Did I say joke? It is treason! Oh! My poor country! Your unworthy sons have forgotten the debt they owe you! But what else can we expect, now, that you have lost your knightly guard, your shield and your arms! I request the blackguard Per Andersson, or whatever his name may be, to withdraw his motion or, by Gad! he shall see that King and country still have loyal servants, able to pick up a stone and fling it at the head of the many-headed hydra of treason."

Applause from the strangers' gallery; indignation in the Chamber.

"Ha! Do you think I'm afraid?"

The speaker made a gesture as if he were throwing a stone, but on every one of the hydra's hundred faces lay a smile. Glaring round, in search of a hydra which did not smile, the speaker discovered it in the reporters' gallery.

"There! There!"

He pointed to the pigeon house and in his eyes lay an expression as if he saw all hell open.

"That's the crows' nest! I hear their croaking, but it doesn't frighten me! Arise, men of Sweden! Cut off the tree, saw through the boards, pull down the beams, kick the chairs to pieces, break the desks into fragments, small as my little finger—he held it up—and then burn the blackguards until nothing of them is left. Then the kingdom will flourish in peace and its institutions will thrive. Thus speaks a Swedish nobleman! Peasants, remember his words!"

This speech which three years ago would have been welcomed with acclamations, taken down verbatim and printed and circulated in national schools and other charitable institutions, was received with universal laughter. An amended version was placed on the record and, strange to say, it was only reported by the opposition papers which do not, as a rule, care to publish outbursts of this description.

The Upsala bench again craved permission to speak. The speaker quite agreed with the last speaker; his acute ear had caught something of the old rattling of swords. He would like to say a few words. He would like to speak of the *idea* of a joint-stock company as an idea, but begged to be allowed to explain to the Chamber that a joint-stock company was not an accumulation of funds, not a combination of people, but a moral personality, and as such not responsible....

Shouts of laughter and loud conversation prevented the reporters from hearing the remainder of the argument, which closed with the remark that the interests of the country were at stake, conformable to the idea, and that, if the motion were rejected the interests of the country would be neglected and the State in danger.

Six speakers filled up the interval until dinner-time by giving extracts from the official statistics of Sweden, Nauman's Fundamental Statutes, the Legal Textbook and the Göteberg Commercial Gazette: the conclusion invariably arrived at was that the country was in danger if his Majesty were to be jointly and severally liable for all joint-stock companies the statutes of which he had sanctioned; and that the interests of the whole country were at stake. One of the speakers was bold enough to say that the interests of the country stood on a throw of the dice; others were of the opinion that they stood on a card, others again that they hung on a thread; the last speaker said they hung on a hair.

At noon the proposition to go into Committee on the motion was rejected; that was to say, there was no need for the country to go through the Committee-mill, the office-sieve, the Imperial chaff-cutter, the club-winnower and the newspaper-hubbub. The country was saved. Poor country!

CHAPTER IX. BILLS OF EXCHANGE

Some time after Arvid Falk's first experience as a reporter Charles Nicholas Falk and his beloved wife were sitting at the breakfast table. He was, contrary to his custom, not in dressing-gown and slippers, and his wife was wearing an expensive morning-gown.

"Yes, they were all here yesterday," said Mrs. Falk, laughing gaily, "all five of them, and they were extremely sorry about the matter."

"I wish the deuce...."

"Nicholas, remember you are no longer standing behind the counter."

"What am I to say then if I lose my temper?"

"One doesn't lose one's temper, one gets annoyed! And it's permissible to say: 'It's very extraordinary!'"

"Very well, then, it's very extraordinary that you have always something unpleasant up your sleeve. Why can't you refrain from telling me things you know will irritate me?"

"Vex you, old man! You expect me to keep my vexations to myself; but you lie——"

"Lay, old girl!"

"I say *lie* your burdens on my shoulders too. Was that what you promised me when we got married?"

"Don't make a scene, and don't let's have any of your logic! Go on! They were all here, mamma and your five sisters?"

"Four sisters! You don't care much for your family!"

"No more do you!"

"No more do I!"

"And they came here to condole with you on account of my brother's discharge? Is that so?"

"Yes! And they were impertinent enough to say that I had no longer any reason to be stuck up...."

"Proud, old girl!"

"They said *stuck up*. Personally I should never have condescended to make use of such an expression."

"What did you say? I expect you gave them a piece of your mind?"

"You may depend on that! The old lady threatened never again to cross our threshold."

"Did she really? Do you think she meant it?"

"No, I don't! But I'm certain that the old man...."

"You shouldn't speak of your father in that tone! Supposing somebody heard you!"

"Do you think I should run that risk? However, the old man—between you and me—will never come here again."

Falk pondered; after a while he resumed the conversation.

"Is your mother proud? Is she easily hurt? I'm always so afraid of hurting people's feelings, as you know; you ought to tell me about her weak points, so that I can take care."

"You ask me whether she is proud? You know; she is, in her own way. Supposing, for instance, she was told that we had given a dinner-party without asking her and my sisters, she would never come here again."

"Wouldn't she really?"

"You may depend upon it."

"It's extraordinary that people of her class——"

"What's that?"

"Oh, nothing; women are so sensitive! How's your association getting on? What did you call it?"

"The Association for the Promotion of Women's Rights."

"What rights do you mean?"

"The wife shall have the right of disposing of her own property."

"Hasn't she got it already?"

"No, she hasn't."

"May I ask what your property is of which you are not allowed to dispose?"

"Half of your's, old man! My dowry."

"The devil! Who taught you such rubbish?"

"It's not rubbish; it's the spirit of the age, my dear. The new law should read like this: 'When a woman marries she becomes the owner of half her husband's property, and of this half she can dispose as she likes.'"

"And when she has run through it, the husband will have to keep her! I should take jolly good care not to."

"Under the new law you would be forced to do so, or go to the poor-house. This would be the penalty for a man who doesn't keep his wife."

"Take care! You are going too far! But, have you any meetings? Who were the women present? Tell me?"

"We are still busy with the statutes, with the preliminaries."

"But who are the women?"

"At present only Mrs. Homan, the controller's wife, and Lady Rehnhjelm."

"Rehnhjelm? A very good name! I think I've heard it before. But didn't you tell me you were going to float a Dorcas Society as well?"

"*Found* a Dorcas Society! Oh, yes, and what d'you think? Pastor Skore is coming one evening to read a paper."

"Pastor Skore is an excellent preacher and moves in good society. I'm glad that you're keeping away from the lower classes. There's nothing so fatal to man or woman as to form low connexions. My father always said that; it was one of his strictest principles."

Mrs. Falk picked up the bread-crumbs from the tablecloth and dropped them into her empty cup. Mr. Falk put his fingers into his waistcoat pocket and brought out a tooth-pick with which he removed some tiny atoms of coffee grounds lodged between his teeth.

Husband and wife felt self-conscious in each other's company. Each guessed the thoughts of the other, and both realized that the first who broke the silence would say something foolish and compromising. They cast about for fresh subjects of conversation, mentally examined them and found them unsuitable; every one of them had some connexion with what had been said, or could be brought into connexion with it. Falk would have liked to have reason for finding fault with the breakfast, so as to have an excuse for expressing indignation; Mrs. Falk looked out of the window, feebly hoping that there might be a change in the weather—in vain.

A maid-servant entered and saved the situation by offering them a tray with the newspapers, at the same time announcing Mr. Levin.

"Ask him to wait," said the master curtly.

For a few moments his boots squeaked up and down the room, preparing the visitor who was waiting in the corridor for his arrival.

The trembling Levin, greatly impressed by the newly invented waiting in the corridor, was ultimately conducted into the master's private room, where he was received like a petitioner.

"Have you brought the bill of exchange with you?" asked Falk.

"I think so," replied the crestfallen Levin, producing a bundle of guarantees and blank bills of various values. "Which bank do you prefer? I have bills on all with the exception of one."

In spite of the grave character of the situation Falk could not help smiling as he looked at the incomplete guarantees on which the name was missing; the bills fully filled up with the exception of an acceptor's name, and those completely filled up, which had not been accepted.

"Let's say the Ropemakers' Bank," he said.

"That's the one impossible one—I'm known there."

"Well, the Shoemakers' Bank, the Tailors' Bank, any one you like, only do be quick about it."

They finally accepted the Joiners' Bank.

"And now," said Falk, with a look as if he had bought the other's soul, "now you had better go and order a new suit; but I want you to order it at a military tailor's, so that they will supply you later on with a uniform on credit."

"Uniform? I don't want——"

"Hold your tongue, and do as you are told! It must be finished on Thursday next, when I'm going to give a big party. As you know, I've sold my shop and warehouse, and to-morrow I shall receive the freedom of the city as a wholesale merchant."

"Oh! I congratulate you!"

"Hold your tongue when I'm speaking! You must go and pay a call now. With your deceitful ways, your unrivalled capacity for talking nonsense, you have succeeded in winning the good graces of my mother-in-law. I want you to ask her what she thought of the party I gave on Sunday last."

"Did you...."

"Hold your tongue and do as I tell you! She'll be jealous and ask you whether you were present. Of course you weren't, for there was no party. You'll both express discontent, become good friends and slander me; I know you're an expert at it. But you must praise my wife. Do you understand?"

"No; not quite."

"Well, it's not necessary that you should; all you've got to do is to carry out my orders. Another thing—tell Nyström that I've grown so proud that I don't want to have anything more to do with him. Tell him that straight out; you'll be speaking the truth for once! No! Hold on! We'll postpone that! You'll go to him, speak of the importance of next Thursday; paint for him the great advantages, the many benefits, the brilliant prospects, and so on. You understand me!"

"I understand."

"Then you take the manuscript to the printers' and—then...."

"We'll kick him out!"

"If you like to call it that, I have no objection."

"And am I to read the verses to your guests and distribute them?"

"Hm—yes! And another thing! Try to meet my brother; find out all you can about his circumstances and friends! Make up to him, worm yourself into his confidence—the latter's an easy job—become his friend! Tell him that I've cheated him, tell him that I am proud, and ask him how much he'll take for changing his name."

A tinge of green, representing a blush, spread over Levin's pale face.

"That's ugly," he said.

"What? And besides—one thing more! I'm a business man and I like order in all my transactions. I guarantee such and such a sum; I must pay it—that's clear!"

"Oh, no!"

"Don't talk rubbish! I have no security in case of death. Just sign this bond made out to the holder and payable at sight. It's merely a formality."

At the word *holder* a slight tremor shook Levin's body, and he seized the pen hesitatingly, although he well knew that retreat was impossible. In imagination he saw a row of shabby, spectacled men, carrying canes in their hands, their breast-pockets bulging with stamped documents; he heard knocking at doors, running on stairs, summonses, threats, respite; he heard the clock on the town hall striking as the men shouldered their canes and led him—with clogged feet—to the place of execution, where he himself was finally released, but where his honour as a citizen fell under the executioner's axe amid the delighted shouts of the crowd. He signed. The audience was over.

CHAPTER X. THE NEWSPAPER SYNDICATE "GREY BONNET"

For forty years Sweden had worked for the right which every man obtains when he comes of age. Pamphlets had been written, newspapers founded, stones thrown, suppers eaten and speeches made; meetings had been held, petitions had been presented, the railways had been used, hands had been pressed, volunteer regiments had been formed; and so, in the end, with a great deal of noise, the desired object had been attained. Enthusiasm was great and justifiable. The old birchwood tables at the Opera Restaurant were transformed into political tribunes; the fumes of the reform-punch attracted many a politician, who, later on, became a great screamer; the smell of reform cigars excited many an ambitious dream which was never realized; the old dust was washed off with reform soap; it was generally believed that everything would be right now; and after the tremendous uproar the country lay down and fell asleep, confidently awaiting the brilliant results which were to be the outcome of all this fuss.

It slept for a few years, and when it awoke it was faced by a reality which suggested a miscalculation. There were murmurs here and there; the statesmen who had recently been lauded to the skies were now criticized. There were even, among the students, some who discovered that the whole movement had originated in a country which stood in very close relationship to the promoter of the Bill, and that the original could be found in a well-known handbook. But enough of it! Characteristic of these days was a certain embarrassment which soon took the form of universal discontent or, as it was called, opposition. But it was a new kind of opposition; it was not, as is generally the case, directed against the Government, but against Parliament. It was a Conservative opposition including Liberals as well as Conservatives, young men as well as old; there was much misery in the country.

Now it happened that the newspaper syndicate *Grey Bonnet*, born and grown up under Liberal auspices, fell asleep when it was called upon to defend unpopular views—if one may speak of the views of a syndicate. The directors proposed at the General Meeting that certain opinions should be changed, as they had the effect of decreasing the number of subscribers, necessary to the continuance of the enterprise. The General Meeting agreed to the proposition, and the *Grey Bonnet* became a Conservative paper. But there was a *but*, although it must be confessed that it did not greatly embarrass the syndicate; it was necessary to have a new chief editor to save the syndicate from ridicule; that no change need be made so far as the invisible editorial staff was concerned, went without saying. The chief editor, a man of honour, tendered his resignation. The editorial management, which had long been abused on account of its red colour, accepted it with pleasure, hoping thereby, without further trouble, to take rank as a better class paper. There only remained the necessity of finding a new chief editor. In accordance with the new programme of the syndicate, he would have to possess the following qualifications: he must be known as a perfectly trustworthy citizen; must belong to the official class; must possess a title, usurped or won, which could be elaborated if necessity arose. In addition to this he must be of good appearance, so that one could show him off at festivals and on other public occasions; he must be dependent; a little stupid, because true stupidity always goes hand in hand with Conservative leanings; he must be endowed with a certain amount of shrewdness, which would enable him to know intuitively the wishes of his chiefs and never let him forget that public and private welfare are, rightly understood, one and the same thing. At the same time he must not be too young, because an older man is more easily managed; and finally, he must be married, for the syndicate, which consisted of business men, knew perfectly well that married slaves are more amenable than unmarried ones.

The individual was discovered, and he was to a high degree endowed with all the characteristics enumerated. He was a strikingly handsome man with a fairly fine figure and a long, wavy beard, hiding all the weak points of his face, which otherwise would have given him away. His large, full, deceitful eyes caught the casual observer and inspired his confidence, which was then unscrupulously abused. His somewhat veiled voice, always speaking words of love, of peace, of honour and above all of patriotism, beguiled many a misguided listener, and brought him to the punch table where the excellent man spent his evenings, preaching straightforwardness and love of the Mother Country.

The influence which this man of honour exerted on his evil environment was marvellous; it could not be seen, but it could be heard. The whole pack, which for years had been let loose on everything time-honoured and venerable, which had not even let alone the higher things, was now restrained and full of love— not only for its old friends—was now—and not merely in its heart—moral and straightforward. They carried out in every detail the programme drawn up by the new editor on his accession, the cardinal points of which, expressed in a few words, were: to persecute all good ideas if they were new, to fight for and uphold all bad ones if they were old, to grovel before those in power, to extol all those on whom fortune was smiling, to push down all those who strove to rise, to adore success and abuse misfortune. Freely translated the programme read: to acknowledge and cheer only the tested and admittedly good, to work against the mania of innovation, and to persecute severely, but justly, everybody who was trying to get on by dishonest means, for honest work only should be crowned with success.

The secret of the last clause which the editorial staff had principally at heart was not difficult to discover. The staff consisted entirely of people whose hopes had been disappointed in one way or another; in most cases by their own fault—through drinking and recklessness. Some of them were "college geniuses," who in the past had enjoyed a great reputation as singers, speakers, poets or wits, and had then justly—or according to them unjustly—been forgotten. During a number of years it had been their business to praise and promote, frequently against their own inclination, everything that was new, all the enterprises started by reformers; it was, therefore, not strange that now they seized the opportunity to attack—under the most honourable pretexts—everything new, good or bad.

The chief editor in particular was great in tracking humbug and dishonesty. Whenever a delegate opposed a Bill which tended to injure the interests of the country for the sake of the party, he was immediately taken to task and called a humbug, trying to be original, longing for a ministerial dress-coat; he did not say portfolio, for he always thought of clothes first. Politics, however, was not his strong, or rather his weak point, but literature. In days long past, on the occasion of the Old Norse Festival at Upsala, he had proposed a toast in verse on woman, and thereby furnished an important contribution to the literature of the world; it was printed in as many provincial papers as the author considered necessary for his immortality. This had made him a poet, and when he had taken his degrees, he bought a second-class ticket to Stockholm, in order to make his début in the world and receive his due. Unfortunately the Stockholmers do not read provincial papers. The young man was unknown and his talent was not appreciated. As he was a shrewd man—his small brain had never been exuberantly imaginative—he concealed his wound and allowed it to become the secret of his life.

The bitterness engendered by the fact that his honest work, as he called it, remained unrewarded specially qualified him for the post of a literary censor; but he did not write himself: his position did not allow him to indulge in efforts of his own, and he preferred leaving it to the reviewer who criticized everybody's work justly and with inflexible severity. The reviewer had written poetry for the last sixteen years under a pseudonym. Nobody had ever read his verses and nobody had taken the trouble to discover the author's real name. But every Christmas his verses were exhumed and praised in the *Grey Bonnet*, by a third party, of course, who signed his article so that the public should not suspect that the author had written it himself—it was taken for granted that the author was known to the public. In the seventeenth year, the author considered it advisable to put his name to a new book—a new edition of an old one. As misfortune would have it, the *Red Cap*, the whole staff of which was composed of young people who had never heard the real name, treated the author as a beginner, and expressed astonishment, not only that a young writer should put his name to his first book, but also that a young man's book could be so monotonous and old-fashioned. This was a hard blow; the old "pseudonymus" fell ill with fever, but recovered after having been brilliantly rehabilitated by the *Grey Bonnet*; the latter went for the whole reading public in a lump, charging it with being immoral and dishonest, unable to appreciate an honest, sound, and moral book which could safely be put into the hands of a child. A comic paper made fun of the last point, so that the "pseudonymus" had a relapse, and, on his second recovery, vowed annihilation to all native literature which might appear in future; it did, however, not apply to quite all native literature, for a shrewd observer would have noticed that the *Grey Bonnet* frequently praised bad books; true, it was often done lamely and in terms which could be read in two ways. The same shrewd observer could have noticed that the miserable stuff in question was always published by the same firm; but this did not necessarily imply that the reviewer was influenced by extraneous circumstances, such as little lunches, for instance; he and the whole editorial staff were upright men who would surely not have dared to judge others with so much severity if they themselves had not been men of irreproachable character.

Another important member of the staff was the dramatic critic. He had received his education and qualified at a recruiting bureau in X-köping; had fallen in love with a "star" who was only a "star" in X-köping. As he was not sufficiently enlightened to differentiate between a private opinion and a universal verdict, it happened to him when he was for the first time let loose in the columns of the *Grey Bonnet* that he slated the greatest actress in Sweden, and maintained that she copied Miss——, whatever her name was. That it was done very clumsily goes without saying, and also that it happened before the *Grey Bonnet* had veered round. All this made his name detested and despised; but still, he had a name, and that compensated him for the indignation he excited. One of his cardinal points, although not at once appreciated, was his deafness. Several years went by before it was discovered, and even then nobody could tell whether or no it had any connexion with a certain encounter, caused by one of his notices, in the foyer of the Opera House, one evening after the lights had been turned down. After this encounter he tested the strength of his arm only on quite young people; and anybody familiar with the circumstances could tell by his critique when he had had an accident in the wings, for the conceited provincial had read somewhere the unreliable statement that Stockholm was another Paris, and had believed it.

The art critic was an old academician who had never held a brush in his hand, but was a member of the brilliant artists club "Minerva," a fact which enabled him to describe works of art in the columns of his paper before they were finished, thereby saving the reader the trouble of forming an opinion of his own. He was invariably kind to his acquaintances, and in criticizing an exhibition never forgot to mention every single one of them. His practice, of many years' standing, of saying something pretty about everybody—and how would he have dared to do otherwise—made it child's play to him to mention twenty names in half a column; in reading his reviews one could not help thinking of the popular game "pictures and devices." But the young artists he always conscientiously forgot, so that the public, which, for ten years had heard none but the old names, began to despair of the future of art. One exception, however, he had made, and made quite recently, in an unpropitious hour; and in consequence of this exception there was great excitement one morning in the editorial office of the *Grey Bonnet*.

What had occurred was this: Sellén—the reader may remember this insignificant name mentioned on a former, and not a particularly important occasion—had arrived with his picture at the exhibition at the very last moment. When it had been hung—in the worst possible place—for the artist was neither a member of the Academy nor did he possess the royal medal—the "professor of Charles IX" arrived; he had been given this nickname because he never painted anything but scenes from the life of Charles IX; the reason again for this was that a long time ago he had bought at an auction a wine glass, a tablecloth, a chair, and a parchment from the period of Charles IX; these objects he had painted for twenty years, sometimes with, sometimes without, the king. But he was a professor now and a knight of many orders, and so there was no help for it. He was with the academician when his eye fell on the silent man of the opposition and his picture.

"Here again, sir?" He put up his pince-nez. "And this, then, is the new style! Hm! Let me tell you, sir! Believe the word of an old man: take that picture away! Take it away! It makes me sick to look at it. You do yourself the greatest service if you take it away. What do you say, old fellow?"

The old fellow said that the exhibition of such a picture was an impertinence, and that if the gentleman would take his kindly meant advice, he would change his profession and become a sign-board painter.

Sellén replied mildly, but shrewdly, that there were so many able people in that profession, that he had chosen an artistic career where success could be obtained far more easily, as had been proved.

The professor was furious at this insolence; he turned his back on the contrite Sellén with a threat which the academician translated into a promise.

The enlightened Committee of Purchases had met—behind closed doors. When the doors were opened again, six pictures had been bought for the money subscribed by the public for the purpose of encouraging native artists. The excerpt from the minutes which found its way into the columns of the newspapers, was worded as follows:

"The Art Union yesterday bought the following pictures: (1) 'Water with Oxen,' landscape by the wholesale merchant K. (2) 'Gustavus Adolphus at the Fire of Magdeburg,' historical painting by the linen draper L. (3) 'A Child blowing its Nose,' genre-picture by lieutenant M. (4) 'S. S. Bore in the Harbour,' marine picture by the shipbroker N. (5) 'Sylvan Scene with Women,' landscape by the royal secretary O. (6) 'Chicken with Mushrooms,' still-life by the actor P."

These works of art, which cost a thousand pounds each on an average, were afterwards praised in the *Grey Bonnet* in two three-quarter columns at fifteen crowns each; that was nothing extraordinary, but the critic, partly in order to fill up the space, and partly in order to seize the right moment for suppressing a growing evil, attacked a bad custom which was beginning to creep in. He referred to the fact that young, unknown adventurers, who had run away from the academy without study, were trying to pervert the sound judgment of the public by a mere running after effect. And then Sellén was taken by the ears and flogged, so that even his enemies found that his treatment was unfair—and that means a great deal. Not only was he denied every trace of talent and his art called humbug; even his private circumstances were dragged before the public; the article hinted at cheap restaurants where he was obliged to dine; at the shabby clothes he was forced to wear; at his loose morals, his idleness; it concluded by prophesying in the name of religion and morality that he would end his days in a public institution unless he mended his ways while there was yet time.

It was a disgraceful act, committed in indifference and selfishness; and it was little less than a miracle that a soul was not lost on the night of the publication of that particular number of the*Grey Bonnet.*

Twenty-four hours later the *Incorruptible* appeared. It reflected on the way in which public moneys were administered by a certain clique, and mentioned the fact that at the last purchase of pictures, not a single one had been bought which had been painted by an artist, but that the perpetrators had been officials and tradesmen, impudent enough to compete with the artists, although the latter had no other market; it went on to say that these pirates lowered the standard and demoralized the artists, whose sole endeavour would have to be to paint as badly as they did if they did not want to starve. Then Sellén's name was mentioned. His picture was the first soulfully conceived work within the last ten years. For ten years art had been a mere affair of colours and brushes; Sellén's picture was an honest piece of work, full of inspiration and devotion, and entirely original; a picture which could only have been produced by an artist who had met the spirit of nature face to face. The critic enjoined the young artist to fight against the ancients, whom he had already left a long way behind, and exhorted him to have faith and hope, because he had a mission to fulfil, etc.

The *Grey Bonnet* foamed with rage.

"You'll see that that fellow will have success!" exclaimed the chief editor. "Why the devil did we slate him quite so much! Supposing he became a success now! We should cover ourselves with ridicule."

The academician vowed that he should not have any success, went home with a troubled heart, referred to his books and wrote an essay in which he proved that Sellén's art was humbug, and that the *Incorruptible* had been corrupted.

The *Grey Bonnet* drew a breath of relief, but immediately afterwards it received a fresh blow.

On the following day the morning papers announced the fact that his Majesty had bought Sellén's "masterly landscape which, for days, had drawn a large public to the Exhibition."

The *Grey Bonnet* received the full fury of the gale; it was tossed hither and thither, and fluttered like a rag on a pole. Should they veer round or steer ahead? Both paper and critic were involved. The chief editor decided, by order of the managing director, to sacrifice the critic and save the paper. But how was it to be done? In their extremity they remembered Struve. He was a man completely at home in the maze of publicity. He was sent for. The situation was clear to him in a moment, and he promised that in a very few days the barge should be able to tack.

To understand Struve's scheme, it is necessary to know the most important data of his biography. He was a "born student," driven to journalism by sheer poverty. He started his career as editor of the Socialist *People's Flag*. Next he belonged to the Conservative *Peasants' Scourge*, but when the latter removed to the provinces with inventory, printing plant and editor, the name was changed into *Peasants' Friend*, and its politics changed accordingly. Struve was sold to the *Red Cap*, where his knowledge of all the Conservative tricks stood him in good stead; in the same way his greatest merit in the eyes of the *Grey Bonnet* was his knowledge of all the secrets of their deadly foe, the *Red Cap*, and his readiness to abuse his knowledge of them.

Struve began the work of whitewashing by starting a correspondence in the *People's Flag*; a few lines of this, mentioning the rush of visitors to the Exhibition, were reprinted in the *Grey Bonnet*. Next there appeared in the *Grey Bonnet* an attack on the academician; this attack was followed by a few reassuring words signed "The Ed." which read as follows: "Although we never shared the opinion of our art critic with regard to Mr. Sellén's justly praised landscape, yet we cannot altogether agree with the judgment of our respected correspondent; but as, on principle, we open our columns to all opinions, we unhesitatingly printed the above article."

The ice was broken. Struve, who had the reputation of having written on every subject—except cufic coins—now wrote a brilliant critique of Sellén's picture and signed it very characteristically Dixi. The *Grey Bonnet* was saved; and so, of course, was Sellén; but the latter was of minor importance.

CHAPTER XI. HAPPY PEOPLE

It was seven o'clock in the evening. The band at Berns' was playing the Wedding March from "A Midsummer Night's Dream," when to the accompaniment of its inspiriting strains Olle Montanus made his entry into the Red Room. None of the members had yet arrived. Olle looked imposing. For the first time since his confirmation he was wearing a high hat. He was dressed in a new suit, and his boots were without holes; he had had a bath, had been newly shaved, and his hair was waved as if he were going to a wedding. A heavy brass chain ornamented his waistcoat, and his left waistcoat pocket bulged visibly. A sunny smile lit up his features; he radiated kindness; one might have thought that he wanted to help all the world with little loans. Taking off his overcoat, no longer cautiously buttoned up, he took the centre of the sofa in the background, opened his coat and tugged at his white shirt front so that it rose with a crackle and stood out like an arch; at every movement the lining of his waistcoat and trousers creaked. This seemed to give him as much pleasure as the knocking of his boot against the leg of the sofa. He pulled out his watch, his dear old turnip, which for a year and a month's grace had been in the pawnbroker's hands, and the two old friends both seemed to enjoy its liberty.

What had happened that this poor fellow should be so inexpressibly happy? We know that he had not drawn the winner in a lottery, that he had not inherited a fortune, that he had not been "honourably mentioned," that he had not won the sweet happiness which baffles description. What had happened then? Something very commonplace: he had found work.

Sellén was the next to arrive. He wore a velvet jacket and patent-leather boots; he carried a rug, a field-glass on a strap, and a cane; a yellow silk handkerchief was knotted round his throat; his hands were covered by flesh-coloured gloves and a flower blossomed in his buttonhole. He was, as usual, cheerful and calm; his lean, intelligent face betrayed no trace of the emotions undergone during the last few days.

Sellén was accompanied by Rehnhjelm; the lad was unusually subdued; he knew that his friend and patron was leaving him.

"Hallo! Sellén," said Olle, "you are happy at last, aren't you, old chap?"

"Happy? What nonsense you are talking! I've sold a piece of work! The first in five years! Is that so overwhelming?"

"But you must have read the papers! Your name's made!"

"Oh! I don't care the toss of a button for that! Don't imagine that I care for such trifles. I know exactly how much I still have to learn before I shall be anybody. Let's talk of it again in ten years' time, Olle."

Olle believed half of what Sellén said and doubted the rest; his shirt front crackled and the lining creaked so that Sellén's attention was aroused.

"By the Lord Harry!" he burst out, "you are magnificent!"

"Think so? You look like a lion."

Sellén rapped his patent-leather boots with his cane, shyly smelt the flower in his buttonhole, and looked indifferent. Olle pulled out his watch to see whether it was not yet time for Lundell to arrive, which gave Sellén an opportunity of sweeping the galleries with his field-glass. Olle was permitted to feel the soft texture of the velvet coat, while Sellén assured him that it was an exceptionally good quality at the price; Olle could not resist asking the cost. Sellén told him, and admired Olle's studs, which were made of shells.

Presently Lundell appeared; he, too, had been given a bone at the great banquet; he was commissioned to paint the altar-piece for the church of Träskola for a small sum; but this had not visibly affected his outward appearance, unless, indeed, his fat cheeks and beaming face hinted at a more generous diet.

Falk was with Lundell. He was grave, but he rejoiced, in the name of the whole world sincerely rejoiced, that merit had found its just reward.

"Congratulations, Sellén!" he said, "but it's no more than your due."

Sellén agreed.

"I have been painting just as well these last five years and all the world has jeered; they were still jeering the day before yesterday, but now! It's disgusting! Look at this letter which I received from the idiot, the professor of Charles IX!"

All eyes opened wide and became keen, for it is gratifying to examine the oppressor closely, have him—on paper at least—in one's hands, at one's mercy.

"'My dear Mr. Sellén,'—Fancy that!—'Let me welcome you among us'—he's afraid of me, the blackguard—'I have always appreciated your talent'—the liar!—let's tear up the rag and forget all about him."

Sellén invited his friends to drink; he drank to Falk, and hoped that his pen would soon bring him to the front. Falk became self-conscious, blushed and promised to do his best when his time came; but he was afraid that his apprenticeship would be a long one, and he begged his friends not to lose patience with him if he tarried; he thanked Sellén for his friendship, which had taught him endurance and renunciation. Sellén begged him not to talk nonsense; where was the merit of endurance when there was no other alternative? And where was the virtue in renouncing what one had no chance of obtaining?

But Olle smiled a kindly smile, and his shirt front swelled with pleasure, so that the red braces could be plainly seen; he drank to Lundell and implored him to take an example from Sellén, and not forget the Land of Promise in lingering over the fleshpots of Egypt. He assured him that his friend, Olle, believed in his talent, that was to say, when he was himself and painted according to his own light; but whenever he humbugged and painted to please others he was worse than the rest; therefore he should look upon the altar-piece as a pot boiler which would put him into a position to follow his own inspiration in art.

Falk tried to seize the opportunity of finding out what Olle thought of himself and his own art, a puzzle which he had long vainly attempted to solve, when Ygberg walked into the Red Room. Everybody eagerly invited him to be his guest, for he had been forgotten during the last hot days, and everyone was anxious to show him that it had not been out of selfishness. But Olle searched in his right waistcoat pocket, and with a movement which he was anxious to hide from all eyes he slipped a rolled-up banknote into Ygberg's coat pocket; the latter understood and acknowledged it by a grateful look.

Ygberg drank to Sellén; he said that one might consider, in one way, that Sellén's fortune was made; but, on the other hand, one might consider, with equal justification, that it was not so. Sellén was not sufficiently developed; he still wanted many years' study, for art was long, as he, Ygberg, had himself experienced. He had had nothing but ill-luck, therefore nobody could suspect him of envying a man of Sellén's reputation.

The envy which peered through Ygberg's words slightly clouded the sunny sky; but it was only for a moment, for everybody realized that the bitterness of a long, wasted life, must be held responsible for it.

All the more gladly Ygberg handed Falk a small newly printed essay, on the cover of which he beheld with consternation the black portrait of Ulrica Eleonora. Ygberg stated that he had delivered the manuscript on the day stipulated. Smith had taken Falk's refusal with the greatest calm, and was now printing Falk's poems.

To Falk's eyes the gas-jets lost their brilliancy; he sat plunged in deep thought; his heart was too full to find vent in words. His poems were to be printed at Smith's expense. This was proof that they were not without merit! The thought was sufficient food for the whole evening.

The evening passed quickly for the happy circle; the band ceased playing and the light was turned out; they were obliged to leave, but, finding the night far too young for breaking up, they strolled along the quays, amid endless conversation and philosophical discussions, until they were tired and thirsty. Lundell offered to take his friends to see Marie, where they could have some beer.

They turned towards the north and came to a street which gave on a fence; the fence enclosed a tobacco field, bordering on the open country. They stopped before a two-storied brick-house with a gable facing the street. From above the door grinned two sandstone faces whose ears and shins were lost in fantastic scrolls. Between the heads hung a sword and an axe. It was formerly the house of the executioner.

Lundell, apparently quite familiar with the neighbourhood, gave a signal before one of the windows on the ground floor; the blind was drawn up; the window opened, and a woman's head looked out; a voice asked whether the caller was Albert? No sooner had Lundell owned to this, his *nom de guerre*, than a girl opened the door and, on the promise of silence, admitted the party. As the promise was readily given, the Red Room was soon in her apartment, and introduced to her under fictitious names.

The room was not a large one; it had once been the kitchen, and the range was still standing in its place. The furniture consisted of a chest of drawers, of a pattern usually found in servants' rooms; on the drawers stood a looking-glass, swathed in a piece of white muslin; above the glass hung a coloured lithograph, representing the Saviour on the Cross. The chest was littered with small china figures, scent bottles, a prayer book, and an ash tray, and with its looking-glass and two lighted tallow candles seemed to form a little house altar. Charles XV, surrounded by newspaper cuttings, mostly representing police constables, those enemies of the Magdalenes, was riding on horseback on the wall above the folding sofa, which had not yet been converted into a bed. On the window-sill stood a stunted fuchsia, a geranium and a myrtle—the proud tree of

Aphrodite in the poor dwelling. A photograph album lay on the work-table. On the first leaf was a picture of the King, on the second and third papa and mamma—poor country folk; on the fourth a student, the seducer; on the fifth, a baby; and on the sixth the fiancé, a journeyman. This was her history, so like the history of most of them. On a nail, close to the range, hung an elegant dress, a velvet cloak, and a hat with feathers—the fairy disguise in which she went out to catch young men. The fairy herself was a tall, ordinary looking young woman of twenty-four. Recklessness and vigils had given her face that white transparency which as a rule distinguishes the untoiling rich, but her hands still showed traces of hard work. In her pretty dressing-gown, with her flowing hair down her back, she was the picture of a Magdalene; her manner was comparatively shy, but she was merry and courteous and on her best behaviour.

The party split up into groups, continued the interrupted discussions and started fresh ones. Falk, who now looked upon himself as a poet and was determined to be interested in everything—be it ever so banal—began a sentimental conversation with Marie, which she greatly enjoyed, for she appreciated the honour of being treated like a human being. As usual the talk drifted to her story and the motives which had shaped her career. She did not lay stress on her first slip, "that was hardly worth speaking about"; but all the blacker was her account of the time she had spent as a servant, leading the life of a slave, made miserable by the whims and scoldings of an indolent mistress, a life of never-ending toil. No, the free life she was leading now was far preferable.

"But when you are tired of it?"

"Then I shall marry Vestergren."

"Does he want you?"

"He's looking forward to the day; moreover, I am going to open a little shop with the money I have saved. But so many have asked me that question: 'Have you got any cigars?'"

"Oh, yes; here you are! But do you mind my talking about it?"

He took the album and pointed out the student—it is always a student, with a white handkerchief round his neck, a white student's hat on his knees, and a gauche manner, who plays Mephisto.

"Who is this?"

"He was a nice fellow."

"The seducer? What?"

"Oh! let it alone! I was every bit as much to blame, and it is always so, my dear; both are to blame! Look, this is my baby. The Lord took it, and I dare say it was for the best. But now let's talk about something else. Who is that gay dog whom Albert has brought here to-night? The one closest to the stove, by the side of the tall one, whose head reaches up to the chimney?"

Olle, very much flattered by her attention, patted his wavy hair which, after the many libations, was beginning to stand up again.

"That is assistant preacher Monsson," said Lundell.

"Ugh! A clergyman! I might have known it from the cunning look in his eyes. Do you know that a clergyman came here last week? Come here, Monsson, and let me look at you!"

Olle descended from his seat where he and Ygberg had been criticizing Kant's Categorical Imperative. He was so accustomed to exciting the curiosity of the sex that he immediately felt younger; he lurched towards the lady whom he had already ogled and found charming. Twirling his moustache, he asked in an affected voice, with a bow which he had not learned at a dancing class:

"Do you really think, miss, that I look like a clergyman?"

"No, I see now that you have a moustache; your clothes are too clean for an artisan—may I see your hand—oh! you are a smith!"

Olle was deeply hurt.

"Am I so very ugly, miss?" he asked pathetically.

Marie examined him for a moment.

"You are very plain," she said, "but you look nice."

"Oh, dear lady, if you only knew how you are hurting me! I have never yet found a woman ready to love me, and yet I have met so many who found happiness although they were plainer than I am. But woman is a cursed riddle, which nobody can solve; I detest her."

"That's right, Olle," came a voice from the chimney, where Ygberg's head was; "that's all right."

Olle was going back to the stove, but he had touched on a topic which interested Marie too much to allow it to drop; he had played on a string the sound of which she knew. She sat down by his side and soon they were deep in a long-winded and grave discussion—on love and women.

Rehnhjelm, who during the whole evening had been more quiet and restrained than usual, and of whom nobody could make anything, suddenly revived and was now sitting in the corner of the sofa near Falk. Obviously something was troubling him, something which he could not make up his mind to mention. He seized his beer-glass, rapped on the table as if he wanted to make a speech, and when those nearest to him looked up ready to listen to him, he said in a tremulous and indifferent voice:

"Gentlemen, you think I am a beast, I know; Falk, I know you think me a fool, but you shall see, friends—the devil take me, you shall see!"

He raised his voice and put his beer-glass down with such determination that it broke in pieces, after which he sank back on the sofa and fell asleep.

This scene, although not an uncommon one, had attracted Marie's attention. She dropped the conversation with Olle, who, moreover, had begun to stray from the purely abstract point of the question and rose.

"Oh! what a pretty boy!" she exclaimed. "How does he come to be with you? Poor little chap! How sleepy he is! I hadn't seen him before."

She pushed a cushion under his head and covered him with a shawl.

"How small his hands are! Far smaller than yours, you country louts! And what a face! How innocent he looks! Albert, did you make him drink so much?"

Whether it had been Lundell or another was a matter of no importance now; the man was drunk. But it also was a fact that he did not need any urging to drink. He was consumed by a constant longing to still an inner restlessness which seemed to drive him away from his work.

The remarks made by his pretty friend had not perturbed Lundell; but now his increasing intoxication excited his religious feelings, which had been blunted by a luxurious supper. And as the intoxication began to be general, he felt it incumbent on him to remind his companions of the significance of the day and the impending leave-taking. He rose, filled his glass, steadied himself against the chest of drawers and claimed the attention of the party.

"Gentlemen,"—he remembered Magdalene's presence—"and ladies! We have eaten and drunk to-night with—to come to the point—an intent which, if we set aside the material which is nothing but the low, sensual animal component of our nature—that in a moment like this when the hour of parting is imminent—we have here a distressing example of the vice which we call drunkenness! Doubtless, it arouses all one's religious emotion if, after an evening spent in a circle of friends, one feels moved to propose a glass to him who has shown more than ordinary talent—I am speaking of Sellén—one should think that self-respect should to a certain extent prevail. Such an example, I maintain, has been manifested here, in higher potency, and therefore I am reminded of the beautiful words which will never cease ringing in my ears as long as I am able to think, and I am convinced they are now in the mind of each one of us, although this spot is anything but suitable. This young man, who has fallen a victim to the vice which we will call drunkenness, has unfortunately crept into our circle and—to cut my speech short—matured a sadder result than anybody could have expected. Your health, noble friend Sellén! I wish you all the happiness which your noble heart deserves! Your health, Olle Montanus! Falk, too, has a noble heart, and will come to the front when his religious sense has acquired the vigour which his character foreshadows. I won't mention Ygberg, for he has at last come to a decision, and we wish him luck in the career upon which he has so splendidly entered—the philosophical career. It is a difficult one, and I repeat the words of the psalmist: Who can tell? At the same time we have every reason to hope for the best in the future, and I believe that we can count on it as long as our sentiments are noble and our hearts are not striving for worldly gain; for, gentlemen, a man without religion is a beast. I therefore ask every gentleman here present to raise his glass and empty it to all that is noble, beautiful, and splendid, and for which we are striving. Your health, gentlemen!"

Religious emotion now overwhelmed Lundell to such a degree that it was thought best to break up the party.

Daylight had been shining through the window-blind for some time and the landscape with the castle and the maiden stood out brilliantly in the first radiance of the morning sun. When the blind was drawn up, day rushed in and illuminated the faces of those nearest the window; they were deadly pale. The red light of the tallow candles fell with magnificent effect on the face of Ygberg, who was sitting on the stove, clutching his glass. Olle was proposing toasts to women, the spring, the sun, the universe, throwing open the window, to give vent to his feelings. The sleepers were roused, the party took their leave of Marie, and filed through the front door.

When they had reached the street, Falk turned round. Magdalene was leaning out of the window; the rays of the sun fell on her pale face; her long, black hair, which shone deep red in the sunlight, seemed to trickle down her throat and over her shoulders and to be falling on the street in little streams. Above her head hung the sword and the axe and the two grinning faces; but in an apple tree on the other side of the road perched a black and white fly-catcher, and sang its frenzied song of joy that the night was over.

CHAPTER XII. MARINE INSURANCE SOCIETY "TRITON"

Levi was a young man born and educated for business and on the point of establishing himself with the assistance of his wealthy father, when the latter died, leaving nothing but a family totally unprovided for.

This was a great disappointment to the young man; he had reached an age when he considered that he might stop working altogether and let others toil for him. He was twenty-five and of good appearance. Broad-shouldered and lean in the flank, his body seemed specially adapted for wearing a frock-coat in the manner which he had much admired in certain foreign diplomatists. Nature had arched his chest in the most elegant fashion, so that he was capable of setting off to the fullest advantage a four-buttoned shirt front, even in the very act of sinking into an easy chair at the foot of a long Board-table occupied by the whole Administrative Committee. A beautiful beard, parted in the middle, gave his young face a sympathetic and trustworthy expression; his small feet were made for walking on the Brussels carpet of a Board-room, and his carefully manicured hands were particularly suitable for very light work, such as the signing of his name, preferably on a printed circular.

In the days which are now called the good days, although in reality they were very bad ones for a good many people, the greatest discovery of a great century was made, namely, that one could live more cheaply and better on other people's money than on the results of one's own efforts. Many, a great many, people had taken advantage of the discovery, and as no patent law protected it, it was not surprising that Levi should be anxious to profit by it, too, more particularly as he had no money himself and no inclination to work for a family which was not his own. He, therefore, put on his best suit one day and called on his uncle Smith.

"Oh, indeed! You have an idea," said Smith, "Let's hear it! It's a good thing to have ideas!"

"I have been thinking of floating a joint stock company."

"Very good. Aaron will be treasurer, Simon secretary, Isaac cashier, and the other boys book-keepers; it's a good idea! Go on! What sort of a company is it going to be?"

"I'm thinking of a marine insurance society."

"Indeed! So far so good; everybody has to insure his property when he goes on a voyage. But your idea?"

"This *is* my idea."

"I don't think much of it. We have the big society 'Neptune.' It's a good society. Yours would have to be better if you intend to compete with it. What would be the novelty in your society?"

"Oh! I understand! I should reduce the premiums and all the patrons of the 'Neptune' would come to me."

"That's better! Very well, then, the prospectus which I would print would begin in this way: 'As the crying need of reducing the marine insurance premiums has long been felt, and it is only owing to the want of competition that it has not yet been done, we, the undersigned, beg to invite the public to take up shares in the new society.... What name?"

"Triton."

"Triton? What sort of a chap was he?"

"He was a sea-god."

"All right, Triton. It will make a good poster! You can order it from Ranch in Berlin, and we will reproduce it in my almanac 'Our Country.' Now for the undersigned. First, of course, my name. We must have big, well-sounding names. Give me the official almanac."

Smith turned over the leaves for some time.

"A marine insurance company must have a naval officer of high rank. Let me see! An admiral."

"Oh! Those sort of people have no money!"

"Bless me! You don't know much about business, my boy! They are only wanted to subscribe, not to pay up! And they receive their dividends for attending the meetings and being present at the directors' dinners! Here we have two admirals; one of them has the Commander's Ribbon of the Polar Star, and the other one has the Russian Order of Anna. What shall we do? I think we had better take the Russian, for there is splendid marine insurance ground in Russia.... There!"

"But is it such a simple matter to get hold of these people?"

"Tut, tut! Next we want a retired minister of State! Yes! Well! They are called Your Excellency! Yes! Good. And a Count! That's more difficult! Counts have lots of money! And we must have a professor! They have no money! Is there such a thing as a Professor of Navigation? That would be a capital thing for our venture! Isn't there a School of Navigation somewhere near the South Theatre? Yes? Very well! Everything is as clear as possible to me. Oh! I nearly forgot the most important point. We must have a legal man! A counsellor of a high court. Here he is!"

"But we have no money yet!"

"Money? What's the use of money in company promoting? Doesn't the man who insures his goods pay us money? What? Or do we pay him? No! Well then, he pays with his premiums."

"But the original capital?"

"One issues debentures!"

"True, but there must be some cash!"

"One pays cash in debentures! Isn't that paying? Supposing I gave you a cheque for a sum, any bank would cash it for you. Therefore, a cheque is money. Very well! And is there a law which ordains that cash shall mean bank-notes? If there were, what about private bank-notes?"

"How large should the capital be?"

"Very small! It's bad business to tie up large sums. A million! Three hundred thousand in cash and the remainder in debentures."

"But—but—but! The three hundred thousand crowns surely must be in bank-notes!"

"Good Lord in Heaven! Bank-notes? Notes are money! If you have notes, well and good; if you haven't, it comes to the same thing. Therefore, we must interest the small capitalists, who have nothing but bank-notes."

"And the big ones? How do they pay?"

"In shares, debenture guarantees, of course. But that will be a matter for later on. Get them to subscribe, and we'll see to the rest."

"And only three hundred thousand? One single great steamer costs as much. Supposing we insured a thousand steamers?"

"A thousand? Last year the 'Neptune' issued forty-eight thousand insurance policies, and did well out of it."

"All the worse, I say! But if—but if—matters should go wrong...."

"One goes into liquidation!"

"Liquidation?"

"Declares oneself insolvent! That's the proper term. And what does it matter if the society becomes insolvent? It isn't you, or I, or he! But one can also increase the number of shares, or issue debentures which the Government may buy up in hard times at a good price."

"There's no risk then?"

"Not the slightest! Besides what have you got to lose? Do you possess one farthing? No! Very well then! What do I risk? Five hundred crowns! I shall only take five shares, you see! And five hundred is as much as this to me!"

He took a pinch of snuff and the matter was settled.

The society was floated and during the first ten years of its activity it paid 6, 10, 10, 11, 20, 11, 5, 10, 36, and 20 per cent. The shares were eagerly bought up, and, in order to enlarge the business, more shares were issued; the new issue of shares was followed by a general meeting of shareholders; Falk was sent to report it for the *Red Cap*, whose assistant reporter he was.

When, on a sunny afternoon in June, he entered the Exchange, the hall was already crowded with people. It was a brilliant assembly. Statesmen, geniuses, men of letters, officers, and civil service men of high rank; uniforms, dress-coats, orders, and ribbons; all those here assembled had one big general interest! The advancement of the philanthropic institution called marine insurance. It required a great love to risk one's money for the benefit of the suffering neighbour whom misfortune had befallen, but here was love! Falk had never seen such an accumulation of it in one spot. Although not yet an entirely disillusioned man, he could not suppress a feeling of amazement.

But he was even more amazed when he noticed the little blackguard Struve, the former Socialist, creeping through the crowd like a reptile, greeted, and sometimes addressed by distinguished people with a familiar nod, a pressure of the hand or a friendly slap on the shoulder. He saw a middle-aged man, wearing a ribbon belonging to a high order, nodding to him, and he noticed that Struve blushed and concealed himself behind an embroidered coat. This brought him into Falk's vicinity, and the latter immediately accosted him and asked him who the man was. Struve's embarrassment increased, but summoning up all his impudence, he replied, "You ought to know that! He's the president of the Board of Payment of Employés' Salaries." No sooner had the words left his lips than he pretended to be called to the other side of the room; but he was in so great a hurry that Falk wondered whether he felt uncomfortable in his society? A blackguard in the company of an honourable man!

The brilliant assembly began to be seated. But the president's chair was still vacant. Falk was looking for the reporter's table, and when he discovered Struve and the reporter for the*Conservative* sitting at a table on the right-hand side of the secretary he took his courage into his hands and marched through the distinguished crowd; just as he had reached the table, the secretary stopped him with a question. "For which paper?" he asked. A momentary silence ensued. "For the *Red Cap*," answered Falk, with a slight tremor in his voice; he had recognized in the secretary the actuary of the Board of Payment of Employés' Salaries. A half-stifled murmur ran through the room; presently the secretary said in a loud voice: "Your place is at the back, over there!" He pointed to the door and a small table standing close to it.

Falk realized in a moment the significance of the word "Conservative," and also what it meant to be a journalist who was not a Conservative. Boiling inwardly he retraced his footsteps, walking to his appointed place through the sneering crowd; he stared at the grinning faces, challenging them with burning eyes, when his glance met another glance, quite in the background, close to the wall. The eyes, bearing a strong resemblance to a pair of eyes now closed in death, which used to rest on his face full of love, were green with malice and pierced him like a needle; he could have shed tears of sorrow at the thought that a brother could thus look at a brother.

He took his modest place near the door, for he was determined not to beat a retreat. Very soon he was roused from his apparent calm by a newcomer who prodded him in the back as he took off his coat and shoved a pair of rubber overshoes underneath his chair. The newcomer was greeted by the whole assembly which rose from their seats as one man. He was the chairman of the Marine Insurance Society Limited "Triton," but he was something else beside this. He was a retired district-marshal, a baron, one of the eighteen of the Swedish Academy, an Excellency, a knight of many orders, etc. etc.

A rap with the hammer and amid dead silence the president whispered the following oration: just delivered by him at a meeting of the Coal Company Limited, in the hall of the Polytechnic.

"Gentlemen! Amongst all the patriotic and philanthropic enterprises there are few—if any—of such a noble and beneficial nature as an Insurance Society."

This statement was received with a unanimous "Hear! hear!" which, however, made no impression on the district-marshal.

"What else is life but a struggle, a life and death struggle, one might say, with the forces of Nature! There will be few among us who do not, sooner or later, come into conflict with them."

"Hear! hear!"

"For long ages man, more especially primitive man, has been the sport of the elements; a ball tossed hither and thither, a glove blown here and there by the wind like a reed. This is no longer the case. I'm correct in saying it is not. Man has determined to rebel; it is a bloodless rebellion, though, and very different to the revolutions which dishonourable traitors to their country have now and again stirred up against their lawful rulers. No! gentlemen! I'm speaking of a revolution against nature! Man has declared war to the natural forces; he has said, 'Thus far shalt thou go and no farther!'"

"Hear! hear!" and clapping of hands.

"The merchant sends out his steamer, his brig, his schooner, his barge, his yacht, and so forth. The gale breaks the vessel to pieces. 'Break away!' says the merchant, for he loses nothing. This is the great aspect of the insurance idea. Imagine the position, gentlemen! The merchant has declared war upon the storms of heaven—and the merchant has won the day!"

A storm of applause brought a triumphant smile to the face of the great man; he seemed thoroughly to enjoy this storm.

"But, gentlemen, do not let us call an Insurance Institution a business. It is not a business; we are not business men. Far from it! We have collected a sum of money and we are ready to risk it. Is this not so, gentlemen?"

"Yes, yes!"

"We have collected a sum of money so as to have it ready to hand over to him whom misfortune has befallen; his percentage—I think he pays 1 per cent.—cannot be called a contribution; it is called a premium, and rightly so. Not that we want any sort of reward—premium means reward—for our little services, which we merely render because we are interested—as far as I am concerned it is purely for this reason. I repeat, I don't think—there can be any question that any one in our midst would hesitate—I don't think that one of us would mind seeing his contribution, if I may be allowed to call the shares by that name, used for the furtherance of the idea."

"No! No!"

"I will now ask the Managing Director to read the annual report."

The director rose. He looked as pale as if he had been through a storm; his big cuffs with the onyx studs could hardly hide the slight trembling of his hand; his cunning eyes sought comfort and strength in Smith's bearded face; he opened his coat and his expansive shirt front swelled as if it were ready to receive a shower of arrows—and read:

"Truly, strange and unexpected are the ways of Providence...."

At the word Providence a considerable number of faces blanched, but the district-marshal raised his eyes towards the ceiling as if he were prepared for the worst (a loss of two hundred crowns).

"The year which we have just completed will long stand in our annals like a cross on the grave of the accidents which have brought to scorn the foresight of the wisest and the calculations of the most cautious."

The district-marshal buried his face in his hands as if he were praying. Struve, believing that the white wall dazzled his eyes, jumped up to pull down the blind, but the secretary had already forestalled him.

The reader drank a glass of water. This caused an outburst of impatience.

"To business! Figures!"

The district-marshal removed his hand from his eyes and was taken aback when he found that it was so much darker than it had been before. There was a momentary embarrassment and the storm gathered. All respect was forgotten.

"To business! Go on!"

The director skipped the preliminary banalities, and plunged right into the heart of the matter.

"Very well, gentlemen, I will cut my speech short!"

"Go on! Go on! Why the devil don't you?"

The hammer fell. "Gentlemen!" There was so much dignity in this brief "Gentlemen" that the assembly immediately remembered their self-respect.

"The Society has been responsible during the year for one hundred and sixty-nine millions."

"Hear! hear!"

"And has received a million and a half in premiums."

"Hear! hear!"

Falk made a hasty calculation and found that if the full receipts in premiums, namely, one million and a half, and the total original capital, one million, were deducted, there remained about one hundred and sixty-six millions for which the society was responsible. He realized what "the ways of Providence" meant.

"Unfortunately the amount paid on policies was one million seven hundred and twenty-eight thousand six hundred and seventy crowns and eight öre."

"Shame!"

"As you see, gentlemen, Providence...."

"Leave Providence alone! Figures! Figures! Dividends!"

"Under the circumstances I can only propose, in my capacity as Managing Director, a dividend of 5 per cent. on the paid-up capital."

Now a storm burst out which no merchant in the world could have weathered.

"Shame! Impudence! Swindler! Five per cent! Disgusting! It's throwing one's money away!"

But there were also a few more philanthropic utterances, such as: "What about the poor, small capitalists who have nothing but their dividends to live on? How'll they manage? Mercy on us, what a misfortune! The State ought to help, and without delay! Oh dear! Oh dear!"

When the storm had subsided a little and the director could make his voice heard, he read out the high praise given by the Supervisory Committee to the Managing Director and all the employés who, without sparing themselves, and with indefatigable zeal, had done the thankless work. The statement was received with open scorn.

The report of the accountants was then read. They stated—after again censuring Providence—that they had found all the books in good—not to say excellent—order, and in checking the inventory all debentures on the reserve fund had been found correct (!) They therefore called upon the shareholders to discharge the directors and acknowledge their honest and unremitting labour.

The directors were, of course, discharged.

The Managing Director then declared that under the circumstances he could not think of accepting his bonus (a hundred crowns) and handed it to the reserve fund. This declaration was received with applause and laughter.

After a short evening prayer, that is to say a humble petition to Providence that next year's dividend might be 20 per cent., the district-marshal closed the proceedings.

CHAPTER XIII. DIVINE ORDINANCE

On the same afternoon on which her husband had attended the meeting of the Marine Insurance Society "Triton," Mrs. Falk for the first time wore a new blue velvet dress, with which she was eager to arouse the envy of Mrs. Homan, who lived in the house opposite. Nothing was easier or more simple; all she had to do was to show herself every now and then at the window while she supervised the preparations in her room, intended to "crush" her guests, whom she expected at seven. The Administrative Committee of the Crèche "Bethlehem" was to meet and examine the first monthly report; it consisted of Mrs. Homan, whose husband, the controller, Mrs. Falk suspected of pride because he was a Government official; Lady Rehnhjelm whom she suspected of the same failing because of her title, and the Rev. Skore, who was private chaplain of all the great families. The whole committee was to be crushed and crushed in the sweetest possible manner.

The new setting for the scene had already been displayed at the big party. All the old pieces which were neither antique nor possessed of any artistic value had been replaced by brand new furniture. Mrs. Falk intended to manage the actors in the little play until the close of the proceedings, when her husband would arrive upon the scene with an admiral—he had promised his wife at least an admiral in full-dress uniform. Both were to crave admission to the society. Falk was to enlarge the funds of the society on the spot by handing over to it a part of the sum which he had been earning so easily as shareholder of the "Triton."

Mrs. Falk had finished with the window and was now arranging the rosewood table, inlaid with mother-of-pearl, on which the proofs of the monthly report were to be laid. She dusted the agate inkstand, placed the silver penholder on the tortoiseshell rack, turned up the seal of the chrysoprase handle so as to hide her commoner's name, cautiously shook the cash-box made of the finest steel wire, so that the value of the few bank-notes it contained could be plainly read. Finally, having given her last orders to the footman dressed up for the parade, she sat down in her drawing-room in the careless attitude in which she desired that the announcement of her friend, the controller's wife, should discover her; Mrs. Homan would be sure to be the first to arrive.

She did arrive first. Mrs. Falk embraced Evelyn and kissed her on the cheek, and Mrs. Homan embraced Eugenia, who received her in the dining-room and retained her there for a few moments in order to ask her opinion of the new furniture. Mrs. Homan wasted no time on the solid oak sideboard dating from the time of Charles XII, with the tall Japanese vases, because she felt small by the side of it; she looked at the chandelier which she found too modern, and the dining-table, which, she said, was not in keeping with the prevailing style; in addition to this she considered that the oleographs were out of place among the old family portraits, and took quite a long time to explain the difference between an oil painting and an oleograph. Mrs. Falk's new silk-lined velvet dress swished against every corner within reach without succeeding in attracting her friend's attention. She asked her whether she liked the new Brussels carpet in the drawing-room; Mrs. Homan thought it contrasted too crudely with the curtains; at last Mrs. Falk felt annoyed with her and dropped her questions.

They sat down at the drawing-room table, clutching at life-buoys in the guise of photographs, unreadable volumes of verse, and so on. A little pamphlet fell into Mrs. Homan's hands; it was printed on gold-edged pink paper and bore the title: "To the wholesale merchant Nicholas Falk, on his fortieth birthday."

"Ah! These are the verses which were read at your party! Who wrote them?"

"A very clever man, a friend of my husband's. His name's Nyström."

"Hm! How queer that his name should be quite unknown! Such a clever man! But why wasn't he at your party?"

"Unfortunately he was ill, my dear; so he couldn't come."

"I see! But, my dear Eugenia, isn't it awfully sad about your brother-in-law? I hear he's so very badly off."

"Don't mention him! He's a disgrace and a grief to the whole family! It's terrible!"

"Yes; it was quite unpleasant when everybody asked about him at your party. I was so sorry for you, dear...."

This is for the oak sideboard, dating from the time of Charles XII, and the Japanese vases, thought the controller's wife.

"For me! Oh, please don't! You mean for my husband?" interrupted Mrs. Falk.

"Surely, that's the same thing!"

"Not at all! I can't be held responsible for all the black sheep in his family."

"What a pity it was that your parents, also, were ill and couldn't come! How's your dear father?"

"Thanks. He's quite well again. How kind of you to think of everybody!"

"Well, one shouldn't think of oneself only! Is he delicate, the old—what *is* his title?"

"Captain, if you like."

"Captain! I was under the impression that my husband said he was—one of the crew of the flagship, but very likely it's the same thing. But where were the girls?"

That's for the Brussels carpet, mentally reflected the controller's wife.

"They are so full of whims, they can never be depended on."

Mrs. Falk turned over the leaves in her photograph album; the binding cracked; she was in a towering rage.

"I say, dear, who was the disagreeable individual who read the verses on the night of your party?"

"You mean Mr. Levin; the royal secretary; he's my husband's most intimate friend."

"Is he really? Hm! How strange! My husband's a controller in the same office where he's a secretary; I don't want to vex you, or say anything unpleasant; I never do; but my husband says that Levin's in such bad circumstances that it's not wise for your husband to associate with him."

"Does he? That's a matter of which I know nothing, and in which I don't interfere, and let me tell you, my dear Evelyn, I never interfere in my husband's affairs, though I've heard of people who do."

"I beg your pardon, dear, I thought I was doing you a service by telling you."

That's for the chandelier and the dining-table. There only remains the velvet dress.

"Well," the controller's wife took up the thread again, "I hear that your brother-in-law...."

"Spare my feelings and don't talk of the creature!"

"Is he really such a bad lot? I've been told that he associates with the worst characters in town...."

At this juncture Mrs. Falk was reprieved; the footman announced Lady Rehnhjelm.

Oh! How welcome she was! How kind of her it was to come!

And Mrs. Falk really was pleased to see the old lady with the kindly expression in her eyes; an expression only found in the eyes of those who have weathered the storms of life with true courage.

"My dear Mrs. Falk," said her ladyship taking a seat; "I have all sorts of kind messages for you from your brother-in-law."

Mrs. Falk wondered what she had done to the old woman that she, too, evidently wanted to annoy her.

"Indeed?" she said, a little stiffly.

"He's a charming young man. He came to see my nephew to-day, at my house; they are great friends! He really is an excellent young man!"

"Isn't he?" joined in Mrs. Homan, always ready for a change of front. "We were just talking about him."

"Indeed? What I most admire in him is his courage in venturing on a course where one easily runs aground; but we need have no apprehensions so far as he is concerned; he's a man of character and principle. Don't you agree with me, Mrs. Falk?"

"I've always said so, but my husband thinks differently."

"Oh! Your husband has always had peculiar views," interposed Mrs. Homan.

"Is he a friend of your nephew's, Lady Rehnhjelm?" asked Mrs. Falk eagerly.

"Yes, they both belong to a small circle, some of the members of which are artists. You must have heard about young Sellén, whose picture was bought by his Majesty?"

"Of course, I have! We went to the Exhibition on purpose to have a look at it. Is he one of them?"

"Yes; they're often very hard up, these young fellows, but that's nothing new in the case of young men who have to fight their way in the world."

"They say your brother-in-law's a poet," went on Mrs. Homan.

"Oh, rather! He writes excellent verse! The academy gave him a prize; the world will hear of him in time," replied Mrs. Falk with conviction.

"Haven't I always said so?" agreed Mrs. Homan.

And Arvid Falk's talents were enlarged upon, so that he had arrived in the Temple of Fame when the footman announced the Rev. Nathanael Skore. The latter entered hastily and hurriedly shook hands with the ladies.

"I must ask your indulgence for being so late," he said, "but I'm a very busy man. I have to be at a meeting at Countess Fabelkrantz's at half-past nine, and I have come straight from my work."

"Are you in a hurry then, dear pastor?"

"Yes, my wide activities give me no leisure. Hadn't we better begin business at once?"

The footman handed round refreshments.

"Won't you take a cup of tea, pastor, before we begin?" asked the hostess, smarting under the unpleasantness of a small disappointment.

The pastor glanced at the tray.

"Thank you, no; I'll take a glass of punch, if I may. I've made it a rule, ladies, never to differ from my fellow-creatures in externals. Everybody drinks punch; I don't like it, but I don't want the world to say that I'm better than anybody else; boasting is a failing which I detest. May I now begin with the proceedings?"

He sat down at the writing-table, dipped the pen into the ink and read:

"'Account of the Presents received by the Administrative Committee of the Crèche "Bethlehem" during the month of May: Signed Eugenia Falk.'"

"Née, if I may ask?"

"Oh, never mind about that," said Mrs. Falk.

"Evelyn Homan."

"Née, if I may make so bold?"

"Von Bähr, dear pastor."

"Antoinette Rehnhjelm."

"Née, madame?"

"Rehnhjelm, pastor."

"Ah! true! You married your cousin, husband dead, no children. But to continue: Presents...."

There was a general—almost general—consternation.

"But won't you sign, too, pastor?" asked Mrs. Homan.

"I dislike boasting, ladies, but if it's your wish! Here goes!"

"Nathanael Skore."

"Your health, pastor! Won't you drink a glass of punch before we begin?" asked the hostess with a charming smile, which died on her lips when she looked at the pastor's glass. It was empty; she quickly filled it.

"Thank you, Mrs. Falk, but we mustn't be immoderate! May I begin now? Please check me by the manuscript."

"'Presents: H.M. the Queen, forty crowns. Countess Fabelkrantz, five crowns and a pair of woollen stockings. Wholesale merchant Schalin, two crowns, a packet of envelopes, six steel nibs, and a bottle of ink. Miss Amanda Libert, a bottle of eau-de-Cologne. Miss Anna Feif, a pair of cuffs. Charlie, twopence halfpenny from his money box. Johanna Pettersson, half-dozen towels. Miss Emily Björn, a New Testament. Grocer Persson, a bag of oatmeal, a quart of potatoes, and a bottle of pickled onions. Draper Scheike, two pairs of woollen under....'"

"May I ask the meeting whether all this is to be printed?" interrupted her ladyship.

"Well, of course," answered the pastor.

"Then I must resign my post on the Administrative Committee."

"But do you imagine, Lady Rehnhjelm, that the society could exist on voluntary contributions if the names of the donors did not appear in print? Impossible!"

"Is charity to shed its radiance on petty vanity?"

"No, no! Don't say that! Vanity is an evil, certainly; we turn the evil into good by transforming it into charity. Isn't that praiseworthy?"

"Oh, yes! But we mustn't call petty things by high-sounding names. If we do, we are boastful!"

"You are very severe, Lady Rehnhjelm! Scripture exhorts us to pardon others; you should pardon their vanity."

"I'm ready to pardon it in others but not in myself. It's pardonable and good that ladies who have nothing else to do should find pleasure in charity; but it's disgraceful if they call it a good action seeing that it is only their pleasure and a greater pleasure than most others on account of the wide publicity given to it by printing."

"Oh!" began Mrs. Falk, with the full force of her terrible logic, "do you mean to say that doing good is disgraceful, Lady Rehnhjelm?"

"No, my dear; but in my opinion it is disgraceful to print the fact that one has given a pair of woollen stockings...."

"But to give a pair of woollen stockings is doing good; therefore it must be disgraceful to do good...."

"No, but to have it printed, my child! You aren't listening to what I'm saying," replied her ladyship, reproving her stubborn hostess who would not give in, but went on:

"I see! It's the printing which is disgraceful! But the Bible is printed, consequently it is disgraceful to print the Bible...."

"Please go on, pastor," interrupted her ladyship, a little annoyed by the tactless manner in which her hostess defended her inanities; but the latter did not yet count the battle as lost.

"Do you think it beneath your dignity, Lady Rehnhjelm, to exchange views with so unimportant a person as I am...?"

"No, my child; but keep your views to yourself; I don't want to exchange."

"Do you call this discussing a question, may I ask? Won't you enlighten us on the point, pastor? Can it be called discussing a question if one party refuses to reply to the argument of the other?"

"Of course it can't, my dear Mrs. Falk," replied the pastor, with an ambiguous smile, which nearly reduced Mrs. Falk to tears. "But don't let us spoil a splendid enterprise by quarrelling over trifles, ladies! We'll postpone the printing until the funds are larger. We have seen the young enterprise shooting up like a seed and we have seen that powerful hands are willing to tend the young plant; but we must think of the future. The Society has a fund; the fund must be administered; in other words, we must look round for an administrator, a practical man, able to transform these presents into hard cash; we must elect a treasurer. I'm afraid we shall not find one without a sacrifice of money—does one ever get anything without such a sacrifice? Have the ladies anybody in view?"

No, the ladies had not thought of it.

"Then may I propose a young man of steady character, who in my opinion is just the right person for the work? Has the Administrative Committee any objection to appointing secretary Ekelund to the post of treasurer at a suitable salary?"

The ladies had no objection to make, especially as the young man was recommended by the Rev. Nathanael Skore; and the Pastor felt the more qualified to recommend him because he was a near relative of his. And so the Crèche had a treasurer with a salary of six hundred crowns.

"Ladies," began the pastor again, "have we worked long enough in the vineyard for one day?"

There was silence. Mrs. Falk stared at the door wondering where her husband was.

"My time's short and I'm prevented from staying any longer. Has anybody any further suggestion to make? No! In calling down the blessing of the Lord on our enterprise, which has begun so auspiciously, I commend all of us to His loving mercy; I cannot do it in a better way than by repeating the words which He Himself has taught us when He prayed: 'Abba, Father—Our Father....'"

He was silent as if he were afraid of the sound of his own voice, and the Committee covered their faces with their hands as if they were ashamed of looking each other in the eyes. The ensuing pause grew long, unbearably long;

yet no one dared to break it; every one looked through the fingers hoping that someone else would make the first move, when a violent pull at the front door bell brought the party down to earth.

The pastor took his hat and emptied his glass; there was something about him of a man who is trying to steal away. Mrs. Falk beamed, for here was the crushing, the vengeance, the rehabilitation.

Revenge was there and the crushing too, for the footman handed her a letter from her husband which contained—the guests were not enlightened as to its contents, but they saw enough to make them declare at once that they had pressing engagements.

Lady Rehnhjelm would have liked to stay and comfort her young hostess, whose appearance betrayed a high degree of consternation and unhappiness. The latter, however, did not encourage her, but on the contrary was so exceedingly eager to help her visitors with their hats and cloaks that it looked as if she wanted to be rid of them as quickly as possible.

They parted in great embarrassment. The footsteps died away on the staircase and the departing guests could tell from the nervous haste with which the hostess shut the door behind them that she longed for solitude in order to be able to give vent to her feelings.

It was quite true. Left by herself in the large rooms Mrs. Falk burst into violent sobs; but her tears were not the tears which fall like a May shower on a wizened old heart; they were the tears of wrath and rage which darken the mirror of the soul and fall like an acid on the roses of health and youth and wither them.

CHAPTER XIV. ABSINTH

A hot afternoon sun was scorching the pavements of the provincial town X-köping.

The large vaults of the town hall were still deserted; fir branches were scattered all over the floor, and it smelt of a funeral. The graduated liqueur bottles stood on the shelves, having an afternoon nap, opposite the brandy bottles which wore the collars of their orders round their necks and were on leave until the evening; the clock, which could never take a nap, stood against the wall like a tall peasant, whiling away the time by contemplating, apparently, a huge playbill, impaled on a clothes peg close by. The vault was very long and narrow; both of the long walls were furnished with birchwood tables, jutting out from the wall, giving it the appearance of a stable, in which the four-legged tables represented the horses tied with their heads to the wall and turning their hind quarters towards the room; at the present moment all of them were asleep; one of them lifted its hind leg a little off the ground, for the floor was very uneven. One could see that they were fast asleep, for the flies were calmly walking up and down their backs.

The sixteen-year-old waiter who was leaning against the tall clock close to the poster was not asleep; he was incessantly waving his white apron at the flies which had just finished their dinner in the kitchen and were now playing about the vaults. Every now and then he leaned back and put his ear to the chest of the clock, as if he were sounding it, or wanting to find out what it had had for dinner. He was soon to be enlightened. The tall creature gave a sob, and exactly four minutes later it sobbed again; a groaning and rumbling in its inside made the lad jump; rattling terribly it struck six times, after which it continued its silent work.

The boy, too, began to work. He walked round his stable, grooming his horses with his apron and putting everything in order as if he were expecting visitors. On one of the tables, in the background, from which a spectator could view the whole long room, he placed matches, a bottle of absinth and two glasses, a liqueur glass and a tumbler; then he fetched a bottle of water from the pump and put it on the table by the side of the inflammables. When everything was ready, he paced up and down the room, occasionally striking quite unexpected attitudes, as if he were imitating somebody. Now he stood with arms folded across his chest, his head bowed, staring fiercely at the faded paper on the old walls; now he stood with legs crossed, the knuckles of his right hand touching the edge of the table holding in his left a lorgnette, made of a piece of wire from a beer bottle through which he sarcastically scanned the mouldings on the ceiling.

The door flew open, and a man of thirty-five entered with assurance, as if he were coming into his own house. His beardless face had the sharply cut features which are the result of much exercise of the facial muscles, characteristic of actors and one other class. Every muscle and ligament was plainly visible under the skin with its bluish shadows on upper lip and chin, but the miserable wirework which set these fine tangents in motion was invisible, for he was not like a common piano which requires a pedal. A high, rather narrow forehead with hollow temples, rose like a true Corinthian capital; black, untidy locks of hair climbed round it like wild creepers, from which small straight snakes darted, trying to reach the sockets of his eyes, but ever failing to do so. In calm moments his large, dark eyes looked gentle and sad, but there were times when they blazed and then the pupils looked like the muzzles of a revolver.

He took his seat at the table which the boy had prepared and looked sadly at the water bottle.

"Why do you always give me a bottle of water, Gustav?"

"So that you won't be burned to death, sir."

"What does it matter to you whether I am or not? Can't I burn if I like?"

"Don't be a nihilist to-day, sir."

"Nihilist? Who talked to you of nihilists? When did you hear that word? Are you mad, boy? Speak!"

He rose to his feet and fired a few shots from his dark revolvers.

Fear and consternation at the expression in the actor's face kept Gustav tongue tied.

"Answer, boy, when did you hear this word?"

"Mr. Montanus said it a few days ago, when he came here from his church," answered the boy timidly.

"Montanus, indeed!" said the melancholy man, sitting down again. "Montanus is my man: he has a large understanding. I say, Gustav, what's the name, I mean the nickname, by which these theatrical blackguards call me? Tell me! You needn't be afraid."

"I'd rather not, sir; it's very ugly."

"Why not if you can please me by doing so? Don't you think I could do with a little cheering up? Do I look so frightfully gay? Out with it! What do they say when they ask you whether I have been here? Don't they say: Has...."

"The devil...."

"Ah, the devil! They hate me, don't they?"

"Yes, they do!"

"Good! But why? Have I done them any harm?"

"No, they can't say that, sir."

"No, I don't think they can."

"But they say that you ruin people, sir."

"Ruin?"

"Yes, they say that you ruined me, sir, because I find that there's nothing new in the world."

"Hm! Hm! I suppose you tell them that their jokes are stale?"

"Yes; everything they say is stale; they are so stale themselves that they make me sick."

"Indeed! And don't you think that being a waiter is stale?"

"Yes, I do; life and death and everything is an old story—no—to be an actor would be something new."

"No, my friend. That is the stalest of all stale stories. But shut up, now! I want to forget myself."

He drank his absinth and rested his head against the wall with its long, brown streak, the track on which the smoke of his cigar had ascended during the six long years he had been sitting there, smoking. The rays of the sun fell through the window, passing through the sieve of the great aspens outside, whose light foliage, dancing in the evening breeze, threw a tremulous net on the long wall. The shadow of the melancholy man's head, with its untidy locks of hair, fell on the lowest corner of the net and looked very much like a huge spider.

Gustav had returned to the clock, where he sat plunged in nihilistic silence, watching the flies dancing round the hanging lamp.

"Gustav!" came a voice from the spider's web.

"Yes sir!" was the prompt response from the clock.

"Are your parents still alive?"

"No, sir, you know they aren't."

"Good for you."

A long pause.

"Gustav!"

"Yes sir!"

"Can you sleep at night?"

"What do you mean, sir?" answered Gustav blushing.

"What I say!"

"Of course I can! Why shouldn't I?"

"Why do you want to be an actor?"

"I don't know! I believe I should be happy!"

"Aren't you happy now?"

"I don't know! I don't think so!"

"Has Mr. Rehnhjelm been here again?"

"No, sir, but he said he would come here to meet you about this time."

A long pause; the door opened and a shadow fell into the spider's net; it trembled, and the spider in the corner made a quick movement.

"Mr. Rehnhjelm?" said the melancholy head.

"Mr. Falander?"

"Glad to meet you! You came here before?"

"Yes; I arrived this afternoon and called at once. You'll guess my purpose. I want to go on the stage."

"Do you really? You amaze me!"

"Amaze you?"

"Yes! But why do you come to me first?"

"Because I know that you are one of our finest actors and because a mutual friend, Mr. Montanus, the sculptor, told me that you were in every way to be trusted."

"Did he? Well, what can I do for you?"

"I want advice."

"Won't you sit down?"

"If I may act as host...."

"I couldn't think of such a thing."

"Then as my own guest, if you don't mind."

"As you like! You want advice?—Hm! Shall I give you my candid opinion? Yes, of course! Then listen to me, take what I'm going to say seriously, and never forget that I said such and such a thing on such and such an evening; I'll be responsible for my words."

"Give me your candid opinion! I'm prepared for anything."

"Have you ordered your horses? No? Then do so and go home."

"Do you think me incapable of becoming an actor?"

"By no means! I don't think anybody in all the world incapable of that. On the contrary! Everybody, has more or less talent for acting."

"Very well then!"

"Oh! the reality is so different from your dream! You're young, your blood flows quickly through your veins, a thousand pictures, bright and beautiful like the pictures in a fairy tale throng your brain; you want to bring them to the light, show them to the world and in doing so experience a great joy—isn't that so?"

"Yes, yes, you're expressing my very thoughts!"

"I only supposed quite a common case—I don't suspect bad motives behind everything, although I have a bad opinion of most things! Well, then, this desire of yours is so strong, that you would rather suffer want, humiliate yourself, allow yourself to be sucked dry by vampires, lose your social reputation, become bankrupt, go to the dogs—than turn back. Am I right?"

"Yes! How well you know me!"

"I once knew a young man—I know him no longer, he is so changed! He was fifteen years old when he left the penitentiary which every community keeps for the children who commit the outrageous crime of being born, and where the innocent little ones are made to atone for their parents' fall from grace—for what should otherwise become of society? Please remind me to keep to the subject! On leaving it he went for five years to Upsala and read a terrible number of books; his brain was divided into six pigeon-holes in which six kinds of information, dates, names, a whole warehouseful of ready-made opinions, conclusions, theories, ideas and nonsense of every description, were stored like a general cargo. This might have been allowed to pass, for there's plenty of room in a brain. But he was also supposed to accept foreign thoughts, rotten, old thoughts, which others had chewed for a life-time, and which they now vomited. It filled him with nausea and—he was twenty years old—he went on the stage. Look at my watch! Look at the second-hand; it makes sixty little steps before a minute has passed; sixty times sixty before it is an hour; twenty-four times the number and it is a day; three hundred and sixty-five times and it is only a year. Now imagine ten years! Did you ever wait for a friend outside his house? The first quarter of an hour passes like a flash! The second quarter—oh! one doesn't mind waiting for a person one's fond of; the third quarter: he's not coming; the fourth: hope and fear; the fifth: one goes away but hurries back; the sixth: Damn it all! I've wasted my time for nothing! the seventh: having waited so long, I might just as well wait a little longer; the eighth: raging and cursing; the ninth: One goes home, lies down on one's sofa and feels as calm as if one were walking arm in arm with death. He waited for ten years! Ten years! Isn't my hair standing on end when I say ten years? Look at it! Ten years had passed before he was allowed to play a part. When he did, he had a tremendous success—at once. But his ten wasted years had brought him to the verge of insanity; he was mad that it hadn't happened ten years before. And he was amazed to find that happiness when at last he held it within his grasp didn't make him happy! And so he was unhappy."

"But don't you think he required the ten years for the study of his art?"

"How could he study it when he was never allowed to play? He was a laughing-stock, the scum of the playbill; the management said he was no good; and whenever he tried to find an engagement at another theatre, he was told that he had no repertoire."

"But why couldn't he be happy when his luck had turned?"

"Do you think an immortal soul is content with happiness? But why speak about it? Your resolution is irrevocable. My advice is superfluous. There is but one teacher: experience, and experience is as capricious, or as calculating, as a schoolmaster; some of the pupils are always praised; others are always beaten. You are born to be praised; don't think I'm saying this because you belong to a good family; I'm sufficiently enlightened not to make that fact responsible for good or evil; in this case it is a particularly negligible quantity, for on the stage a man stands or falls by his own merit. I hope you'll have an early success so that you won't be enlightened too soon; I believe you deserve it."

"But have you no respect for your art, the greatest and most sublime of all arts?"

"It's overrated like everything about which men write books. It's full of danger and can do much harm! A beautifully told lie can impress like a truth! It's like a mass meeting where the uncultured majority turns the scale. The more superficial the better—the worse, the better! I don't mean to say that it is superfluous."

"That can't be your opinion!"

"That *is* my opinion, but all the same, I may be mistaken."

"But have you really no respect for your art?"

"For mine? Why should I have more respect for my art than for anybody else's?"

"And yet you've played the greatest parts! You've played Shakespeare! You've played Hamlet! Have you never been touched in your inmost soul when speaking that tremendous monologue: To be or not to be...."

"What do you mean by tremendous?"

"Full of profound thought."

"Do explain yourself! Is it so full of profound thought to say: Shall I take my life or not? I should do so if I knew what comes hereafter, and everybody else would do the same thing; but as we don't know, we don't take our lives. Is that so very profound?"

"Not if expressed in those words."

"There you are! You've surely contemplated suicide at one time or another? Haven't you?"

"Yes; I suppose most people have."

"And why didn't you do it? Because, like Hamlet, you hadn't the courage, not knowing what comes after. Were you very profound then?"

"Of course I wasn't!"

"Therefore it's nothing but a banality! Or, expressed in one word it is—what is it, Gustav?"

"Stale!" came a voice from the clock, a voice which seemed to have waited for its cue.

"It's stale! But, supposing the poet had given us an acceptable supposition of a future life, that would have been something new."

"Is everything new excellent?" asked Rehnhjelm. Under the pressure of all the new ideas to which he had been listening, his courage was fast ebbing away.

"New ideas have one great merit—they are new! Try to think your own thoughts and you will always find them new! Will you believe me when I say that I knew what you wanted before you walked in at that door? And that I know what you are going to say next, seeing that we are discussing Shakespeare?"

"You are a strange man! I can't help confessing that you're right in what you're saying, although I don't agree with you."

"What do you say to Anthony's speech over the body of Cæsar? Isn't it remarkable?"

"That's exactly what I was going to speak about. You seem to be able to read my thoughts."

"Exactly what I was telling you just now. And is it so wonderful considering that all men think the same, or at any rate say the same thing? Well, what do you find in it of any great depth?"

"I can't explain in words...."

"Don't you think it a very commonplace piece of sarcastic oratory? One expresses exactly the reverse of one's meaning, and if the points are sharpened, they are bound to sting. But have you ever come across anything more beautiful than the dialogue between Juliet and Romeo after their wedding night?"

"Ah! You mean where he says, 'It is the nightingale and not the lark'...."

"What other passage could I mean? Doesn't every one quote that? It is a wonderful poetical conception on which the effect depends. Do you think Shakespeare's greatness depends on poetical conceptions?"

"Why do you break up everything I admire? Why do you take away my supports?"

"I am throwing away your crutches so that you may learn to walk without them. But let me ask you to keep to the point."

"You are not asking, you are compelling me to do so."

"Then you should steer clear of me. Your parents are against your taking this step?"

"Yes! How do you know?"

"Parents always are. Why overrate my judgment? You should never exaggerate anything."

"Do you think we should be happier if we didn't?"

"Happier? Hm! Do you know anybody who is happy? Give me your own opinion, not the conventional one."

"No!"

"If you don't believe anybody is happy, how can you postulate such a condition as being happier? Your parents are alive then? It's a mistake to have parents."

"Why? What do you mean?"

"Don't you think it unfair of an older generation to bring up a younger one in its antiquated inanities? Your parents expect gratitude from you, I suppose?"

"And doesn't one owe it to one's parents?"

"For what? For the fact that with the connivance of the law they have brought us into this world of misery, have half-starved us, beaten us, oppressed us, humiliated us, opposed all our wishes? Believe me, a revolution is needed—two revolutions! Why don't you take some absinth? Are you afraid of it? Look at the bottle! It's marked with the Geneva cross! It heals those who have been wounded on the battlefield, friends and foes alike; it lulls all pain, blunts the keen edge of thought, blots out memories, stifles all the nobler emotions which beguile humanity into folly, and finally extinguishes the light of reason. Do you know what the light of reason is? First, it is a phrase, secondly, it is a will-o'-the-wisp; one of those flames, you know, which play about spots where decaying fish have engendered phosphoretted hydrogen; the light of reason is phosphoretted hydrogen engendered by the grey brain substance. It is a strange thing. Everything good on this earth perishes and is forgotten. During my ten years' touring, and my apparent idleness, I have read through all the libraries one finds in small towns, and I find that all the twaddle and nonsense contained in the books is popular and constantly quoted; but the wisdom is neglected and pushed aside. Do remind me to keep to the point...."

The clock went through its diabolical tricks and thundered seven. The door was flung open and a man lurched noisily into the room. He was a man of about fifty, with a huge, heavy head, fixed between a pair of lumpy shoulders like a mortar on a gun carriage, with a permanent elevation of forty-five degrees, looking as if it were going to throw bombs at the stars. To judge from the face, the owner was capable of all possible crimes and impossible vices, but too great a coward to commit any. He immediately threw a bombshell at the melancholy man, and harshly ordered a glass of grog made of rum, in grammatical, uncouth language and in the voice of a corporal.

"This is the man who holds your fate in his hands," whispered the melancholy man to Rehnhjelm. "This is the tragedian, actor-manager, and my deadly foe."

Rehnhjelm could not suppress a shudder of disgust as he looked at the terrible individual who, after having exchanged a look of hatred with Falander, now closed the passage of arms by repeated expectorations.

The door opened again, and in glided the almost elegant figure of a middle-aged man with oily hair and a waxed moustache. He familiarly took his place by the side of the actor-manager, who gave him his middle finger on which shone a ring with a large cornelian.

"This is the editor of the Conservative paper, the defender of throne and altar. He has the run of the theatre and tries to seduce all the girls on whom the actor-manager hasn't cast his eye. He started his career as a Government official, but had to resign his post, I'm ashamed to tell you why," explained Falander. "But I am also ashamed to remain in the same room with these gentlemen, and, moreover, I have asked a few friends here, to-night, to a little supper in celebration of my recent benefit. If you care to spend the evening in bad company, among the most unimportant actors, two notorious ladies and an old blackguard, you are welcome at eight."

Rehnhjelm hesitated a moment before he accepted the invitation.

The spider on the wall climbed through his net as if to examine it and disappeared. The fly remained in its place a little longer. The sun sank behind the cathedral, the meshes of the net were undone as if they had never existed, and the aspens outside the window shivered. The great man and stage-director raised his voice and shouted—he had forgotten how to speak:

"Did you see the attack on me in the *Weekly*?"

"Don't take any notice of such piffle."

"Take no notice of it? What the devil do you mean? Doesn't everybody read it? Of course the whole town does! I should like to give him a horse-whipping! The impertinent rascal calls me affected and exaggerated."

"Bribe him! Don't make a fuss!"

"Bribe him? Haven't I tried it? But these Liberal journalists are damned queer. If you are on friendly terms with them, they'll give you a nice enough notice; but they won't be bribed however poor they may be."

"Oh! You don't go about it in the right way! You shouldn't do it openly, you could send them presents which they can turn into cash, or cash, if you like, but anonymously, and never refer to it."

"As I do in your case! No, old chap, the trick doesn't work in their case. I've tried it! It's hell to reckon with people with opinions."

"Who do you think was the victim in the devil's clutches, to change the subject?"

"That's nothing to do with me."

"Oh, but I think it has! Gustav! Who was the gentleman with Mr. Falander?"

"His name's Rehnhjelm! He wants to go on the stage."

"What do you say? He wants to go on the stage? He!" shouted the actor-manager.

"Yes, that's it!" replied Gustav.

"And, of course, act tragedy parts? And be Falander's protégé? And not come to me? And take away my parts? And honour us by playing here? And I know nothing about the whole matter? I? I? I'm sorry for him! It's a pity! Bad prospects for him. Of course, I shall patronize him! I'll take him under my wing! The strength of my wings may be felt even when I don't fly! They have a way of pinching now and then! He was a nice looking lad! A smart lad! Beautiful as Antinous! What a pity he didn't come to me first, I should have given him Falander's parts, every one of them! Oh! Oh! Oh! But it isn't too late yet! Hah! Let the devil corrupt him first! He's still a little too fresh! He really looked quite an innocent boy! Poor little chap! I'll only say 'God help him!'"

The sound of the last sentence was drowned in the noise made by the grog drinkers of the whole town who were now beginning to arrive.

CHAPTER XV. THE THEATRICAL COMPANY "PHŒNIX"

On the following day Rehnhjelm awoke late in the morning in his hotel bed. Memories of the previous night arose like phantoms and crowded round him.

He saw again the pretty, closely shuttered room, richly decorated with flowers, in which the orgy had been held. He saw the actress, a lady of thirty-five who, thanks to a younger rival, had to play the parts of old women; he saw her entering the room, in a frenzy of rage and despair at the fresh humiliations heaped upon her, throwing herself full length on the sofa, drinking glass after glass of wine and, when the temperature of the room rose, opening her bodice, as a man opens his waistcoat after a too-plentiful dinner.

He saw again the old comedian who, after a very short career, had been degraded from playing lead to taking servant's parts; he now entertained the tradespeople of the town with his songs, and, above all, with the stories of his short glory.

But, in the very heart of the clouds of smoke and his drunken visions Rehnhjelm saw the picture of a young girl of sixteen, who had arrived with tears in her eyes, and told the melancholy Falander that the great actor-manager had again been persecuting her with insulting proposals, vowing that in future, unless she would accede to them, she should play only the very smallest parts.

And he saw Falander, listening to everybody's troubles and complaints, breathing on them until they vanished; he watched him, reducing insults, humiliations, kicks, accidents, want, misery, and grief to nothing; watched him teaching his friends and warning them never to exaggerate anything, least of all their troubles.

But again and again his thoughts reverted to the little girl of sixteen with the innocent face, with whom he had made friends, and who had kissed him when they parted, hungrily, passionately. To be quite candid, her kiss had taken him by surprise. But what *was* her name?

He rose, and stretching out his hand for the water-bottle, he seized a tiny handkerchief, spotted with wine. Ah! Here was her name, ineffaceable, written in marking ink—Agnes! He kissed the handkerchief twice on the cleanest spot and put it into his box.

When he had carefully dressed himself, he went out to see the actor-manager, whom he confidently expected to find at the theatre between twelve and three.

To be on the safe side, he arrived at the office at twelve o'clock; he found no one there but a porter, who asked him what he wanted and put himself at his service.

Rehnhjelm did not think that he would need his help, and asked to see the actor-manager; he was told that the actor-manager was at the present moment at the factory, but would no doubt come to the office in the course of the afternoon.

Rehnhjelm supposed factory to be a slang expression for theatre, but the porter explained to him that the actor-manager was also a match manufacturer. His brother-in-law, the cashier, was a post office employé and never came to the theatre before two o'clock; his son, the secretary, had a post in the telegraph office, and his presence could never be safely relied upon. But the porter, who seemed to guess the object of Rehnhjelm's visit, handed him, on his own responsibility and in the name of the theatre, a copy of the statutes; the young gentleman was at liberty to amuse himself with it until one of the managerial staff arrived.

Rehnhjelm possessed his soul in patience and sat down on the sofa to study the documents. It was half-past twelve when he had finished reading them. He talked to the porter until a quarter to one, and then set himself to fathom the meaning of paragraph 1 of the statutes. "The theatre is a moral institution," it ran, "therefore the members of the company should endeavour to live in the fear of God, and to lead a virtuous and moral life." He turned and twisted the sentence about, trying to throw light upon it, without succeeding. "If the theatre is a moral institution," he mused, "the members who—in addition to the manager, the cashier, the secretary, the machinists, and scene-shifters—form the institution, need not endeavour to practise all these beautiful things. If it said: The theatre is an immoral institution and therefore ... there would be some sense in it; but that, surely, the management does not intend to convey."

He thought of Hamlet's "words, words," but immediately remembered that to quote Hamlet was stale, and that one ought to clothe one's thoughts in one's own words; he chose his own term, and called the regulations nonsense, but discarded the expression again, because it was not original; but then the original was not original either.

Paragraph 2 helped him to while away a quarter of an hour in meditation on the text: "The theatre is not a place for amusement; it does not merely exist to give pleasure." In one place it said the theatre is not a place for amusement and in another the theatre does not "merely" exist to give pleasure, therefore it did exist to give pleasure—to a certain extent.

He reflected under what circumstances the theatre ministered to one's pleasure. It was amusing to see children, especially sons, defrauding their parents, more particularly when the parents were thrifty, goodhearted, and sensible; it was amusing to see wives deceiving their husbands; especially when the husband was old and required his wife's care. Besides this he remembered having laughed very heartily at two old men who nearly died of starvation because their business was on the decline, and that to this day all the world laughed at it in a piece written by a classical author. He also recollected having been much amused by the misfortune of an elderly man who had become deaf; and that, together with six hundred other men and women, he had shouted with laughter at a priest, who tried, by natural means, to cure his insanity, the result of self-restraint; his mirth had been particularly stimulated by the hypocrisy displayed by the wily priest in order to gain the object of his desire.

Why does one laugh? he wondered. And as he had nothing else to do, he tried to find an answer. One laughed at misfortune, want, misery, vice, virtue, the defeat of good, the victory of evil.

This conclusion, which was partly new to him, put him into a good temper; he found a great deal of amusement in playing with his thoughts. As the management still remained invisible, he went on playing, and, before the lapse of five minutes, he had come to the following conclusion: In a tragedy one weeps at just those things which in comedy make one laugh.

At this point his thoughts were arrested; the great actor-manager burst into the room, brushed past Rehnhjelm without apparently being aware of his presence and entered a room on the left, whither, a moment afterwards, the violent ringing of a bell summoned the porter. In less than half a minute he had gone in and come out again, announcing that his Highness was ready to receive the visitor.

As Rehnhjelm entered the director had already fired his shot and his mortar was fixed at an angle which quite prevented him from perceiving the nervous mortal who was timidly coming into the room. But he had no doubt heard him, for he asked him immediately, in an offensive manner, what he wanted.

Rehnhjelm stammered that he was anxious to make his début on the stage.

"What? A début? Have you a repertory, sir? Have you played 'Hamlet,' 'Lear,' 'Richard Sheridan'; been called ten times before the curtain after the third act? What?"

"I've never played a part."

"Oh, I see! That's quite another thing!"

He sat down in an easy-chair painted with silver paint and covered with blue brocade. His face had become a mask. He might have been sitting for a portrait for one of the biographies of Suetonius.

"Shall I give you my candid opinion, what? Leave the theatrical profession alone!"

"Impossible!"

"I repeat, leave it alone! It's the worst of all professions! Full of humiliations, unpleasantnesses, little annoyances, and thorns which will embitter your life so that you'll wish you had never been born."

He looked as if he were speaking the truth, but Rehnhjelm's resolution was not to be shaken.

"I beg you to take my advice! I solemnly adjure you to drop this idea. I tell you that the prospects are so bad, that for years to come you'll have simply to walk on. Think of it! And don't come to me with complaints when it is too late. The theatrical career is so infernally difficult, sir, that you would not dream of taking it up, if you had the least knowledge of it! It's a hell! believe me. I have spoken."

It was a waste of breath.

"Well, wouldn't you prefer an engagement without a début? The risk is less great."

"I shall be only too pleased; I never expected more."

"Then you'd better sign this agreement. A salary of twelve hundred crowns and a two years' engagement. Do you agree?"

He pulled a filled-up agreement, signed by the management, from underneath the blotting-pad, and gave it to Rehnhjelm. The latter's brain was whirling at the thought of the twelve hundred crowns and he signed it without a look at the contents.

When he had signed the actor-manager held out his large middle finger with the cornelian ring, and said: "Be welcome!" He flashed at him with the gums of his upper jaw and the yellow and bloodshot whites of his eyes with their green irises.

The audience was over. But Rehnhjelm—in whose opinion the whole business had been hurried through far too quickly—instead of moving, took the liberty of asking whether he had not better wait until all the members of the management were assembled.

"The management?" shouted the great tragedian. "I am the management. If you have any questions to ask, address yourself to me! If you want advice, come to me! To me, sir! To nobody else! That's all! You can go now!"

The skirt of Rehnhjelm's coat must have caught on a nail, for he turned on the threshold to see what the last words looked like; but he saw only the red gums, which had the appearance of an instrument of torture, and the bloodshot eyes; he felt no desire to ask for an explanation, but went straight to the vaults of the town hall to have some dinner and meet Falander.

Falander was sitting at one of the tables, calm and indifferent, as if he were prepared for the worst. He was not surprised to hear that Rehnhjelm had been engaged, although this news considerably increased his gloom.

"And what did you think of the manager?" he asked.

"I wanted to box his ears, but I hadn't the courage."

"Nor has the management, and therefore he rules autocratically—brutality always rules! Perhaps you know that he is a playwright as well as all the rest?"

"I've heard about it."

"He writes a sort of historical play which is always successful. The reason is that he writes parts instead of creating characters; he manipulates the applause at the exits and trades on so-called patriotism. His characters never talk, they quarrel; men and women, old and young, all of them; for this reason his popular piece, *The Sons of King Gustavus*, is rightly called a historical quarrel in five acts; it contains no action, nothing but quarrels: family rows, street brawls, scenes in Parliament, and so on. Questions are answered by sly cuts, which do not provoke scenes, but the most terrible scuffles. There is no dialogue, nothing but squabbling, in which the characters insult each other, and the highest dramatic effect is attained by blows. The critics call his characterisation great. What has he made of Gustavus Vasa in the play I just mentioned? A broad-shouldered, long-bearded, bragging, untenable fellow of enormous strength; at the meeting of Parliament at Västeros, he breaks a table with his fist, and at Vadstena he kicks a door panel to pieces. On one occasion however the critics said there was no meaning in his plays; it made him angry, and he resolved to write comedies with plenty of meaning. He had a boy at school—the blackguard's married—who had been playing pranks and got a thrashing. Immediately his father wrote a comedy in which he drew the masters and exposed the inhuman treatment boys receive at school in these days. On another occasion he was criticized by an honest reviewer, and immediately he wrote a comedy, libelling the liberal journalists of the town. But I'll say no more about him!"

"Why does he hate you?"

"Because I said, at a rehearsal, Don Pasquale, in spite of his maintaining that the proper pronunciation was Pascal. Result: I was ordered, on penalty of a fine, to pronounce the word in *his*way. It was immaterial to him, he said, how the rest of the world pronounced the word, at X-köping it was to be pronounced Pascal, because it was his wish."

"Where does he come from? What was he before?"

"Can't you guess that he was a wheelwright? He'd poison you if he thought you knew it. But let us change the subject; how do you feel after last night's revels?"

"Splendid! I quite forgot to thank you!"

"Don't mention it! Are you fond of the girl? I mean Agnes?"

"Yes, I'm very fond of her."

"And she loves you? That's all right, then! Take her!"

"What nonsense you talk! We couldn't be married for a long time!"

"Who told you to be married?"

"What are you driving at?"

"You're eighteen, she's sixteen! You're in love with each other! If you're agreed, only the most private detail is wanting."

"I don't understand what you mean! Are you trying to encourage me to behave like a scoundrel towards her?"

"I am trying to encourage you to obey the great voice of nature and snap your fingers at the petty commands of men. It's only envy if men condemn your conduct; their much-talked-of morality is nothing but malice, in a suitable, presentable guise. Hasn't nature called you for some time to her great banquet, the delight of the gods and the horror of society afraid of having to pay alimony?"

"Why don't you advise me to marry her?"

"Because that's quite another thing! One doesn't bind oneself for life after having spent one evening together; it doesn't follow that he who has enjoyed the rapture, must also undergo the pain. Matrimony is an affair of souls; there can be no question of this in your case. However, there's no need for me to spur you on; the inevitable is bound to happen. Love each other while you're young, before it's too late; love each other as birds love, without worrying about how to furnish a home; love as the flowers of the species Diœcia."

"You've no right to talk disrespectfully of the girl. She is good, innocent, and to be pitied, and whoever denies it is a liar. Have you ever seen more innocent eyes than hers? Doesn't truth proclaim itself in the sound of her voice? She is worthy of a great and pure love, not merely of the passion you speak of. Don't ever talk to me about her in this way again. You can tell her that I shall look upon it as the greatest happiness, the highest honour, to ask her to marry me when I'm worthy of her."

Falander shook his head so violently that the snakes on his forehead wriggled.

"Worthy of her? Marriage? What stuff!"

"I mean it!"

"Dreadful! And if I should tell you that the girl does not only lack all the qualities which you ascribe to her, but possesses all the reverse ones, you wouldn't believe me, but would deprive me of your friendship?"

"Yes!"

"The world is so full of lies, that nobody will believe a man when he speaks the truth."

"How can a man believe you, who have no morals?"

"That word again! What an extraordinary word it is! It answers all questions, cuts off all discussions, excuses all failings—one's own, not those of others—strikes down all adversaries, pleads for or against a cause, just like a lawyer. For the moment you have defeated me with it, next time I shall defeat you. I must be off, I have a lesson at three! Good-bye, good luck!"

And he left Rehnhjelm to his dinner and his reflections.

When Falander arrived home, he put on a dressing-gown and slippers, as if he were expecting no visitors. But he seemed full of an uncontrollable restlessness. He walked up and down the room, stopping every now and then at the window and gazing at the street from behind the curtain. After a while he stopped before the looking-glass, took his collar off and laid it on the sofa table. For a few more minutes he continued his promenade, but suddenly, coming to a standstill before a card-tray, he took up the photograph of a lady, placed it under a strong magnifying glass and examined it as if it were a microscopic slide. He lingered a long time over his examination.

Presently he heard the sound of footsteps on the stairs; quickly concealing the photograph in the place from where he had taken it, he jumped up and went and sat at his writing-table, turning his back to the door. He was apparently absorbed in writing when a knocking—two short, gentle raps—broke the silence.

"Come in," he called, in a voice which was anything but inviting.

A young girl, small but well-proportioned, entered the room. She had a delicate, oval face, surrounded by an aureole of hair which might have been bleached by the sun, for it was of a less pronounced tint than the usual natural blond. The constant play of the small nose and exquisitely cut mouth produced roguish curves which were incessantly changing, like the figures in a kaleidoscope; when, for instance, she moved the wings of her nose, so that the bright red cartilage showed like the leaf of the liverwort, her lips fell apart and disclosed the edges of very small, straight teeth which, although her own, were too white and even to inspire confidence. Her eyes were drawn up at the root of the nose and slanted towards the temples; this gave them a pleading, pathetic expression, which stood in bewitching contrast to the lower, roguish parts of her face; she had restless pupils, small like the point of a needle at one moment, and distended at the next, like the objective of a night-telescope.

On entering the room, she removed the key from the lock and shot the bolt.

Falander remained sitting at his table, writing.

"You are late to-day, Agnes," he said.

"Yes, I know," she replied, defiantly, taking off her hat.

"We were up late last night."

"Why don't you get up and say how do you do to me? You can't be as tired as all that!"

"I beg your pardon, I forgot all about it!"

"You forgot? I have noticed for some time that you've been forgetting yourself in many ways."

"Indeed? Since when have you noticed it?"

"Since when? What do you mean? Please change your dressing-gown and slippers."

"This is the first time you have found me in them, and you said for some time. Isn't that funny? Don't you think it is?"

"You are laughing at me! What's the matter with you? You've been strange for some time."

"For some time? There you are at it again! Why do you say for some time? Is it because lies have got to be told? Why should it be necessary to tell lies?"

"Are you accusing me of telling lies?"

"Oh! no, I'm only teasing you!"

"Do you think I can't see that you are tired of me? Do you think I didn't see last night how attentive you were to that stupid Jenny? You hadn't a word for me!"

"Do you mean to say you're jealous?"

"Jealous! No, my dear, not in the least! If you prefer her to me, well and good! I don't care a toss!"

"Really? You're not jealous? Under ordinary circumstances this would be an unpleasant fact."

"Under ordinary circumstances? What do you mean by that?"

"I mean—quite plainly—that I'm tired of you, as you just suggested."

"It's a lie! You're not!"

The wings of her nose trembled, she showed her teeth and stabbed him with the needles.

"Let's talk of something else," he said. "What do you think of Rehnhjelm?"

"I like him very much! He's a dear boy!"

"He's fallen in love with you!"

"Nonsense!"

"And the worst of it is he wants to marry you!"

"Please spare me these inanities!"

"But as he's not twenty, he's going to wait until he's worthy of you, so he said."

"The little idiot!"

"By worthy he means when he's made a name as an actor. And he can't succeed in that until he's allowed to play parts. Can't you manage it for him?"

Agnes blushed, threw herself back on the sofa cushions and exhibited a pair of elegant little boots with gold tassels.

"I? I can't manage it for myself! You're making fun of me!"

"Yes, I am!"

"You're a friend, Gustav, you really are!"

"Perhaps I am, perhaps I'm not. It's difficult to say. But as a sensible girl...."

"Oh! shut up!"

She took up a keen-edged paper knife and threatened him in fun, but it looked very much as if she were in earnest.

"You are very beautiful to-day, Agnes," said Falander.

"To-day? Why to-day? Has it never struck you before?"

"Of course it has!"

"Why are you sighing?"

"Too much drink last night!"

"Let me look at you! What's the matter with your eyes?"

"No sleep last night, my dear!"

"I'll go, then you can take a nap."

"Don't go! I can't sleep anyhow!"

"I must be off! I really only came to tell you that."

Her voice softened; her eyelids dropped slowly, like the curtain after a death scene.

"It was kind of you to come and tell me that it's all over," said Falander.

She rose and pinned on her hat before the glass.

"Have you any scent?" she asked.

"Not here; at the theatre."

"You should stop smoking a pipe; the smell hangs about one's clothes."

"I will."

She stooped and fastened her garter.

"I beg your pardon," she said, looking at Falander, pleadingly.

"What for?" he asked, absent-mindedly.

As she made no reply, he took courage and drew a deep breath.

"Where are you going?" he said.

"To be fitted for a dress; you needn't be afraid," she replied, innocently, as she thought.

Falander could easily tell that it was an excuse.

"Good-bye, then," he said.

She went to him to be kissed. He took her in his arms and pressed her against him as if he wanted to crush her; then he kissed her on the forehead, led her to the door, pushed her outside, and said briefly: "Good-bye!"

CHAPTER XVI. IN THE WHITE MOUNTAINS

One afternoon in August, Falk was again sitting in the garden on Moses Height; but he was alone, and he had been alone during the whole summer. He was turning over in his mind all that had happened to him during the three months which had passed since his last visit, when his heart was brimful of hope, courage, and strength. He felt old, tired, indifferent; he had seen the houses at his feet from the inside, and on every occasion his expectations had been disappointed. He had seen humanity under many aspects, aspects which are only revealed to the eye of the poor man's doctor or the journalist, with the only difference that the journalist generally sees men as they wish to appear, and the doctor as they are. He had every opportunity of studying man as a social animal in all possible guises; he had been present at Parliamentary meetings, church councils, general meetings of shareholders, philanthropic meetings, police court proceedings, festivals, funerals, public meetings of working men; everywhere he had heard big words and many words, words never used in daily intercourse, a particular species of words which mean nothing, at least not what they ought to mean. This had given him a one-sided conception of humanity; he could see in man nothing but the deceitful social animal, a creature he is bound to be because civilization forbids open war. His aloofness blinded him to the existence of another animal, an animal which "between glass and wall" is exceedingly amiable, as long as it is not exasperated, and which is ready to come out with all its failings and weaknesses when there are no witnesses. He was blind to it and that was the reason why he had become embittered.

But the worst of it all was he had lost his self-respect. And that had happened without his having committed a single action of which he need have been ashamed. He had been robbed of it by his fellow-creatures, and it had not been a very difficult thing to do. He had been slighted everywhere, and how could he, whose self-confidence had been destroyed in his early youth, respect a person whom everybody despised? With many a bitter pang he saw that all Conservative journalists, that was to say men who defended and upheld everything that was wrong—or if they could not defend it, at least left it untouched—were treated with the utmost courtesy. He was despised, not so much as a pressman as in his character of advocate of all those who were down-trodden and hardly dealt with.

He had lived through times of cruel doubt. For instance: in reporting the General Meeting of Shareholders of the Marine Insurance Society "Triton," he had used the word swindle. In replying to his report, the *Grey Bonnet* had published a long article proving so clearly that the society was a national, patriotic, philanthropic institution that he had almost felt convinced of having been wrong, and the thought of having recklessly played with the reputation of his fellow citizens was a nightmare to him for many days to come.

He was now in a state of mind which alternated between fanaticism and callousness; his next impulse would decide the direction his development was to take.

His life had been so dreary during the summer that he welcomed with malicious pleasure every rainy day, and it was a comparatively pleasant sensation to watch leaves rustling along the garden paths.

He sat absorbed in grimly humorous meditations on life and its purposes, when one lean, bony hand was laid on his shoulder, and another clutched his arm; he felt as if death had come to take him at his word. He looked up and started: before him stood Ygberg, pale as a corpse, emaciated and looking at him with those peculiarly washed out eyes which only starvation produces.

"Good morning, Falk," he whispered, almost inaudibly, and his whole body seemed to rattle.

"Good morning, Ygberg," replied Falk, suddenly brightening up. "Sit down and have a cup of coffee! How are you? You look as if you had been lying under the ice."

"Oh! I've been so ill, so ill!"

"You seem to have had as jolly a summer as I had!"

"Have you had a hard time, too?" asked Ygberg, a faint hope that it had been the case brightening his yellow face.

"I can only say: Thank God that the cursed summer is over! It might be winter all the year round for all I care! Not only that one is suffering all the time, but one also has to watch others enjoying themselves! I never put a foot out of town; did you?"

"I haven't seen a pine tree since Lundell left Lill-Jans in June! And why should one want to see pine trees? It isn't absolutely essential; nor is a pine tree anything extraordinary! But that one can't have the pleasure, that's where the sting comes in."

"Oh, well! Never mind! It's clouding over in the east, therefore it will rain to-morrow; and when the sun shines again, it will be autumn. Your health!"

Ygberg looked at the punch as if it were poison, but he drank it nevertheless.

"But you wrote that beautiful story of the guardian angel, or the Marine Insurance Society 'Triton,' for Smith," remarked Falk. "Didn't it go against your convictions?"

"Convictions? I have no convictions."

"Haven't you?"

"No, only fools have convictions."

"Have you no morals, Ygberg?"

"No! Whenever a fool has an idea—it comes to the same thing whether it is original or not—he calls it his conviction, clings to it and boasts of it, not because it is *a* conviction, but because it is *his* conviction. So far as the Marine Insurance Society is concerned, I believe it's a swindle! I'm sure it injures many men, the shareholders at all events, but it's a splendid thing for others, the directors and employés, for instance; so it does a fair amount of good, after all."

"Have you lost all sense of honour, old friend?"

"One must sacrifice everything on the altar of duty."

"I admit that."

"The first and foremost duty of man is to live—to live at any price! Divine as well as human law demands it."

"One must never sacrifice honour."

"Both laws, as I said, demand the sacrifice of everything—they compel a poor man to sacrifice his so-called honour. It's cruel, but you can't blame the poor man for it."

"Your theory of life is anything but cheerful."

"How could it be otherwise?"

"That's true!"

"But to talk of something else: I've had a letter from Rehnhjelm. I'll read it to you, if you like."

"I heard he had gone on the stage."

"Yes, and he doesn't seem to be having a good time of it."

Ygberg took a letter from his breast-pocket, put a piece of sugar into his mouth and began to read.

"If there is a hell in a life after this, which is very doubtful...."

"The lad's become a free-thinker!"

"It cannot be a worse place than this. I've been engaged for two months, but it seems to me like two years. A devil, formerly a wheelwright, now theatrical manager, holds my fate in his hand, and treats me in such a way that three times a day I feel tempted to run away. But he has so carefully drafted the penal clauses in the agreement, that my flight would dishonour my parents' name.

"I have *walked on* every single night, but I've never been allowed to open my lips yet. For twenty consecutive evenings I have had to smear my face with umber and wear a gipsy's costume, not a single piece of which fits me; the tights are too long, the shoes too large, the jacket is too short. An under-devil, called the prompter, takes good care that I don't exchange my costume for one more suitable; and whenever I try to hide myself behind the crowd, which is made up of the director-manufacturer's factory hands, it opens and pushes me forward to the footlights. If I look into the wings, my eyes fall on the under-devil, standing there, grinning, and if I look at the house, I see Satan himself sitting in a box, laughing.

"I seem to have been engaged for his amusement, not for the purpose of playing any parts. On one occasion I ventured to draw his attention to the fact that I ought to have practice in speaking parts if I was ever going to be an actor. He lost his temper and said that one must learn to crawl before one can learn to walk. I replied that I could walk. He said it was a lie and asked me whether I imagined that the art of acting, the most beautiful and difficult of all arts, required no training. When I said that that was exactly what I did imagine, and that I was impatiently waiting for the beginning of my training, he told me I was an ignorant puppy, and he would kick me out. When I remonstrated, he asked me whether I looked upon the stage as a refuge for impecunious youths. My reply was a frank, unconditional glad Yes. He roared that he would kill me.

"This is the present state of my affairs.

"I feel that my soul is flickering out like a tallow candle in a draught, and I shall soon believe that 'Evil will be victorious, even though it be concealed in clouds,' as the Catechism has it.

"But the worst of all is that I have lost all respect for this art, which was the dream and the love of my boyhood. Can I help it when I see that men and women without education or culture, spurred on by vanity and recklessness, completely lacking in enthusiasm and intelligence are able to play in a few months' time character parts, historical parts, fairly well, without having a glimmer of knowledge of the time in which they move, or the important part which the person they represent played in history?

"It is slow murder, and the association with this mob which keeps me down—some of the members of the company have come into collision with various paragraphs of the penal code—is making of me what I've never been, an aristocrat. The pressure of the cultured can never weigh as heavily on the uncultured.

"There is but one ray of light in this darkness: I am in love. She is purest gold among all this dross. Of course she, too, is persecuted and slowly murdered, just as I am, since she refused the stage-manager's infamous proposals. She is the only woman with a living spirit among all these beasts, wallowing in filth, and she loves me with all her soul. We are secretly engaged. I am only waiting for the day when I shall have won success, to make her my wife. But when will that be? We have often thought of dying together, but hope, treacherous hope, has always beguiled us into continuing this misery. To see my innocent love burning with shame when she is forced to wear improper costumes, is more than I can bear. But I will drop this unpleasant subject.

"Olle and Lundell wish to be remembered. Olle is very much changed. He has drifted into a new kind of philosophy, which tears down everything and turns all things upside down. It sounds very jolly and sometimes seems true, but it must be a dangerous doctrine if carried out.

"I believe he owes these ideas to one of the actors here, an intelligent and well-informed man, who lives a very immoral life; I like and hate him at the same time. He is a queer chap, fundamentally good, noble and generous; a man who will sacrifice himself for his friends. I cannot fix on any special vice, but he is immoral, and a man without morality is a blackguard—don't you think so?

"I must stop, my angel, my good spirit is coming. There is a happy hour in store for me; all evil spirits will flee, and I shall be a better man.

"Remember me to Falk and tell him to think of me when life is hard on him.
"Your friend R."

"Well, what do you think of that?"

"It's the old story of the struggle of the wild beasts. I'll tell you what, Ygberg, I believe one has to be very unscrupulous if one wants to get on in the world."

"Try it! You may not find it so easy!"

"Are you still doing business with Smith?"

"No, unfortunately not! And you?"

"I've seen him on the subject of my poems. He has bought them, ten crowns the folio, and he can now murder me in the same way as the wheelwright is murdering Rehnhjelm. And I'm afraid something of the sort is going to happen, for I haven't heard a word about them. He was so exceedingly friendly that I expect the worst. If only I knew what's going on! But what's the matter with you? You're as white as a sheet."

"The truth is," replied Ygberg, clutching the railings, "all I've had to eat these last two days has been five lumps of sugar. I'm afraid I'm going to faint."

"If food will set you right, I can help you; fortunately I have some money."

"Of course it will set me right," whispered Ygberg faintly.

But it was not so. When they were sitting in the dining-room and food was served to them, Ygberg grew worse, and Falk had to take him to his room, which fortunately was not very far off.

The house was an old, one-story house built of wood; it had climbed on to a rock and looked as if it suffered from hip-disease. It was spotted like a leper; a long time ago it was going to be painted, but when the old paint had been burned off, nothing more was done to it; it looked in every respect miserable, and it was hard to believe the legend of the sign of the Fire Insurance Office, rusting on the wall, namely, that a phœnix should rise from the ashes.

At the base of the house grew dandelions, nettles, and roadweed, the faithful companions of poverty; sparrows were bathing in the scorching sand and scattering it about; pale-faced children with big stomachs, looking as if they were being brought up on 90 per cent. of water, were making dandelion chains and trying to embitter their sad lives by annoying and insulting each other.

Falk and Ygberg climbed a rotten, creaking staircase and came to a large room. It was divided into three parts by chalk lines. The first and second divisions served a joiner and a cobbler as workshops; the third was exclusively devoted to the more intimate pursuits of family life.

Whenever the children screamed, which happened once in every quarter of an hour, the joiner flew into a rage and burst out scolding and swearing; the cobbler remonstrated with quotations from the Bible. The joiner's nerves were so shattered by these constant screams, the unceasing punishments and scoldings, that five minutes after partaking of the snuff of reconciliation offered by the cobbler, he flew into a fresh temper in spite of his firm resolve to be patient. Consequently he was nearly all day long in a red-hot fury. But the worst passages were when he asked the woman, "why these infernal females need bring so many children into the world;" then the woman in question came on the tapis and his antagonist gave him as good as he brought.

Falk and Ygberg had to pass this room to gain the latter's garret, and although both of them went on tiptoe, they wakened two of the children; immediately the mother began humming a lullaby, thereby interrupting a discussion between cobbler and joiner; naturally the latter nearly had a fit.

"Hold your tongue, woman!"

"Hold your tongue yourself! Can't you let the children sleep?"

"To hell with the children! Are they my children? Am I to suffer for other people's immorality? Am I an immoral man? What? Have I any children? Hold your tongue, I say, or I'll throw my plane at your head."

"I say, master, master!" began the cobbler; "you shouldn't talk like that of the children; God sends the little ones into the world."

"That's a lie, cobbler! The devil sends them! The devil! And then the dissolute parents blame God! You ought to be ashamed of yourselves!"

"Master, master! You shouldn't use such language! Scripture tells us that the kingdom of heaven belongs to the children."

"Oh, indeed! They have them in the kingdom of heaven, have they?"

"How dare you talk like that!" shrilled the furious mother. "If you ever have any children of your own, I shall pray that they may be lame and diseased; I shall pray that they shall be blind and deaf and dumb; I shall pray that they shall be sent to the reformatory and end on the gallows; see if I won't."

"Do so for all I care, you good-for-nothing hussy! I'm not going to bring children into the world to see them living a dog's life. You ought to be sent to the House of Correction, for bringing the poor things into all this misery. You are married, you say? Well! Need you be immoral because you are married?"

"Master, master! God sends the children."

"It's a lie, cobbler! I read in a paper the other day that the damned potato is to blame for the large families of the poor; don't you see, the potato consists of two substances, called oxygen and nitrogen; whenever these substances occur in a certain quantity and proportion, women become prolific."

"But what is one to do?" asked the angry mother, whom this interesting explanation had calmed down a little.

"One shouldn't eat potatoes; can't you see that?"

"But what is one to eat if not potatoes?"

"Beef-steak, woman! Steak and onions! What! Isn't that good? Or steak à la Châteaubriand! Do you know what that is? What? I saw in the 'Fatherland' the other day that a woman who had taken womb-grain very nearly died as well as the baby."

"What's that?" asked the mother, pricking up her ears.

"You'd like to know, would you?"

"Is it true what you just said about womb-grain?" asked the cobbler, blinking his eyes.

"Hoho! That brings up your lungs and liver, but there's a heavy penalty on it, and that's as it should be."

"Is it as it should be?" asked the cobbler dully.

"Of course it is! Immorality must be punished; and it's immoral to murder one's children."

"Children! Surely, there's a difference," replied the angry mother, resignedly; "but where does the stuff you just spoke about come from, master?"

"Haha! You want more children, you hussy, although you are a widow with five! Beware of that devil of a cobbler! He's hard on women, in spite of his piety. A pinch of snuff, cobbler?"

"There is really a herb then...."

"Who said it was a herb? Did I say so? No; it's an organic substance. Let me tell you, all substances—nature contains about sixty—are divided into organic and inorganic substances. This one's Latin name is cornuticus secalias; it comes from abroad, for instance from the Calabrian Peninsula."

"Is it very expensive, master?" asked the cobbler.

"Expensive!" ejaculated the joiner, manipulating his plane as if it were a carbine. "It's awfully expensive!"

Falk had listened to the conversation with great interest. Now he started; he had heard a carriage stopping underneath the window, and the sound of two women's voices which seemed familiar to him.

"This house looks all right."

"Does it?" said an older voice. "I think it looks dreadful."

"I meant it looks all right for our purpose. Do you know, driver, whether any poor people are living in this house?"

"I don't know," replied the driver, "but I'd stake my oath on it."

"Swearing is a sin, so you had better not. Wait for us here, while we go upstairs to do our duty."

"I say, Eugenia, hadn't we better first talk a little to the children down here?" said Mrs. Homan to Mrs. Falk, lagging behind.

"Perhaps it would be just as well. Come here, little boy! What's your name?"

"Albert," answered a pale-faced little lad of six.

"Do you know Jesus, my laddie?"

"No," answered the child with a laugh, and put a finger into his mouth.

"Terrible!" said Mrs. Falk, taking out her note-book. "I'd better say: Parish of St. Catherine's. White Mountains. Profound spiritual darkness in the minds of the young. I suppose darkness is the right word?" She turned to the little fellow: "And don't you want to know him?"

"No!"

"Would you like a penny?"

"Yes!"

"You should say please! Indescribably neglected, but I succeeded, by gentleness, in awakening their better feelings."

"What a horrible smell! Let's go, Eugenia," implored Mrs. Homan.

They went upstairs and entered the large room without knocking.

The joiner seized his plane and began planing a knotty board, so that the ladies had to shout to make themselves heard.

"Is anybody here thirsting for salvation?" shouted Mrs. Homan, while Mrs. Falk worked her scent-spray so vigorously that the children began to cry with the smarting of their eyes.

"Are you offering us salvation, lady?" asked the joiner, interrupting his work. "Where did you get it from? Perhaps there's charity to be had, too, and humiliation and pride?"

"You are a ruffian; you will be damned," answered Mrs. Homan.

Mrs. Falk made notes in her note-book. "He's all right," she remarked.

"Is there anything else you'd like to say?" asked Mrs. Homan.

"We know the sort you are! Perhaps you'd like to talk to me about religion, ladies? I can talk on any subject. Have you ever heard anything about the councils held at Nicæa, or the Smalcaldic Articles?"

"We know nothing about that, my good man."

"Why do you call me good? Scripture says nobody is good but God alone. So you know nothing about the Nicene Council, ladies? How can you dare to teach others, when you know nothing yourselves? And if you want to dispense charity, do it while I turn my back to you, for true charity is given secretly. Practise on the children, if you like, they can't defend themselves; but leave us in peace. Give us work and pay us a just wage and then you needn't run about like this. A pinch of snuff, cobbler!"

"Shall I write: Great unbelief, quite hardened, Evelyn?" asked Mrs. Falk.

"I should put *impenitent*, dear."

"What are you writing down, ladies? Our sins? Surely your book's too small for that!"

"The outcome of the so-called working men's unions...."

"Very good," said Mrs. Homan.

"Beware of the working men's unions," said the joiner. "For hundreds of years war has been made upon the kings, but now we've discovered that the kings are not to blame. The next campaign will be against all idlers who live on the work of others; then we shall see something."

"That's enough!" said the cobbler.

The angry mother, whose eyes had been riveted on Mrs. Falk during the whole scene, took the opportunity of putting in a word.

"Excuse me, but aren't you Mrs. Falk?" she asked.

"No," answered that lady with an assurance which took even Mrs. Homan's breath away.

"But you're as like her as its possible to be! I knew her father, Ronock, who's now on the flagship."

"That's all very nice, but it doesn't concern us.... Are there any other people in this house who need salvation?"

"No," said the joiner, "they don't need salvation, they need food and clothes, or, better still, work; much work and well-paid work. But the ladies had better not go and see them, for one of them is down with small-pox...."

"Small-pox!" screamed Mrs. Homan, "and nobody said a word about it! Come along Eugenia, let's at once inform the police! What a disgusting set of people they are!"

"But the children? Whose children are these? Answer!" said Mrs. Falk, holding up her pencil, threateningly.

"They're mine, lady," answered the mother.

"But your husband? Where's your husband?"

"Disappeared!" said the joiner.

"We'll set the police on his track! He shall be sent to the Penitentiary. Things must be changed here! I said it was a good house, Evelyn."

"Won't the ladies sit down?" asked the joiner. "It's so much easier to keep up a conversation sitting down. We've no chairs, but that doesn't matter; we've no beds either; they went for taxes, for the lighting of the street, so that you need not go home from the theatre in the dark. We've no gas, as you can see for yourselves. They went in payment of the water-rate—so that your servants should be saved running up and down stairs; the water's not laid on here. They went towards the keeping up of the hospitals, so that your sons will not be laid up at home when...."

"Come away, Eugenia, for God's sake! This is unbearable!"

"I agree with you, ladies, it is unbearable," said the joiner. "And the day will come when things will be worse; on that day we shall come down from the White Mountains with a great noise, like a waterfall, and ask for the return of our beds. Ask? We shall take them! And you shall lie on wooden benches, as I've had to do, and eat potatoes until your stomachs are as tight as a drum and you feel as if you had undergone the torture by water, as we...."

But the ladies had fled, leaving behind them a pile of pamphlets.

"Ugh! What a beastly smell of eau-de-Cologne! It smells of prostitutes!" said the joiner. "A pinch of snuff, cobbler!"

He wiped his forehead with his blue apron and took up his plane while the others reflected silently.

Ygberg, who had been asleep during the whole of the scene, now awoke and made ready to go out again with Falk. Once more Mrs. Homan's voice floated through the open window:

"What did she mean when she said your father was on the flagship? Your father is a captain, isn't he?"

"That's what he's called. It's the same thing. Weren't they an insolent crowd? I'll never go there again. But it will make a fine report. To the restaurant Hasselbacken, driver!"

CHAPTER XVII. NATURA....

Falander was at home studying a part one afternoon, when he was disturbed by a gentle tapping, two double-raps, at his door. He jumped up, hastily donned a coat and opened.

"Agnes! This is a rare visit!"

"I had to come and see you, it's so damned slow!"

"What dreadful language!"

"Let me curse! It relieves my feelings."

"Hm! hm!"

"Give me a cigar; I haven't had a smoke these last six weeks. This education makes me frantic."

"Is he so severe?"

"Curse him!"

"For shame, Agnes!"

"I've been forbidden to smoke, to curse, to drink punch, to go out in the evening! But wait until we are married! I'll let him see!"

"Is he really serious about it?"

"Absolutely! Look at this handkerchief!"

"A. R. with a crown and nine balls."

"Our initials are the same and he's making me use his design. Isn't it lovely?"

"Yes, very nice. It's gone as far as that, has it?"

The angel, dressed in blue, threw herself on the sofa and puffed at her cigar. Falander looked at her body as if he were making an estimate, and said:

"Will you have a glass of punch?"

"Rather!"

"Are you in love with your fiancé?"

"He doesn't belong to the class of men with whom one can really be in love. But I don't know. Love? Hm! What is love?"

"Yes, what is it?"

"Oh, you know what I mean. He's very respectable, awfully respectable, but, but, but...."

"But?"

"He's so proper."

She looked at Falander with a smile which would have saved the absent fiancé, if he could have seen it.

"He isn't demonstrative enough?" asked Falander curiously, in an unsteady voice.

She drank her glass of punch, paused, shook her head, and said with a theatrical sigh:

"No!"

The reply seemed to satisfy Falander; it obviously relieved him. He continued his cross-examination.

"It may be a long time before you can get married. He's never played a single part yet."

"No, I know."

"Won't you find the waiting dull?"

"One must be patient."

I must use the thumbscrew, thought Falander.

"I suppose you know that Jenny and I are lovers?"

"The ugly, old hag!"

A whole shower of white northern lights flamed across her face and every muscle twitched, as if she were under the influence of a galvanic battery.

"She isn't as old as all that," said Falander coldly. "Have you heard that the waiter Gustav is going to play Don Diego in the new piece, and that Rehnhjelm has been given the part of his servant? The waiter is bound to have a success, for the part plays itself; but poor Rehnhjelm will die with shame."

"Good heavens! Is it true?"

"It's true enough."

"It shan't happen!"

"Who's to prevent it?"

She jumped up from the sofa, emptied her glass and began to sob wildly.

"Oh! How bitter the world is, how bitter!" she sobbed. "It's just as if an evil power were spying on us, finding out our wishes, merely to cross them; discerning our hopes, so as to shatter them; anticipating our thoughts so as to paralyse them. If it were possible to long for evil to happen to oneself, one ought to do it just for the sake of making a fool of that power."

"Quite true, my dear; therefore one should always be prepared for a bad ending. But that's not the worst. I'll give you a thought which will comfort you. You know that every success you attain entails someone else's failure; if you are given a part to play, some other woman is disappointed; it makes her writhe like a worm trodden under foot, and without knowing it you have committed a wrong; therefore, even happiness is poisoned. Be comforted in misfortune by the thought that every piece of ill-luck which falls to your share is equivalent to a good action, even though it be a good action committed without your knowing it; and the thought of a good action is the only pure enjoyment which is given to us mortals."

"I don't want to do any good actions! I don't want any pure joys! I have the same right to success as everybody else! And I—will—be successful!"

"At any price?"

"I won't play your mistress's maid at any price."

"You're jealous! Learn to bear failure gracefully! That's greater—and much more interesting."

"Tell me one thing! Is she in love with you?"

"I'm afraid she loves me only too well."

"And you?"

"I? I shall never love any woman but you!"

He seized her hand.

She jumped up from the sofa, showing her stockings.

"Do you believe in what is called love?" she asked, gazing at him with distended pupils.

"I believe there are several kinds of love."

She crossed the room towards the door.

"Do you love me wholly and entirely?" She put her hand on the door-handle.

He pondered for two seconds. Then he replied:

"Your soul is evil, and I don't love evil."

"I don't care a fig for my soul! Do you love me? Me?"

"Yes! So deeply...."

"Why did you send me Rehnhjelm?"

"Because I wanted to find out what life without you would be like."

"Did you lie when you said you were tired of me?"

"Yes, I lied."

"Oh! You old devil!"

She took the key out of the lock and he drew down the blind.

CHAPTER XVIII. NIHILISM

As Falk was walking home one rainy September evening and turning into Count-Magni-Street, he saw to his amazement that his windows were lit up. When he was near enough to be able to cast a glance into his room from below, he noticed on the ceiling the shadow of a man which seemed familiar, although he could not place it. It was a despondent-looking shadow, and the nearer he came the more despondent it looked.

On entering his room he saw Struve sitting at his writing-table with his head on his hands. His clothes were soaked with rain and clung heavily to his body; there were little puddles on the floor which slowly drained off through the chinks. His hair hung in damp strands from his head, and his usually English whiskers fell like stalactites on his damp coat collar. He had placed his black hat beside him on the table; it had collapsed under its own weight, and the wide crape band which it was wearing suggested that it was mourning for its lost youth.

"Good evening," said Falk. "This is an unexpected honour."

"Don't jeer at me," begged Struve.

"And why not? I see no reason why I should spare you."

"I see! You're done!"

"Yes! I shall turn Conservative too, before long. You're in mourning, I see; I hope I may congratulate you."

"I've lost a little son."

"Then I'll congratulate him! But what do you want here? You know I despise you! I expect you do yourself. Don't you?"

"Of course I do! But isn't life bitter enough without our unnecessarily embittering it still further? If God, or Providence, is amused at it, need it follow that man should equally degrade himself?"

"That sounds reasonable and does you honour. Won't you put on my dressing-gown while you are drying your clothes? You must be cold."

"Thank you! But I mustn't stay."

"Oh! Stay a little while! It will give us a chance of having things out."

"I don't like talking about my misfortunes."

"Then talk about your crimes!"

"I haven't committed any!"

"Oh, yes, you have! You have committed great crimes! You have put your heavy hand on the oppressed; you have kicked the wounded; you have sneered at the wretched. Do you remember the last strike when you were on the side of power?"

"The side of the law, brother!"

"Haha! The law! Who has dictated the law which governs the life of the poor man, you fool! The rich man! That is to say, the master made the law for the slave."

"The law was dictated by the whole nation and the universal sense of right. God gave the law."

"Save your big words when you talk to me. Who wrote the law of 1734? Mr. Kronstedt! Who is responsible for the law of corporal punishment? Colonel Sabelman—it was his Bill, and his friends, who formed the majority at that time, pushed it through. Colonel Sabelman is not the nation and his friends are not the universal sense of right. Who is responsible for the law concerning joint stock companies? Judge Svindelgren. Who is responsible for the new Parliamentary laws? Assessor Vallonius. Who has written the law of 'legal protection,' that is to say the protection of the rich from the just claims of the poor? Wholesale merchant grocer. Don't talk to me! I know your claptrap. Who has written the new law of succession? Criminals! The forest laws? Thieves! The law relating to bills of private banks? Swindlers! And you maintain that God has done it? Poor God!"

"May I give you a piece of advice, bought with my own experience, advice which will be useful to you all your life? If you want to escape self-immolation, a fate which in your fanaticism you are fast approaching, change your point of view as soon as possible. Take a bird's-eye view of the world, and you will see how small and insignificant everything is. Start with the conviction that the whole world is a rubbish heap; that men are the refuse, no better than egg-shells, carrot stalks, cabbage leaves, rags; then nothing will take you by surprise, you will never lose an illusion; but, on the contrary, you will be filled with a great joy whenever you come across a fine thought, a good action; try to acquire a calm contempt of the world—you needn't be afraid of growing callous."

"I have not yet attained to that point of view, it's true, but I have a contempt for the world. But that is my misfortune; for directly I hear of a single act of generosity or kindness, I love humanity again, and overrate my fellowmen, only to be deceived afresh."

"Be more selfish! Let the devil take your fellowmen!"

"I'm afraid I can't."

"Try another profession; join your brother; he seems to get on in this world. I saw him yesterday at the church council of the Parish of St. Nicholas."

"At the church council?"

"Yes; that man has a future. The pastor primarius nodded to him. He'll soon be an alderman, like all landed proprietors."

"What about the 'Triton'?"

"They work with debentures now; but your brother hasn't lost anything by it, even though he hasn't made anything. No, he's other fish to fry!"

"Don't let us talk of that man."

"But he's your brother!"

"That isn't his merit! But now tell me what you want."

"My boy's funeral is to-morrow, and I have no dress-coat...."

"I'll lend you mine."

"Thank you, brother. You're extricating me from an awkward position. That was one thing, but there is something else, of a rather more delicate nature...."

"Why come to me, your enemy, with your delicate confidences? I'm surprised...."

"Because you are a man of heart."

"Don't build on that any longer! But go on."

"How irritable you've grown! You're not the same man; you used to be so gentle."

"We discussed that before! Speak up!"

"I want to ask you whether you would come with me to the churchyard."

"I? Why don't you ask one of your colleagues from the *Grey Bonnet*?"

"There are reasons. I don't see why I shouldn't tell you. I'm not married."

"Not married! You! The defender of religion and morality, have broken the sacred bonds!"

"Poverty, the force of circumstances! But I'm just as happy as if I were married! I love my wife and she loves me, and that's all. But there's another reason. The child has not been baptized; it was three weeks old when it died, and therefore no clergyman will bury it. I don't dare to tell this to my wife, because she would fret. I've told her the clergyman would meet us in the churchyard; I'm telling you this to prevent a possible scene. She, of course, will remain at home. You'll only meet two other fellows; one of them, Levi, is a younger brother of the director of the 'Triton,' and one of the employés of that society. He's a decent sort, with an unusually good head and a still better heart. Don't laugh, I can see that you think I've borrowed money from him—and so I have—he's a man you'll like. The other one is my old friend, Dr. Borg, who treated the little one. He is very broad-minded, a man without any prejudices; you'll get on with him! I can count on you, can't I? There'll be four of us in the coach, and the little coffin, of course."

"Very well, I'll come."

"There's one more thing. My wife has religious scruples and is afraid that the little one won't go to heaven because he died without baptism. She asks everybody's opinion on the subject, so as to ease her mind."

"But what about the Augsburg Confession?"

"It's not a question of confessions."

"But in writing to your paper, you always uphold the official faith."

"The paper is the affair of the syndicate; if it likes to cling to Christianity, it may do so for all I care! My work for the syndicate is a matter apart. Please agree with my wife if she tells you that she believes that her child will go to heaven."

"I don't mind denying the faith in order to make a human heart happy, particularly as I don't hold it. But you haven't told me yet where you live."

"Do you know where the White Mountains are?"

"Yes! Are you living in the spotted house on the mountain rock?"

"Do you know it?"

"I've been there once."

"Then perhaps you know Ygberg, the Socialist, who leads the people astray? I am the landlord's deputy—Smith owns the property—I live there rent free on condition that I collect the rents; whenever the rents are not forthcoming, the people talk nonsense which he has put into their heads about capital and labour, and other things which fill the columns of the Socialistic press."

Falk did not reply.

"Do you know Ygberg?"

"Yes, I do. But won't you try on my dress-coat now?"

Struve tried it on, put his own damp coat over it, buttoned it up to the chin, lit the chewed-up end of his cigar, impaled on a match, and went.

Falk lighted him downstairs.

"You've a long way to go," he said, merely to say something.

"The Lord knows it! And I have no umbrella."

"And no overcoat. Would you like my winter coat?"

"Many thanks. It's very kind of you."

"You can return it to me by and by."

He went back to his room, fetched the overcoat and gave it to Struve, who was waiting in the entrance hall. After a brief good-night they parted.

Falk found the atmosphere in his room stifling; he opened the window. The rain was coming down in torrents, splashing on the tiles and running down into the dirty street. Tattoo sounded in the barracks opposite; vespers were being sung in the lodgment; fragments of the verses floated through the open window.

Falk felt lonely and tired. He had been longing to fight a battle with a representative of all he regarded as inimical to progress; but the enemy, after having to some extent beaten him, had fled. He tried to understand clearly what the quarrel was about, but failed in his effort; he was unable to say who was right. He asked himself whether the cause he served, namely, the cause of the oppressed, had any existence. But at the next moment he reproached himself with cowardice, and the steady fanaticism which glowed in him burst into fresh flames; he condemned the weakness which again and again had induced him to yield. Just now he had held the enemy in his hand, and not only had he not shown him his profound repugnance, but he had even treated him with kindness and sympathy; what would he think of him?

There was no merit in this good nature, as it prevented him from coming to a firm decision; it was nothing but moral laxity, making him incapable of taking up a fight which seemed more and more beyond him. He realized that he must extinguish the fire under the boilers; they would not be able to stand the pressure, as no steam was being used. He pondered over Struve's advice, and brooded until his mind was chaos in which truth and lies, right and wrong, danced together in complete harmony; his brain in which, owing to his academic training, all conceptions had been so neatly pigeon-holed, would soon resemble a pack of well-shuffled cards.

He succeeded beyond expectation in working himself into a state of complete indifference; he looked for fine motives in the actions of his enemies, and gradually it appeared to him that he had all along been in the wrong; he felt reconciled to the existing order of things, and ultimately came to the fine conclusion that it was quite immaterial whether the whole was black or white. Whatever was, had to be; he was not entitled to criticize it. He found this mood pleasant, it gave him a feeling of restfulness to which he had been a stranger all those years during which he had made the troubles of humanity his own.

He was enjoying this calm and a pipe of strong tobacco, when a maid servant brought him a letter just delivered by the postman. It was from Olle Montanus and very long. Parts of it seemed to impress Falk greatly.

MY DEAR FELLOW, [it ran,]

Although Lundell and I have now finished our work and will soon be back in Stockholm, I yet feel the need of writing down my impressions, because they have been of great importance to myself and my spiritual development. I have come to a conclusion, and I am as full of amazement as a chicken which has just been hatched, and stares at the world with its newly opened eyes, trampling on the egg-shell which had shut out the light for so long. The conclusion, of course, is not a new one; Plato propounded it before Christianity was: the world, the visible world, is but a delusion, the reflexion of the ideas; that is to say, reality is something low, insignificant, secondary and accidental. Yes! but I will proceed synthetically, begin with the particular and pass on from it to the general.

I will speak of my work first, in which both Government and Parliament have been interested. On the altar of the church at Träskola two wooden figures used to stand; one of them was broken, but the other one was whole. The whole one, the figure of a woman, held a cross in her hand; two sacks of fragments of the broken one were preserved in the sacristy. A learned archæologist had examined the contents of the two sacks, in order to determine the appearance of the broken figure, but the result had been mere conjecture.

But he had been very thorough. He had taken a specimen of the white paint with which the figure had been grounded, and sent it to the Pharmaceutical Institute; the latter had reported that it contained lead and not zinc; therefore, the figure must date from before 1844, because zinc-white did not come into use until after that date. (What can one say to such a conclusion, seeing that the figure might have been painted over!) Next he sent a sample of the wood to the Stockholm timber office; he was informed that it was birch. The figure was therefore made of birchwood and dated from before 1844.

But that was not all he was striving for. He had a reason (!) in plain words, he wished for his own aggrandisement, that the carved figures should be proved to date from the sixteenth century; and he would have preferred that they should be the work of the great—of course *great*, because his name had been so deeply carved in oak that it has been preserved to our time—Burchard von Schiedenhanne, who had carved the seats in the choir of the Cathedral of Västeros.

The learned research was carried on. The professor stole a little plaster from the figures in Västeros and sent it, together with a specimen from the sacristy of Träskola to the Ekole Pollytechnik (I can't spell it). The reply completely crushed the scoffers; the analysis proved that the two specimens of plaster were identical; both contained 77 per cent. of chalk and 35 of sulphuric acid; therefore (!) the figures must date from the same period.

The age of the figures had now been settled; a sketch was made of the whole one and "sent in" (what a terrible passion these learned men have for "sending things in") to the Academy; the only thing which remained to be done was to determine and reconstruct the broken one. For two whole years the two sacks travelled up and down between Upsala and Lund; the two professors differed and carried on a lively dispute. The professor of Lund, who had just been made rector, took the figure as the subject of his inaugural address and crushed the professor of Upsala. The latter replied in a brochure. Fortunately at the very moment a professor of the Stockholm Academy of Art appeared with a totally new opinion; then Herod and Pilate "compromised," as is always the case, and attacked the man from the capital, rending him with the unbridled fury of provincials.

This was their compromise: the broken figure had represented Unbelief, because the other one must have been meant for Faith, whose symbol is the cross. The supposition (advanced by the professor of Lund) that the broken figure had been intended to represent Hope, arrived at because one of the sacks contained an anchor, was rejected, because that would have postulated a third figure, Love, of which there was no trace, and for which there could have been no room; moreover, it was proved by specimens from the rich collection of arrow-heads in the historical museum, that the fragment in question was not an anchor, but an arrowhead, which forms a part of the weapons belonging to the symbols of Unbelief. The shape of the arrowhead, which resembled in every detail those from the period of the Vice-regent Sture, removed the last doubt as to the age of the figure.

It was my task to make a statue of Unbelief, as a companion to the figure of Faith, in accordance with the directions of the professors. I was given my instructions and I did not hesitate. I looked for a male model, for the figure was to be a man; I had to look for a long time, but I found him in the end; I really believe I met the personification of Unbelief—and I succeeded brilliantly.

And there he now stands, Falander, the actor, to the left of the altar, with a Mexican bow (used in the drama *Ferdinand Cortez*) and a robber's cloak (from *Fra Diavolo*), but the people say that it is Unbelief throwing down his arms before Faith. And the Deputy-Superintendent, who preached the inaugural sermon, spoke of the splendid gifts which God sometimes gives to man, and which, in this case, he had given to me; and the Count, who gave the inaugural dinner, declared that I had created a masterpiece, fit to stand side by side with the antiques (he's been in Italy); and a student who occupies some post in the Count's household, seized the opportunity to write and circulate some verses, in which he developed the conception of the Sublimely Beautiful, and gave a history of the Myth of the Devil.

Up to now I have, like a true egoist, spoken only of myself. What am I to say about Lundell's altar-piece? I will try to describe it to you. Christ (Rehnhjelm) hangs on the cross in the background; to the left is the impenitent thief (I; and the rascal has made me worse-looking than I am); to the right the repenting thief (Lundell himself, squinting with hypocritical eyes at Rehnhjelm); at the foot of the cross Mary Magdalene (you will remember Marie—in a very low dress), and a Roman centurion (Falander) on horseback (stallion belonging to Alderman Olsson).

I cannot describe the awful impression made on me when, after the sermon, the picture was unveiled, and I saw all these well-known faces staring from the wall above the altar at the community rapturously listening to the words of the preacher on the great importance of art, particularly art in the service of religion. As far as I am concerned, a veil has been lifted from many things; I will tell you by and by my thoughts on Faith and Unbelief. I am going to embody my views on art and its high mission in an essay, and read it at some public hall as soon as I am back in town.

It goes without saying that Lundell's religious sense has tremendously developed during those "dear" days. He is, comparatively speaking, happy in his colossal self-deception, and has no idea what a rascal he really is.

I think I have told you everything now; anything else verbally when we meet. Until then, good-bye. I hope you are in good health and spirits.

Your friend,
OLLE MONTANUS.

P.S. I must not forget to tell you the result of the antiquarian research. The end of it all was that old Jan, an inmate of the almshouses, remembered having seen the figures when he was a child. He said there had been three: Faith, Hope, and Love; and as Love was the greatest of these, it had stood above the altar. In the first decade of this century a flash of lightning had struck Love and Faith. The figures had been the work of his father who was a carver of figure-heads in the naval port Karlskrona.

O. M.

When Falk had read the letters, he sat down at his writing-table, examined his lamp to see whether there was plenty of oil in it, lit his pipe, took a manuscript from his table-drawer, and began to write.

CHAPTER XIX. FROM CHURCHYARD TO PUBLIC-HOUSE

The September afternoon lay grey and warm and still over the capital as Falk climbed the hills in the south. When he had arrived at the churchyard of St. Catherine's he sat down to rest; he noticed with a feeling of genuine pleasure that the maples had turned colour during the recent cold nights, and he welcomed autumn with its darkness, its grey clouds, and falling leaves.

Not a breath stirred; it was as if Nature were resting, tired after the work of the short summer. Everything was asleep; the dead were lying beneath the sod, calm and peaceful, as if they had never been alive; he wished that he had all men there, and that he, himself, was with them.

The clock on the tower chimed the hour, and he rose and continued his walk. He went down Garden Street, turned into New Street—which looked as if it had been new a hundred years ago at least—crossed the New Market, and came to the White Mountains.

He stood still before the spotted house, listening to the children's chatter, for, as usual, there were children playing about the street; they talked loudly and unreservedly while they were busy polishing little pieces of brick, presently to be used in a game of hop-scotch.

"What did you have for dinner, Janne?"

"That's my business!"

"Your business? Did you say it was your business? Mind what you're about or you'll get a hiding."

"Don't brag! You with your eyes!"

"Who shoved you into the lake the other day?"

"Oh! shut up!"

Janne received a thrashing, and peace was restored.

"I say! You stole cress in the churchyard the other day, didn't you, Janne?"

"That cripple Olee split on me!"

"And you were nabbed by the police, weren't you?"

"Who cares for the police? I don't!"

"Don't you? Come along of us to-night then; we're going to pinch some pears."

"There's a savage dog behind the fence!"

"Garn! Chimney-sweep's Peter'll climb over and a kick'll do for the dog."

The polishing was interrupted by a maid-servant who came out of the house and began to scatter pine branches on the grass-grown street.

"Who's going to be buried?"

"The deputy's wife's baby!"

"He's a proper old Satan, the deputy, isn't he?"

Instead of replying, the other began whistling an unknown and very peculiar tune.

"Let's thrash his red-haired cubs when they come home from school! I say! Doesn't his old woman fancy herself? The old she-devil locked us out in the snow the other night because we couldn't pay the rent, and we had to spend the night in the barn."

The conversation flickered out; the last item of conversation had not made the smallest impression on Janne's friend.

After this introduction to the status of the tenants by the two urchins, Falk entered the house not with the pleasantest of sensations. He was received at the door by Struve, who looked distressed, and took Falk's arm as if he were going to confide a secret to him, or suppress a tear—he had to do something, so he embraced him.

Falk found himself in a big room with a dining-table, a sideboard, six chairs, and a coffin. White sheets were hanging before the windows through which the daylight filtered and broke at the red glow of the tallow candles; on the table stood a tray with green wine glasses, and a soup tureen filled with dahlias, stocks, and white asters.

Struve seized Falk's hand and led him to the coffin where the baby lay bedded on shavings, covered with tulle, and strewn with fuchsias.

"There!" he said, "there!"

Falk felt nothing but the quite commonplace emotion the living always feel in the presence of the dead; he could think of nothing suitable to say, and therefore he confined himself to pressing the father's hand. "Thank you, thank you," stammered Struve, and disappeared in an adjoining room.

Falk was left alone; he could hear excited whispering behind the door through which Struve had vanished; then it grew still for a while; but presently a murmur from the other end of the room penetrated the matchboard wall. A strident treble seemed to be reciting long verses with incredible volubility.

"Babebibobubybäbö—Babebibobubybäbö—Babebibobubybäbö," it sounded.

An angry man's voice answered to the accompaniment of a plane which said hwitcho—hwitcho—hwitch—hwitch—hitch—hitch.

And a long-drawn, rumbling mum-mum-mum-mum-mum-mum-mum-*m*um replied, seemingly anxious to calm the storm. But the plane spat and sneezed again its hwitch—hwitch, and immediately after a storm of Babili—bebili—bibili—bobili—bubili—bybili—bäbili—bö—broke out with fresh fury.

Falk guessed the subject under discussion, and a certain intonation gave him the idea that the dead baby was involved in the argument.

The whispering, occasionally interrupted by loud sobs, began again behind the door through which Struve had disappeared; finally it was pushed open and Struve appeared leading by the hand a woman who looked like a laundress; she was dressed in black, and her eyelids were red and swollen with weeping. Struve introduced her with all the dignity of a father of a family:

"My wife, Mr. Falk, my old friend."

Falk clasped a hand, hard as a beetle, and received a vinegary smile. He cast about for a few platitudes containing the words "wife" and "grief," and as he was fairly successful, he was rewarded by Struve with an embrace.

Mrs. Struve, anxious not to be left out in the cold, began brushing the back of her husband's coat.

"It's dreadful how you seem to pick up every bit of dirt, Christian," she said; "your back's always dusty. Don't you think that my husband always looks like a pig, Mr. Falk?"

There was no need for poor Falk to reply to this tender remark; behind the mother's back now appeared two heads, regarding the visitor with a grin. The mother patted them affectionately.

"Have you ever seen plainer boys before, Mr. Falk?" she asked. "Don't they look exactly like young foxes?"

This statement was so undeniably accurate that Falk felt compelled to deny it eagerly.

The opening of the hall door and the entrance of two men stopped all further civilities. The first of the new-comers was a man of thirty, broad-shouldered, with a square head, the front of which was supposed to represent the face; the skin looked like the half-rotten plank of a bridge in which worms have ploughed their labyrinths; the wide mouth, always slightly open, showed the four shining eye-teeth; whenever he smiled his face seemed to split into two parts; his mouth opened as far back as the fourth back tooth; not a single hair grew in the barren soil; the nose was so badly put on that one could see through it far into the head; on the upper part of the skull grew something which looked like cocoa-nut matting.

Struve, who possessed the faculty of ennobling his environment, introduced Candidate Borg as Dr. Borg. The latter, without a sign of either pleasure or annoyance, held out his arm to his companion, who pulled off the coat and hung it on the hinge of the front door, an act which drew from Mrs. Struve the remark that the old house was in such bad repair that there was not even a hall-stand.

The man who had helped Borg off with his overcoat was introduced as Mr. Levi. He was a tall, overgrown youth; the skull seemed but a backward development of the nasal bone, and the trunk which reached to the knees, looked as if it had been drawn through a wire plate, in the way in which wire is drawn; the shoulders slanted like eaves; there was no trace of hips, the shanks ran up into the thighs; the feet were worn out of shape like a pair of old shoes; the instep had given way. The legs curved outward and downward, like the legs of a working man who has carried heavy loads, or stood for the greater part of his life. He was a pure slave-type.

The candidate had remained at the door; he had taken off his gloves, put down his stick, blown his nose, and put back the handkerchief into his pocket without taking the least notice of Struve's repeated attempts to introduce him; he believed that he was still in the entrance hall; but now he took his hat, scraped the floor with his foot and made a step into the room.

"Good morning, Jenny! How are you?" he said, seizing Mrs. Struve's hand with as much eagerness as if it were a matter of life and death. He bowed, hardly perceptibly, to Falk, with the snarl of a dog who sees a strange dog in its yard.

Young Mr. Levi followed at the heels of the candidate, responding to his smiles, applauding his sarcasms, and generally kow-towing to his superiority.

Mrs. Struve opened a bottle of hock and filled the glasses. Struve raised his glass and welcomed his guests. The candidate opened his mouth, made a canal of his tongue, poured the contents of the glass on it, grinned as if it were physic and swallowed it.

"It's awfully sour and nasty," said Mrs. Struve; "would you prefer a glass of punch, Henrik?"

"Yes, it *is* very nasty," agreed the candidate, and Levi eagerly seconded him.

The punch was brought in. Borg's face brightened; he looked for a chair, and immediately Levi brought him one.

The party sat down round the dining-table. The strong scent of the stocks mingled with the smell of the wine; the candles were reflected in the glasses, the conversation became lively, and soon a column of smoke stood above the candidate's chair. Mrs. Struve glanced uneasily at the little sleeper near the window, but nobody saw her look.

Presently a coach stopped in the street outside the house. Everybody rose except the candidate. Struve coughed, and in a low voice, as if he had something unpleasant to say, he whispered:

"Shall we get ready now?"

Mrs. Struve went to the coffin and stooped over it, weeping bitterly; when, in drawing back, she saw her husband standing behind her with the coffin lid, she burst into loud sobs.

"There, there, compose yourself," said Struve, hastening to screw down the lid as if he wanted to hide something. Borg, looking like a yawning horse, gulped down another glass of punch. Mr. Levi helped Struve to screw down the lid, displaying quite extraordinary skill; he seemed to be packing a bale of goods.

The men shook hands with Mrs. Struve, put on their overcoats and went; the woman warned them to be careful in going downstairs; the stairs were old and rotten.

Struve marched in front, carrying the coffin; when he stepped into the street and became aware of the little crowd which had collected before the house, he felt flattered, and the devil of pride took possession of him. He scolded the driver who had omitted to open the door and let down the steps; to heighten the effect of his words, he spoke with contemptuous familiarity to the tall man in livery who, hat in hand, hastened to carry out his commands.

From the centre of the crowd, where the boy Janne was standing, came a short, scornful cough; but when the boy saw that he was attracting universal attention, he raised his eyes towards the chimneys, and seemed to be eagerly looking for the sweep.

The door of the coach slammed behind the four men; a lively conversation broke out between some of the younger members of the mass-meeting, who now felt more at their ease.

"I say, what a swell coffin! Did you see it?"

"Yes! But did you see that there was no name on it?"

"Wasn't there?"

"No! Didn't you see it? It was quite plain."

"Why was that, then?"

"Don't you know? Because he was a bastard...."

The whip cracked, and the coach rumbled off. Falk's eyes strayed to the window; he caught a glimpse of Mrs. Struve, who had already removed some of the sheets, blowing out the candles; and he saw the two cubs standing by the side of her, each with a glass of wine in his hand.

The coach rattled along, through street after street; nobody attempted to speak. Struve, sitting with the coffin on his knees, looked embarrassed; it was still daylight; he longed to make himself invisible.

It was a long journey to the churchyard, but it finally came to an end. They arrived.

A row of coaches stood before the gate. They bought wreaths and the gravedigger took possession of the coffin. After a lengthy walk, the small procession stopped quite at the back on the north side of the churchyard, close to a new sandfield.

The gravedigger placed the coffin in position.

Borg commanded:

"Hold tight! Ease off! Let go!"

And the little nameless child was lowered three yards into the ground.

There was a pause; all heads were bowed and all eyes looking into the grave, as if they were waiting for something.

A leaden sky gloomed dismally over the large, deserted sandfield, the white poles of which looked like the shadows of little children who had lost their way. The dark wood might have been the background in a magic lantern show; the wind was hushed.

All of a sudden a voice rose, tremulous at first, but growing in clearness and intensity, as if it were speaking from an inner conviction. Levi was standing on the pall, bare-headed:

"In the safe keeping of the Most High, resting in the shadow of His omnipotence, I say to the Eternal: Oh, Thou my stronghold, my defence in all eternity, my God in whom I trust—Kaddisch. Lord, Almighty God, let Thy holy name be worshipped and sanctified in the whole world. Thou wilt, in Thy own time, renew the world. Thou wilt awaken the dead and call them to a new life. Everlasting peace reigns in Thy kingdom. Give us and all Israel Thy peace. Amen.

"Sleep soundly, little one, to whom no name had been given. He who knoweth His own will give you a name; sleep soundly in the autumn night, no evil spirits will trouble you, although you never received the holy water; rejoice that you are spared the battle of life; you can dispense with its pleasures. Count yourself happy that you were permitted to go, before you knew the world; pure and stainless your soul left its delicate tenement; therefore we will not throw earth on your coffin, for earth is an emblem of dissolution; we will bed you in flowers, for as a flower pierces the soil, so your soul shall rise from the dark grave to the light; from spirit you came, to spirit you will return."

He dropped his wreath into the little grave and covered his head. Struve took a few steps towards him, seized his hand, and shook it warmly; tears rolled down his cheeks, and he begged Levi for the loan of his handkerchief. Borg, after throwing his wreath into the grave, turned to go, and the others followed slowly.

Falk stood gazing into the open grave, plunged in deep thought. At first he saw only a square of darkness; but gradually a bright spot appeared which grew and took shape; it looked like a disc and shone with the whiteness of a mirror—it was the blank shield on which the life of the child should have been recorded.

It gleamed brightly in the darkness, reflecting the unbroken daylight. He dropped his wreath. There was a faint, dull thud, and the light went out. He turned and followed the others.

Arrived at the coach, there was a brief discussion. Borg cut it short.

"To the Restaurant Norrbacka!" he said, briefly.

A few minutes later the party was standing in the large room on the first floor; they were received by a girl whom Borg embraced and kissed; this done, he pushed his hat underneath the sofa, commanded Levi to help him off with his overcoat, and ordered a quart of punch, twenty-five cigars, half a pint of brandy, and a sugar-loaf. Finally he took off his coat and sat down in shirt sleeves on the only sofa in the room.

Struve's face beamed when he saw the preparations for an orgy, and he shouted for music. Levi went to the piano and strummed a waltz, while Struve put his arm into Falk's and walked with him up and down the room. He touched lightly on life in general, on grief and joy, the inconstant nature of man, and so on, all of which went to prove that it was a sin to mourn what the gods—he said gods, because he had already said sin and did not wish to be taken for a pietist—had given and taken.

This reflexion was apparently made by way of an introduction to the waltz which he immediately after danced with the girl who brought the bowl.

Borg filled the glasses, called Levi, nodded towards a glass, and said:

"Let's drink to our brotherly love now; later on we can be as rude as we like."

Levi expressed his appreciation of the honour.

"Your health, Isaac!" said Borg.

"My name's not Isaac!"

"What the dickens do I care what your name is? I call you Isaac, my Isaac."

"You're a jolly devil...."

"Devil! Shame on you, Jew!"

"We were going to be as rude as we liked...."

"We? I was, as far as you are concerned!"

Struve thought he had better interfere.

"Thank you, brother Levi, for your beautiful words," he said. "What prayer was that?"

"Our funeral prayer!"

"It was beautiful!"

"Nothing but empty words," interposed Borg. "The infidel dog prayed only for Israel; therefore the prayer couldn't have been meant for the child."

"All those who are not baptized are looked upon as belonging to Israel," replied Levi.

"And then you attacked baptism," continued Borg. "I don't allow anybody to attack baptism—we can do that ourselves. And furthermore you attacked the doctrine of justification by faith. Leave it alone in future; I don't permit any outsiders to attack our religion."

"Borg's right there," said Struve; "we should draw the line at attacking either baptism or any other of the sacred truths; and I must beg of you not to indulge in any frivolous discussion of these things to-night."

"You must beg of us?" sneered Borg. "Must you really? All right! I'll forgive you if you'll hold your tongue. Play something, Isaac! Music! Why is music mute at Cæsar's feast? Music! But none of your old chestnuts! Play something new!"

Levi went to the piano, and played the overture to "The Mute."

"Now, let's talk," said Borg. "You are looking depressed, Mr. Falk; have a glass with me."

Falk, who felt a certain embarrassment in Borg's company, accepted the offer with mental reservations. But conversation languished, everybody seemed to dread a collision.

Struve fluttered about like a moth in search of pleasure, but unable to find it he again and again returned to the punch-table; every now and then he danced a few steps, to keep up the fiction that the meeting was merry and festive; but this was not the case by any means.

Levi see-sawed between piano and punch. He attempted to sing a cheerful song, but it was so stale that nobody would listen to it.

Borg talked at the top of his voice, "in order to raise his spirits," as he said, but the party grew more and more silent, one might almost have said uneasy.

Falk paced up and down the room, taciturn, portentous like a thundercloud.

At Borg's order a tremendous supper, a "sexa" was served. The convives took their seats amidst ominous silence. Struve and Borg drank immoderate quantities of brandy; in the face of the latter red spots appeared here and there, and the white of the eyes looked yellow. But Struve resembled a varnished Edam cheese; he was uniformly red and greasy. Beside them Falk and Levi looked like children, eating their last supper in the society of giants.

Borg looked at Levi. "Hand the salmon to the scandal-monger," he commanded, in order to break the monotonous silence.

Levi handed the dish to Struve. The latter pushed his spectacles on to his forehead and spat venom.

"Shame on you, Jew," he foamed, throwing his dinner-napkin in Levi's face.

Borg laid a heavy hand on Struve's bald pate.

"Silence, you blackguard!" he said.

"What dreadful company to be mixed up with! Let me tell you, gentlemen, I'm too old to be treated like a schoolboy," said Struve, tremulously, forgetting his usual *bonhomie*.

Borg, who had had enough to eat, rose from the table.

"Ugh!" he said, "what a beastly crowd you are! Pay, Isaac, I'll pay you back later on; I'm going."

He put on his overcoat, put his hat on his head, filled a tumbler with punch, added brandy to it, emptied it at one gulp, blew out some of the candles in passing, smashed a few of the glasses, pocketed a handful of cigars and a box of matches, and staggered out of the room.

"What a pity that such a genius should drink like that," said Levi solemnly.

A moment later Borg re-entered the room, went to the dining-table, took the candelabrum, lighted his cigar, blew the smoke into Struve's face, put out his tongue, showed his back teeth, extinguished the lights, and departed again. Levi rolled on the floor screaming with laughter.

"To what scum have you introduced me?" asked Falk gravely.

"Oh, my dear fellow, he's intoxicated to-night, but he's the son of Professor Dr...."

"I didn't ask who his father was, I asked who he was," said Falk, cutting him short, "I understand now why you allow such a dog to bully you; but can you tell me why he associates with you?"

"I reserve my reply to all these futilities," answered Struve stiffly.

"Do reserve it, but reserve it for yourself!"

"What's the matter with you, brother Levi?" asked Struve officiously; "you look so grave."

"It's a great pity that a genius like Borg should drink so much," replied Levi.

"How and when does he show his genius?" asked Falk.

"A man can be a genius without writing verse," said Struve pointedly.

"I dare say; writing verse does not pre-suppose genius, nor is a man a genius if he behaves like a brute," said Falk.

"Hadn't we better pay and go?" remarked Struve, hurrying towards the door.

Falk and Levi paid. When they stepped into the street it rained and the sky was black; only the reflexion of the gas-lit town faintly illuminated the sky. The coach had driven away; there was nothing left for them but to turn up their collars and walk.

They had gone as far as the skittle-alley, when they were startled by terrible yells above their heads.

"Curse you!" screamed a voice, and looking up they saw Borg rocking himself on one of the highest branches of a lime tree. The branch nearly touched the ground, but at the next moment it described a tremendous curve upwards.

"Oh! Isn't it colossal!" screamed Levi. "Colossal!"

"What a madman," smiled Struve, proud of his protégé.

"Come along, Isaac!" bellowed Borg, high up in the air, "come along, Jew, let's borrow money from each other!"

"How much do you want?" asked Levi, waving his pocket book.

"I never borrow less than fifty!"

At the next moment Borg had slid to the ground and pocketed the note. Then he took off his overcoat.

"Put it on again immediately!" commanded Struve.

"What do you say? I'm to put it on again? Who are you to order me about? What? Do you want a fight?"

He smashed his hat against the tree, took off coat and waistcoat, and let the rain beat on his shirt.

"Come here, you rascal! Let's have a fight!"

He seized Struve round the waist, and, staggering backwards, both of them fell into the ditch.

Falk hurried away as fast as he could. And for a long time he could hear behind him outbursts of laughter and shouts of bravo. He could distinguish Levi's voice yelling: "It's divine, it's colossal—it's colossal!" And Borg's: "Traitor! Traitor!"

CHAPTER XX. ON THE ALTAR.

The clock in the Town-hall Vaults of X-köping thundered the seventh hour of an October evening as the manager of the Municipal Theatre came in. He beamed as a toad may beam after a good meal; he looked happy, but his facial muscles, not accustomed to express such emotions, drew the skin into worried folds and disfigured him still more than usual. He nodded patronizingly to the little shrivelled head-waiter who was standing behind the bar counting the guests.

"Well, and how's the world treating you?" screamed the manager in German—he had dropped the habit of speaking long ago.

"Thank you!" replied the head-waiter in the same language, and as this was all the German the two gentlemen knew, the conversation was continued in Swedish.

"Well, what do you think of the lad Gustav? Wasn't his Don Diego excellent? Don't you admit that I can make actors? What?"

"There's no denying that! Fancy, that boy! It's quite true what you said, sir. It's easier to do something with a man who hasn't been ruined by book-learning."

"Books are the ruin of a good many people. Nobody knows that better than I do. However, do you know anything about books? I do! You will see queer things when young Rehnhjelm plays Horatio! I've promised him the part, because he gave me no peace; but I've also warned him not to look to me for any assistance. I don't want to be held responsible for his failure; I also told him that I was allowing him to play the part to show him how difficult it is to act when one has no talent. Oh! He shall have such a snub that he'll never look at a part again. See if he won't! But that isn't what I want to say to you! Have you got two vacant rooms?"

"The two small ones?"

"Just so!"

"They're at your disposal, sir!"

"Supper for two, the best you can do! You'd better do the waiting yourself."

He did not shout the last few words; the head-waiter bowed; he had understood.

At this moment Falander entered the room. He took his accustomed seat without as much as a look at the manager. The latter rose immediately. "At eight then," he whispered, as he passed the bar and went out.

The head-waiter brought Falander a bottle of absinth, and all the usual trimmings. As the actor seemed disinclined to enter into conversation, the head-waiter wiped the table with his napkin; when that was no good, he refilled the match-stand, and said:

"Supper to-night, the small rooms! Hm!"

"Of whom and of what are you talking?"

"Of him who's just gone out."

"I see! But that's unusual, he's generally so mean. Supper for one?"

"For two," replied the head-waiter, winking. "In the small rooms, hm!"

Falander pricked up his ears, but at the same time he felt ashamed to be listening to gossip and dropped the subject; but that was not what the head-waiter wanted.

"I wonder who it is? His wife is ill, and...."

"What does it matter to us? Let the monster sup with whom he likes! Have you an evening paper?"

The head-waiter was saved a reply. Rehnhjelm was approaching the table, radiant, like a man who sees a ray of light on his path.

"Leave the absinth alone to-night," he said, "and be my guest. I am happy, I could cry."

"What has happened?" asked Falander uneasily. "Surely, he hasn't given you a part?"

"He has, you pessimist! I'm to play Horatio...."

Falander's face clouded.

"And she'll play Ophelia."

"How do you know?"

"I feel it."

"You and your premonitions! But after all, it wasn't so difficult to guess. Don't you think she deserves it? Have they a better Ophelia in the whole company?"

"No, I admit that! Do you like your part?"

"Oh! It's splendid!"

"It's extraordinary how opinions differ."

"What do *you* think?"

"I think that he is the greatest rascal at the whole court; he says Yes to everything: 'Yes, my prince; yes, my good prince.' If he were really Hamlet's friend, he would sometimes say No, and not always agree with him like any other sycophant."

"Are you going to overthrow another of my ideals?"

"I will overthrow all your false idols! How can you—as long as you look upon all paltry creations of man as great and splendid—strive after the eternal? If you see perfection and excellence in everything here below, how can you yearn for the really perfect? Believe me, pessimism is the truest idealism! It is a Christian doctrine too, if that will salve your conscience, for Christianity teaches us that the world is a vale of tears from which death will deliver us!"

"Can't you let me believe that the world is beautiful? Can't you let me be grateful to Him who is the giver of all good things, and rejoice in the happiness life has to offer?"

"Yes, yes, my boy, rejoice, rejoice and believe and hope! As all men strive for the same thing—happiness—you will have the 1,439,134,300th part of a chance of winning it, seeing that the denominator of this fraction represents the number of people on this earth. Is the happiness which has come to you to-day worth the torture and humiliations of the last few months? And moreover—what is this great piece of luck? You have been given a part to play, a part in which you cannot make a success—by which I don't mean that you necessarily need be a failure. Are you sure that...."

He paused for breath.

"That Agnes will have a success in the part of Ophelia? She may make good use of the rare chance and get as much out of the part as most actresses do. I am sorry I made you feel sad; don't believe what I said; after all, who knows whether I am right or wrong?"

"If I didn't know you better, I might believe you that you're jealous."

"No, my boy; nothing would please me more than to see yours and all men's wishes speedily fulfilled; then the thoughts of men might turn to higher things. Perhaps that is the meaning of life."

"You can afford to say that so calmly; you have had success long ago."

"Isn't this a state of mind much to be desired? We do not yearn for happiness so much, as for the faculty of being able to smile at our ardent efforts. I say *ardent* advisedly."

Eight strokes thundered through the room. Falander rose hastily as if he were going to leave, brushed his hand across his forehead and sat down again.

"Has Agnes gone to see Aunt Beata to-night?" he asked casually.

"What makes you think so?"

"I'm merely supposing it because you are sitting here so quietly. She told you she would read her part to her, as the time is so short, didn't she?"

"Yes; have you seen her to-night?"

"No! On my word of honour, I haven't! Only I can't think of anything else which would prevent her from spending a free evening with you."

"You guessed correctly. She urged me to go out and spend the evening with friends; she thinks I'm too much at home. The dear girl! She has such a tender and loving little heart."

"Yes, very tender!"

"I only once waited for her in vain; her aunt had kept her till late and forgotten to send me word. I thought I was going mad and couldn't sleep all night."

"You are referring to the evening of the sixth of July, I suppose?"

"You startle me! Are you watching us?"

"Why should I? I know of your engagement and aid you in every way I can. And why shouldn't I know that it was Tuesday the sixth of July? You've told me about it more than once."

"That's true!"

Neither of them spoke for a while.

"It's extraordinary," said Rehnhjelm, suddenly breaking the silence, "that happiness can make one feel melancholy; I feel uneasy to-night, and would much rather have spent the evening with Agnes. Let's go to the small rooms and send for her. She could say that friends had arrived from the country."

"She wouldn't do that; she couldn't tell a lie."

"Oh, nonsense! The woman who can't isn't born yet!"

Falander stared at Rehnhjelm with so peculiar an expression, that the latter felt puzzled.

"I'll go and see whether the little rooms are vacant," he said after a short pause; "we can send her a message, if they are."

"Come along then!"

Rehnhjelm made ready to follow him, but Falander kept him back.

"I'll be back in two minutes!"

He returned with a very white face, but perfectly calm.

"They are engaged," he said quietly.

"What a nuisance!"

"Let's keep each other company and be as jolly as we can!"

And they kept each other company, ate and drank and talked of life and love and human malice; and when they had eaten and drunk and talked enough, they went home and to bed.

CHAPTER XXI. A SOUL OVERBOARD

Rehnhjelm awoke on the following morning at four o'clock; somebody had called his name. He sat up in bed and listened—there was not a sound. He drew up the blind and looked out on a grey autumn morning, windy and rainy. He went back to bed and tried to sleep, but in vain. There were strange voices in the wind; they moaned and warned and wept and whimpered. He tried to think of something pleasant: of his happiness. He took his part and began to learn it; it seemed to be nothing but *yes, my prince*; he thought of Falander's words and could not help admitting that he was to some extent right. He tried to picture himself on the stage as Horatio; he tried to picture Agnes in the part of Ophelia, and could see in her nothing but a hypocritical schemer, spreading nets for Hamlet at Polonius's advice. He attempted to drive away the thought, and instead of Agnes he saw the coquettish Miss Jacquette, who had been the last to play the part at the Municipal Theatre.

He tried in vain to drive away these disagreeable fancies; they followed him like gnats. At last, exhausted with the strain, he fell asleep, but only to suffer the same torment in his dream; he roused himself with an effort, but soon dropped off to sleep again, and immediately the same visions disturbed him. About nine o'clock he awoke with a scream, and jumped out of bed as if he were fleeing from evil spirits. When he looked into the glass he saw that his eyes were red with weeping. He dressed hastily and as he picked up his boot, a big spider ran across the floor. The sight pleased him for he believed in the superstition that a spider is a harbinger of happiness; his good-humour was restored and he came to the conclusion that if a man wanted an undisturbed night's rest, he should avoid crabs for supper. He drank his coffee and smoked a pipe and smiled at the rain-showers and the wind. A knock at the door aroused him from his reverie; he started, for he was afraid of news, he could not tell why; but he thought of the spider and calmly opened the door.

A servant handed him a letter from Falander, begging him to come to his rooms at ten, on very important business.

Again he was assailed by the indescribable feeling of fear which had troubled his morning slumber; he tried to while away the time until ten. It was impossible; he dressed and went to Falander's house.

The latter had risen early; his room had been put straight and he was ready to receive his friend. He greeted Rehnhjelm cordially, but with unusual gravity. Rehnhjelm overwhelmed him with questions, but Falander refused to reply before ten o'clock. Rehnhjelm's anxiety grew and he wanted to know whether there was unpleasant news; Falander replied that nothing on earth was unpleasant as long as one looked at things in the right light. And he declared that many so-called unbearable situations could be borne quite easily if only one did not exaggerate their importance.

The time passed slowly, but at last it struck ten. A gentle double-rap at the door relieved the tension. Falander opened at once and admitted Agnes.

Without a look at those present she drew the key from the lock, and locked the door from the inside. A momentary embarrassment seized her when, on turning round, she was confronted by two men instead of only one, but her embarrassment gave way to pleasant surprise when she recognized Rehnhjelm. Throwing off her water-proof, she ran towards him; he took her in his arms and passionately pressed her to his heart, as if he had not seen her for a year.

"You've been away a long time, Agnes!"

"A long time? What do you mean?"

"I feel as if I hadn't seen you for a life-time. How splendid you are looking! Did you sleep well?"

"Do you think I look better than usual?"

"Yes! You are flushed and there are little dimples in your cheeks! Won't you say good morning to Falander?"

The latter stood quietly listening to the conversation, but his face was deadly white and he seemed to be absorbed in thought.

"How worn you are looking," said Agnes, crossing the room with the graceful movements of a kitten, as Rehnhjelm released her from his arms.

Falander made no reply. Agnes looked at him more keenly, and all at once became aware of his thoughts. A fleeting expression of trouble passed across her face, as the surface of a pond is rippled by the breeze; but she immediately regained her usual serenity, glanced at Rehnhjelm, realized the situation, and was prepared for anything.

"May we be told what important business has brought us together here, at this early hour?" she asked gaily, putting her hand on Falander's shoulder.

"Certainly," said the latter, with such firm resolution that her face paled; but at the same moment he threw back his head, as if he wanted to force his thoughts into another groove, "it's my birthday, and I want you to have breakfast with me."

Agnes, who had seen the train rushing straight at her, felt relieved; she burst into merry laughter and embraced Falander.

"But as breakfast has been ordered for eleven, we'll have to wait a while. Won't you sit down?"

There was an ominous silence.

"An angel is passing through the room," said Agnes.

"You!" said Rehnhjelm, respectfully and ardently kissing her hand.

Falander looked as if he had been thrown out of his saddle, and was making violent efforts to regain it.

"I saw a spider this morning," said Rehnhjelm, "that predicts happiness."

"*Araignée matin: chagrin*," said Falander. "Have you never heard that?"

"What does that mean?" asked Agnes.

"A spider on the morrow: grief and sorrow."

"Hm!"

154

Again they grew silent. The only sound which disturbed the stillness was the sound of the rain beating in gusts against the windows.

"I read an awfully tragic book last night," presently remarked Falander. "I hardly slept a wink."

"What book was that?" asked Rehnhjelm, without betraying very much interest.

"Its title was 'Pierre Clément,' and its subject the usual woman's game. But it was told so well that it made a great impression on me."

"May I ask what the usual woman's game is?" said Agnes.

"Faithlessness and treachery!"

"And this Pierre Clément?"

"He was, of course, betrayed. He was a young artist, in love with another man's mistress...."

"I remember the book; I liked it very much. Wasn't she later on engaged to a man whom she really loved? Yes, that was it, and during all the time she kept up her old *liaison*. The author wanted to show that a woman can love in two ways; a man only in one. That's true enough, isn't it?"

"Certainly! But the day came when her fiancé was going to compete with a picture. To cut my tale short, she gave herself to the president, and Pierre Clément was happy and could be married."

"And by this the author wanted to show that a woman will sacrifice everything to the man she loves—a man, on the other hand...."

"That is the most infamous statement I ever heard!" burst out Falander.

He rose, went to his writing-desk, threw open the flap and took out a black box.

"Here," he said, handing it to Agnes; "go home and rid the world of a monster."

"What's that?" laughed Agnes, opening the box and taking out a six-barrelled revolver. "I say, what a sweet thing! Didn't you use this as Carl Moor? I believe it is loaded."

She raised the revolver and fired up the chimney.

"Lock it up," she said, "this is no toy, my friends."

Rehnhjelm had watched the scene speechlessly. He understood the meaning well enough, but he was unable to say a word; and he was so much under the girl's spell, that he could not even feel angry with her. He realized that he had been stabbed, but he had as yet not had time to feel the pain.

The girl's impudence disconcerted Falander; he wanted time to recover; his moral execution had been a complete failure, and his *coup de théâtre* had been disastrous to himself.

"Hadn't we better go now?" asked Agnes, straightening her hat before the glass.

Falander opened the door.

"Go and be damned to you!" he said. "You have ruined an honest man's peace of mind."

"What are you talking about? Shut the door! It's none too warm here."

"I see, I have to speak more plainly. Where were you last night?"

"Hjalmar knows, and it's no business of yours."

"You were not at your aunt's! You had supper with the manager!"

"It's a lie!"

"I saw you at nine in the vaults of the Town-hall."

"I say it's a lie! I was at home at that time! Go and ask aunt's maid who saw me home."

"I should never have expected this from you!"

"Hadn't we better stop talking nonsense now and be off? You shouldn't read stupid books all night; then you wouldn't be in a bad temper on the next day. Put on your hats and come."

Rehnhjelm put his hand to his head to feel whether it was in its accustomed place, for everything seemed to him to be turned upside down. When he found that it was still there, he attempted to come to a clear understanding of the matter, but he was unable to do so.

"Where were you on the sixth of July?" asked Falander, with the sternness of a judge.

"What an idiotic question to ask! How can I remember what happened three months ago?"

"You were with me, but you told Hjalmar you were with your aunt."

"Don't listen to him," said Agnes, going up to Rehnhjelm and caressing him. "He's talking nonsense."

Rehnhjelm's hand shot out; he seized her by the throat and flung her on her back behind the stove, where she fell on a little pile of wood and remained lying still and motionless.

He put on his hat, but Falander had to help him with his coat, for he trembled violently.

"Come along, let's be off," he said, spitting on the hearthstone.

Falander hesitated for a moment, felt Agnes' pulse and then followed Rehnhjelm with whom he caught up in the lower hall.

"I admire you!" he said; "the matter was really beyond discussion."

"Then let it for ever remain so! We haven't much time to enjoy each other's company. I am leaving for home by the next train, to work and to forget! Let's go to the vaults now."

They went to the vaults and engaged a private room, where breakfast was served to them.

"Has my hair turned grey?" asked Rehnhjelm, passing his hand over his hair which was damp and clung closely to his skull.

"No, old man, that doesn't often happen; even I'm not grey."

"Is she hurt?"

"No!"

"It was in this room—I met her for the first time."

He rose from the table, staggered to the sofa, and threw himself on his knees by the side of it. Burying his head in the cushions, he burst into tears like a child crying in his mother's lap.

Falander took his head in both his hands, and Rehnhjelm felt something hot and scalding dropping on his neck.

"Where's your philosophy now, old fellow? Out with it! I'm drowning! Give me a straw to clutch at!"

"Poor boy! poor old boy!"

"I must see her! I must ask her forgiveness! I love her in spite of it! In spite of it! Are you sure she isn't hurt? Oh! my God, that one can be so unhappy and yet not die!"

At three o'clock in the afternoon Rehnhjelm left for Stockholm. Falander slammed the carriage door behind him and turned the handle.

CHAPTER XXII. HARD TIMES

To Sellén also the autumn had brought great changes. His powerful patron had died, and all memory of him was to be blotted out; even the memories of his kind actions were not to survive him. That Sellén's stipend was stopped went without saying, especially as the artist could not bring himself to petition for its continuance. He did not believe that he required further assistance, after having been given a helping hand once, and, moreover, there were so many younger members of his profession in greater need of it.

But he was made to realize that not only was the sun extinguished but that the smaller planets, too, suffered from total eclipse. He had worked strenuously during the summer and had made great progress in his art, but nevertheless the president declared that it had deteriorated, and that his success in the spring had been nothing more than a stroke of luck; the professor of landscape-painting had told him as a friend that he would never be a great artist, and the academician had seized the opportunity to rehabilitate himself, and clung to his first opinion. In addition to this the public taste in pictures had changed; the ignorant wealthy handful of people who were in the habit of buying pictures and therefore set the fashion, did not want landscapes, but portraits of the watering-places and summer resorts they knew; and it was difficult to sell even these; the only demand was for sentimental genre-pictures and half-nude figures.

Therefore Sellén had fallen on evil days, for he could not bring himself to paint against his better judgment. He was now renting a former photographic studio on the top of a house in Government Street. The accommodation consisted of the studio itself, with its rotten floor and leaking roof—the latter defect was not felt at present, for it was winter and the roof was covered with snow—and the old dark-room which smelt of collodium, and for this reason could only be used as a wood-or coal-shed, when circumstances permitted the purchase of fuel. The only piece of furniture was a wooden garden seat, studded with protruding nails. It was so short that a man using it as a bed—and it was always used as a bed when the owner, or rather the borrower, spent the night at home—had either to draw his knees up to his chin, or allow his legs to dangle over the side. The bedding consisted of half a rug—the other half was at the pawnbroker's—and a leather case, stuffed to bursting-point with studies and sketches.

In the dark-room was a water tap and a basin with a waste pipe—the only substitute for a dressing-table.

On a cold afternoon, a short time before Christmas, Sellén was standing before his easel, painting for the third time a new picture on an old canvas. He had just risen from his hard bed; no servant had come in to light his fire—partly because he had no servant, and partly because he had nothing with which to make a fire—no servant had brushed his clothes or brought his coffee. And yet he was standing before his easel whistling merrily, engaged in painting a brilliant sunset, when there came four knocks at the door. Sellén opened without hesitation and admitted Olle Montanus, very plainly and very lightly clad, without an overcoat.

"Good morning, Olle! How are you? Did you sleep well?"

"Thanks."

"How's the cash-box?"

"Oh! Bad!"

"And the notes?"

"There are so few in circulation."

"I see! They won't issue any more? And the valuables?"

"There aren't any."

"Do you think it's going to be a hard winter?"

"I saw a great many chatterers this morning; that means a hard winter."

"You took a morning stroll?"

"I've walked about all night, after leaving the Red Room at midnight."

"You were at the Red Room last night?"

"Yes; and I made two new acquaintances: Dr. Borg and a man called Levin."

"Oh! Those rascals! I know them! Why didn't you spend the night with them?"

"They turned up their noses at me because I had no overcoat, and I felt ashamed. But I am worn out; I'll rest for a few moments on your sofa! I've walked through the whole town and round half of it; I must try and get work to-day at a stone-mason's or I shall starve."

"Is it true that you are a member of the Workmen's Union 'Star of the North'?"

"Quite true; I'm going to lecture there on Sunday next, on Sweden."

"A good subject! Plenty to say!"

"If I should fall asleep on your sofa, don't waken me; I'm dead-beat."

"All right, old chap! Go to sleep!"

A few moments later Olle was fast asleep and snoring loudly. His head was hanging over one of the side-railings which supported his thick neck, and his legs over the other.

"Poor devil!" muttered Sellén, covering him up with his rug.

There was another knock, but as it was unfamiliar Sellén judged it wise to take no notice of it; thereupon the clamour became so furious that it dissipated his apprehensions and he opened the door to Dr. Borg and Levin. Borg was the first to speak.

"Is Falk here?"

"No!"

"Who is that sack of wood over there?" continued Borg, pointing at Olle with his snow-boot.

"Olle Montanus."

"Oh! That extraordinary fellow who was with Falk last night! Is he asleep?"

"Yes."

"Did he spend the night here?"

"Yes."

"Why haven't you a fire? It's beastly cold."

"Because I have no wood."

"Send for some then! Where's the servant? I'll make her trot."

"Gone to early service."

"Wake up that sleeping ox over there and send him!"

"No, let him sleep," objected Sellén, covering up Olle, who was still snoring loudly.

"Then I must show you another way. What's the floor-packing? Earth or rubbish?"

"I don't understand these matters," replied Sellén, carefully stepping on some sheets of cardboard which were lying on the floor.

"Have you got another piece of cardboard?"

"What are you driving at?" asked Sellén, colouring up to the roots of his hair.

"I want it, and a pair of fire-tongs."

Sellén gave him the required articles, took his sketching stool and sat down on the pieces of cardboard as if he were guarding a treasure.

Borg took off his coat, and with the help of the fire-tongs loosened a board in the floor, rotted by rain and acids.

"Confound you! What are you doing?" exclaimed Sellén.

"I used to do this in my college days at Upsala," said Borg.

"But you can't do that sort of thing at Stockholm!"

"Hang it all, I'm cold! I must have a fire."

"But there's no necessity to break up the floor in the middle of the room! It shows too much!"

"What does that matter to me! I don't live here. But this is too hard."

Meanwhile he had approached Sellén, and all of a sudden he pushed him and the stool over; in falling the artist dragged the pieces of cardboard with him, exposing the bare floor-packing underneath.

"Miscreant! To have a perfect timber-yard and not to say a word about it!"

"The rain's done it!"

"I don't care who's done it! Let's light a fire!"

He wrenched off a few pieces of wood with his strong hands and soon a fire was blazing in the grate.

Levin had watched the scene, quiet, neutral, and polite. Borg sat down before the fire and made the tongs red-hot.

Again there was a knock: three short raps and a longer one.

"That's Falk," said Sellén, opening the door.

Falk entered, looking a little hectic.

"Do you want money?" said Borg to the newcomer, laying his hand on his breast-pocket.

"What a question to ask," said Falk, looking at him doubtfully.

"How much do you want? I can let you have it."

"Are you serious?" asked Falk, and his face cleared.

"Serious? Hm! How much? The figure! The amount!"

"I could do with, say, sixty crowns."

"Good Lord, how modest you are," remarked Borg, and turned to Levin.

"Yes, it *is* very little," said the latter. "Take as much as you can get Falk while the purse is open."

"I'd rather not! Sixty crowns is all I want, and I can't afford to take up a bigger loan. But how is it to be paid back?"

"Twelve crowns every sixth month, twenty-four crowns per annum, in two instalments," said Levin promptly and firmly.

"Those are easy terms," replied Falk. "Where do you get money on those terms?"

"From the Wheelwrights' Bank. Give me paper and a pen, Levin!"

Quick as lightning Levin produced a promissory note, a pen, and a pocket inkstand. The note had already been filled up by the others. When Falk saw the figure eight hundred he hesitated for a moment.

"Eight hundred crowns?" he asked.

"You can have more if you are not satisfied."

160

"No, I won't; it's all the same who takes the money as long as it is paid up all right. But can you raise money on a bill of this sort, without security?"

"Without security? You are forgetting that we are guaranteeing it," replied Levin, with contemptuous familiarity.

"I don't want to depreciate it," observed Falk. "I'm grateful for your guarantees, but I don't believe that the bill will be accepted."

"Oh, won't it! It's accepted already," said Borg, bringing out a *bill of acceptance*, as he called it. "Go on, Falk, sign!"

Falk signed his name.

Borg and Levin were watching him, looking over his shoulders like policemen.

"Assessor," dictated Borg.

"No, I'm a journalist," objected Falk.

"That's no good; you are registered as assessor, and as such you still figure in the directory."

"Did you look it up?"

"One should be correct in matters of form," said Borg gravely.

Falk signed.

"Come here, Sellén, and witness," commanded Borg.

"I don't know whether I ought to," replied Sellén, "I've seen at home, in the country, so much misery arising from such signatures...."

"You are not in the country now, and you are not dealing with peasants. There's no reason why you shouldn't witness that Falk's signature is genuine."

Sellén signed, shaking his head.

"And now rouse that draught-ox over there and make him, too, witness the signature."

When all shaking was in vain Borg took the tongs, which were now red-hot, and held them under the sleeper's nostrils.

"Wake up, you dog, and you shall have something to eat!"

Olle jumped up and rubbed his eyes.

"You are to witness Falk's signature. Do you understand?"

Olle took the pen and wrote his name in obedience to the two guarantors' dictation. When he had done so, he turned to the bench to lie down again but Borg prevented him.

"Wait a minute," he said, "Falk must first sign a counter-guarantee."

"Don't do it, Falk," said Olle; "it'll end badly, there'll be trouble."

"Silence, you dog," bellowed Borg. "Come here, Falk! We've just guaranteed your bill, as you know; all we want now from you is a counter-guarantee in place of Struve's, against whom an action has been brought."

"What do you mean by a counter-guarantee?"

"It's only a matter of form; the loan was for eight hundred crowns on the Painters' Bank; the first payment has been made, but now that Struve has been proceeded against, we must find a substitute. It's a safe old loan and there are no risks; the money was due a year ago."

Falk signed and the other two witnessed.

Borg carefully folded the bills and gave them to Levin who immediately turned to go.

"I'll give you an hour," said Borg. "If you are not back with the money by then, I'll set the police on your track."

And satisfied with his morning's work, he stretched himself out on the seat on which Olle had been lying.

The latter staggered to the fire, lay down on the floor and curled himself up like a dog.

For a little while nobody spoke.

"I say, Olle," said Sellén presently, breaking the silence, "supposing we signed a bill of this sort...."

"You would be sent to Rindö," said Borg.

"What is Rindö?" asked Sellén.

"A convict prison in the Skerries; but in case the gentlemen should prefer the Lake of Mälar, there's a prison there called Longholm."

"But seriously," said Falk, "what happens if one can't pay on the day when the money falls due?"

"One takes up a fresh loan at the Tailors' Bank, for instance," replied Borg.

"Why don't you go to the Imperial Bank?" questioned Falk.

"Because it's rotten!" answered Borg.

"Can you make head or tail out of all this?" said Sellén to Olle.

"I don't understand a word of it," answered the latter.

"You will, when you are members of the Academy, and your names appear in the Directory."

CHAPTER XXIII. AUDIENCES

Nicholas Falk was sitting in his office; it was the morning of the day before Christmas Eve. He was a little changed; time had thinned his fair hair, and the passions had delved little channels in his face, for the acids which the parched soil distilled. He was stooping over a little book of the shape and size of the Catechism, and his busy pen seemed to prick out designs.

There was a knock at the door; immediately the book disappeared beneath the flap of his writing-desk, and was replaced by the morning paper. Falk was absorbed in its perusal when his wife entered.

"Take a seat," he said, politely.

"No, thank you; I'm in a hurry. Have you read the morning paper?"

"No!"

"But you are reading it at this very minute!"

"I've only just taken it up."

"Have you seen the review of Arvid's poems?"

"Yes."

"Well? They were much praised."

"He wrote the review himself."

"You said the same thing last night when you were reading the *Grey Bonnet*."

"What have you come here for?"

"I've just met the admiral's wife; she's accepted our invitation and said she would be delighted to meet the young poet."

"Did she really?"

"She did, indeed."

"Hm! Of course it's possible to make a mistake, although I don't admit that I made one. I suppose you're again wanting money?"

"Again? How long ago is it since you gave me any?"

"Here you are, then! But now go, and don't bother me again before Christmas; you know it's been a bad year."

"Indeed! I don't know that at all! Everybody says it's been a splendid year."

"For the agriculturist yes, but not for the insurance societies. Run away now!"

Mrs. Falk went, making way for Fritz Levin, who entered cautiously, as if he were afraid of a trap.

"What have you come for?" asked Falk.

"Oh, I just wanted to wish you a good morning in passing."

"A good idea! I've been wanting to see you."

"Have you really?"

"You know young Levi?"

"Of course I do!"

"Read this paper, aloud, please!"

Levin read, in a loud voice: "Magnificent bequest: With a generosity which is not now infrequently met with among the merchant class, the wholesale merchant Mr. Charles Nicholas Falk, in order to commemorate the anniversary of a happy marriage, has bequeathed to the crèche 'Bethlehem' the sum of twenty thousand crowns, one half of it to be paid at once, and the other half after the death of the generous donor. The bequest is all the more significant as Mrs. Falk is one of the founders of the philanthropic institution."

"Will that do?" asked Falk.

"Splendidly! The new year will bring you the order of Vasa!"

"I want you to take the deed of gift and the money to the Administrative Committee of the crèche, that is to say, to my wife, and then go and find young Levi. Do you understand?"

"Quite."

Falk gave him the deed of gift, written on parchment, and the amount.

"Count the money to see whether it is right."

Levin opened a packet of papers and stared, wide-eyed, at fifty sheets covered with lithographic designs, in all possible colours.

"Is that money?" he asked.

"These are securities," answered Falk; "fifty shares at two hundred crowns each in the 'Triton,' which I bequeath to the crèche Bethlehem."

"Haha! It's all over with the 'Triton,' then, and the rats are leaving the sinking ship!"

"I didn't say that," replied Falk, laughing maliciously.

"But if it should be the case, the crèche will be bankrupt."

"That doesn't concern me, and it concerns you even less. But there is something else I want you to do. You must—you know what I mean when I say you must...."

"I know, I know, bailiffs, promissory notes—go on!"

"You must induce Arvid to come here to dinner on Bank Holiday...."

"It will be about as easy as bringing you three hairs out of the giant's beard. Now do you admit that I was wise when I refused to give him your message of last spring? Haven't I always predicted this?"

"Did you? Well, never mind, hold your tongue and do as you are told! So much for that! There's another thing! I have noticed symptoms of remorse in my wife. She must have met her mother, or one of her sisters. Christmas is a sentimental season. Go to my mother-in-law and stir up a little strife!"

"A very unpleasant commission!"

"Off you go! Next man...."

Levin went. The next visitor was schoolmaster Nyström, who was admitted by a secret door in the background. At his entrance the morning paper was dropped, and the long, narrow book reappeared.

Nyström had gone to pieces. His body was reduced to a third of its former size, and his clothes were extremely shabby. He remained humbly standing at the door, took a much-used pocket-book out of his pocket and waited.

"Ready?" asked Falk, keeping the place in the book with his first finger.

"Ready," replied Nyström, opening the pocket-book.

"No. 26. Lieutenant Kling, 1500 crowns. Paid?"

"Not paid."

"Prolong, with extra interest and commission. Call at his private address."

"Never receives at home."

"Threaten him by post with a visit at the barracks."

"No. 27. Judge Dahlberg, 800 crowns. Let's see. Son of the wholesale merchant Dahlberg, estimated at 35,000. Grant a respite at present, but see that he pays the interest. Keep an eye on him."

"He never pays the interest."

"Send him a postcard to his office."

"No. 28. Captain Stjernborst, 4000. Good for nothing fellow, that! Paid?"

"Not paid."

"Good. Instructions: Call on him at noon at the guards room. Dress—you that is—compromisingly. Your red overcoat with the yellow seams, you know what I mean."

"No use! I've called on him at the guards room in the depth of the winter without any overcoat."

"Then go to his guarantors!"

"I've been and they told me to go to hell. They said that a guarantee was only a matter of form."

"Then call on him on a Wednesday afternoon at one o'clock at the offices of the 'Triton'; take Andersson with you, then there'll be two of you."

"Been done already."

"Has it? How did the directors take it?" asked Falk, rising.

"They were embarrassed."

"Really? Much embarrassed?"

"Much embarrassed."

"And he himself?"

"He took us into the corridor and promised to pay if we never called on him there again."

"Indeed! He spends two hours a week there, and receives six thousand crowns, because his name is Stjernborst. Let's see! It's Saturday to-day. Be at the 'Triton' punctually at half-past twelve; if you should see me there, which I expect you will, not a flicker of an eyelid. Do you understand? Right! Any fresh business?"

"Thirty-five new requests."

"Yes, yes, it's Christmas Eve to-morrow."

Falk turned over a bundle of promissory notes; every now and then he smiled, or muttered a word.

"Good Heavens! Has he come to that? And this one—and that one—who was looked upon as such a steady fellow! Yes, yes—hard times are in store for all of us. Oh! He, too, wants money? Then I shall buy his house...."

Another knock at the door. The desk was closed, papers and catechism vanished into thin air, and Nyström disappeared through the secret door.

"At half-past twelve," whispered Falk, as he went. "One thing more! Have you finished the poem?"

"Yes," replied a muffled voice.

"Right! Keep Levin's promissory note in readiness, so that it can be submitted to his head office at any time. Some day I shall smash him. The rascal's deceitful."

He arranged his tie, pulled out his cuffs and opened the door leading to a little waiting-room.

"Ah! Good morning, Mr. Lundell! Very glad to see you! Please come in! How are you? I had locked my door for a few moments."

It really was Lundell; Lundell dressed in the height of fashion like a shop assistant; he wore a watch-chain, rings, gloves and overshoes.

"I am not calling at an inconvenient time, I hope?"

"Not at all! Do you think, Mr. Lundell, that you will be able to finish it by to-morrow?"

"Must it be finished by to-morrow?"

"It absolutely must! It will be a red-letter day for the crèche to-morrow; Mrs. Falk will publicly present my portrait to the institution, to be hung in the dining-room."

"Then we must not let any obstacles stand in our way," replied Lundell, taking an easel and an almost finished canvas from a cupboard. "If you will sit to me for a few moments, sir, I will give the picture the finishing touches."

"With all the pleasure in the world."

Falk sat down in a chair, crossed his legs, threw himself into the attitude of a statesman and tried to look aristocratic.

"Won't you talk, sir? Although your face is an exceedingly interesting one when at rest, yet the more characteristics I can bring out, the better."

Falk smirked; a glimmer of pleasure and gratification lit up his coarse features.

"I hope you'll be able to dine with us on bank holiday, Mr. Lundell?"

"Thank you...."

"You'll be able to study the faces of many men of distinction, then, men whose features deserve being fixed on canvas far more than mine do."

"Perhaps I may have the honour of painting them?"

"You will, if I recommend you."

"Oh, do you really think so?"

"Certainly I do!"

"I just caught a new expression in your face. Try and keep it for a few moments. There! This is excellent! I'm afraid I shall have to work at this portrait all day long. There are so many details which one only discovers gradually. Your face is rich in interesting features."

"In that case we had better dine together! We must see a good deal of each other, Mr. Lundell, so that you may have an opportunity of studying my face for a second edition, which it is always well to have. Really, I must say, there are few people to whom I felt so strongly drawn from the first moment, as I did to you, Mr. Lundell."

"Oh, my dear sir!"

"And let me tell you that my eyes are keen and well able to distinguish truth from flattery."

"I knew that from the first," answered Lundell unscrupulously. "My profession has given me an insight into human character."

"You are a very keen observer indeed. Not everybody understands me. My wife, for instance...."

"Oh! Women cannot be expected...."

"No, that wasn't altogether what I meant. But may I offer you a glass of good old port?"

"Thank you, sir; I never drink when I'm working, on principle...."

"Quite right! I respect this principle—I always respect principles—all the more because I share it."

"But when I'm not at work, I enjoy a glass."

"Just as I do."

It struck half-past twelve. Falk rose.

"Excuse me, I must leave you for a short time, on business. I shall be back almost immediately."

"Certainly, business first."

Falk put on his hat and coat and went. Lundell was left alone.

He lit a cigar and studied the portrait. No observer, however keen, could have guessed his thoughts; he had acquired sufficient knowledge of the art of life to hide his opinions even when he was alone; nay, more than that, he was afraid of coming to a clear understanding with himself.

CHAPTER XXIV. ON SWEDEN

They had arrived at the dessert. The champagne sparkled in the glasses which reflected the rays of light from the chandelier in Nicholas Falk's dining-room. Arvid was greeted on all sides with friendly hand-shakes, compliments and congratulations, warnings and advice; everybody wanted to be present and share in his triumph, for he had had a decided success.

"Assessor Falk! I'm delighted!" said the President of the Board of Payment of Employés' Salaries, nodding to him across the table. "I fully appreciate your talent."

Arvid tranquilly pocketed the insulting compliment.

"Why are your poems so melancholy?" asked a young beauty on the poet's right. "One might almost think you were suffering from an unhappy love-affair."

"Assessor Falk, allow me to drink your health," said the chief editor of the *Grey Bonnet*, from the left, stroking his long, blond beard. "Why don't you write for my paper?"

"I shouldn't think you would print my articles," replied Arvid.

"I don't see why we shouldn't."

"Our opinions differ so very widely...."

"Oh! That isn't half as bad as you think. One compromises. We have no opinions."

"Your health, Falk!" shouted the excited Lundell, from the other side of the table. "Your health!"

Levi and Borg had to hold him, otherwise he would have risen and made a speech. It was for the first time that Lundell was invited to a dinner of this sort, and the brilliant assembly and luxurious food and drink intoxicated him; but as all the guests were more or less merry, he fortunately excited no unpleasant attention.

Arvid Falk's heart beat faster at the sight of all these people who had readmitted him to their circle without asking for explanations or apologies. It gave him a sense of security to sit on those old chairs, which had been a part of the home of his childhood. With a feeling of melancholy he recognized the tall table-centre which in the old times had only seen daylight once a year. But the number of new people distracted him; their friendly faces did not deceive him; certainly they did not wish him evil, but their friendship depended on a combination of circumstances.

Moreover, he saw the whole entertainment in the light of a masquerade. What mutual interest could possibly form a bond between his uncultured brother and Professor Borg, the man with the great scientific reputation? They were shareholders in the same company! What was the proud Captain Gyllenborst doing here? Had he come for the sake of the dinner? Impossible, even though a man will go a long way for the sake of a good dinner. And the President? The Admiral? There must have been invisible ties, strong, unbreakable ties perhaps.

The mirth increased, but the laughter was too shrill; the lips were overflowing with wit, but the wit was biting. Falk felt ill at ease; it seemed to him that his father's eyes were looking angrily at the assembly from the painted canvas which hung over the piano.

Nicholas Falk beamed with satisfaction; he neither saw nor heard any unpleasantness, but he avoided meeting his brother's eyes as much as possible. They had not spoken to each other yet, for Arvid, in compliance with Levin's instructions, had not arrived until after all the guests had been assembled.

The dinner was approaching its end. Nicholas made a speech on "the stamina and firm resolution" which are necessary to accomplish a man's purpose: the achievement of financial independence and a good social position. "These two qualities," said the speaker, "raise a man's self-respect and endow him with that firmness without which his efforts are unavailing, at any rate as far as the general good is concerned. And the general welfare, gentlemen, must always be our highest endeavour; I have no doubt that—if the truth were known—it is the ambition of every one here present. I drink the health of all those who have this day honoured my house, and I hope that I may often—in the future—enjoy the same privilege."

Captain Gyllenborst, who was slightly intoxicated, replied in a lengthy, facetious speech which, delivered at a different house, before people in a different mood, would have been called scandalous.

He abused the commercial spirit which was spreading, and declared that he had plenty of self-respect, although he was by no means financially independent; he had been obliged, this very morning, to settle some business of a most disagreeable nature—but in spite of this he had sufficient strength of character to be present at the banquet; and as far as his social position was concerned, it was second to none—he felt sure that this was everybody's opinion, for otherwise he would not be sitting at this table, the guest of so charming a host.

When he had concluded, the party drew a breath of relief. "It was as if a thundercloud had passed over our heads," remarked the beauty, and Arvid Falk heartily agreed.

There was so much humbug, so much deceit in the atmosphere that Arvid longed to take his leave. These people, who appeared so honest and respectable, seemed to be held by an invisible chain at which they tore every now and then with suppressed fury. Captain Gyllenborst treated his host with open, though facetious contempt. He smoked a cigar in the drawing-room, generally behaved like a boor, and took no notice whatever of the ladies. He spat in the fire-place, mercilessly criticized the oleographs on the walls, and loudly expressed his contempt for the mahogany furniture. The other gentlemen were indifferent; they gave Falk the impression that they were on duty.

Irritated and upset, he left the party unnoticed.

In the street below stood Olle waiting for him.

"I really didn't think you would come," said Olle. "It's so beautifully light up there."

"What a reason! I wish you'd been there!"

"How is Lundell getting on in smart society?"

"Don't envy him. He won't have an easy time if he's going to make his way as a portrait-painter. But let's talk of something else. I have been longing for this evening, so as to study the working man at close quarters. It will be like a breath of fresh air after these deadly fumes; I feel as if I were allowed to take a stroll in the wood, after having long been laid up in a hospital. I wonder whether I shall be disillusioned."

"The working man is suspicious; you will have to be careful."

"Is he generous? Free from pettiness? Or has the pressure which has lain on him for so long spoiled him?"

"You'll be able to see for yourself. Most things in this world differ from our expectations."

"That's true, unfortunately."

Half an hour later they had arrived in the great hall of the working men's union "Star of the North." The place was already crowded. Arvid's black dress-coat did not create a good impression; he caught many an unfriendly glance from angry eyes.

Olle introduced Arvid to a tall, gaunt man with a face full of passion, who seemed to be troubled with an incessant cough.

"Joiner Eriksson!"

"That's me," said the latter, "and is this one of those gentlemen who want to put up for election? He doesn't look big enough for that."

"No, no," said Olle, "he's here for the newspaper."

"Which newspaper? There are so many different sorts. Perhaps he's come to make fun of us?"

"No, no, nothing of the sort," said Olle. "He's a friend, and he'll do all he can for you."

"I see! That alters the matter. But I don't trust those gentlemen; one of them lived with us, that is to say, we lived in the same house, in the White Mountains; he was the landlord's agent—Struve was the rascal's name."

There was a rap with the hammer. The chair was taken by an elderly man, Wheelwright Löfgren, alderman and holder of the medal *Litteris et artibus*. He had held many offices and acquired a great deal of dramatic routine. A certain venerability, capable of quelling storms and silencing noisy meetings, characterized him. His broad face, ornamented by side-whiskers and a pair of spectacles, was framed by a judge's wig.

The secretary who sat at his side was one of the supernumeraries of the great Board of Functionaries; he wore eye-glasses and expressed with a peasant's grin his dissatisfaction with everything that was said.

The front bench was filled by the most aristocratic members of the Union: officers, Government officials, wholesale merchants; they supported all loyal resolutions, and with their superior parliamentary skill voted against every attempt at reform.

The secretary read the minutes, which the front bench approved.

Next the first item of the agenda was read:

"The Preparatory Committee would suggest that the working men's union 'Star of the North' should express the dissatisfaction which every right-thinking citizen must feel in regard to the unlawful movements which under the name of strikes are spreading nearly all over Europe."

"Is this the pleasure of the Union?"

"Yes, yes!" shouted the front bench.

"Mr. President!" called out the joiner from the White Mountains.

"Who is making so much noise at the back?" asked the chairman, looking over his spectacles with a face which suggested that he would presently have recourse to the cane.

"Nobody is making any noise; I am asking for permission to speak."

"Who is I?"

"Master-joiner Eriksson."

"Are you a master? Since when?"

"I am a journeyman out of my time; I have never had the means to be made free of the city, but I am every bit as skilful as any other master and I work on my own account."

"I request the journeyman-joiner Eriksson to sit down and stop interfering. Is it the pleasure of the Union to reply to the question in the affirmative?"

"Mr. Chairman!"

"What is the matter?"

"I ask permission to speak! Let me speak!" bellowed Eriksson.

There was a murmur on the back benches: "Eriksson's turn to speak."

"Journeyman Eriksson—do you spell your name with an x or a z?" asked the chairman, prompted by the secretary.

The front bench shook with laughter.

"I don't spell, gentlemen, I discuss," said the joiner with blazing eyes. "I discuss, I say. If I had the gift of making speeches, I should show you that the strikers are right; for if masters and principals grow fat because they have nothing to do but to fawn and cringe at levees, and similar ceremonies, the working man must pay the piper with his sweat. We know why you won't pay us just wages; it's because we should get the Parliamentary vote, and that's what you are afraid of...."

"Mr. Chairman!"

"Captain von Sporn!"

"Mr. Chairman, gentlemen! It is much to be regretted that at a meeting of this Union, which has a reputation for dignified conduct (last displayed at the Royal wedding), people without the smallest trace of Parliamentary tact should be permitted to compromise a respectable society by a shameless and reckless contempt of all seemliness. Believe me, gentlemen, such a thing could never have happened in a country where from early youth military discipline...."

"Conscription," said Eriksson to Olle.

"... had been the rule; where the habit of controlling oneself and others had been acquired! I believe I am expressing the general feeling of the meeting when I say that I hope that such a distressing scene may never again occur amongst us. I say us—for I, too, am a working man—we all are in the sight of the Eternal—

and I say it as a member of this Union. The day would be a day of mourning when I should find myself compelled to withdraw the words which I recently uttered at another meeting (it was at the meeting of the National League of Promoters of Conscription), the words: 'I have a high opinion of the Swedish working man.'"

"Hear, hear! Hear, hear!"

"Does the meeting accept the suggestion of the Preparatory Committee?"

"Yes! Yes!"

"Second item: At the instigation of several members of the Union, the Preparatory Committee submit to the meeting the proposal to collect a sum, not exceeding three thousand crowns, as a testimonial to the Duke of Dalsland at his forthcoming confirmation. The gift is to be an expression of the gratitude of the working man to the Royal Family and, more especially, of his disapproval of those working men's disturbances which under the name of 'Commune' devastated the French capital."

"Mr. Chairman!"

"Doctor Haberfeld!"

"No, it's I, Eriksson; I ask permission to say a few words."

"Oh! Well! Eriksson has permission to speak."

"I merely want to point out that not the working men, but officials, lawyers, officers—conscripts—and journalists were to blame for the Commune at Paris. If I had the gift of making speeches, I should ask those gentlemen to express their ideas in an album of confessions."

"Does the meeting agree to the proposal?"

"Yes, yes!"

And the clerks began to write and to check and to chatter, exactly as they had done at the Parliamentary meetings.

"Are things always managed in this way?" asked Falk.

"Don't you think it amusing, sir?" said Eriksson. "It's enough to turn one's hair grey. I call it corruption and treachery. Nothing but meanness and selfishness. There isn't a man amongst them who has the cause really at heart. And therefore the things which must happen will happen."

"What things?"

"We'll see!" said the joiner, taking Olle's hand. "Are you ready? Hold your own ground, you'll be sharply criticized."

Olle nodded slyly.

"Stonemason, journeyman, Olle Montanus has announced a lecture on Sweden; the subject is a big one. But if he will promise not to exceed half an hour, we will hear what he has got to say. What do you say, gentlemen?"

"Hear! Hear!"

"If you please, Mr. Montanus."

Olle shook himself like a dog about to jump, and threaded his way through the assembly, who examined him with curious eyes.

The chairman began a brief conversation with the front bench, and the secretary yawned before taking up a newspaper, to show the meeting that he, for one, was not going to listen.

Olle stepped on the platform, lowered his heavy eyelids and moved his jaws, pretending to be speaking; when the room had grown really silent, so silent that everybody could hear what the chairman said to the captain, he began:

"On Sweden. Some points of view."

And after a pause:

"Gentlemen! It might be more than an unfounded supposition to say that the most productive idea and the most vigorous striving of our times is the suppression of short-sighted patriotism, which divides nations and pits them against one another as foes; we have seen the means used to gain this object, namely, international exhibitions and their results: honorary diplomas."

The audience looked puzzled. "What's he driving at?" said Eriksson. "It's rather unexpected, but it sounds all right."

"Now, as in the past, Sweden marches at the head of civilization; she has more than any other nation spread the cosmopolitan ideal, and if one may rely on statistics, she has attained a great deal. Exceptionally favourable circumstances have contributed to this result. I will examine them shortly, and then pass on to lighter subjects such as the form of government, the ground-tax, and so on."

"It's going to be rather long," said Eriksson, nudging Arvid, "but he's an amusing chap."

"Sweden, as everybody knows, was originally a German colony, and the Swedish language, which has been preserved fairly pure to our days, is neither more nor less than Low-German and its twelve dialects. This circumstance—I mean the difficulty of communicating with one another, experienced by the provinces—has been a powerful factor in counteracting the development of that unhealthy national feeling. Other fortunate facts have opposed a one-sided German influence which had reached its pinnacle when Sweden became a German province under Albrecht of Mecklenburg. The foremost of these facts is the conquest of the Danish provinces: Scania, Halland, Bleking, Bohuslän, and Dalsland; Sweden's richest provinces are inhabited by Danes who still speak the language of their country and refuse to acknowledge the Swedish rule."

"What in the name of fortune is he getting at? Is he mad?"

"The inhabitants of Scania, for instance, to this day look upon Copenhagen as their capital, and constitute the opposition in Parliament. The same thing applies to the Danish Göteborg, which does not acknowledge Stockholm as the capital of the realm. An English settlement has sprung up there and English influence is predominant. These people, the English people, fish in the waters near the coast, and during the winter very nearly all the wholesale trade is in their hands; they return to their own country in the summer and enjoy their winter profits in their villas in the Scotch Highlands. Very excellent people, though! They have even their own newspaper, in which they commend their own actions, without, it must be admitted, blaming those of others.

"Immigration is another factor of the utmost importance. We have the Fins in the Finnish forests, but we also have them in the capital, where they took refuge when the political situation drove them out of their own country. In all our more important iron-works you will find a fair number of Walloons; they came over in the seventeenth century and to this day speak their broken French. You all know that we owe the new Swedish constitution to a Walloon. Capable people, these Walloons, and very honest!"

"What in the name of heaven does it all mean?"

"In the reign of King Gustavus Adolphus a whole cargo of Scotch scum landed on our coast and took service in the army; they eventually forced their way into the House of Knights. At the East coast there are many families who cherish traditions of their immigration from Livland and other Slavonic provinces, and so it is not surprising that we frequently meet here pure Tartar types.

"I maintain that the Swedish nation is fast becoming denationalized. Open a book on heraldry and count the Swedish names! If they exceed 25 per cent. you may cut off my nose, gentlemen! Open the directory at random! I counted the letter G, and of four hundred names two hundred were foreign.

"What is the cause of this? There are many causes, but the principal ones are the foreign dynasties and the wars of conquest. If one thinks of all the scum that has sat on the Swedish throne at one time or another, one cannot help marvelling that the nation is so loyal to the king. The constitutional law that the kings of Sweden shall be foreigners is bound to be of the greatest assistance in the work of denationalization; this has been proved to be a fact.

"I am convinced that the country will gain by its alliance with foreign nations; it cannot lose anything—because it has nothing to lose. The country has no nationality; Tegnér discovered that in 1811, and short-sightedly bemoaned the fact. But his discovery came too late, for the race had already been ruined by the constant recruiting for the foolish wars of conquest. Of the one million men which inhabited the country in the days of Gustavus Adolphus, seventy thousand enlisted and were killed in the wars. I do not know for how many Charles X, Charles XI, and Charles XII were responsible; but it is easy to picture the offspring of those who remained behind, the men whom the crown had rejected as unfit for service.

"I repeat my statement that Sweden has no nationality. Can anybody tell me of anything Swedish in Sweden except her firs, pine trees, and iron-mines? And the latter will soon disappear from the market. What is our folk-lore but bad translations of French, English, and German ballads? What are the national costumes, the disappearance of which we so keenly regret, other than fragments and tatters of the aristocratic mediæval costumes? In the days of Gustavus I the dalesmen demanded that all those who wore low-cut or many-coloured dresses should be punished. Probably the gay court-dress from Burgundy had not yet filtered down to the daleswomen. But since then the fashion has changed many times.

"Tell me of a Swedish poem, a work of art, a piece of music, so specifically Swedish that it differs from all other not-Swedish ones! Show me a Swedish building! There isn't one, and if there were, it would either be bad architecture or built in a foreign style.

"I don't think I'm exaggerating when I maintain that the Swedish nation is a stupid, conceited, slavish, envious, and uncouth nation. And for this reason it is approaching its end, and approaching it with giant strides."

A tumult arose in the hall, but shouts of Charles XII could be heard above the turmoil.

"Gentlemen, Charles XII is dead; let him sleep until his next jubilee. To no one are we more indebted for our denationalisation than to him, and therefore, gentlemen, I call for three cheers for Charles XII! Gentlemen, long live Charles XII!"

"I call the meeting to order!" shouted the chairman.

"Is it possible to imagine that a nation can be guilty of a greater piece of folly than to go to foreign nations in order to learn to write poetry?

"What unsurpassable oxen they must have been to walk for sixteen hundred years behind the plough and never conceive the idea of inventing a song!

"Then a jolly fellow of the court of Charles XII came along and destroyed the whole work of denationalization. The literary language, which up to now had been German, was henceforth to be Swedish: Down with the dog Stjernhjelm!

"What was his name? Edward Stjernström!"

The chairman's hammer came down on the table with a bang. The disturbance grew. "Stop him! Down with the traitor! He's laughing at us!"

"The Swedish nation can scream and brawl, I am aware of that! They can do nothing else! And as you will not allow me to continue my lecture and discuss the Government and the royal copyholds, I will conclude by saying that the servile louts whom I have heard to-night are ripe for the autocracy which they are sure to get. Believe my words: You will have an absolute monarchy before very long!"

A push from the back jerked the words of the speaker out of his throat. He clung to the table:

"And an ungrateful race who will not listen to the truth...."

"Kick him out! Tear him to pieces!"

Olle was dragged from the platform; but to the last moment, while knocks and blows rained down on him, he yelled like a madman: "Long live Charles XII! Down with George Stjernhjelm!"

At last Olle and Arvid were standing in the street.

"Whatever were you thinking of?" asked Falk. "You must have taken leave of your senses!"

"I believe I had! I had learnt my speech by heart for the last six weeks; I knew to a word what I was going to say; but when I stood on the platform and saw all those eyes gazing at me, it all went to pieces; my artificial arguments broke down like a scaffolding; the floor underneath my feet gave way, and my thoughts became confusion. Was it very crazy?"

"Yes, it was bad, and the papers will pull you to pieces."

"That's a pity, I admit. I thought I was making it all so clear. But it *was* fun to give it them for once."

"You only injured your cause; they'll never let you speak again."

Olle sighed.

"Why in the name of fortune couldn't you leave Charles XII alone? That was your worst mistake."

"Don't ask me! I don't know!"

"Do you still love the working man?" asked Falk.

"I pity him for allowing himself to be humbugged by adventurers, and I shall never abandon his cause, for his cause is the burning question of the near future, and all your politics aren't worth a penny in comparison."

The two friends were making their way back to old Stockholm, and finally entered a café.

It was between nine and ten and the room was almost empty. A single customer was sitting near the counter. He was reading from a book to a girl who sat beside him doing needlework. It was a pretty, domestic scene, but it seemed to make a strong impression on Falk, who started violently and changed colour.

"Sellén! You here? Good evening, Beda!" he said, with artificial cordiality which sat strangely on him, shaking hands with the girl.

"Hallo! Falk, old chap!" said Sellén. "So you are in the habit of coming here too? I might have guessed it, you are hardly ever at the Red Room now."

Arvid and Beda exchanged glances. The young girl looked too distinguished for her position; she had a delicate, intelligent face, which betrayed a secret sorrow; and a slender figure. Her movements were full of self-confidence and modesty; her eyes were set in her face at a slightly upward angle; they seemed to be peering skyward as if they were anticipating evil to drop down from the clouds; with this exception they looked as if they were ready to play all the games which the whim of the moment might dictate.

"How grave you are," she said to Arvid, and her gaze dropped to her sewing.

"I've been to a grave meeting," said Arvid, blushing like a girl. "What were you reading?"

"I was reading the Dedication from Faust," said Sellén, stretching out his hand and playing with Beda's needlework.

A cloud darkened Arvid's face. The conversation became forced and restrained. Olle sat plunged in meditations, the subject of which must have been suicide.

Arvid asked for a paper and was given the *Incorruptible*. He remembered that he had forgotten to look for the review of his poems. He hastily opened the paper and on page three he found what he sought.

His eyes met neither compliments nor abuse; the article was dictated by genuine and deep interest. The reviewer found Arvid's poetry neither better nor worse than the average, but just as selfish and meaningless; he said that it treated only of the poet's private affairs, of illicit relations, real or fictitious; that it coquetted with little sins, but did not mourn over great ones; that it was no better than the English fashion-paper poetry, and he suggested that the author's portrait should have preceded the title-page; then the poems would have been illustrated.

These simple truths made a great impression on Arvid; he had only read the advertisement in the *Grey Bonnet*, written by Struve, and the review in the *Red Cap*, coloured by personal friendship. He rose with a brief good-night.

"Are you going already?" asked Beda.

"Yes; are we going to meet to-morrow?"

"Yes, as usual. Good-night."

Sellén and Olle followed him.

"She's a rare child," said Sellén, after they had proceeded a little way in silence.

"I should thank you to be a little more restrained in your criticism."

"I see. You're in love with her!"

"Yes. I hope you don't mind."

"Not in the least. I shan't get into your way!"

"And I beg you not to believe any evil of her...."

"Of course I won't! She's been on the stage...."

"How do you know? She never told me that!"

"No, but she told me; one can never trust these little devils too far."

"Oh well! there's no harm in that! I shall take her away from her surroundings as soon as I possibly can. Our relations are limited to meeting in the Haga Park at eight in the morning and drinking the water from the well."

"How sweet and simple! Do you never take her out to supper?"

"I never thought of making such an improper suggestion; she would refuse it with scorn. You are laughing! Laugh if you like! I still have faith in a woman who loves whatever class she may belong to, and whatever her past may have been. She told me that her life had not been above reproach, but I have promised never to ask her about her past."

"Is it serious then?"

"Yes, it is serious."

"That's another thing; Good-night, Falk! Are you coming with me, Olle?"

"Good night."

"Poor Falk!" said Sellén to Olle. "Now it's his turn to go through the mill. But there's no help for it; it's like changing one's teeth; a man is not grown up until he has had his experience."

"What about the girl?" asked Olle, merely in order to show a polite interest, for his thoughts were elsewhere.

"She's all right in her way, but Falk takes the matter seriously; she does too, apparently, as long as she sees any prospect of winning him; but unless Falk's quick about it, she will grow tired of waiting, and who knows whether she won't amuse herself meanwhile with somebody else? No, you don't understand these things; a man shouldn't hesitate in a love-affair, but grab with both hands; otherwise somebody else will step in and spoil the game. Have you ever been in love, Olle?"

"I had an affair with one of our servants at home; there were consequences, and my father turned me out of the house. Since then I haven't looked at a woman."

"That was nothing very complicated. But to be betrayed, as it is called, that's what hurts, I can tell you! One must have nerves like the strings of a violin to play that game. We shall see what sort of a fight Falk will make; with some men it goes very deep, and that's a pity.

"The door is open, come in Olle! I hope the beds are properly made, so that you will lie softly; but you must excuse my old bed-maker, she cannot shake up the feather-beds; her fingers are weak, don't you see, and the pillow, I'm afraid, may be hard and lumpy."

They had climbed the stairs and were entering the studio.

"It smells damp, as if the servant had aired the room or scrubbed it."

"You are laughing at yourself! There can be no more scrubbing, you have no longer a floor."

"Haven't I? Ah! That makes a difference! But what has become of it? Has it been used for fuel? There's nothing for it then, but to lie down on our mother earth, or rubbish, or whatever it may be."

They lay down in their clothes on the floor-packing, having made a kind of bed for themselves of pieces of canvas and old newspapers, and pushed cases filled with sketches underneath their heads. Olle struck a match, produced a tallow candle from his trousers pocket and put it on the floor beside him. A faint gleam flickered through the huge, bare studio, passionately resisting the volumes of darkness which tried to pour in through the colossal windows.

"It's cold to-night," said Olle, opening a greasy book.

"Cold! Oh no! There are only twenty degrees of frost outside, and thirty in here because we are so high up. What's the time, I wonder?"

"I believe St. John's just struck one."

"St. John's? They have no clock! They are so poor that they had to pawn it."

There was a long pause which was finally broken by Sellén.

"What are you reading, Olle?"

"Never mind!"

"Never mind? Hadn't you better be more civil, seeing that you are my guest?"

"An old cookery book which I borrowed from Ygberg."

"The deuce you did! Do let's read it; I've only had a cup of coffee and three glasses of water to-day."

"What would you like?" asked Olle, turning over the leaves. "Would you like some fish? Do you know what a mayonnaise is?"

"Mayonnaise? No! Read it! It sounds good!"

"Well, listen! No. 139. Mayonnaise: Take some butter, flour, and a pinch of English mustard, and make it into a smooth paste. Beat it up with good stock, and when boiling add the yolks of a few eggs; beat well and let it stand to cool."

"No, thank you; that's not filling enough...."

"Oh, but that's not all. Then take a few spoonfuls of fine salad oil, vinegar, a spoonful of cream, some white pepper—oh, yes, I see now, it's no good. Do you want something more substantial?"

"Try and find toad-in-the-hole. It's my favourite dish."

"I can't go on reading."

"Do!"

"No, leave me alone!"

They were silent. The candle went out and it was quite dark.

"Good-night, Olle; wrap yourself well up, or you'll be cold."

"What with?"

"I don't know. Aren't we having a jolly time?"

"I wonder why one doesn't kill oneself when one is so cold."

"Because it would be wrong. I find it quite interesting to live, if only to see what will come of it all in the end."

"Are your parents alive, Sellén?"

"No; I'm illegitimate. Yours?"

"Yes; but it comes to the same thing."

"You should be more grateful to Providence, Olle; one should always be grateful to Providence—I don't quite know why. But I suppose one should."

Again there was silence. The next time it was Olle who broke it.

"Are you asleep?"

"No; I'm thinking of the statue of Gustavus Adolphus; would you believe me when I...."

"Aren't you cold?"

"Cold? It's quite warm here."

"My right foot is frozen."

"Pull the paint box over you, and tuck the brushes round your sides, then you'll be warmer."

"Do you think anybody in the world is as badly off as we are?"

"Badly off? Do you call us badly off when we have a roof over our heads? Some of the professors at the Academy, men who wear three-cornered hats and swords now, were much worse off than we are. Professor Lundström slept during nearly the whole of April in the theatre in the Hop garden. There was style in that! He had the whole of the left stage-box, and he maintains that after one o'clock there wasn't a single stall vacant; there was always a good house in the winter and a bad one in the summer. Good night, I'm going to sleep now."

Sellén snored. But Olle rose and paced the room, up and down, until the dawn broke in the east; then day took pity on him and gave him the peace which night had denied him.

CHAPTER XXV. CHECKMATE

The winter passed; slowly for the sufferers, more quickly for those who were less unhappy. Spring came with its disappointed hopes of sun and verdure, and in its turn made room for the summer which was but a short introduction to the autumn.

On a May morning Arvid Falk, now a member of the permanent staff of the *Workman's Flag*, was strolling along the quay, watching the vessels loading and discharging their cargoes. He looked less well-groomed than in days gone by; his black hair was longer than fashion decreed, and he wore a beard à la Henri IV, which gave his thin face an almost savage expression. An ominous fire burned in his eyes, a fire denoting the fanatic or the drunkard.

He seemed to be endeavouring to make a choice among the vessels, but was unable to come to a decision. After hesitating for a considerable time, he accosted one of the sailors, who was wheeling a barrow full of goods on to a brig. He courteously raised his hat.

"Can you tell me the destination of this ship?" he asked timidly, imagining that he was speaking in a bold voice.

"Ship? I see no ship?"

The bystanders laughed.

"But if you want to know where this brig's bound for, go and read that bill over there!"

Falk was disconcerted, but he forced himself to say, angrily:

"Can't you give a civil reply to a civil question?"

"Go to hell, and don't stand there swearing at a fellow!—'tention!"

The conversation broke off, and Falk made up his mind. He retraced his footsteps, passed through a narrow street, crossed a market-place, and turned the first corner. Before the door of a dirty-looking house he stopped. Again he hesitated; he could never overcome his besetting sin of indecision.

A small, ragged boy with a squint came running along, his hands full of proofs in long strips; as he was going to pass Falk, the latter stopped him.

"Is the editor upstairs?" he asked.

"Yes, he's been here since seven," replied the boy, breathlessly.

"Has he asked for me?"

"Yes, more than once."

"Is he in a bad temper?"

"He always is."

The boy shot upstairs like an arrow. Falk, following on his heels, entered the editorial office. It was a hole with two windows looking on a dark street; before each of the windows stood a plain deal table, covered with paper, pens, newspapers, scissors and a gum bottle.

One of the tables was occupied by his old friend Ygberg, dressed in a ragged black coat, engaged in reading proofs. At the other table, which was Falk's, sat a man in shirt sleeves, his head covered by a black silk cap of the kind affected by the communards. His face was covered by a red beard, and his thick-set figure with its clumsy outlines betrayed the man of the people.

As Falk entered, the communard's legs kicked the table violently: he turned up his shirt-sleeves, displaying blue tattoo marks representing an anchor and an Anglo-Saxon R, seized a pair of scissors, savagely stabbed the front page of a morning paper, cut out a paragraph, and said, rudely, with his back to Falk:

"Where have you been?"

"I've been ill," replied Falk, defiantly, as he thought, but humbly as Ygberg told him afterwards.

"It's a lie! You've been drinking! I saw you at a café last night...."

"Surely I can go where I please."

"You can do what you like; but you've got to be here at the stroke of the clock, according to our agreement. It's a quarter past eight. I am well aware that gentlemen who have been to college, where they imagine they learn a lot, have no idea of method and manners. Don't you call it ill-bred to be late at your work? Aren't you behaving like a boor when you compel your employer to do your work? What? It's the world turned upside down! The employé treats the master—the employer, if you like—as if he were a dog, and capital is oppressed."

"When did you come to these conclusions?"

"When? Just now, sir! just now! And I trust these conclusions are worth considering, in spite of that. But I discovered something else; you are an ignoramus; you can't spell! Look at this! What's written here? Read it! 'We hope that all those who will have to go through their drill next year....' Is it possible? '*Who ... next year....*'"

"Well, that's quite right," said Falk.

"Right? How dare you say it's right? It's customary to say *who in the next year*, and consequently it should also be written in this form."

"That's right, too; definitions of time govern either the accusative or...."

"None of your learned palaver! Don't talk nonsense to me! Besides this you spell ex-ercise with an x only, although it should be spelt *ex-sercise*. Don't make excuses—is it ex-ercise or ex-sercise?"

"Of course people say...."

"People say—therefore ex-sercise is right; the customary pronunciation must be correct. Perhaps, all things considered, I'm a fool? Perhaps I can't spell correctly? But enough, now! Get to work and another time pay a little more attention to the clock."

He jumped up from his chair with a yell, and boxed the ears of the printer's boy.

"Are you sleeping in bright daylight, you young scamp? I'll teach you to keep awake. You are not yet too old for a thrashing."

He seized the victim by the braces, threw him on a pile of unsold papers, and beat him with his belt.

"I wasn't asleep! I wasn't asleep! I was only closing my eyes a little," howled the boy.

"What, you dare to deny it? You've learned to lie, but I will teach you to speak the truth! Were you asleep or were you not asleep? Tell the truth or you'll be sorry for it."

"I wasn't asleep," whimpered the boy, too young and inexperienced to get over his difficulty by telling a lie.

"I see, you mean to stand by your lie, you hardened little devil! You insolent liar!"

He was going to continue the thrashing when Falk rose, approached the editor, and said firmly:

"Don't touch him! I saw that he was not asleep!"

"By jove! Listen to him! Who the dickens are you? Don't touch him! Who said those words? I must have heard a gnat buzzing. Or perhaps my ears deceived me. I hope so! I do hope so! Mr. Ygberg! You are a decent fellow. You haven't been to college. Did you happen to see whether this boy, whom I'm holding by the braces like a fish, was asleep or not?"

"If he wasn't asleep," replied Ygberg, phlegmatically and obligingly, "he was just on the point of dropping off."

"Well answered! Would you mind holding him, Mr. Ygberg, while I give him a lesson with my cane in telling the truth?"

"You've no right to beat him," said Falk. "If you dare to touch him, I shall open the window and call for the police."

"I am master in my own house and I always thrash my apprentices. He is an apprentice and will be employed in the editorial office later on. That's what's going to be done, although there are people who imagine that a paper can only be properly edited by a man who has been to college. Speak up, Gustav, are you learning newspaper work? Answer, but tell the truth, or...."

Before the boy had time to reply, the door was opened and a head looked in—a very striking head, and certainly not one that might have been expected in such a place; but it was a well-known head; it had been painted five times.

At the sight of it the editor strapped his belt round him, hastily put on his coat, bowed and smiled.

The visitor asked whether the editor was disengaged? He received a satisfactory reply, and the last remnant of the working man disappeared when a quick movement swept the communard's cap off the editor's head.

Both men went into an inner office and the door closed behind them.

"I wonder what the Count's after?" said Ygberg, with the air of a schoolboy, when the master had left the class-room.

"I don't wonder in the least," said Falk; "I think I know the kind of rascal he is, and the kind of rascal the editor is. But I am surprised to find that you have changed from a mere blockhead into an infamous wretch, and that you lend yourself to these disgraceful acts."

"Don't lose your temper, my dear fellow! You were not at the House last night?"

"No! In my opinion Parliament is a farce, except in so far as private interests are concerned. What about the 'Triton'?"

"The question was put to the vote, and it was resolved that the Government, in view of the greatness, the patriotism, which characterized the enterprise, should take over the debentures while the society went into liquidation, that is to say, settled the current affairs."

"Which means that Government will prop up the house while the foundation crumbles away, so as to give the directors time to get out of harm's way."

"You would rather that all those small...."

"I know what you are going to say, all those small capitalists. Yes, I would rather see them working with their small capital than idling away their time and lending it out at interest; but, above all things, I should like to see those sharpers in prison; it would help to put a stop to these swindles. But they call it political economy! It's vile! There's something else I want to say: You covet my post. You shall have it! I hate the idea of your sitting in your corner with a heart filled with bitterness, because you have to sweep up after me in reading proofs. There are already too many of my unprinted articles lying on the desk of this contemptible apostle of liberty to tempt me to go on telling cock-and-bull stories. The *Red Cap* was too Conservative to please me, but the *People's Flag* is too dirty."

"I am glad to see you relinquishing your chimeras and listening to common sense. Go to the *Grey Bonnet*, you'll have a chance there."

"I have lost the illusion that the cause of the oppressed lies in good hands, and I think it would be a splendid mission to enlighten the people on the value of public opinion—especially printed public opinion—and its origin; but I shall never abandon the cause."

The door to the inner room opened again, and the editor came out. He stood still in the middle of the office and said, in an unnaturally conciliatory voice, almost politely:

"I want you to look after the office for a day, Mr. Falk. I have to go away on important business. Mr. Ygberg will assist you so far as the daily business is concerned. His Lordship will be using my room for a few minutes. I hope, gentlemen, you will see that he has everything he wants."

"Oh, please don't trouble," came the Count's voice from inside the room, where he was sitting bent over a manuscript.

The editor went and, strange to say, two minutes later the Count went also; he had waited just long enough to avoid being seen in the company of the editor of the *Workman's Flag*.

"Are you sure that he's gone?" asked Ygberg.

"I hope so," said Falk.

"Then I'll go and have a look at the market. By-the-by, have you seen Beda since?"

"Since when?"

"Since she left the café and went to live in a room by herself."

"How do you know she did?"

"Do control your temper, Falk. You'll never get on in the world unless you do."

"Yes, you're right. I must take matters more calmly, or else I'll go out of my mind! But that girl, whom I loved so dearly! How shamefully she has treated me! To give to that clumsy boor all she denied to me! And then to have the face to tell me that it proved the purity of her love for me!"

"Most excellent dialectics! And she is quite right too, for her first proposition is correct. She does love you, doesn't she?"

"She's running after me, anyhow."

"And you?"

"I hate her with all my soul, but I am afraid to meet her."

"Which proves that you are still in love with her."

"Let's change the subject!"

"You really must control yourself, Falk! Take an example from me! But now I'll go and sun myself; one should enjoy life as much as possible in this dreary world. Gustav, you can go and play buttons for an hour, if you like."

Falk was left alone. The sun threw his rays over the steep roof opposite and warmed the room; he opened the window and put out his head for a breath of fresh air, but he only breathed the pungent odours of the gutter. His glance swept the street on the right and far away in the distance he saw a part of a steamer, a few waves of the Lake of Mälar glittering in the sunlight, and a hollow in the rocks on the other side, which were just beginning to show a little green here and there. He thought of the people whom that steamer would take into the country, who would bathe in those waves and feast their eyes on the young green. But at this moment the whitesmith below him began to hammer a sheet of iron, so that house and window panes trembled; two or three labourers went by with a rattling, evil-smelling cart, and an odour of brandy, beer, sawdust, and pine-branches poured out of the inn opposite. He shut the window and sat down at his table.

Before him lay a heap of about a hundred provincial papers, from which it was his task to make cuttings. He took off his cuffs and began to look through them. They smelt of oil and soot and blackened his hands—that was their principal feature. Nothing he considered worthy of reprinting was of any use, for he had to consider the programme of his paper. A report to the effect that the workmen of a certain factory had given the foreman a silver snuff-box had to be cut out; but the notice of a manufacturer having given five hundred crowns to his working-men's funds had to be ignored. A paragraph reporting that the Duke of Halland had handselled a pile-driver, and Director Holzheim celebrated the event in verses, had to be cut out and reproduced in full "because the people liked to read this kind of thing"; if he could add a little biting sarcasm, all the better, for then "they were sure to hear about it."

Roughly speaking, the rule was to cut out everything said in favour of journalists and working men and everything depreciating clergymen, officers, wholesale merchants (not retail), the professions, and famous writers. Moreover, at least once a week, it was his business to attack the management of the Royal Theatre, and severely criticize the frivolous musical comedies produced in the Little Theatre, in the name of morality and public decency—he had noticed that the working men did not patronize these theatres. Once a month the town councillors had to be accused of extravagance. As often as opportunity arose the form of government, not Government itself, had to be assailed. The editor severely censored all attacks on certain members of Parliament and ministers. Which? That was a mystery unknown to even the editor; it depended on a combination of circumstances which only the secret proprietor of the paper could deal with.

Falk worked with his scissors until one of his hands was black. He had frequent recourse to the gum-bottle, but the gum smelt sour and the heat in the room was stifling. The poor aloe, capable of enduring thirst like a camel, and patiently receiving countless stabs from an irritated steel-nib, increased the terrible resemblance to a desert. It had been stabbed until it was covered with black wounds; its leaves shot, like a bundle of donkeys' ears out of the parched mould. Falk probably had a vague consciousness of something of this sort, as he sat, plunged in thought, for before he could realize what he was doing, he had docked off all the ear lobes. When he perceived what he had done, he painted the wounds with gum and watched it drying in the sun.

He vaguely wondered for a few moments how he was to get dinner, for he had strayed on to that path which leads to destruction, so-called *poor circumstances*. Finally he lit a pipe and watched the soothing smoke rising and bathing, for a few seconds in the sunshine. It made him feel more tolerant of poor Sweden, as she expressed herself in these daily, weekly, and monthly reports, called the Press.

He put the scissors aside and threw the papers into a corner; he shared the contents of the earthen water-bottle with the aloe; the miserable object looked like a creature whose wings had been clipped; a spirit standing in a bog on its head, digging for something; for pearls, for instance, or at any rate, for empty shells.

Then despair, like a tanner, seized him again with a long hook, and pushed him down into the vat, where he was to be prepared for the knife, which should scrape his skin off and make him like everybody else. And he felt no remorse, no regret at a wasted life, but only despair at having to die in his youth, die the spiritual death, before he had had an opportunity of being of use in the world; despair that he was being cast into the fire as a useless reed.

The clock on the German church struck eleven, and the chimes began to play "Oh blessed land" and "My life a wave"; as if seized by the same idea, an Italian barrel-organ, with a flute accompaniment, began to play "The Blue Danube." So much music put new life into the tinsmith below, who began hammering his iron-sheet with redoubled energy.

The din and uproar prevented Falk from becoming aware of the opening of the door and the entrance of two men. One of them had a tall, lean figure, an aquiline nose and long hair; the other one was short, blond, and thick set; his perspiring face much resembled the quadruped which the Hebrews consider more unclean than any other. Their outward appearance betrayed an occupation requiring neither much mental nor great physical strength; it had a quality of vagueness, pointing to irregularity of work and habits.

"Hsh!" whispered the tall man, "are you alone?"

Falk was partly pleased, partly annoyed at the sight of his visitors.

"Quite alone; the Red One's left town."

"Has he? Come along then and have some dinner."

Falk had no objection; he locked the office and went with his visitors to the nearest public-house, where the three of them sat down in the darkest corner.

"Here, have some brandy," said the thick-set man, whose glazed eyes sparkled at the sight of the brandy bottle.

But Falk who had only joined his friends because he was yearning for sympathy and comfort, paid no attention to the proffered delights.

"I haven't been as miserable as this for a long time," he said.

"Have some bread and butter and a herring," said the tall man. "We'll have some caraway cheese. Here! Waiter!"

"Can't you advise me?" Falk began again. "I can't stand the Red One any longer, and I must...."

"Here! Waiter! Bring some black bread! Drink, Falk, and don't talk nonsense."

Falk was thrown out of the saddle; he made no second attempt to find sympathy with his mental difficulties, but tried another, not unusual way.

"Your advice is the brandy bottle?" he said. "Very well, with all my soul, then!"

The alcohol flowed through his veins like poison, for he was not accustomed to take strong drink in the morning; the smell of cooking, the buzzing of the flies, the odour of the faded flowers, which stood by the side of the dirty table-centre, induced in him a strange feeling of well-being. And his low companions with their neglected linen, their greasy coats, and their unwashed gaol-bird faces harmonized so well with his own degraded position, that he felt a wild joy surging in his heart.

"We were in the Deer Park last night and, by Jove! we did drink," said the stout man, once more enjoying the past delights in memory.

Falk had no answer to this, and moreover, his thoughts were running in a different groove.

"Isn't it jolly to have a morning off?" said the tall man, who seemed to be playing the part of tempter.

"It is, indeed!" replied Falk, trying to measure his freedom, as it were, with a glance through the window; but all he saw was a fire-escape and a dust-bin in a yard which never received more than a faint reflexion of the summer sky.

"Half a pint! That's it! Ah! Well and what do you say to the 'Triton'? Hahaha!"

"Don't laugh," said Falk; "many a poor devil will suffer through it."

"Who are the poor devils? Poor capitalists? Are you sorry for those who don't work, but live on the proceeds of their money? No, my boy, you are still full of prejudices! There was a funny tale in the *Hornet* about a wholesale merchant, who bequeathed to the crèche Bethlehem twenty thousand crowns, and was given the order of Vasa for his munificence; now it has transpired that the bequest was in 'Triton' shares with joint liability, and so the crèche is of course bankrupt. Isn't that lovely? The assets were twenty-five cradles and an oil painting by an unknown master. It's too funny! The portrait was valued at five crowns! Hahahaha!"

The subject of conversation irritated Falk, for he knew more of the matter than the two others.

"Did you see that the *Red Cap* unmasked that humbug Schönström who published that volume of miserable verses at Christmas?" said the stout man.

"It really was a rare pleasure to learn the truth about the rascal. I have more than once given him a sound slating in the *Copper-Snake*."

"But you were rather unjust; his verses were not as bad as you said," remarked the tall man.

"Not as bad? They were worse than mine which the *Grey Bonnet* tore to shreds. Don't you remember?"

"By-the-by, Falk, have you been to the theatre in the Deer Park?" asked the tall man.

"No!"

"What a pity! That Lundholm gang of thieves is playing there. Impudent fellow, the director! He sent no seats to the *Copper-Snake*, and when we arrived at the theatre last night, he turned us out. But he'll pay for it! You give it to the dog! Here's paper and pencil. Heading: 'Theatre and Music. Deer Park Theatre.' Now, you go on!"

"But I haven't seen the company."

"What does that matter? Have you never written about anything you hadn't seen?"

"No! I've unmasked humbugs, but I have never attacked unoffending people, and I know nothing about this company."

"They are a miserable lot. Just scum," affirmed the stout man. "Sharpen your pen and bruise his heel; you are splendid at it."

"Why don't you bruise him yourselves?"

"Because the printers know our handwriting and some of them walk on in the crowds. Moreover Lundholm is a violent fellow; he will be sure to invade the editorial office; then it will be a good thing to be able to tell him that the criticism is a communication from the public. And while you write up the stage, I will do the concerts. There was a sacred concert last week. Wasn't the man's name Daubry? With a 'y'?"

"No, with an 'i,'" corrected the fat man. "Don't forget that he's a tenor and sang the 'Stabat Mater.'"

"How do you spell it?"

"I'll tell you in a minute."

The stout editor of the *Copper-Snake* took a packet of greasy newspapers from the gas-meter.

"Here's the whole programme, and, I believe, a criticism as well."

Falk could not help laughing.

"How could a criticism appear simultaneously with the advertisement?"

"Why shouldn't it? But we shan't want it; I will criticize that French mob myself. You'd better do the literature, Fatty!"

"Do the publishers send books to the *Copper-Snake*?" asked Falk.

"Are you mad?"

"Do you buy them yourselves for the sake of reviewing them?"

"Buy them? Greenhorn! Have another glass and cheer up, and I'll treat you to a chop."

"Do you read the books which you review?"

"Who do you think has time for reading books? Isn't it enough to write about them? It's quite sufficient to read the papers. Moreover, it's our principle to slate everything."

"An absurd principle!"

"Not at all! It brings all the author's enemies and enviers on one's side—and so one's in the majority. Those who are neutral would rather see an author slated than praised. To the nobody there is something edifying and comforting in the knowledge that the road to fame is beset with thorns. Don't you think so?"

"You may be right. But the idea of playing with human destinies in this way is terrible."

"Oh! It's good for young and old; I know that, for I was persistently slated in my young days."

"But you mislead public opinion."

"The public does not want to have an opinion, it wants to satisfy its passions. If I praise your enemy you writhe like a worm and tell me that I have no judgment; if I praise your friend, you tell me that I have. Take that last piece of the Dramatic Theatre, Fatty, which has just been published in book form."

"Are you sure that it has been published?"

"I am certain of it. It's quite safe to say that there isn't enough action in it; that's a phrase the public knows well; laugh a little at the 'beautiful language'; that's good, old, disparaging praise; then attack the management for having accepted such a play and point out that the moral teaching is doubtful—a very safe thing to say about most things. But as you haven't seen the performance, say that want of room compels us to postpone our criticism of the acting. Do that, and you can't make a mistake."

"Who is the unfortunate author?" asked Falk.

"Nobody knows."

"Think of his parents, his friends, who will read your possibly quite unjust remarks."

"What's that got to do with the *Copper-Snake*? They were hoping to see a friend slated; they know what to expect from the *Copper-Snake*."

"Have you no conscience?"

"Has the public which supports us, a conscience? Do you think we could survive if it did not support us? Would you like to hear a paragraph which I wrote on the present state of literature? I can assure you it will give you plenty to think about. I have a copy with me. But let us have some stout first. Waiter! Here! Now I'm going to give you a treat; you can profit by it if you like."

"'We have not heard so much whining in the Swedish verse-factory for many years; this constant puling is enough to drive a man into a lunatic asylum. Robust rascals caterwaul like cats in March; they imagine that anæmia and adenoids will arouse public interest now that consumption is played out. And withal they have backs broad as brewers' horses and faces red as tapsters. This one whimpers about the infidelity of women, although all he has to go on is the bought loyalty of a wanton; that one tells us that he has no gold, but that his "harp is all he possesses in the world"—the liar! He has five thousand crowns dividend per annum and the right to an endowed chair in the Swedish Academy. A third is a faithless, cynical scoffer, who cannot open his lips without breathing forth his impure spirit and babbling blasphemies. Their verses are not a whit better than those which thirty years ago clergymen's daughters sang to the guitar. They should write for confectioners at a penny a line, and not waste the time of publishers, printers, and reviewers with their rhymes. What do they write about? About nothing at all, that is to say about themselves. It is bad form to talk about oneself, but it is quite the right thing to write about oneself. What are they bemoaning? Their incapacity to achieve a success? Success? That is the word! Have they produced one single thought, capable of benefiting their fellow-creatures; the age in which they live? If they had but once championed the cause of the helpless, their sins might be forgiven them; but they have not. Therefore they are as sounding brass—nay, they are as a clanking piece of tin and the cracked bell of a fool's cap—for they have no other love than the love of the next edition of their books, the love of the Academy and the love of themselves.'"

"That's sarcasm, isn't it? What?"

"It's unjust," said Falk.

"I find it very impressive," said the stout man. "You can't deny that it is well written. Can you? He wields a pen which pierces shoe-leather."

"Now, lads, stop talking and write; afterwards you shall have coffee and liqueurs."

And they wrote of human merit and human unworthiness and broke hearts as if they were breaking egg-shells.

Falk felt an indescribable longing for fresh air; he opened the window which looked on the yard; it was dark and narrow like a tomb; all he could see was a small square of the sky if he bent his head far back. He fancied that he was sitting in his grave, breathing brandy fumes and kitchen smells, eating the funeral repast at the burial of his youth, his principles and his honour. He smelt the elder-blossoms which stood on the table, but they reeked of decay; once more he looked out of the window eager to find an object which would not inspire him with loathing; but there was nothing but a newly tarred dust-bin—standing like a coffin—with its contents of cast-off finery and broken litter. His thoughts climbed up the fire-escape which seemed to lead from dirt, stench, and shame right up into the blue sky; but no angels were ascending and descending, and no love was watching from above—there was nothing but the empty, blue void.

Falk took his pen and began to shade the letters of the headline "Theatre," when a strong hand clutched his arm and a firm voice said:

"Come along, I want to speak to you!"

He looked up, taken back and ashamed. Borg stood beside him, apparently determined not to let him go.

"May I introduce...." began Falk.

"No, you may not," interrupted Borg, "I don't want to know any drunken scribblers, come along."

He drew Falk to the door.

"Where's your hat? Oh, here it is! Come along!"

They were in the street. Borg took his arm, led him to the nearest square, marched him into a shop and bought him a pair of canvas shoes. This done, he drew him across the lock to the harbour. A cutter lay there, fast to her moorings, but ready to go to sea; in the cutter sat young Levi reading a Latin grammar and munching a piece of bread and butter.

"This," said Borg, "is the cutter *Urijah*; it's an ugly name, but she is a good boat and she is insured in the 'Triton.' There sits her owner, the Hebrew lad Isaac, reading a Latin grammar—the idiot wants to go to college—and from this moment you are engaged as his tutor for the summer—and now we'll be off for our summer residence at Nämdö. All hands on board! No demur! Ready? Put off!"

CHAPTER XXVI. CORRESPONDENCE

CANDIDATE BORG *to* JOURNALIST STRUVE

NÄMDÖ, *June 18—*

OLD SCANDAL-MONGER!—As I am convinced that neither you nor Levin have paid off your instalments of the loan made by the Shoemakers' Bank, I am sending you herewith a promissory note, so that you may raise a new loan from the Architects' Bank. If there is anything over after the instalments have been paid up, we will divide it equally amongst us. Please send me my share by steamer to Dalarö, where I will call for it.

I have now had Falk under treatment for a month, and I believe he is on the road to recovery.

You will remember that after Olle's famous lecture he left us abruptly and, instead of making use of his brother and his brother's connexions, went on the staff of the *Workman's Flag*, where he was ill-treated for fifty crowns a month. But the wind of freedom which blew there must have had a demoralizing effect on him, for he became morose and neglected his appearance. With the help of the girl Beda I kept my eye on him, and when I considered him ripe for a rupture with the communards, I went and fetched him away.

I found him in a low public-house called "The Star," in the company of two scandal writers with whom he was drinking brandy—I believe they were writing at the same time. He was in a melancholy condition, as you would say.

As you know, I regard mankind with calm indifference; men are to me geological preparations, minerals; some crystallize under one condition, others under another; it all depends on certain laws or circumstances which should leave us completely unmoved. I don't weep over the lime-spar, because it is not as hard as a rock-crystal.

Therefore I cannot regard Falk's condition as melancholy; it was the outcome of his temperament (heart you would say) plus the circumstances which his temperament had created.

But he was certainly "down" when I found him. I took him on board our cutter and he remained passive. But just as we had pushed off, he turned round and saw Beda standing on the shore, beckoning to him; I can't think how she got there. On seeing her, our man went clear out of his mind. Put me ashore! he screamed, threatening to jump overboard. I seized him by the arms, pushed him into the cabin and locked the door.

As we passed Vaxholm, I posted two letters; one to the editor of the *Workman's Flag*, begging him to excuse Falk's absence, and the other to his landlady, asking her to send him his clothes.

In the meantime he had calmed down, and when he beheld the sea and the skerries, he became sentimental and talked a great deal of nonsense: he had lost all hope of ever seeing God's (?) green earth again, he said, and so on.

But presently he began to suffer from something like qualms of conscience. He maintained that he had no right to be happy and take a holiday when there were so many unhappy people in the world; he imagined that he was neglecting his duty towards the scoundrel who edits the *Workman's Flag*, and begged us to row him back. When I talked to him of the terrible time he had just gone through, he replied that it was the duty of all men to work and suffer for one another. This view had almost become a religion with him, but I have cured him of it with soda water and salt baths. He was completely broken, and I had great difficulty in patching him up, for it was hard to say where the physical trouble ended and the psychical began.

I must say that in a certain respect he excites my astonishment—I won't say admiration, for I never admire anybody. He seems to suffer from an extraordinary mania which makes him act in direct contradiction to his own interest. He might have been in a splendid position, if he had not thrown up his career in the Civil Service, particularly as his brother would, in that case have helped him with a sum of money. Instead of that he cast his reputation to the winds and slaved for a brutal plebeian; and all for the sake of his ideals! It is most extraordinary!

But he seems to be mending at last, more particularly after a lesson he had here. Can you believe it, he called the fishermen "sir," and took off his hat to them. In addition he indulged in cordial chats with the natives, in order to find out "how these people lived." The result was that the fishermen pricked up their ears, and one of them asked me one day whether "this Falk" paid for his own board, or whether the doctor (I) paid for him? I told Falk about it and it depressed him; he is always despondent, whenever he is robbed of a delusion. A few days later he talked to our landlord on the subject of universal suffrage; later on our landlord asked me whether Falk was in poor circumstances.

During the first few days he ran up and down the shore like a madman. Often he swam far out into the fjord, as if he never meant to return again. As I always looked upon suicide as the sacred right of every individual, I did not interfere.

Isaac told me that Falk had opened his heart to him on the subject of the girl Beda; she seems to have made an awful fool of him.

A propos of Isaac! He is one of the shrewdest fellows I ever met. He has, after one month's study, mastered the Latin grammar, and he reads his Cæsar as we read the *Grey Bonnet*; and what's more, he knows all about it, which we never did. His brain is receptive, that is to say, capable of assimilating knowledge, and in addition to this it is practical; this combination has produced many a genius, in spite of gross stupidity in many other respects. Every now and then he indulges his business instincts; the other day he gave us a brilliant example of his talent in that direction.

I know nothing about his financial position—for in that respect he is very reticent—but a little while ago he had to pay a few hundred crowns. He was very fidgety, and as he did not want to apply to his brother (of the "Triton") with whom he is not on friendly terms, he asked me to lend him the sum. I was not in a position to do so. Thereupon he sat down, took a sheet of note-paper, wrote a letter and sent it off by special messenger. For a few days nothing happened.

In front of our cottage grew a pretty little oakwood which shaded us from the sun and sheltered us from the strong sea breezes. I don't know much about trees and things pertaining to nature, but I love to sit in the shade when the days are hot. One morning, on pulling up my blind, I was dumbfounded; I was looking at the open fjord and a yacht riding at anchor about a cable-length from the shore. Every tree had gone, and Isaac was sitting on a stump reading Euclid and counting the trunks as they were being carried on board the yacht.

I wakened Falk; he was furious and had a quarrel with Isaac who made a thousand crowns on the deal. Our landlord received two hundred, all he had asked for. I could have killed Isaac, not because he had had the trees cut down, but because I had not thought of it first.

Falk said it was unpatriotic, but Isaac swears that the removal of the "rubbish" has improved the view; he declares that he will take a boat next week and visit the neighbouring islets with the same object.

Our landlord's wife cried all day long, but her husband went to Dalarö to buy her a new dress; he remained away for two whole days, and when he returned at last, he was drunk; there was nothing in the boat, and when his wife asked for the new dress, the fisherman confessed that he had forgotten all about it.

Enough for the present. Write soon and tell me a few new scandals, and be careful how you manipulate the loan.

Your deadly enemy and security, H. B.

P.S. I read in the papers that a Civil Service Bank is about to be established. Who is going to put money into it? Keep an eye on it, so that we can place a bill there when the time comes.

Please put the following paragraph into the *Grey Bonnet*; it will affect my medical degree.

Scientific Discovery: Cand. Med. Henrik Borg, one of our younger distinguished medical men has, while engaged in zootomic research on the skerries near Stockholm, discovered a new species of the family Clypeaster, to which he has given the very pertinent name of *maritimus*. Its characteristics may be described as follows: Cutaneous laminæ in five porous ambulacral shields and five interambulacral shields, with warts instead of pricks. The animal has excited much interest in the scientific world.

ARVID FALK *to* BEDA PETTERSON

NÄMBÖ, *August 18—*

As I walk along the seashore and see the roadweed growing in sand and pebbles, I think of you blossoming for a whole winter in an inn of old Stockholm.

I know nothing more delightful than to lie full length on a cliff and feel the fragments of gneiss tickling my ribs while I gaze seaward. It makes me feel proud, and I imagine that I am Prometheus, while the vulture—that is you—has to lie in a feather bed in Sandberg Street and swallow mercury.

Seaweed is of no use while it grows at the bottom of the sea; but when it decays on the shore it smells of iodine which is a cure for love, and bromide, which is a cure for insanity.

There was no hell until Paradise was quite complete, that is to say until woman was created (chestnut!).

Far away, by the open sea, there lives a pair of eider ducks, in an old quarter cask. If one considers that the stretched out wings of the eider measure two feet, it seems a miracle—and love is a miracle. The whole world is too small for me.

BEDA PETTERSON *to* MR. FALK

STOCKHOLM, *August 18—*

DEAR FRENT,—i have just receeved your letter, but i cannot say that i have understood it, i see you think that i am in Sandberg Street, but that is a grate lie and i can undertand why that blackgard says i am, it is a grate lie and i sware that i love you as much as befor, i often long to see you but it canot be yet.

Your fathfull Beda.

P. S. Dear Arvid, if you could lent me 30 crowns till the 15th, i sware i will pay it back on the 15th becos i shall receeve money then, i have been so ill and i am often so sad that i wish i was dead. The barmaid in the café was a horrid creechur who was jelous becaus of the stout Berglund and that is why i left. All they say of me is lies i hope you are well and dont forget your

The same.

You can send the money to Hulda in the Café then i shall get it.

CANDIDATE BORG to JOURNALIST STRUVE

NÄMDÖ, *August 18—*

CONSERVATIVE BLACKGUARD,—You must have embezzled the money, for instead of receiving cash, I received a request for payment from the Shoemakers' Bank. Do you imagine a man has a right to steal because he has a wife and children? Render an account at once, else I shall come up to town and make a row.

I have read the paragraph, which, of course, was not without errors. It said zoologic instead of zootomic, and Crypeaster instead of Clypeaster. Nevertheless, I hope it will serve its purpose.

Falk went mad after receiving a letter in a feminine handwriting a day or two ago. One minute he was climbing trees, at the next he was diving to the bottom of the sea. I expect it was the crisis—I'll talk to him like a father a little later on.

Isaac has sold his yacht without asking my permission, and for this reason we are, at the moment, enemies. He is at present reading the second book of Livy and founding a Fishing Company.

He has bought a strömming-net, a seal-gun, twenty-five pipe stems, a salmon line, two bass-nets, a shed for drag-nets and a—church. The latter seems incredible, but it is quite true. I admit it was scorched a little by the Russians in 1719, but the walls are still standing. The parish possesses a new one which serves the ordinary purpose; the old one was used as a parochial store-room. Isaac is thinking of making the Academy a present of it, in the hope of receiving the order of Vasa.

The latter has been given for less. Isaac's uncle, who is an innkeeper, received it for treating the deaf and dumb to bread and butter and beer when they used the riding-ground in the autumn. He did it for six years. Then he received his reward. Now he takes no more notice of the deaf and dumb, which proves how fatal the order of Vasa may be under certain circumstances.

Unless I drown the rascal Isaac, he won't rest until he has bought all Sweden.

Pull yourself together and behave like an honourable man, or I shall bear down upon you like Jehu, and then you'll be lost.

H. B.

P.S. When you write the notice relating to the distinguished strangers at Dalarö, mention me and Falk, but ignore Isaac; his presence irritates me—he went and sold his yacht.

Send me some blank bills (blue ones, sola-bills) when you send the money.

CANDIDATE BORG *to* JOURNALIST STRUVE

NÄMDÖ, *September 18—*

MAN OF HONOUR!—Money arrived! Seems to have been exchanged, for the Architects' Bank always pays in Scanian bills of fifty. However, never mind!

Falk is well; he has passed the crisis like a man; he has regained his self-confidence—a most important quality as far as worldly success goes, but a quality which, according to statistics is considerably weakened in children who lose their mothers at an early age. I gave him a prescription which he promised to try all the more readily as the same idea had occurred to him. He will return to his former profession, but without accepting his brother's help—his last act of folly of which I do not approve—re-enter society, register his name with the rest of the cattle, become respectable, make himself a social position, and hold his tongue until his word bears weight.

The latter is absolutely necessary, if he is to remain alive; he has a tendency to insanity, and is bound to lose his reason unless he forgets all about these ideas which I really cannot understand; and I don't believe that he himself could define what it is he wants.

He has begun the cure and I am amazed at his progress. I'm sure he'll end as a member of the Royal Household.

That is what I believed until a few days ago when he read in a paper an account of the Commune at Paris. He at once had a relapse and took to climbing trees again. He got over it, though, and now he does not dare to look at a paper. But he never says a word. Beware of the man when his apprenticeship is over.

Isaac is now learning Greek. He considers the text-books too stupid and too long; therefore he takes them to pieces, cuts out the most important bits and pastes them into an account book which he has arranged like a summary for his forthcoming examinations.

Unfortunately, his increasing knowledge of the classics makes him impudent and disagreeable. So, for instance, he dared to contradict the pastor the other day while playing a game of draughts with him, and maintain that the Jews had invented Christianity and that all those baptized were really Jews. Latin and Greek have ruined him! I am afraid that I have nursed a dragon in my hairy bosom; if this is so, then the seed of the woman must bruise the serpent's head.

H. B.

P.S. Falk has shaved his American beard and no longer raises his hat to the fishermen.

You'll not hear from me again from Nämdö. We are returning to town on Monday.

CHAPTER XXVII. RECOVERY

It was autumn again. On a clear November morning Arvid Falk was walking from his elegantly furnished rooms in Great Street to ... man's Boarding School near Charles XII Market, where he had an appointment as master of the Swedish language and history.

During the autumn months he had made his way back into civilized society, a proceeding which had brought home to him the fact that he had become a perfect savage during his wanderings. He had discarded his disreputable hat and bought a high one which he found difficult, at first, to keep on his head; he had bought gloves, but in his savagery he had replied "fifteen" when the shopgirl asked for his size, and blushed when his reply brought a smile to the face of every girl in the shop.

The fashion had changed, since he had last bought clothes; as he was walking through the streets, he looked upon himself as a dandy, and every now and then examined his reflexion in the shop windows, to see whether his garments set well.

Now he was strolling up and down the pavement before the Dramatic Theatre and waiting for the clock on St. James' Church to strike nine; he felt uneasy and embarrassed, as if he were a schoolboy going to school himself; the pavement was so short, and as again and again he retraced his footsteps he compared himself to a dog on a chain.

For a moment he had a wild thought of taking a wider range, a very much wider range, for if he went straight on, he would come to Lill-Jans, and he remembered the spring morning when that very pavement had led him away from society, which he detested, into liberty, nature, and—slavery.

It struck nine. He stood in the corridor; the schoolroom doors were closed; in the twilight he saw a long row of children's garments hanging against the wall: hats, boas, bonnets, wraps, gloves, and muffs were lying on tables and window sills, and whole regiments of button boots and overshoes stood on the floor. But there was no smell of damp clothes and wet leather as in the halls of the Parliamentary Buildings and in the Working-men's Union "Phœnix," or—he became conscious of a faint odour of newly mown hay—it seemed to come from a little muff lined with blue silk and trimmed with tassels, which looked like a white kitten with black dots. He could not resist taking it in his hand and smelling the perfume—new-mown hay—when the front door opened and a little girl of about ten came in accompanied by a maid.

She looked at the master with big fearless eyes, and dropped a coquettish little curtsey; the almost embarrassed master replied with a bow which made the little beauty smile—and the maid, too. She was late; but she was quite unconcerned and allowed her maid to take off her outdoor garments and overshoes as calmly as if she had come to a dance.

From the class-room came a sound which made his heart beat—what was it? Ah! The organ—the old organ! a legion of children's voices were singing

"Jesus, at the day's beginning...." He felt ill at ease, and forced himself to fix his mind on Borg and Isaac in order to control his feelings.

But matters went from bad to worse: "Our Father, which art in Heaven...." The old prayer—it was long ago....

The silence was so profound that he could hear the raising of all the little heads and the rustling of collars and pinafores; the doors were thrown open; he looked at a huge, moving flower-bed composed of little girls between eight and fourteen. He felt self-conscious like a thief caught in the act, when the old headmistress shook hands with him; the flowers waved to and fro, and there was much excited whispering and exchanging of significant glances.

He sat down at the end of a long table, surrounded by twenty fresh faces with sparkling eyes; twenty children who had never experienced the bitterest of all sorrows, the humiliations of poverty; they met his glance boldly and inquisitively, but he was embarrassed and had to pull himself together with an effort; before long, however, he was on friendly terms with Anna and Charlotte, Georgina and Lizzy and Harry; teaching was a pleasure. He made allowances, and let Louis XIV and Alexander be termed great men, like all others who had been successful; he permitted the French Revolution to be called a terrible event, during which the noble Louis XVI and the virtuous Marie Antoinette perished miserably, and so on.

When he entered the office of the Board of Purveyance of Hay for the Cavalry Regiments, he felt young and refreshed. He stayed till eleven reading the *Conservative*; then he went to the offices of the Committee on Brandy Distilleries, lunched, and wrote two letters, one to Borg and one to Struve.

On the stroke of one he was in the Department for Death Duties. Here he collated an assessment of property which brought him in a hundred crowns; he had time enough before dinner to read the proofs of the revised edition of the Forest Laws, which he was editing.

It struck three. Anybody crossing the Riddarhus Market at that time could have met on the bridge a young, important-looking man, with pockets bulging with manuscripts, and hands crossed on his back; he is strolling slowly along, accompanied by an elderly, lean, grey-haired man of fifty, the actuary of the dead. The estate of every citizen who dies has to be declared to him; according to the amount he takes his percentage; some say that this is his duty; others that he represents the Earth, and has to watch that the dead take nothing away with them, as everything is a loan—without interest. In any case, he is a man more interested in the dead than the living, and therefore Falk likes his company; he, on the other hand, is attached to Falk because, like himself, he collects coins and autographs, and because he possesses that excellent quality, tolerance, which is rarely found in a young man.

The two friends enter the Restaurant Rosengren, where they are fairly certain not to meet young men and where they can discuss numismatics and autography. They take their coffee in the Café Rydberg and look at catalogues of coins until six. At six o'clock the official *Post* appears, and they read the promotions.

Each enjoys the other's company, for they never quarrel. Falk is so free from fixed opinions that he is the most amiable man in the world, liked and appreciated by chiefs and colleagues.

Occasionally they dine in the Hamburg Exchange and take a liqueur or two at the Opera Restaurant, and to see them walking along arm in arm, at eleven o'clock, is really quite an edifying sight.

Moreover, Falk has become a regular guest at family dinners and suppers in houses into which Borg's father has introduced him. The women find him interesting, although they do not know how to take him; he is always smiling and expert at sarcastic little pleasantries.

But when he is sick of family life and the social life, he visits the Red Room, and there he meets the redoubtable Borg, his admirer Isaac, his secret enemy and envier Struve, the man who never has any money, and the sarcastic Sellén, who is gradually preparing his second success, after all his imitators have accustomed the public to his manner.

Lundell, who, after the completion of his altar-piece, gave up painting sacred pictures and became a fat Epicurean, only comes to the Red Room when he has no money to pay for his dinner; he makes a living by portrait painting, a profession which brings him countless invitations to dinners and suppers; Lundell maintains that these invitations are essential for making character studies.

Olle, who is still employed by the stonemason, has become a gloomy misanthrope after his great failure as a politician and orator. He refuses "to impose on" his former friends and lives a solitary life.

Falk is in a boisterous, riotous mood whenever he visits the Red Room, and Borg is of opinion that he does him credit; he is a veritable *sappeur* to whom nothing is sacred—except politics; this is a subject on which he never touches. But if, while he lets off his fireworks for the amusement of his friends, he should catch, through the dense tobacco smoke, a glimpse of the morose Olle on the other side of the room, his mood changes, he becomes gloomy like a night on the sea, and swallows large quantities of strong liquor, as if he wanted to extinguish a smouldering fire.

But Olle has not been seen for a long time.

CHAPTER XXVIII. FROM BEYOND THE GRAVE

The snow was falling lightly and silently, clothing the street in pure white, as Falk and Sellén were walking to the infirmary in the south-eastern suburb of Kingsholm, to call for Borg on their way to the Red Room.

"It's strange that the first snow should create an almost solemn impression," said Sellén. "The dirty ground is transformed to...."

"Are you sentimental?" scoffed Falk.

"Oh, no! I was merely talking from the point of view of a landscape painter."

They continued their way in silence, wading through the whirling snow.

"The Kingsholm with its infirmaries always strikes me as uncanny," remarked Falk, after a pause.

"Are you sentimental?" scoffed Sellén.

"Not at all, but this part of the town always makes that impression on me."

"Nonsense! It doesn't make any impression at all; you imagine it does. Here we are, and Borg's windows are lit up. Perhaps he's got some nice corpses to-night."

They were standing before the door of the institute. The huge building with its many dark windows glared at them as if it were inquiring what they wanted at that hour of the night. They passed the round flower bed, and entered the small building on the right.

At the very back of the room Borg was sitting alone in the lamplight, working at the mutilated body of a man who had hanged himself.

"Good evening," said Borg, laying aside his knife. "Would you like to see an old friend?"

He did not wait for the answer—which was not forthcoming—but lighted a lantern, took his overcoat and a bunch of keys.

"I didn't know that we had any friends here," said Sellén, desperately clinging to a flippant mood.

"Come along!" said Borg.

They crossed the yard and entered the large building; the creaking door closed behind them, and the little piece of candle, a remnant from the last card party, threw its red, feeble glimmer on the white walls. The two strangers tried to read Borg's face, wondering whether he was up to some trick, but the face was inscrutable.

They turned to the left and went along a passage which echoed to their footsteps in a way which suggested that they were being followed. Falk kept close behind Borg and tried to keep Sellén at his back.

"Over there!" said Borg, standing still in the middle of the passage.

Nobody could see anything but walls. But they heard a low trickling sound, like the falling of a gentle rain and became aware of a strange odour, resembling the smell of a damp flower-bed or a pine-wood in October.

"To the right!" said Borg.

The right wall was made of glass, and behind it, on their backs, lay three white bodies.

Borg selected a key, opened the glass door, and entered.

"Here!" he said, standing still before the second of the three.

It was Olle. He lay there as quietly, with his hands folded across his chest, as if he were taking an afternoon nap. His drawn-up lips created the impression that he was smiling. He was well-preserved.

"Drowned?" asked Sellén, who was the first to regain his self-possession.

"Drowned," echoed Borg. "Can either of you identify his clothes?"

Three miserable suits were hanging against the wall. Sellén at once picked out the right one; a blue jacket with sporting buttons, and a pair of black trousers, rubbed white at the knees.

"Are you certain?"

"Ought to know my own coat—which I borrowed from Falk."

Sellén drew a pocket-book from the breast pocket of the jacket, it was saturated with water and covered with green algæ, which Borg called enteromorph. He opened it by the light of the lantern and examined its contents—two or three overdue pawn-tickets and a bundle of papers tied together, on which was written: To him who cares to read.

"Have you seen enough?" asked Borg. "Then let's go and have a drink."

The three mourners (friend was a word only used by Levin and Lundell when they wanted to borrow money) went to the nearest public-house as representatives of the Red Room.

Beside a blazing fire and behind a battery of bottles, Borg began the perusal of the papers which Olle had left behind, but more than once he had to have recourse to Falk's skill as an "autographer," for the water had washed away the words here and there; it looked as if the writer's tears had fallen on the sheets, as Sellén facetiously remarked.

"Stop talking now," said Borg, emptying his glass of grog with a grimace which exhibited all his back teeth; "I am going to read, and I beg of you not to interrupt me.

"'TO HIM WHO CARES TO READ.

"'I have a right to take my life, all the more so because not only does my act not interfere with the interests of a fellow-creature, but rather it contributes to the happiness, as it is called, of at least one person; a place and four hundred cubic feet of air will become vacant.

"'My motive is not despair, for an intelligent individual never despairs, but I take this step with a fairly calm conscience; that an act of this kind throws one's mind into a certain state of excitement will be easily understood by everybody; to postpone it from fear of what might come hereafter is only worthy of a slave clutching at any excuse, so that he might stay in a world where he cannot have suffered much. At the thought of going, a burden seems to fall from my shoulders; I cannot fare worse, I might fare better. If there is no life beyond the grave, death must be happiness; as great a happiness at least as sleep in a soft bed after hard physical labour. Nobody who has ever observed how sleep relaxes every muscle, and how the soul gradually steals away, can fear death.

"'Why does humanity make so much ado about death? Because it has burrowed so deeply into the earth, that a tearing away from it is bound to be painful. I put off from the shore long ago; I have no family bonds, no social, national, or legal ties which could hold me back, and I'm going simply because life has no longer any attraction for me.

"'I do not want to encourage those who are well content to follow my example; they have no reason to do so, and therefore they cannot judge my act. I have not considered the point whether it is cowardly or not—to that aspect of the question I am indifferent; moreover, it is a private matter; I never asked to come here and therefore I have a right to go when I please.

"'My reason for going? There are so many reasons and they are so complicated that I have neither the time nor the ability to explain them. I will only mention the most obvious, those which had the greatest influence on myself and on my act.

"'My childhood and youth were one long continuation of manual labour; you who do not know what it means to labour from sunrise to sunset, only to fall into a heavy sleep when the toil is over, you have escaped the curse of the fall, for it is a curse to feel one's spiritual growth arrested while one's body sinks deeper and deeper into the earth. A man who walks behind the ploughing cattle day in day out, and sees nothing but the grey clouds, will end by forgetting the blue sky above his head; a man who takes a spade and digs a hole while the sun scorches his skin, will feel that he is sinking into the parched ground and digging a grave for his soul. You know nothing of this, you who play all day long, and work a little only during an idle hour between luncheon and dinner; you who rest your spirit when the earth is green and enjoy nature as an ennobling and elevating spectacle. The toiler on the land never sees the spirit of Nature. To him the field is bread, the forest timber, the sea a wash-tub, the meadow cheese and milk—everything is earth, soulless earth!

"'When I saw one-half of humanity engaged in fostering their spiritual growth, while the other half had merely time to attend to their bodily needs, I thought at first that there existed two laws for two different species of man. But my intellect denied this. My spirit rebelled and I resolved that I, too, would escape the curse of the fall—I became an artist.

"'I can analyse the much-talked-of artistic instinct because I was endowed with it myself. It rests on a broad base of longing for freedom, freedom from profitable labour; for this reason a German philosopher defined Beauty as the Unprofitable; as soon as a work of art is of practical use, betrays a purpose or a tendency its beauty vanishes. Further-more the instinct rests on pride; man wants to play God in art, not that he wants to create anything new—he can't do that—but because he wants to improve, to arrange, to recreate. He does not begin by admiring his model, Nature, but by criticizing it. Everything is full of faults and he longs to correct them.

"'This pride, spurring a man on to never-ceasing effort, and the freedom from work—the curse of the fall—beget in the artist the illusion that he is standing above his fellow creatures; to a certain extent this is true, but unless he were constantly recalling this fact he would find himself out, that is to say find the unreal in his activity and the unjustifiable in his escape from the profitable. This constant need of appreciation of his unprofitable work makes him vain, restless, and often deeply unhappy; as soon as he comes to a clear understanding of himself he becomes unproductive and goes under, for only the religious mind can return to slavery after having once tasted freedom.

"'To differentiate between genius and talent, to look upon genius as a separate quality, is nonsense, and argues a faith in special manifestation. The great artist is endowed with a certain amount of ability to acquire some kind of technical skill. Without practice his ability dies. Somebody has said: genius is the infinite capacity for taking pains. This is, like so many other things, a half-truth. If culture be added—a rare thing because knowledge makes all things clear, and the cultured man therefore rarely becomes an artist—and a sound intellect, the result is genius, the natural product of a combination of favourable circumstances.

"'I soon lost faith in the sublime character of my hobby—heaven forbid that I should call it my profession—for my art was incapable of expressing a single idea; at the most it could represent the body in a position expressing an emotion accompanying a thought—or, in other words, express a thought at third hand. It is like signalling, meaningless to all who cannot read the signals. I only see a red flag, but the soldier sees the word of command: Advance! After all, even Plato, who was a fine intellectualist and an idealist into the bargain, realized the futility of art, calling it but the semblance of a semblance (-reality); wherefore he excluded the artist from his ideal state. He was in earnest!

"'I tried to find my way back into slavery, but I could not. I tried to find in it my most sacred duty; I tried to resign myself, but I did not succeed. My soul was taking harm, and I was on the way to becoming a beast; there were times when I fancied that all this toil was a positive sin, in as far as it checked the greater aim of spiritual development; at such times I played truant for a day, and fled to nature, absorbed in unspeakably blissful meditations. But then again this bliss appeared to me in the light of a selfish pleasure as great, greater even, than the pleasure I used to feel in my artistic work; conscience, the sense of duty, overtook me like a fury and drove me back to my yoke, which then seemed beautiful—for a day.

"'To escape from this unbearable state of mind, and win light and peace, I go to face the Unknown. You who behold my dead body, say—do I look unhappy in death?

"'NOTES MADE WHILE WALKING:

"'The plan of the world is the deliverance of the idea from the form; art, on the other hand, attempts to imprison the idea in a sensuous form, so as to make it visible. Therefore....

"'Everything corrects itself. When artistic traffic in Florence surpassed all bounds Savonarola came—the profound thinker! and spoke his "All this is futile." And the artists—and what artists they were! made a pyre of their masterpieces—Oh! Savonarola!

"'What was the object of the iconoclasts in Constantinople? What did the baptists and breakers of images want in the Netherlands? I dare not state it for fear of being branded.

"'The great striving of our time: division of labour benefits the species but sentences the individual to death. What is the species? The conception of the whole; the philosophers call it the idea and the individuals believe what they say and lay down their lives for the idea!

"'It is a strange thing that the will of the princes and the will of the people always clashes. Isn't there a very simple and easy remedy?

"'When, at a riper age, I again read through my school-books, I was astonished to find that we human beings are so little removed from the beasts in the fields. I reread Luther's Catechism in those days; I made a few annotations, and drafted a plan for a new Catechism. (Not to be sent in to the Commissioners; what I am going to say now is all that I have written.)

"'The first Commandment destroys the doctrine of one God, for it assumes other gods, an assumption granted by Christianity.

"'Note. Monotheism which is so highly extolled has had an adverse influence on humanity; it has robbed it of the love and respect for the One and True God, by leaving Evil unexplained.

"'The second and third Commandments are blasphemous; the author puts petty and stupid commands in the mouth of the Lord; commands which are an insult to His omniscience; if the author were living in our days, a charge of blasphemy would be brought against him.

"'The fifth Commandment should read as follows: "Your inbred feeling of respect for your parents shall not induce you to admire their faults; you shall not honour them beyond their deserts; under no circumstances do you owe your parents any gratitude; they have not done you a service by bringing you into this world; selfishness and the civil code of laws compel them to clothe and feed you. The parents who expect gratitude from their children (there are some who even demand it) are like usurers; they are willing to risk the capital as long as the interest is being paid."'"

"'Note 1. The reason why parents (more especially fathers) hate their children so much more frequently than they love them arises from the fact that the presence of children has an adverse influence on the financial position of the parents. There are parents who treat their children as if they were shares in a joint stock company, from which they expect constant dividends.

"'Note 2. This Commandment has resulted in the most terrible of all forms of government, in the tyranny of the family, from which no revolution can deliver us. There is more need for the foundation of societies for the protection of children than for societies for the protection of animals.

"'To be continued.

"'Sweden is a colony which has passed her prime, the period when she was a great power, and like Greece, Italy, and Spain, she is now sinking into eternal sleep.

"'The terrible reaction which set in after 1865, the year of the death of all hope, has had a demoralising effect on the new generation. History has not witnessed for a long time a greater indifference to the general welfare, a greater selfishness, a greater irreligiousness.

"'In the world outside the nations are bellowing with fury against oppression; but in Sweden all we do is to celebrate jubilees.

"'Pietism is the sole sign of spiritual life of the sleeping nation; it is the discontent which has thrown itself into the arms of resignation to avoid despair and impotent fury.

"'Pietists and pessimists start from the same principle, the misery of the world, and have the same aim: to die to the world and live to God.

"'The greatest sin man can commit is to be a Conservative from selfish motives. It is an attempt against the plan of the world for the sake of a few shillings; the Conservative tries to stem evolution; he plants his back against the rolling earth and says: "Stand still!" There is but one excuse: stupidity. Poor circumstances are no excuse, merely an explanation.

"'I wonder whether Norway is not going to prove a new patch on an old garment, as far as we are concerned?'"

"Well, what do you think of it?" asked Borg laying down the papers and drinking a small brandy.

"Not bad," said Sellén, "it might have been expressed more wittily."

"What do you think, Falk?"

"The usual cry—nothing more. Shall we go now?"

Borg looked at him, wondering whether he was speaking ironically, but he saw no danger-signal in Falk's face.

"And so Olle has gone to happier hunting-grounds," said Sellén. "He's well off, need no longer trouble about his dinner. I wonder what the head-waiter at the 'Brass-Button' will say to it? Olle owed him a little money."

"What heartlessness! What brutality! Shame on you!" burst out Falk, throwing a few coins on the table, and putting on his overcoat.

"Are you sentimental?" scoffed Sellén.

"Yes, I am! Good night."

And he had gone.

CHAPTER XXIX. REVUE

Licentiate Borg at Stockholm *to the* Landscape Painter Sellén at Paris

Dear Sellén,—You have waited a whole year for a letter from me; now I have news to tell you. If I were acting on my principles, I should begin with myself; but as I had better conform to the rules of politeness laid down by civilized society—seeing that I am about to go out into the world to earn my own living—I will begin with you.

I heartily congratulate you on the success of your recently exhibited picture. Isaac took the notice to the *Grey Bonnet*, and it was printed without the knowledge of the editor, who was furious when he read it; he had firmly made up his mind that you should be a failure. But now that your genius has been acknowledged abroad, you are famous at home too, and I need no longer be ashamed of you.

In order to forget nothing, and to be as brief as possible—for I am lazy as well as tired after a day's work at the hospital—I will write my letter in the shape of a report and the style of the Grey Bonnet; this will have the additional advantage that you can more easily skip those parts which do not interest you.

The political situation is becoming more and more interesting; all parties have corrupted one another by presents and counter-presents, and now all of them are grey. This reaction will probably end in Socialism. There is a talk of increasing the number of the districts to forty-eight, and the Ministerial career is the one which offers the best chances of promotion, more especially as a man need not even have passed the examination of an elementary school-teacher. I met a school-friend the other day who is already a pensioned Cabinet Minister; he told me that it was far easier to become a Minister than a secretary of one of the departments; they say the work is very much like the work of a man who signs guarantees—it is only a matter of a signature now and then! It doesn't matter so much about the payment, there is always a second guarantor.

The Press—well, you know the Press. Roughly speaking it is just business, that is to say, it always adopts the opinion of the majority, and the majority, or, in other words, the greater number of subscribers, is reactionary. One day I asked a Liberal journalist how it was that he wrote in such laudatory terms about you, of whom he knew nothing. He said it was because public opinion, i.e. the largest number of subscribers, was on your side.

"But supposing public opinion turned against him?" I asked.

"Then, of course," he said, "I shall turn against him too."

You will understand that under these circumstances the whole generation which grew up after 1865, and which is not represented in Parliament, is in despair; and therefore they are either Nihilists—in other words, they don't care a d—— for anything—or they find their advantage in turning Conservative. To be a Liberal in these days is the devil's own job.

The financial position is depressed. The supply of bills, mine at least, reduced; no bank will look at the safest bills, even if they are signed by two doctors.

The "Triton" went into liquidation, as you know. Directors and liquidators took over the printed shares, but the shareholders and depositors received a number of lithographed ones from the well-known society at Norrköping, which alone managed to weather this period of frauds and swindles. I met a widow who had a handful of papers connected with a marble quarry; they were large, beautiful sheets, printed in red and blue, on which 1000 Cr., 1000 Cr., was engraved; and below the figures, just as if they were standing security, appeared the names of well-known persons; three of them, at least, are knights of the Order of the Seraphim.

Nicholas Falk, the friend and brother, sick of his private money-lending business, because it detracted from the full value of his civic authority, which is far from being the case when the business is a public one, decided to combine with a few experts(?) and found a bank. The novel feature of the undertaking was expressed as follows:

"As experience—truly a melancholy experience" (Levin is the author, as you may guess) "has proved that deposit receipts are not in themselves a sufficient guarantee for the return of deposits—that is deposited money—we, the undersigned, actuated by unselfish zeal for the welfare of home industry, and desirous of giving greater security to the well-to-do public, have founded a bank, under the title of 'Deposit Guarantee Society Limited.' The novel and safe feature of the enterprise—and not everything new is safe—consists in the fact that the depositors instead of receiving deposit receipts, are given securities to the full value of the deposited sums, etc. etc."

They do a brisk business, and you may imagine what sort of securities they issue instead of deposit receipts.

Levin. Falk, with his keen eye for business, recognized at once the great advantage to be reaped from the services of a man with Levin's experience and colossal knowledge of people, acquired through his money-lending business. But to train him for all eventualities, and make him familiar with all the by-ways of the business, he felled him to the ground with his promissory note, and forced him into bankruptcy. Having done so, he appeared in the rôle of his saviour and made him his confidential clerk with the title of secretary. And now Levin is installed in a little private office; but on no account is he permitted to show his face in the bank.

Isaac Levi is employed in the same bank as cashier. He passed his examinations (with Latin, Greek and Hebrew) first class in all subjects. The *Grey Bonnet*, of course, reported his achievements. Now he is reading for the law, and doing a little business on his own account. He is like the eel; he has nine lives and lives on nothing. He takes no alcohol; he does not smoke; I don't know whether he has any vices, but he is formidable. He has an ironmongers shop at Hernösand, a tobacconists at Helsingförs, and a fancy goods shop at

Södertelje; in addition he owns a few cottages at Stockholm, S. People say he is the coming man; I say the man has come.

After the winding-up of the "Triton," his brother retired with a considerable fortune, I am told, and is now doing business privately. I heard that he proposed buying the forest monastery near Upsala, and rebuilding it in a new style invented by his uncle of the Academy of Arts. But his offer was refused. Levi, very much offended, sent a notice to the *Grey Bonnet* under the heading: "Persecution of the Jews in the Nineteenth Century." It won him the lively sympathy of the whole cultured public; the affair would win him a seat in Parliament if he cared for that distinction. A vote of thanks was presented to him by his co-religionists—(as if Levi had any religion) which was printed in the *Grey Bonnet*. They thanked him for standing up for the rights of the Jews (to buy the forest monastery). The address was handed to him at a banquet, to which also a great many Swedes (I always refer the Jewish question to its rightful domain, the ethnographical one) had been bidden, to feast on bad salmon and uncorked wine. The deeply moved hero of the day (vide *Grey Bonnet*) received on the same occasion a present of 20,000 crowns (in shares) for the foundation of a Home for Fallen Boys of the Evangelical Denomination.

I was present at the banquet, and saw a sight I had never seen before—I saw Isaac the worse for drink! He shouted that he hated me, and you, and Falk, and all "Whites"; he alternately called us "whites," and "natives," and *roche*; I had never heard the last word before, but no sooner had he uttered it than a large number of "blacks" crowded round us, looking so ominous that Isaac thought it better to take me into an adjoining room. There he poured out all his soul to me; he spoke of his sufferings as a schoolboy; of the ill-treatment to which master and school-fellows had subjected him, the daily knocks and cuffs from the street arabs. But what roused my indignation more than anything else was an incident which had happened to him during his military service; he was called up to the front at vespers and ordered to recite the Lord's Prayer. As he did not know it, he was scoffed and jeered at. His account made me change my opinion of him and his race.

Religious swindle and charitable fraud are more rampant than ever, and make life in our country very unpleasant. You will remember two imps of Satan, Mrs. Falk and Mrs. Homan, the two pettiest, vainest and most malicious creatures who ever idled away their days. You know the crèche they had founded and its end. Their latest achievement is a Home for Fallen Women, and the first inmate—received on my recommendation—was Marie! The poor girl had lent all her savings to a fellow who absconded with them. She was only too happy to find a home where she would be kept free of charge, and be able to retrieve her character. She told me that she did not mind all the religious palaver, which is, unfortunately, inseparable from an enterprise of this sort, as long as she could count on her cup of coffee in the morning.

The Rev. Skore, whom you will no doubt remember, has not been made *pastor primarius*, and from sheer annoyance he is begging for funds to build a new church. Printed begging-letters, signed by all the wealthiest magnates of Sweden, are sent out to appeal to the charitable public. The church, which is to be three times the size of the church on the Blasieholm and connected with a sky-high tower, is to be built on the old site of St. Catherine's. The latter is supposed to be too small to satisfy the great spiritual needs from which the Swedish nation is suffering at the moment, and is, therefore, to be pulled down. The sum collected has already reached such dimensions that a treasurer had to be appointed (with free lodging and fuel). Who do you think is the treasurer? You would never guess! Struve!

Struve has become somewhat religious these days—I say *somewhat*, because it is not much—only just enough for his position, for he is patronized by the faithful. This does, however, not interfere with his journalism and his drinking. But his heart is not soft, on the contrary, he is most bitter against all those who have not come down; between you and me, he has very much deteriorated; therefore he hates you and Falk, and he has sworn to slate you next time you are heard of. He had to submit to the marriage ceremony for the sake of the free lodging and fuel. He was married to his wife in the White Mountains. I was one of the witnesses. His wife, too, has been converted, for she is under the impression that religion is good form.

Lundell has left the religious sphere, and is painting nothing but portraits of directors; he has been made assistant at the Academy of Arts. He has also become immortal, for he has managed to smuggle a painting of his into the National Museum. It was accomplished by a very simple trick and ought to encourage imitators. Smith made a present to the National Museum of one of Lundell's genre pictures, a service which Lundell repaid by painting his portrait gratis! Splendid! Isn't it?

The end of a romance. One Sunday morning, at the hour when the Sabbath peace is not disturbed by the terrible church bells, I was sitting in my room, smoking. There was a knock at the door, and a tall, well-made man, whose face seemed familiar to me, entered—it was Rehnhjelm. We cross-examined each other. He is manager of a large factory and quite satisfied with his lot.

Presently there was another knock. It was Falk. (More of him later on.)

We revived old memories and discussed mutual friends. But by and by there was a pause, that strange silence which so frequently occurs after a lively conversation. Rehnhjelm took up a book, turned over the leaves and read out:

"A Cæsarean Operation: An academic treatise which, with the permission of the illustrious medical faculty, will be publicly discussed in the little lecture room of the University." What horrible diagrams! "Who in the world is the unfortunate being cursed thus to haunt the living after his death?"

"You will find it on page 2," I said.

He went on reading.

"The pelvis which, as No. 38, is preserved in the pathological collection of the Academy...." No—that can't be it. "Agnes Rundgren, spinster...."

The man's face turned as white as chalk. He got up and drank some water.

"Did you know the woman?" I asked, in order to distract his thoughts.

"Did I know her? She was on the stage, and I knew her at X-köping; after leaving X-köping, she was engaged in a Stockholm café, under the name of Beda Petterson."

Then you should have seen Falk! It came to a scene which ended in Rehnhjelm's cursing all women, and Falk, greatly excited, replying, that there were two kinds of women, which differed from each other as much as angels and devils. He was so moved that Rehnhjelm's eyes filled with tears.

And now to Falk! I purposely left him to the last. He is engaged to be married! How did it happen? He himself says: "We just met one another!"

As you know, I have no rigid opinions, but cultivate an open mind; but from what I have seen up to now, it is undeniable that love is something of which we bachelors know nothing—what we call love is nothing but frivolity. You may laugh if you like, you old scoffer!

Only in very bad plays have I seen such a rapid development of character, as I had occasion to watch in Falk. You won't be surprised to hear that his engagement was not all plain sailing. The girl's father, an old widower, a selfish army pensioner, looked upon his daughter as an investment, hoping that she would marry well and thereby secure him a comfortable old age. (Nothing at all unusual!) He therefore bluntly refused his consent. You should have seen Falk! He called on the old man again and again; he was kicked out, and yet he called again and told the old egoist to the face that he would marry his daughter without his consent, if he continued to object. I am not sure, but I believe it actually came to fisticuffs.

One evening Falk had accompanied his sweetheart home. They had both spent the evening at the house of one of the girl's relatives to whom Falk had introduced himself. When they turned the corner of the street in which the girl lives, they saw by the light of the street lamp that her father was leaning out of the window—he lives in a small house which belongs to him. Falk knocked at the garden gate; but nobody came to open it. At last he climbed over and was on the other side attacked by a large dog; he got the better of the brute and shut it up in the dust-bin. (Imagine the nervous Falk.) Then he compelled the porter to get up and open the gate. Now they had gained the yard and stood before the front door. He hammered it with a large stone, but no reply came from within; he searched the garden and found a ladder, by means of which he reached the old man's window. Open the door, he shouted, or I'll smash the window!

"If you smash the window, you rascal," yelled the old man, "I'll shoot you!"

Falk immediately smashed the window.

For a few moments there was silence. Finally a voice came from within the fortress:

"You are my man! I consent."

"I'm not fond of smashing windows," explained Falk, "but there's nothing I would not do to win your daughter."

The matter was settled, and they became engaged.

I don't know whether you know that Parliament has carried through its reorganization of the public offices, doubling the salaries and the number of posts, so that a young man in the first division is now in a position to marry. Falk is going to be married in the autumn.

His wife will keep her post at the school. I know next to nothing of the Woman's Question—it doesn't interest me—but I believe that our generation will get rid of the last remnant of the Eastern conception which still clings to marriage. In the days to come, husband and wife will enter into a partnership where both will retain their independence; they will not try to convert each other, but will mutually respect their weaknesses, and live together in a life-long friendship which will never be strained by the demands of one of the partners for amorous demonstrations.

I look upon Mrs. Nicholas Falk, the charitable she-devil, as nothing more than a *femme entretenue*, and I am sure she does so herself. Most women marry for a home where they need not work—be their own mistress, as it is called. The fact that marriage is on the decline is as much the woman's fault as the man's.

But I cannot make Falk out. He is studying numismatics with an almost unnatural zeal; he told me the other day that he was engaged in writing a text-book on numismatics, which he would endeavour to introduce into the schools where this science is to be taught.

He never reads a paper; he does not know what is going on in the world, and he seems to have abandoned the idea of writing. He lives only for his work and his fiancée, whom he worships.

But I don't trust his calm. Falk is a political fanatic, well aware that he would be consumed if he allowed the fire to burn freely; therefore he tries to stifle it with hard, monotonous work; but I don't think that he will succeed; in spite of all his restraint the day is bound to come when he will cast aside all self-control and burst out into fresh flames.

Between you and me—I believe he belongs to one of those secret societies which are responsible for the reaction and militarism on the Continent. Not very long ago, at the reading of the King's Speech in Parliament, I saw him, dressed in a purple cloak, with a feather in his hat, sitting at the foot of the throne (at the foot of the throne!) and I thought—no, it would be a sin to say what I thought. But when the Prime Minister read his Majesty's gracious propositions respecting the state of the country and its needs, I saw a look in Falk's eyes which plainly said: What on earth does his Majesty know of the condition and needs of the country?

That man, oh! that man!

I conclude my review without having forgotten anybody. Enough for to-day. You shall soon hear from me again.

H. B. 1879.

THE END

Printed in Great Britain
by Amazon